SHE'S THEIR...

KARMA

NEW YORK TIMES BESTSELLING AUTHOR

K.A. KNIGHT

Karma

Written by K.A. Knight

Edited By Jess from Elemental Editing and Proofreading.

Proofreading by Norma's Nook.

Internal Formatting by The Nutty Formatter.

Formatting art by Dily Iola Designs & Galactixy_illustrations

Cover by The Pretty Little Design Co

For the women that don't need a man to save them, but sure as shit don't mind saving the men - especially if they are sexy as hell, rich and call them good girl while fucking them senseless.

READER CONSIDERATIONS

This is a very dark book not meant for anybody under the age of 18.

Content includes: explicit sex, explicit violence, torture, stalking, gore, depression, murder, imprisonment, PTSD, loss of a family member, sexual assault, child abuse, loss of limbs, misuse of narcotics, dubious consent and much more.

1

BEXLEY

Fuck, I am so late.

That mouthy little brat is never going to let me hear the end of this. It won't matter to her that I was building the new princess bed she wanted. No, she'll just point out the fact that I am always late and then call attention to all my other flaws until she makes me feel worse than all the dates I've been on combined. If you think men can cut you to size, try kids.

God, I fucking love that kid.

Her sister says she gets her attitude from me. I mean, it's probably true. She has grown up around me, so she's bound to pick up some of my habits, good or bad.

A sleek black Mercedes cuts me off, pulling into my lane, and I have to swerve my lime-green Kawasaki Ninja so I'm not flattened like a pancake. Anger courses through me, and I ignore my best friend's voice in my head, which reminds me to try the breathing exercises she taught me, and speed up, cutting around the car and flipping the older man in the driver's seat off.

He flips me off in return and purposely swerves again before speeding away.

Oh no, he fucking didn't.

Did that idiot just try to outrun me? I'm on a fucking bike, moron.

Leaning down, I race after him, speeding through the light that changes to red. I ignore honking cars as I weave through traffic. He is trying to get away, and when he stops at the next light, feeling safe, I skid in front of his car so he can't drive off, and then I swing my leg over my bike.

Leaving my helmet on, I stalk toward his shiny Mercedes, rapping my gloved knuckles on his window. He ignores me, studiously staring straight ahead, and my annoyance flares higher. I slam my fist into his window and urge him to roll it down.

I could walk away and ignore what happened, but why the fuck should I?

I ask myself WWAMWAD—*aka what would a man with audacity do*—and I channel the audacity that men seem to carry around with them and slam my fist into his window again. If this mouth breather doesn't open it, I am going to lose my shit.

"I'm already late, and you are making me later. Have you ever faced the wrath of a ten-year-old before?" I snarl as I slam my fist into his window again. "I'm not fucking around, limp dick. Roll it down and talk to me or I'll make you."

His grip tightens on the wheel, the only sign he can hear me. I can sense others in the cars around us, watching, but I ignore them.

"Fine, have it your way. I have a lot of rage to get out today anyway, since my sparring partner didn't turn up. Lucky you, huh?"

Wandering to the front of his car, I point at his face through the front window. "Last chance to open up and apologize."

His lips purse ever so slightly, his graying hair catching the sunlight as he leans back in his seat. The light behind us has turned green, but I don't give a flying fuck.

Slamming my hands into his shiny fucking hood, I glare at him through his front window. His eyes narrow, and his car jerks forward. I leap back to avoid being hit.

"Did you just try to ram me?" I shout.

Oh, fuck no.

I bang my hands down his shiny hood once more and kick at his car as he revs the engine again, ready to come at me.

Sirens cut through the air, and the man slumps in relief. I chuckle. He thinks that will save him. I step back and drive my steel-toed boots into his front lights on both sides, smashing them as he shouts from the safety of his locked car. Picking up a rock, I toss it a few times in my hand, testing the weight before hurling it right at his face. The windshield cracks as he yelps. The sirens grow louder, so I flip him off once more and climb back on my bike, walking it backwards, then I shoot off into traffic.

My speed increases, and the sirens fade as I cross the bridge into downtown. By the time I pull up at the venue, I am alone and scot-free. Even if the idiot comes after me, he'll get a rude surprise. Pulling off my helmet, I rest it on my handlebar as I look up at the place and check the address again.

"Who the fuck holds a kid's party in a bar?" I mutter. "Why the fuck is she letting her come to a kid's party in a bar?" As I talk to myself, I pull off my gloves and unzip my jacket as I head toward the closed doors.

Pushing inside, I take a moment to look around. I've been here before—most in my line of work have. It's a good meeting place, the type that doesn't ask too many questions. Just who the fuck is this kid who's celebrating their birthday anyway? I really should read the calendar.

Luckily, it seems to be closed for the event. There are streamers and banners spread around, and there's even a cake on one of the back booths where, just last week, I fucked someone's brains out.

Kids are running around and playing, and horror sparks through me at the sheer volume of tiny people. It's like a small, annoying army.

"You're late." The sharp, commanding voice makes me grin as I search through the crowd. Lauren stands with her arms crossed over her chest, her eyebrows raised as she taps one foot. It's the same fucking pose her sister adopts when she knows I've been up to bad shit. Lauren might not have come from me, but I sure as shit love her like she's my own, which is shocking since I hate every other child on the planet. I mean, come on, babies? They all look like fucking aliens. I've never met a cute baby, and everyone always insists on shoving them in your face or showing you pictures, and when you point out that it looks like an alien? Well, they tend to get a little touchy. And kids? Annoying little fuckers, just like the one currently running around me, screaming, Lauren, though... Nah, she's alright when she isn't stealing my ice cream.

"Am I?" I say as I wind through the tables. I stop when a kid kicks my ankle and starts to laugh. Frowning down at the snotty boy, I trip the same foot as he goes to run away, and he falls and hits the floor.

"Idiot. Didn't they teach you not to pick on someone bigger?" I ask as I step over him and head to Lauren, who sighs, looking from the crying kid to me.

"Really, Aunt Bexley?"

I wince. "Shit, kid, why are you full naming me? I'm here, aren't I?"

"And you are late, as always. Taylor won't be happy," she warns, narrowing her sassy eyes.

I shrug. "Then let's not tell your sister."

"It will cost you," she retorts.

"Doesn't it always?" I mutter as I lean down and get in her face. "Fine, what do you want this time, you little blackmailer?"

"Three weeks of doing my chores." Her smile is slow and evil. Fuck, I taught her well.

"Two," I counter.

"Two and a half," she negotiates.

"One," I offer.

"Bex, that is not how this works." She sighs like I'm the annoying one.

"Fine, two is my final offer." I hold out my pinkie.

I watch her fight a smile, and she finally drops her arms and hooks her tiny pinkie around mine, our matching flower nails catching the light. Hers are white and yellow, while mine are black and pink. It was my last blackmail gift, a treat day on me. The little minx drained me dry.

"Deal. Let's go. I need to get back and finish my homework," she says.

"Fuck, kid, have some fun. Lighten up!"

"Some of us would like a successful future and to not end up riding around all day on our bike, babysitting a twelve-year-old like a fucking moron," she derides, arching her eyebrow as if to dare me to argue.

"Honestly, who taught you those words? And you have such an attitude," I grumble.

"You," she scoffs.

"Touché." I ruffle her curly hair and glance at the bar. "Did you get your cake or whatever the fuck you do at these parties?"

"Cake is not good for you." It is something she's told me a million times, her eyes tightening at me messing up her perfect schedule.

"Cake is always good for you," I tell her as I walk backwards. "Wait there, I'll grab you a slice to go."

"I won't eat it!" she yells.

"Then I will!" I wave at her as I round the corner of the bar and step into the kitchen, knowing my way pretty well. There are two more cakes in here, and I grab a knife and carve the biggest slice I can. We both know she will see me eat some and want to try it, and if her annoying sister, my best friend, Taylor, is home, well, she'll eat it too. Honestly, there are some things that should not be shared.

Cake is one of them.

The things I do for these idiots.

Wrapping it in a handy little bag, I suck the icing from my fingers as I walk back out into the bar, only to freeze. The atmosphere changed in the two minutes I was in the kitchen.

Kids are cowering and hiding, and there are three men in designer suits standing next to Lauren and a little boy who's about her age. They appear to be protecting her, which is the only reason they are still breathing. Following all the other eyes, I see the problem.

Working their way through the bar are five tatted-up assholes. I scan them, noting the pyramid and spider design on most of their necks, which tells me exactly who they are.

Sucking my fingers clean, I head toward Lauren in the silence and stop next to her, ignoring everyone else. "Are you okay?"

She nods, her wide, scared eyes darting behind me, but she's holding one arm in the other. Kneeling, I turn to the little boy next to her. "Can you hold this?" I hand him the cake, and he takes it, holding it protectively as I turn back to Lauren and carefully pull her arm away from the other.

She whimpers, and fury fills me, demanding to be let out. Breathing slowly so I don't scare her, I turn her arm over to see a hand-print there that will bruise.

"We will handle this. We apologize for them touching her. We did not see them in time." The dark, seductive voice comes from one of the suits next to me.

I glance up at him, blinking at the three men staring down at me. Their faces resemble each other's, so they are probably related, but that's where the similarities end. They scream money, wearing custom suits—only something custom would fit their muscles like that—Rolex watches, and diamond rings. It's subtle, but the signs are there.

The one closest to me who spoke looks to be the oldest, maybe mid-thirties, with deep brown hair that has pale blond highlights. It shouldn't work, but it does as it perfectly frames his face. Brown stubble surrounds full lips, which sit below a strong nose, and he has the darkest eyes I've ever seen. The one on his left looks younger than him, probably more around my age. His hair is black, like his suit, and messily falls into his face. One of his eyebrows has a slit in it, and unlike the older man, his eyes are a striking gray and his stubble is almost nonexistent. I also see earrings along his right ear and ink peeking from the top of his shirt.

The one on the right has closely shaved hair, with some length on the top, and it's a mix of colors. His face is thicker than the others', with mismatched eyes—one gray and one black. His eyebrows are pulled together in a severe frown that suits his thick features.

I note that all in the time it takes for them to blink at me.

"Hot," I say before clearing my throat. "No, you won't."

The one who spoke to me blinks in confusion. He's obviously not used to being questioned or ignored. "Excuse me?"

"Handle it. I will. She's my responsibility, my family." Glancing at Lauren, I kiss her bruised arm. "Which one was it, sweetie?"

She looks up at me, and I see fear on her face.

"Lauren, look at me and only me. You know I will never let anyone hurt you, don't you?" She nods, and I smile. "Just point. Which one?"

She lifts her injured arm and points at a bald-headed fucker standing a few feet away.

"Good job, sweetie. Can you go get me some water? I'm thirsty. The kitchen is just down there." I point it out.

"If you are going to kick their asses, can I at least watch?" she murmurs, some of her usual spark returning. "Taylor stopped letting me watch your shows. She said they were too dark, so I need some entertainment."

"Next time. Go," I order.

She sighs dramatically and spins on her heel, heading the way I indicated.

When she's out of sight, I rip my jacket off and toss it on the closest table. My cropped black vest is low-cut and armless, exposing all of my tattoos, and I see the moment they realize who they fucked with. They all take a step back, their faces paling.

"Shit," the bald-headed one says as I prowl toward him. He stumbles backward and holds his hands up. "I didn't know it was you, Karma. I didn't know she was yours. I'm fucking sorry, okay?"

"He's right. We'll leave. We don't want any issues," another adds. "The boss didn't know, we swear!"

I ignore their panicked pleas and grab a Coke bottle from a table, then I smash it on the edge, my body filled with fury. He must see it in my eyes because he tries to get away.

I kick out, sending him back into the table. He hits the floor hard, and I'm on him in an instant.

"This is going to fucking hurt. Stay still," I growl. Grabbing his left arm, I slam it against the floor then hold it there with my boot, pressing the sharp edge of the bottle against his skin. I start to slice, his screams filling the bar, and when I press the bottle deeper to carve it through tendon and bone, his cry turns high-pitched. His blood squirts across my face when I hit a juicy vein, but I keep going. When I'm satisfied, I lift my head and stomp on the raw meat of his wrist, snapping his bone, then I yank on his hand until it rips free and toss it onto his chest as I blow my black hair from my face.

"You should have known better than to touch what isn't yours," I tell him. His chest is heaving and his eyes are wide in shock.

"It was the other hand," one of the suits calls helpfully, his voice laced with amusement. I glance at him with a frown, and he arches his eyebrow. "His right hand touched Lauren."

"Thank you." I toast him with the bottle and turn back to the guy. "Sorry, my mistake. Hold on, let me fix that."

"Wait, wait, no!" He starts to scream again, and this time the process is easier since I know the best way to angle the bottle. After tossing that hand next to the first, I step back and turn to the others, who are watching me.

Three linger near the door, and they incline their heads out of respect. "We are sorry, Karma. We really are." They hightail it out of here. Smart boys.

The other? Not so much.

He heads my way, shaking his fists as anger contorts his square face. He has hair, but he looks somewhat similar to the man on the floor, except he has hands.

"Really?" I scoff incredulously.

"That's my brother!" he roars.

"Your brother likes to touch little girls. I did the world a favor. I guess we could end your family line here though." I duck under his punch and drive my fist up into his stomach. He stumbles back, a breath whooshing from his lips as I arch a brow.

"You know who I am, and you really think you can beat me? I guess neither of you were born with brains," I tease, and he roars as he throws himself at me.

He's strong, but I'm faster, and I weave under his punches,

laughing and taunting until I get bored. Kicking his chest, I spin with the movement and leap, knocking him down as I wrap my legs around his throat and slam my elbow into his face. His nose busts as he groans. I climb up off him and dig my boot into his dick, grinding down until his face turns red, then purple.

"You know why they call me Karma?" I demand of him.

His eyes are bloodshot and bugging from his head, and he slaps my feet to get me off his precious manhood. "Because you make things right," he rasps.

"Good boy. I would end you, but there are a lot of kids here. Apparently, seeing that shit fucks them up. I don't know how. I mean, I saw my first dead body at five and I turned out just fine, but oh well. You're lucky today. When I step back, you better run as far and as fast as you can. Get out of town because if I find you when I hunt tonight, you're dead."

Lifting my boot, I step back and wait. Will he fight or run?

He climbs to his feet, glancing at his brother, and hesitates before he makes up his mind and runs to the door.

Picking up one of his brother's hands, I use it to wave at him as he scrambles from the bar, leaving his brother behind. I guess family loyalty only goes so far.

I turn back to the party to find Lauren standing with the boy holding the cake and the three suits, a cup of water in her hand. She arches one eyebrow at me, but she isn't scared anymore.

Heading her way, I take the cup and wash my face with it before winking at her.

"Who the fuck are you?" one of the suits asks, finally breaking the silence.

"This is my aunt, Bexley, who is going to be in so much trouble with my sister when she finds out she hurt someone in front of me again," Lauren answers. "Bexley, this is my best friend's, Tommy's, family, the Sais."

"Four weeks of chores," I implore her.

"Nope. You're done for," she threatens.

"Lauren," I whine, narrowing my eyes. "I'll let you ride in the 'stang!"

"Deal!" she squeals.

Turning to Tommy, I take my cake back. "Thanks for holding it, and, uh . . . happy birthday, I guess."

"That was awesome," he murmurs.

Grinning, I tug Lauren closer and glance at the three suits. Uncles? Brothers? Father? It's hard to tell. "Sorry for the blood." I pull out a wad of cash and hand it over. "This will help with the cleanup."

They are obviously connected in some way. Everything about them hints at money, and I can spy at least two guns on their hips, not to mention they didn't even blink when I carved into that man, so they can handle it.

"This is unnecessary." The older one hands the cash back. "I said we would handle it."

"Yeah, well, I never let anyone handle my business." I shrug and glance at Lauren. "Let's go. We still need to finish those episodes of *Alice in Borderland* before Taylor gets home."

"Is he dead?" she asks curiously, pointing at the man on the ground. I block her view with my body and grin.

"He's just sleeping. He's very tired," I tell her.

"Bexley," she snaps. "I'm twelve, not a moron."

"Right, well, time to go." I nod at the men. "Thanks for inviting her."

Before they can ask me anything else, I steer Lauren out of the door and hand her the spare helmet I keep. After helping her put it on, I lift her onto the bike. "What's the deal with your best friend's family?" I ask.

She shrugs, tightening her backpack. "All he said was they owned a lot of businesses and most people were scared of them."

"Great," I mutter as I get on. "Hold on, kid."

"Stop calling me a kid," she mumbles, but she wraps her arms around me, and I tear off before they come after us.

If they are who I think they are, then I just gained the attention of one of the most dangerous mafia families in the city, which is not good news for someone like me.

I lie low for a reason, silent and faceless karma.

I guess that's all up in smoke now.

2

KANE

C limbing from one of the Mercedes outside of our family home, I glance at Dodge. "Find them," I order as I button my suit. "I want them all here in the next two hours."

I don't even have to tell him who. He knows. We let them go for the children, but that doesn't mean they are free.

They invaded my younger brother's birthday party.

They dared to threaten my family and lay hands on innocents.

Despite . . . her, Bexley, making them pay, she is not family, so they will answer for this.

Dodge inclines his head out of respect as I meet with my three younger brothers before the steps to our home, which is more of a hotel. That's what it used to be before I bought it and turned it into a haven for our family and security.

Ruffling Tommy's hair, I grin down at him. "Did you have a good birthday?"

It was our consolation. He had been so sad about his birthday, wanting a normal party like the other kids. The bar we owned was our compromise, and I hate that it was disturbed, but our enemies don't care about the importance of family time. They only care about trying to end us—the three heads of the Sai family.

As the oldest, it is my responsibility to keep my family safe. Neo is a few years younger than me and has taken over the construction side of the business, helping me keep our companies and men in line. Zayn, the youngest, recently graduated law school and has started keeping our family safe that way. Together, we are unstoppable, and everyone knows it.

No law can touch us.

There isn't any other leading family who can challenge us, but it doesn't stop them from trying in underhanded ways. This was a local gang, though, not a leading family, which is surprising. They rarely make a move against us because they know better.

"Yes, it was good." Tommy perks up and tugs on Zayn's suit leg. "Can we go watch *Howl's Moving Castle* now?"

"Go get it ready. I'll be there soon," he promises, nodding at me. He knows what to do. He'll make the calls to cover up the mess the girl made at our bar.

Neo pulls his phone out when Tommy hurries inside, ready to make calls. "I'm going to ask some of our informants what happened."

"Neo." I catch his arm. "Ask about her too. Find out who she is."

He grins. "I thought you'd like her."

I arch a brow at that. "I'm just curious. I don't know her, but they did, and I don't like secrets."

"Sure, big brother, whatever you say." He heads inside, followed by Zayn, before I roll my shoulders with a sigh and glance up at our home.

I am doing everything I can to keep them safe. It isn't easy, but it's my responsibility, something that has been driven into me since birth. Our upbringing was intense, but my father knew what we would face and wanted to prepare us for a world where everyone is either out to use or kill us.

It's a lesson I quickly learned.

"Mr. Sai." The guards bow as I pass, heading inside to speak to my father. He will want to know what happened today. Despite him handing leadership over to us when he deemed we were ready, everyone knows he is still the head of this house, and out of respect and love for him, we keep him apprised of everything.

He built our empire with his bare hands, a kid from the streets with nothing but a name—one he turned into a brand and a threat to the world that hurt him.

Sitting across from my father, I watch him contemplate the chess board, his brown eyes covered by his thick-rimmed glasses. Even now, he is in his designer suit, his jacket unbuttoned as he leans back in a decorative chair on the veranda overlooking the back garden. He spends hours out here, refusing to let anyone else touch his flowers and plants, nor his fish in his pond. He said he needed purpose when he "retired," but I think he just uses it as an excuse to avoid us.

Raising four killers isn't easy.

"Sir." Dodge bows, and when my father nods and waves his hand, he smiles.

"How many times do I have to tell you that you can freely speak and not wait for me to allow it?" He sighs as he leans over the board and moves a piece.

I cover my smirk with my hand, but he catches it. "I never should have taught you chess."

"You said it would help me with our business. Don't blame me, old man, for always beating you now."

"Dodge, what is it? Tell me before I shoot my own son."

Dodge smirks and glances at me. "They are here."

I nod, dismissing him, and he bows before leaving again. Standing, I button my suit and move my king. "Checkmate," I say, and my father sits back heavily.

"Sometimes I think I raised you too well. You are too devious for your own good." He waves me off. "Go deal with things. I will ask one of my guards to play with me. Probably West. He's good with a gun but terribly stupid. It might make me feel better."

"Hey!" West protests from his post to the left.

Laughing, I lean down and press a kiss to my father's head. "You could still beat me if you tried, Father. We both know that." My smile drops as I turn and head inside, taking one of the many central elevators down to the ground floor.

I stride into the formal sitting room. The men are on their knees on the marble floor, the large windows allowing light to shine down on them. Ignoring them for a moment, I walk over to the bar where Neo sits, looking at his iPad. Pouring two drinks, I slide one over to him before pouring a third, and a moment later, Zayn wanders in, still on the phone.

When he's done, he takes the drink and leans back against the bar. I continue to ignore the men, letting them sweat to show them they are nothing to us. Mind games are just as important as physical torture in my line of business.

"Well?" I prompt.

"I've asked around, but nobody seems to know her," Neo scoffs. "It's a lie, and I will keep digging."

"Tommy is watching his movie with his guards, so he will be busy for a while," Zayn adds, and I turn to follow his gaze to the thugs who are waiting nervously.

They know nobody walks out of this house alive.

Enemies come in, but they never go out.

It is a fortress for a reason, and a death sentence.

Nobody fucks with my family.

Draining my glass, I wander over, dangling it from my fingertips, and when I reach the biggest man on the left, I smash it into his head. I hold one of the shards, driving it into his eye as he screams. Blood pours down my hand and arm, and I see one of my newer guards wince and look away. I take note of it, and when I look at Dodge, I see him doing the same.

He is the head of security for a reason, and he has been with us since we were boys.

It is his job to train new recruits and break them of any fear or morality they might have. They can't afford to have any of that in this line of work. We demand the best. We make killers and sinners, but we also pay the most. That's why they flock to us.

Stepping back, I let the glass fall to the floor as he continues to scream. "Be quiet, you're annoying me."

He keeps shrieking, however, covering his eye, and I nod at the closest guard. He approaches and stuffs something in the screamer's mouth to silence him as I look at the others. "You dared to attack me and my family on a special day. I'm curious to know why."

"You made a move on our territory," the one on the right spits. "The boss just wanted to remind you who it belongs to."

"To me." I arch a brow pointedly. "You're nothing but bothersome little boys playing gangster. I take what I want, and I want that land, so it's mine. You and your boss were stupid to attack us—my family. Did you really think it would get you anywhere?"

"You're not as untouchable as you think," the one in the middle sneers.

"No, I know we are," I respond. "Never mind, I will send your boss a message he won't forget. He only lives because I say he can. He works and earns money only because I allow him to. I'm sure he'll understand, and you'll help me send that message, but first, I have one more question." Pulling my gun out, I approach the mouthy one.

"Karma," I murmur, tipping his head up with my muzzle. "That is what you called her, did you not? I want to know everything about the woman who was there earlier."

His face pales, and for a moment, he looks truly terrified, and not of my gun. Interesting. Just who is this woman, and why don't I know about her? "You might as well kill me. I won't betray her. I fear her more than you, so do your worst."

"As you wish." I pull the trigger, and before his body even hits the floor, I turn to the others. I have other ways to get the information. If they know her, others will too.

I don't negotiate, ever.

I raise my gun. "Wait—" I pull the trigger twice, then put it away. The only one left alive is the one who's still bleeding, and he spits the tie from his mouth. He glances at the glass on the floor then back to me.

I see the moment he makes his decision. He grabs for a shard and tries to dive at me, ready to slice my throat. I do not even flinch as he gets inches away.

The shot is loud, ringing around the room, and he drops back with a hole in his forehead.

I glance over to Neo, who's putting his gun away, not even looking up from his iPad. "You getting sloppy, brother?" he teases without looking.

Zayn smirks. "It's his old age."

"Old age my ass. I'm thirty-five," I snap as I accept the drink Zayn gives me and turn back to our guards.

"Cut off their hands and heads, then send them to their boss in boxes. Make it clear that if he makes a move again, I will destroy everything he loves before I kill him," I order as I stroll over to the bar and wipe my hand on my handkerchief. "And find Karma. I want to meet the woman they are all so afraid of."

"Yes, sir." Dodge looks at the guards, and they spring into action as I sit between my brothers.

"What are you going to do when you find her? Tommy knows her niece," Neo murmurs, looking at me.

I shrug, knowing my smile is dark. "I'm just intrigued."

They both groan, knowing that isn't good news.

For her at least.

3

BEXLEY

"W ill you—" I duck under the bowl flying at my head. It shatters against the board behind me, and I sigh as I glance from it to Taylor. "That was my favorite cereal bowl."

"I know," she snaps, crossing her arms. She is a bigger version of Lauren, attitude and all. They even look the exact same, especially when they are mad.

She gave me the same look when we met when we were five and I called her an idiot. She kicked me in the shins and glowered at me.

We have been best friends ever since, more like sisters, so when her parents died unexpectedly, I took both her and Lauren in, giving them a home and helping her raise her little sister.

I bought us a house, carving out a safe and stable life for them. They are my family, the only one I have.

"You cut off a man's hand in front of her," Taylor scoffs when I just stare.

Rolling my eyes, I hop onto the counter, ignoring the broken bowl, and sip my coffee. "It wasn't in front of her, just in her vicinity," I mutter.

"Bexley fucking Adams," she growls. "You promised me, no more adult shit. She's seen enough. I want her to grow up norma—"

"Taylor." I sigh, and she drops her arms. "That kid was never going to grow up normal. She has seen more shit than most adults, but normal is overrated. Plus, she's turned out well so far, but if you think I will apologize for harming the man who touched her, then you do not know me very well."

"I love that you are willing to kill to protect us, Bex," she starts. "I just wish you didn't have to and that she didn't have to know this side of life."

"Don't we both," I agree. "She never stood a chance. I would say I would try to change, but everything I do is to keep our family safe, and I will not apologize for that. This world will eat us alive if we aren't careful."

"I know," she whispers, but she doesn't really. I have sheltered her from the truth of what I've had to do to keep us together and safe. We were not born with money, and when her family died, she had nothing.

Nothing good ever comes of three kids alone on the streets. It made me who I am.

"Taylor, you shouldn't reprimand her," Lauren comments as she walks in, holding a book in one hand. "I am not scared of Bexley or her actions."

"That's what worries me," Taylor replies.

Lauren looks from her to me. "You said yourself that without Bex, we would either be dead or something worse. There are people out there who kill for fun and even eat other people." She shrugs. "The way I see it, Bex is the lesser of evils."

"Jesus Christ, stop watching TV with her," Taylor begs her sister.

"It's called the internet, dummy." Lauren sighs, like she is the adult in this situation, and looks between us. "Now, don't forget that someone needs to buy some groceries. Oh, and clean up that bowl before you cut yourselves. I'm not helping drag Taylor's fat ass to the sofa when she faints again when she sees blood." She grabs an apple and leaves, and Tay and I share a look.

"She takes after you," we say at the same time and share a smile.

20

Shoulders slumping, she approaches me, leaning into my side. "I'm fucking this up, aren't I? Raising her?"

"Nah, she's a good kid," I assure her. "Smart, funny, strong . . . She'll go far. You're doing incredible, Taylor, and for what it's worth, I will try to keep her exposure to killing to a minimum . . . maybe."

"How about only one murder a week?" she teases.

"At least three," I counter.

"Two," she says, and I grin.

"Fine, but you have to clean this up and get the groceries." I hop down then, over the bowl. "I have to work."

"Remember to leave your damn clothes outside. I washed the floors today!" she yells after me. I wave her off and lean over the sofa, kissing Lauren's head.

"Be good for your sister. She's struggling," I murmur. "Look after her for me."

Lauren looks up at me and nods. "She always gets like this when she is on her period."

I can't help but laugh and ruffle Lauren's hair. "Too smart for your own good."

"Be safe, Bexley." She frowns. "I will make sure Taylor is okay while you're gone."

"What would I do without you, huh?" Heading to the door, I shove my feet in my boots and make my way to the garage out back. I scan my hand and input the code no one else knows, especially Lauren, then step inside, letting the door shut behind me.

Lights turn on as I walk down the aisles of weapons and supplies. I can never be too prepared. Whistling to myself, I select a handgun and a couple of blades. Hopefully this will just be a civilized talk, but you can never be too careful.

One wrong move in this game and you're just fucking dead.

That won't happen tonight, or any night after.

I will never leave my family.

I will never make them grieve for someone again.

It's a promise I made, and one I intend to keep.

Just because I'm here to talk, doesn't mean I'm going to knock nicely.

The casino sits in the poor end of the city, known as Hell's End for its connections with the mob and gangbangers. It's a haven for sinners, but it isn't open this early in the evening. That doesn't stop me.

The man guarding the front flies through the door, smashing it in. Gangbangers jump to their feet and aim their guns at me. When they realize who it is, more guns are drawn. Ignoring them, I walk through the entrance of the casino and wait, looking up at the second floor.

"Knock, knock," I call loudly. "Anybody home?"

It's silent for a moment, and then he appears, leaning over the balcony, and he groans when he sees me. "Lower your weapons, you idiots, unless you all want to die." He heads down the stairs, not stopping until he's in front of me. "Karma." He nods.

"Jakob." I smile, knowing it's not a nice one. "I thought we would discuss what happened earlier today."

"Come." He turns his head, and I follow him into the bar area, where we sit at a sticky table. He leans back, looking tired. "I didn't know you were involved in any way. I swear it. My men never returned. Your handiwork?"

"Not mine, probably the Sai family. Really, what were you thinking, fucking with them like that?"

His bald head shines under the light, covered in ink, and one of his ears is blown into a cauliflower since he made his name through street fighting and worked his way up. Compared to the likes of the Sais, he's a small fish in a big pond, but on these streets? Yeah, enough people fear and respect him.

I'm one of the latter. We have always had an understanding—he doesn't fuck with me, and I don't fuck with him.

In another world, we could have even been friends.

He waves his hand to order us a drink then rubs his head. "I just wanted to make them aware that they couldn't fuck with us without repercussions," he admits. "They moved in on our territory without even a warning. I know they think they are untouchable, but I just wanted to prove they aren't, not start a war."

"It's like a chihuahua nipping at a giant's ankles," I scoff. "We have survived the streets because we play it smart and lie low, and that wasn't smart."

"Well, I never said I was smart," he mutters as two tumblers are placed before us. I sip mine as he rubs his face. "I fucked up, didn't I?"

"Kinda," I reply. "I'm glad your men are dead though. I was going to finish them off. They touched something that was mine. A neutral."

He winces. "I'm sorry, Karma, for what it's worth. I can't get the right staff these days. They are all too fucking eager to earn their name, and they don't know the rules we grew up with."

"Teach them," I tell him as I drain my glass. "Or next time, I will," I warn as I stand. "The next time I'm here, it won't be for a drink. Understand?"

He nods, looking at his glass, and I sigh at how forlorn he appears. If he disappears, another person will take his place, and I'll have to break them in all over again. "Go apologize and beg for forgiveness. Lose your fucking dignity. It's better than losing your head," I tell him. "Or stay silent and let them come here and kill you. Your choice, but we both know a family like Sai doesn't forget, and they definitely don't forgive easily."

I stride toward the front door I kicked in when his voice stops me. "Karma. Thank you for not killing us." He smiles. "Back in the day, I wouldn't have offered the same niceties, but I guess that's why they call you Karma."

"No, they call me Karma because I'm a bitch." I smirk.

4

NEO

Sitting in the booth, I rest my ankle on my opposite knee, my suit pants rising with the movement. My silk shirt falls farther open, exposing some of my chest. I took my tie off after the zoning meeting. Nobody ever prepared me for how boring it would be to be head of construction for the family, but it has to be done.

"Did the new permits get approved?" Kane asks as he sips his wine and leans back, mirroring my pose, his arm stretched across the other side of the booth.

Zayn eyes me as he forks another piece of steak into his mouth.

The entire restaurant is empty, but it always is when we eat here.

The eighty-story building slowly rotates around, giving us the best views of the city. It's a famous restaurant for that very reason, and it's also why I purchased it a year ago. After all, it's my job to expand our legal businesses and snap things up when I see potential.

"Mr. Sai." Our waiter bows and pours us more wine. We wait for him to leave before I continue speaking, knowing better than to be overheard.

"Yes, I had to grease a few hands on the opposing counsel, since they weren't happy about the noise pollution, but the casino is a go, and we will begin construction straight away," I inform as I reach for my glass and drain it with a sigh.

"Long day, big brother?" Zayn mocks.

"And you?" I arch a brow.

"Nobody to keep out of jail for once." He smirks as he leans back, wiping his mouth. "I'm sure you'll rectify that soon enough."

"Any news on the woman I asked you to look into?" Kane asks, his voice sharp and commanding. There is a reason he leads the family. He shoulders all the burdens and our father's expectations. He's been serious and calculating since he was young. His brain works in ways I've never seen before. He's highly intelligent, but I see his fingers dancing across his thigh, no doubt itching to play.

If he had a choice, he would have followed that dream, but he didn't—none of us did. This is family, and family sticks together, so his passion was forgotten, replaced by his duty. Although I know he enjoys what he does now and loves protecting us, I worry for him.

He's so straightlaced that he might explode one day.

"Not yet. It's like she's a ghost," I admit.

"Same here," Zayn adds. "Nobody wants to talk. I've offered bribes and deals. Nothing. It's like she doesn't exist."

Kane frowns, clearly annoyed. He hates to be denied what he wants, and he always finds a way. This will be no different, I'm sure.

"Mr. Sai, I am sorry to interrupt, but you have a visitor. He is, uh . . . rather persistent."

I look up at the waiter with a frown. "Who is it?" I ask.

"It's me." A bald man storms across the restaurant. Our guards step forward, drawing their guns. He's alone, though, and I lift my hand, stopping them.

If we can't handle one man, then we don't deserve to be in charge.

He doesn't stop until he barrels through the room and reaches our table. I run my eyes down him. His suit pants are cheap and a little ripped, and his shirt is nice but messy. The tattoos indicate who he is, however, and Kane must make the connection as well.

"Jakob, head of that ragtag bunch I killed yesterday?" he asks, swirling his wine in his glass as he eyes the man.

Jakob nods, clenching his jaw.

"And why are you here?" Kane muses, taking a sip and setting the glass down. "To kill us?"

"I wouldn't have made it two steps," he grumbles. "I'm here to beg for forgiveness."

"Begging is done on your knees. Don't you agree, brother?" Zayn smirks.

"I do," Kane answers casually.

Jakob sighs, and with an expression showing his pain and embarrassment, he drops to his knees. "I apologize for the stupid attack. I was angry and lashed out. You stole our land, so I retaliated. My men are dead. Now we are even."

"Not even close." I toast him before I drink my wine.

Kane looks him over. "You don't strike me as the kind who would feel regret or ask for forgiveness, so why are you?"

"Someone told me to sacrifice my dignity and beg for my life before it's too late. I trust them, so that's what I'm doing," he admits, bowing his head out of respect and fear. Smart. He knew we would eventually deal with him. Nobody gets away with coming at our family, but he wasn't at the top of our list. He's a minor player, no one important.

"And who was that, I wonder?" Kane asks, something in his eyes flashing. I groan at his expression. It's one we know well, and Zayn and I share a knowing look. Kane's like a dog with a bone when he gets started.

Jakob stays quiet for a moment, glancing around. "Who it was doesn't matter. This isn't their business. Now, what do I have to do to keep my people and myself alive?"

"For starters, you can tell us who. I'm curious," Kane retorts.

Jakob's nostrils flare, and he looks resigned as he utters one word. "Karma." My eyes narrow as I sit up. "She came to me and told me to beg after she threatened to kill us for going near what is hers. I trust her, so I'm here."

"Interesting," Kane mutters, and Zayn and I shoot him a look. "I'll tell you what. If you tell us everything we want to know about Karma, everything useful, then we will forgive you. We have already punished your men, so I see no reason to end your entire little . . . family. You could be valuable in the future."

"No, I won't betray her," he snaps.

"We'll even let you keep your land. Isn't that nice of us?" Zayn says, sweetening the pot. I use force, and Kane uses his brain, but Zayn? He uses this silky composure. He can talk you 'round and 'round in a circle and convince you it was your idea to start with. "All you have to do is tell us what we want to know."

Jakob glances between us. "What do you want with her?"

"Your loyalty is commendable," Kane comments as he picks up his wine, "but foolish. This is your only chance. If you want your land and your life, then you will tell us what we want to know while I'm asking nicely."

His face pales and he closes his eyes for a moment, and when they open, his shoulders slump. "I'll tell you, but if you are going to try to kill her, I would caution you against it—even you wouldn't win."

"We don't want to kill her." I smirk. "We just want to . . . talk. Now, do not make us ask again. Tell us and we will decide if it's good enough for you to live or not."

5

BEXLEY

Putting my phone away, I repeat the list Taylor texted me to pick up from the convenience store on my way home. As I push through the glass door, the bell rings overhead, and I look up, taking in the scene before me.

There are two men in masks. One waves a gun around the customers who are crouched, looking terrified, while the other presses a gun to the clerk's head. The cash register is open, and a bag of money is open on the counter. The display that usually houses scratchers is smashed on the floor beside them.

I tell myself it isn't my problem.

Not my fucking problem.

Turning to the first aisle, I grab the pasta I need then cheese and bread before heading down the second aisle toward checkout.

The store is silent, and every eye is on me as I calmly place my items on the counter, pull some bills out, and glance up at the terrified clerk. "Can I pay for these, please?"

"Um, sure," he squeaks, his big brown eyes wide as he scans them. The man aiming the gun at him stares at me in confusion. "Fifteen."

I hand the cash over with a smile, grab what I need, and start to head for the door.

No bodies. Not my problem, I repeat to myself, but when a cry splits the air, I freeze and breathe deeply.

Not my problem. Not my problem. No more bodies this week. I've reached my quota—

The cry comes again, and I glance over my shoulder to see the other robber dragging a young schoolgirl to her feet.

He slides his hands across her shirt, trying to rip it open. When she kicks him, he presses the gun into her mouth. "Do you want to fucking die?" he snarls at her. Tears fall down her cheeks, but she kicks him again, and he presses it deeper until she chokes. "Do you want to fucking die?"

Ah, fuck it. As long as I don't kill them, Taylor won't be too mad.

I drop the groceries in my hand and turn. "No, do you?" I snarl and rush toward him, kicking out. He flies backwards into the glass freezer, and I duck under his friend's shot. Turning, I race to the counter, jump across it, and knock him back. He hits the floor, and I grab his hand and snap his wrist, catching the gun as it goes flying.

Grinning at the wide-eyed clerk, I hand him the weapon. "Hold this for me." I roll back over the counter and head toward the other robber, who's trying to extract himself from the broken freezer.

When he sees me coming, he raises his gun again.

Ducking left, I avoid the shot and then dart right, and when I reach him, I slam my fist into his face. "Do *you* want to die?" I ask him.

He tries to raise his gun, but I smash my fist into his face again and feel his nose bust like a grapefruit. Grabbing his hair, I slam his face into the door before dragging him across the floor. He cries out, tugging my wrists as I throw him at the feet of the girl before grabbing his gun and pressing it to his head. "Apologize."

He stutters, and I shake him.

"Apologize!" I roar as she gapes.

"I'm sorry! I'm sorry!" he yells, turning his eyes up to me.

"Not good enough." Crouching, I drag the gun down his face. "I can understand the need to steal or even murder, sure, but that? That was for fun, not survival." Pressing the gun against his lips, I meet his eyes. "Open your mouth."

Tears slide down his cheeks as he struggles to breathe.

"Now," I order.

He opens it, and I shove the gun inside. He chokes, slapping me as his face turns purple. "Not nice, is it? Remember, there is always someone stronger than you. These are my streets. If I catch you doing shit like this again, I will make you wish I pulled the trigger. Understood?"

He nods, even as he gags, and I pull the gun out. Emptying the clip, I pop the bullet from the chamber and dismantle it before tossing it into the freezer. "You will stay here until the police arrive and tell them what you did. You will serve your time, and when you come out, you will get clean. There are other ways to earn money."

I blow my hair from my face and glance around at the mess, then I head back to the counter and hold out my hand. The wide-eyed assistant passes the gun over, and I dismantle it and lay it on the counter before looking around again.

Pulling out more cash, I set it on the counter with a tap. "For the mess," I say as I walk to the door, glass crunching under my feet. I stop to pick up the items Taylor wanted, and then I head outside toward my bike.

"Wait!" I turn as the young girl and her friends run out. She's wiping her tears away but smiling at me. "Thank you. That was so fucking cool! Oh my god!"

"You're welcome. Go home, okay?" I tell her as I stow my stuff and grab my helmet. She follows me, and I raise an eyebrow as I swing my leg over my bike and lean against the tank. "What is it?"

"You're, like, so cool. I want to learn to fight like that. Can you teach me?" she gushes.

"No, but there's a gym two blocks down. Reacher will teach you," I reply. If she wants to learn, I won't stop her. Everyone should be able to protect themselves.

"Thank you, I will, seriously. You're so cool. Straight up mommy material." She giggles.

"Please don't ever call me that again," I grumble as I pull my helmet on.

"Sure thing, Mother." She smirks.

Rolling my eyes, I slam my visor down and point at her. "I mean it. Go home and behave."

"Bye, Mommy!" she calls loudly over the revving of my engine. Scoffing, I pull out.

Kids these days. Fuck, I sound old.

I should head home, but Taylor is still in a mood, so instead I drive to Night Tails for a drink so I can work up my courage to face her wrath. When I pull up outside and park my bike, I eye the two black Mercedes idling in front of the bar. A man in a suit nods at me, and I tilt my head.

Nobody like that comes to a place like this. It's a dive bar. They have good liquor and music, but it's mostly a safe place for us street kids to hang out—neutral territory.

Who is here starting trouble? I have an idea, and I know I should turn around and leave, but if it is them, then they won't give up that easily. It's better to see it through now and discover what they want.

Sighing, I stow my helmet. Can't a bitch have just one day without a man causing trouble and making her have to clean up his mess?

One would assume I hate men, and most of the time, I do, but I also love them when I need them. I just don't really need a man for anything. Fucking? I could probably fuck myself better. Protection? No thanks, I can handle that.

Money? I have plenty.

The thing is, men sense that about me, and it makes them insecure. They don't know how to react when they can't manipulate a situation or lord something over me. It usually makes them act in one of two ways—feral or angry.

I'm going to bet on feral with the three Sai boys.

They aren't used to being denied, born with silver spoons in their mouths and told they are God's gifts to our world. They were bred and raised to be the best and lead their family, and now they are here.

Pushing through the padded leather door, I scan the bar and find them in the back booth, the pole right next to them. The music is low, which is unusual, even for a slow night. The other patrons look nervous, and there are men wearing suits lining every single wall with guns at their waists.

I guess having the three heads of the Sai family in one place makes them nervous.

Ignoring them, I walk across the sticky floor, past the tables, and slide onto a stool at the long black bar.

I grab some ice and wrap it around my hand, ignoring the men staring at me. "Vodka, please, babe." I smile sweetly at Sash. She moves behind the bar, pouring it for me, and when she slides it over, she leans in. "They are chasing my customers away."

"Got it." Downing my drink, I keep my knuckles wrapped as I slip from the stool and head their way.

They watch me approach, their drinks untouched before them.

I know enough about them now to tell them apart—Kane, Neo, and Zayn Sai.

Their guards shuffle as I stride right to their table, not stopping until I'm next to it. "What can I do for you?"

"Ah, we were just waiting for you." Zayn toasts me. "Take a seat."

"No thanks." I eye their drinks. "Don't be rude. Drink your drinks and then get the fuck out," I say sweetly. "There is nothing here for you to wait for."

The big asshole, Kane, bursts into laughter, and we all turn to look at him in surprise.

Chuckling softly, he leans back and watches me with dark eyes. "Now I'm even more interested. Sit, Karma. Now."

This dick . . .

6

ZAYN

I can actually see her gearing up to rip my older brother a new one, and he can too, though he seems more amused than anything as he waits for her vicious tongue.

Have I ever heard my older brother laugh before? No, I don't think I have.

I eye her once more, even more curious now.

"I suggest you change your tone before I decide that your men aren't here for a gang bang and are actually a threat," she warns and smiles sweetly, but it's terrifying. "Now, Mr. Sai, what can I do for you?"

"Talk," Kane replies, and then he gestures to the chair by the booth. "Sit, please," he tacks on when she raises an eyebrow.

Neo and I share a shocked look, but he ignores us, and she sits in the chair, eyeing us. Most people would be terrified, but she doesn't look the least bit intimidated, more irritated than anything.

"Karma, I have learned a lot about you recently," Kane begins.

"Is that supposed to scare me?" she scoffs and grabs Kane's drink, downing it before holding up the glass. "Babe, can I get another? It seems our guests don't want to leave on their own."

"You don't seem scared of us," I remark.

She runs her eyes over me. "Darling, I have scarier men bringing me my mail. You're just rich boys playing gangsters. Now, last chance, why are you here?"

Kane's face loses all its amusement, going cold, and his guards react, standing straighter. She simply arches a brow. "I have been polite, but I do not appreciate insults. Your attitude may be acceptable around here, but you will speak to me with respect—"

"Or what?" She lifts her chin. "What will you do, Mr. Sai? Kill me? Many people have tried. Torture me? Been there. What will you do to me?" He grinds his jaw as she smirks. "Just as I thought. You have money and power, but not here. These are my streets, not yours. I don't know what you thought would happen when you came here, but you were wrong."

"We came to thank you," I interrupt as they glare at each other, "for helping with the mess on our brother's birthday. We didn't come to fight."

"Then you shouldn't have brought an army," she snaps as a drink appears for her. She accepts the tumbler and sips it as she looks at me. "You seem like the smart one here. Is that what you all want? Because you can go now."

"Our brother and your . . . niece are friends," Neo hedges. "We should get along."

"No, we really shouldn't," she retorts as she takes a drink and stands. "Have a good night—"

"We are being nice, yet you keep running from us," Kane comments.

Turning, she leans down until he has no choice but to tilt back. "Bitch, please. I don't run from anyone. I drive fast." She smirks.

"Is it bravery or stupidity that makes you so bold?" he retorts.

"Neither. It's experience and the ability to back it up," she responds then presses the drink to his lips. "You're being rude. This is good whiskey."

Opening his mouth, he swallows as she tips the liquid down his throat, and then she steps back. "It is good," he says with a grin. "We got off on the wrong foot. We truly did wish to thank you."

"A card would have sufficed, or flowers, not bringing an all-you-can-eat man buffet." She runs her gaze over our guards. "Though, that one is cute." She blows a kiss that way, and Kane's eyes narrow. I wouldn't be surprised if the guard was fired before the night was through.

The door opens, and a group of men storms inside, scanning the bar. When their eyes land on our table, it's clear they are here for us. I nod my head at Kane, but he shakes it as they stomp our way.

"The fuck are you doing here, Sai?" the big bastard at the front barks. "This isn't your turf."

"Just having a drink," I say as I look them over. "You have us at a disadvantage. You know us, but we don't know you."

"We ar—"

"Oh, no, we don't really care," I say, toasting him with my drink. "Just thought you should know since you seem slow."

"You fucking—" He slams his fist on the table, but whatever he was going to say is cut off as Karma suddenly stands.

Every eye turns to her, and the big guy actually shrinks back. "You are being rude to my guests," she says conversationally as she eyes them. "Now, if you want to kill them, you will do it outside of my bar. Is that understood?"

"Yes, Karma. I'm sorry." He bows his head, eyeing his men. "We didn't know they were here on your invitation. We apologize."

"Good, now be good boys and get out of here before my mood darkens because I have to look at your ugly fucking face." She waves them off, and they hurry away as swiftly as they arrived.

"I'm both turned on and afraid," I comment with a grin.

"Just the way I like it." She winks.

We lapse into silence as the men leave the bar and she sits down, eyeing us. "You said your thanks."

"I still have a drink," Kane replies.

She rolls her eyes but doesn't protest. Maybe she's warming up to us? It couldn't hurt to have someone like her on our side. Whatever she's into, it's obvious she holds power around here and has a reputation. Others show her respect and fear. I wonder what a woman like her has done to deserve it, because there is one thing I know for sure—you do not earn it easily.

My phone rings, and I check the ID and sigh. Staring at Kane, I answer it. "Tell me you haven't been arrested."

I listen carefully, and when I hang up, I shoot Karma a look before focusing on Kane. "I need to go. The men we sent to speak to the chief have been detained."

His eyes tighten in annoyance. We knew it was a risk, but we had no choice. It was a smart business decision. Kane relaxes, and I arch a brow as an evil grin curves his lips, one that means I'm going to be doing a whole lot of paperwork. "Use it."

"What do you—" Realization dawns on me. "You want me to frame the police chief for illegally detaining our men?"

"Or threaten him with it. Get what we need." Kane shrugs.

Chuckling, I stand. "Got it, brother."

"Neo, go with him," Kane orders.

"What about you?" I ask.

"If these twenty men can't keep me alive, then I deserve to die," he scoffs.

I look around then back at Karma, who just watches us, smiling innocently. "I won't kill your brother, unless he annoys me, then all bets are off."

"Why don't I feel comforted by that?" I mutter. Shooting Kane a look, I narrow my eyes. "Don't annoy her. I don't want to have to take over your role. It seems like way too much work." I step past her, and with Neo on my heels, we stalk to the door, ready to leverage with the police to get what we want.

We leave our brother to play with the woman everyone else is afraid of.

Let's just hope he can keep his mouth shut for once.

7

KANE

I watch my brothers depart, knowing they can handle it, then I look
back at Karma. She's an unknown, and I don't like not knowing.
"One thing does fascinate me . . ."

"I am on the edge of my seat, waiting to hear what," she deadpans.

I hide my smile at her sass. Something about it is strangely endearing. Nobody else speaks to me like that. They cower in terror. Even my
brothers, despite their ribbing, don't dare cross that line. Everyone
fears me, and I don't blame them.

There is a reason I have the reputation I do. There is a reason I am
the head of this family.

I will do whatever it takes.

She doesn't seem to care, however, and I don't know if it's bravery
on her part or just plain stupidity, but I do not mind as I speak to her.
She's . . . different from those who surround us, desiring money,
power, or clout. She doesn't seem to care for any of it, but uses them
just as well as weapons. Karma is rough, her voice speaking of the
streets, and her clothes aren't designer, yet she wears them like they
are. She's as comfortable in this bar as I assume she would be in a
mansion.

She's a puzzle, one I want to pick apart and put back together.

39

We stare at each other for a moment. "Well?" she prompts.

"I was waiting for you to ask politely. I don't like foulmouthed people."

Her laughter rings through the bar. "Fuck off. You're surrounded by killers and mobsters." She leans closer, her eyes sparkling viciously. "You say you don't like my mouth, but are you sure about that? You've been staring at it a lot."

Her meaning is clear, yet I can't stop myself from tracing her lips with my eyes, and she smirks, thinking she's winning. I change the game again, running my thumb across hers. Her lips part, soft as petals, as I murmur, "I like the look of it, but the words make me want to silence it another way. Now, ask nicely about what intrigues me."

"You think I care enough to ask?" she retorts against my thumb.

People are watching us, but I don't care. We are so close, I can smell her sweet perfume. It wraps around me, stroking my skin, speaking of nights in silk sheets with untold pleasure. The challenge in her eyes promises I'd enjoy it, and as her wicked lips part, I watch as she sucks my thumb into her mouth. Her hot tongue wraps around it, teasing my skin. My eyes widen in surprise and pleasure, and then she bites down.

Hissing, I jerk away. She laughs, my blood on her lips.

Before she can move away, I wrap my hand around her throat and squeeze. "Nobody who draws even a drop of my blood lives," I growl.

"Then try to kill me," she dares, and I feel the hard press of a gun against my dick. "You might manage it, but I'll also pull the trigger, then we'll both be dead. Won't that be fun?"

"You truly do have a death wish," I mumble as I stare into her eyes. Her outward beauty hides such a vicious little thing.

"Maybe, or maybe I'm just itching for you to give me an opening," she replies. "Now, release my throat. If it's not during sex, it just isn't worth it."

Surprise fills me, and laughter tumbles free as I release her and sit back. She watches me with an arched eyebrow. "You look a lot more handsome when you laugh."

"Is that right?" I grin. "I don't usually have a reason to, so I guess you'll have to make it happen more often. Now, how about you remove your gun from my dick? I'm quite attached to it."

"I bet." She drops her arm and sits back like nothing happened.

"Boss!" someone yells.

Karma glances over, but she aims her gun at me. Smart girl. "Call," the same person adds.

Throwing me one last look, she stands and tucks her weapon away. "Well, that ends this delightful yet strange conversation. Have a good evening, Mr. Sai." She wanders away.

I watch her go, staring at her tight ass, and when she answers the phone, I make no move to leave. I even sit back and get comfortable.

"Sir, shall I get the car?" one of my guards asks.

"Not yet. I'm enjoying myself." I continue to watch her, more than intrigued.

Who is this woman?

"Alright, stalker." She places her palms on the table and leans into me two hours later. I've watched her the entire time and observed how others direct questions to her and respond. It's been interesting and enlightening. "Are you planning on staying all night? You're scaring away the customers."

"Am I?" I murmur. "Tell me your real name and I'll leave."

"You want my name?" she flirts, sliding her hand across mine on the table. "Why? So you can scream it?"

"Planning on making me scream?" I flirt back.

"Not in the way you're thinking." She flutters her lashes inno-cently. "And no name. I don't give out information for free. You should know better. Nothing in this world is free, and information is power."

"What do you want in return?" I ask. For some reason, I need to know it—not just so I can figure out who this woman is, but so I can call her by it.

"Nothing you can offer," she purrs.

"I have enough money to buy the entire world ten times over, more land than God, and more men than I can count. I have everything. Tell me what it costs."

"You have everything, but not me." She smirks. "And not my name. This is one thing your status, money, or power can't buy. I am not for sale."

"Everything is for sale," I counter. "It's just the price that differs, so tell me, what's yours?"

Pulling out a revolver, one of many guns she's undoubtedly carrying, she sets it on the table before me. "Here, pull the trigger and see if you die or not. If you survive, I'll tell you my name." When I don't move, she grins. "That's what I thought. You'll gamble land and money, but not your life. From a man who looks like a bad *Godfather* reject and will have his hairline snatched back in two years, it isn't surprising. I obviously have more to fill out my pants than you."

I have to bite back my smile. Why are her insults so fucking endearing?

I can't let her think of me that way though. For some reason, I want to prove her wrong.

Picking up the gun, I meet her eyes and press it to my head without hesitation.

"Sir—"

I pull the trigger, never once looking away or flinching, and then I hand it back to her. "Well?"

"That's it." One of my guards steps up next to her, aiming his pistol at her. "Sir, she is trying to kill you."

"Really? Wasn't that obvious before now?" I smirk, but he doesn't lower his arm, and something about it makes my smile dissolve.

"Motherfucker, really?" She pulls another gun, this time a Glock 17, and presses the barrel to his head so they are in a standoff.

My other guards draw their weapons, outnumbering her.

My eyes narrow. There are so many guns aimed at her, yet she doesn't seem concerned. It bothers me, though I'm not sure why.

"The next person to aim at her dies," I warn, my voice ice-cold.

I don't like them pointing guns at her.

"You heard your master. Drop them," she teases, still smiling, but her eyes are tight and she's scanning them like they are threats. I have no doubt she would take most of them out before they could kill her.

"Sir—"

I pull out my trusty Sig Sauer P226 and shoot the man who's speaking. He crumples to the floor. "Last warning. Drop them now!" I roar.

The bar is silent as my men slowly obey. Karma smirks, stepping back and lowering hers as I stand and fasten my suit jacket. "Until next time," I murmur into her ear as I pass, and I frown at the corpse. "Take care of that," I order.

She grabs my arm, and I realize she is a woman of her word as she presses up on her tiptoes, her lips against my ear. "Bexley."

Holding back my shiver of desire, I watch her walk away before shaking off my stupor and prowling to the door, then I leave her and the bar behind me.

I don't know much more than when I came, but I know one thing for sure—I want Bexley carnally.

Bexley . . .

She was right. I want to scream it.

8

BEXLEY

It's been a few days since the Sai brothers invaded my bar. I've been waiting for the other shoe to drop, but it doesn't, so I relax. I don't know what they want, but they won't get it from me. They might be fun to play with, but that's all.

I have much more important things to deal with, like avoiding the punch heading my way.

I manage it at the last second, and the boxer across from me stumbles back when I kick him. "Focus, Bex!" Reacher barks.

Groaning, I pull my gloves off and lean into the ropes. "Why do I have to train the newbies?"

"Because you lost the bet," he reminds me, his arms crossed. "Plus, I trained you, so you train them. It's a fair turnaround."

"I have other things to do," I begin.

"I don't care," he snaps, the only person besides Taylor who would dare to talk to me like that. Maybe it's because he's too old to care whether he lives or dies. "Now get your ass back in there before I let all of them in to beat your ass."

Sighing, I pull my gloves on and turn as a new fighter advances on me. He's brutal and fierce, and he's trying to prove himself, but he picked the wrong person to challenge.

I let him tire himself out. His swings are forceful, but his footwork is sloppy, and I dance around him as the crowd grows. He's going to be a champion, but they all know me, and the bets taking place in our audience only annoy him.

He thinks he's too good for me, so I play with him. I land a few soft hits and dance out of reach. "You're too big. You can't move, can you? If you're going to let a little girl beat you, I might as well bend you over and make you my bitch."

His eyes narrow and he snarls, exposing his mouth guard as he lunges for me again. Laughing, I dodge his feral attack, which only angers him more. I roll under a brutal grab and punch that probably would have broken my neck, then I taunt him until his face is red and covered in sweat. He looks like he's ready to murder me.

This is fun . . . until my phone rings.

I decide to stop toying with him and end it. I pull back my fist and slam it into his head the next time he comes at me. He goes down for the count within a second, and I pull off my gloves as the spectators cheer and hand over their bets. I skip to my bag and pull my cell out, grabbing a wad of cash since I bet too.

"Yo?" I answer, wedging the phone between my shoulder and ear as I count to make sure it's the right amount.

"Bex." The sob makes the blood freeze in my veins. "Bexley— hel—"

Taylor's voice ends in a scream, and my heart stops as a soft, maniacal chuckle sounds. "If you ever want to see your friend again, I suggest you find us." The line goes dead.

I am out of the door in an instant, ignoring everyone's worried looks and yells.

I race home faster than I've ever driven, my heart pounding in fear. Our front door is closed, and a bad feeling builds within me. Pulling my gun out, I slide along the wall and crouch to avoid the window, then I peek in before crouching again, but I saw six guys waiting for me.

Idiots.

Since they probably expect me to come through the front or back doors, I go to the side of the house and put my gun away, then I hook my hand in a pipe and scale it. It's something I practiced and perfected. There are ridges on it to assist in a quick escape, but to everyone else, it looks like nothing but a pipe.

Once I reach the slightly lower roof over the bathroom, I flip over and hang down so I can grab the ledge and drop to it. I press against the glass there as I slow my heart and balance on the three-inch ledge. Sliding down, I carefully open the window.

I drop silently onto the bathmat and listen. When there's no noise, I redraw my weapon and move to the door, twisting the knob. I swing it open soundlessly—I only oiled it the other week, so there's no squeak, which I'm thankful for as I crouch walk along the corridor to the top of the stairs and peek over.

Two men are sitting on our sofa like nothing is happening, flipping through our magazines.

One is smoking in my house, and the disrespect pisses me off more.

One is at the back door, and there are two more at the front.

Furniture is overturned and a lamp is shattered, indicating there was a struggle. Taylor's bag sits forgotten by the front door, where they obviously snatched her. I take it all in within seconds.

I could play it safe and try to speak to them, but they came into my house and touched my friend.

They are smoking in my fucking living room, and that one bastard has his feet up on my table.

It's just rude, and I hate rude people.

Standing, I take aim as I whistle. They turn to me. "Waiting for me, idiots?" I call as they fumble for their weapons.

Too late.

I don't even give them time to speak. I fire rapidly as I descend the stairs, my boots loud, bullets ripping through my living room and their bodies.

By the time my feet hit the bottom step, they are all dead.

Taylor is going to be so mad, but as I look around, I don't care.

Walking over to Taylor's bag, I inspect it. Her keys are near it. She obviously dropped them when she opened the door and was attacked. Her phone is gone, but her purse is still here.

They were sending a message. Carefully picking up the contents, I put it on the sofa and step over the bodies. My blood flows coldly, my anger getting the best of me.

They touched her.

If I find out they hurt one hair on her head, I will tear them limb from limb.

A phone rings, and I crouch, taking it from one of the bodies, and answer, but I don't speak.

"Well, do you have her?" an impatient voice asks.

Smirking, I look around. "Your men won't be coming back anytime soon, nor do they have me, but don't worry. I'm coming to you anyway. I'll be seeing you soon." I hang up, ignoring it as it rings again.

I got lucky. Lauren is staying with a friend tonight, but I still call and check. My voice probably sounds odd, but I try to calm down so I don't alert her that anything is wrong.

"Hey, kiddo," I greet when she answers. "You all ready for bed?"

"Yep. You're picking me up tomorrow, right?" she replies happily, and I hear giggling in the background.

"Sure thing. You're all okay?" I ask.

"Of course, why wouldn't I be?" She laughs at something her friend says. "Tell Tay I'm okay. I'll call her in the morning."

"Will do, kid. Have a good night." I hang up, my expression turning cold.

They took Taylor.

This has to be because of the Sai brothers—one of their enemies. No one else would dare come against me or take a neutral. They are off-limits for a reason.

I heard rumors over the last few days. They spread like wildfire after the two bar incidents. They say that I'm in bed with them. The rumors are wrong, of course, but it seems their enemies don't care about that. They can't touch them, so they came for me.

That was their first mistake.

The second was thinking I would let them live.

Grabbing my phone, I put in a call. "Trace the two numbers I'm sending you. Keep it quiet and consider it a personal favor." I hang up without explaining. She knows what to do. A minute later, a message comes through. Both numbers are at one location.

That's where they have her.

I could call in reinforcements, but this is my family. Maybe it's time I remind everyone who I am and what I can do so they never make this mistake again.

They dared to touch what is mine.

They will regret it.

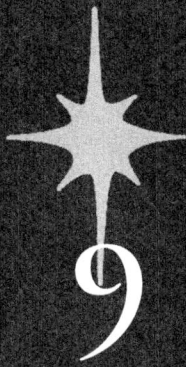

9

BEXLEY

I don't know who it is, but I don't care.

I stand in front of their house, on the border of the rich and poor sides. Kids come and go, no doubt running drugs, and they have guards with guns patrolling the perimeter. I watch it all.

They aren't expecting one woman.

I could kill all of them, but I don't need to. I just need to cut the head off the snake and get Taylor out of there safely. Everyone else can suffer later.

No, this will be a reminder, but first, I'll get my family to safety.

As I run my eyes over the perimeter again, a plan forms. Hopping down from the roof of the abandoned house next door, I wait for the guards to turn away and speak to the new batch of teenagers heading inside, and then I make my move. Rushing across the paved driveway, I duck under one of the cars and strap on a homemade device before rolling out the other side near the wall. When there are no alarms or shouts, I hurry to the bushes and wait.

Exactly thirty seconds later, the car goes up in flames in a massive explosion. The guards race toward it, their guns raised, and I use the chaos to my advantage. I slip through their masses completely unseen and walk through the front door.

I keep my head ducked and walk into the first room. Once there are no more footsteps, I shut the front door and lock it. It will buy me a little time. I head upstairs, where most of the guards came from. It doesn't take a genius to guess where he is hiding, but I check every room as I pass just in case.

There's a closed door at the end of the hallway, with indents from guards' boots on either side of it. They are gone now, the morons.

Whistling happily, I kick in the door, announcing myself as it slams shut behind me. I step into the carpeted office and look around, but the idiot doesn't even have any guards up here with him. Either he's under-estimating me or he's dumb.

Either way, one of us should be offended.

"What the fuck?" he roars as he climbs to his feet, and I finally focus on him.

"What? I got your invitation, and this is me accepting," I reply sweetly. He isn't a player I recognize, which is surprising. He either must be new or good at hiding. Whichever, it doesn't matter, not after what he did.

He went after a neutral.

He touched my family.

Pulling my gun out, I scratch my head with it as he sits, his Adam's apple bobbing. He's a big guy—not fat, just big. He fills out the chair behind his desk, his shaved head shining under the light. He has to be at least fifty, and judging by the diamonds on his fat fingers, he's prob-ably new money. Only they show off like that.

I stroll around his office as he watches me from his chair, fear and anger in his eyes. He isn't used to being outplayed. He isn't used to people not fearing him. He thought I was an easy target.

He's an idiot, and he'll pay for it.

"You sent all those people to kill me . . . Well, I'm right here in front of you." I spread my arms as I grin. "Kill me! Oh, wait, I forgot. You're too much of a pussy so you make others do your dirty work—teenagers and easily led men. You can't do it, can you?" I smirk as his nostrils flare.

"What do you want?" he demands, his face turning red as I

continue to wander around his office before stopping at the edge of his desk.

"What do I want?" I muse as I run my fingers over his desk to a chessboard. "I wanted a simple, quiet life, but you ruined it." Picking up some of the pieces, I make him wait. "You stole that from me." I place the king down as I lift my eyes to his. "So now I'm going to do the same to you." I flick the king over, and it hits the board, making him jump. "If I can't have the life I want, then neither can you."

He glances at the computer on his desk, and I see his shoulders slump in relief. It gives me the second I need to react.

I turn as the door bursts open and fire, killing the men coming to rescue him.

Turning back to him, I grin. "Tell me where she is and I won't shoot you."

He looks from his dead men to me, and I arch my eyebrow. "She's downstairs in the kitchen," he snaps.

"Good boy," I praise as I step around his desk. Once there, I set my gun on the top, and he glances at it. I wag my finger in warning as I reach over and undo his tie, then I use it to bind his feet to his chair before grabbing my gun and looking at the tray of liquor behind him. Smirking, I reach over and grab a bottle.

"Good year." I nod in appreciation. "Must have cost you a few million." Uncorking it with my teeth, I meet his eyes as I take a big gulp, and when he doesn't react, I roll my eyes. "Boring." Tipping the bottle over, I pour it over him and then throw it across the office, covering the carpet as he sputters and gasps. I prowl around the desk, stopping next to the chessboard once more.

Picking up the queen, I pocket it with a wink and walk toward the door, pulling my lighter out and dropping it to the floor as I go.

"You said you wouldn't!" he roars as he fights to get to his feet as the liquor ignites, whooshing across the carpet and straight for him.

"I said I wouldn't shoot you," I reply as I lay my hand on the door and turn to look at him. "I never said anything about not killing you. I would stay to watch, but I have to get home. Enjoy the fire you started."

I shut the door and walk down the corridor, his screams filling the air as he burns to death.

Descending the stairs, I head back into a corridor as flames consume the second story, and I find Taylor in a wooden kitchen chair, her eyes wide and mouth gagged. Two men hesitate on either side of her. Rolling my eyes, I aim at them. "Go, before I kill you. Last chance."

They share a look, but both lift their guns. "I guess that's a no. See, Tay, this is what I get for being nice."

Her eyes narrow as she yells something behind her gag, but I can't hear her, so I focus on the two men.

"Friends?" I offer instead, and they share a look, confused and unsure. I have that effect on people.

Lifting my arm, I shoot, but the mag's empty. "Oops," I say with a grin. "Guess I got carried away. How about we talk instead?" I drop to the floor as they fire and leap at the first man, knocking him back to the kitchen counter. "I guess not," I mutter, slamming his hand into the marble. He releases the gun, so I grab it and pull him up in front of me as a shield as his friend swings around to us.

He hesitates.

I don't.

I shoot, but he darts to the side, the bullet cutting through his shoulder when the man I'm holding elbows me, making me double over with a grunt. I kick out, and he stumbles, falling over the kitchen rug before righting himself.

He kicks as well, though, and catches my hand, causing me to drop the pistol, which spins across the room and under a counter. How fucking annoying. I hear the flames growing closer and know I need to end this.

His fist slams into my jaw, and I spin before turning and spitting blood across his face. He roars as he wipes it away. "You bitch!"

"Nope, my mamma didn't raise no bitch. Well, technically, she didn't raise me at all, but you get the point," I joke, ducking under his punch. "Damn, you don't like dead parent jokes? Yeah, we wouldn't be good friends."

Tay struggles in the chair, and she falls to the floor with a crash, wiggling on her side. I kick out, and the man stumbles over her and plummets to his ass on the other side as his bleeding friend comes at me with a kitchen knife. Leaping back, I duck and weave to avoid the blade until I spot my opening. Grabbing a kitchen towel, I stretch it between my hands and wrap it around his wrist on his next upward swing, twist, and turn. The knife goes flying, and I whip the fabric across his face. He howls as he steps back, covering his eyes.

"Damn," I whisper as I look at the towel. "Who knew?"

There's a grumble, and I glance up in time to see them both heading toward me once more. "You really don't give up, huh? Does he pay well? Good benefits? I'm curious what the going rate for hired idiots is."

"You're dead," the one I shot snarls.

"And you need a thesaurus or a dictionary. Come on, where's the verbal repartee? The sassy comebacks? Spice it up a bit, you know?" I sigh as the heat in the kitchen starts to creep up from the fire.

I grab a pan and throw it at the blockheaded idiot. It smacks him dead in the face, bursting his nose, and his friend comes at me when I'm distracted.

He grabs me from behind, lifting me into the air. I use it to my advantage as his friend comes at me and lift both legs, kicking his chest and sending him to his ass.

He lifts me higher, and I throw my weight back so we both fall backwards. He hits the ground hard, and I make sure to elbow his junk on the way down so his hold loosens. Flipping over, I grab his head and snap his neck. It's a quicker death than I'd like, but it's getting hot in here, and I don't want to be a Bexley kebab. Sliding across the floor, I grab the towel and wrap it around the other guy's neck as he struggles to his feet. Leaping up, I press one foot to his shoulder and the other to the floor, then I heave with all my strength. He slaps at me, his face turning purple, and when he stops, I let go.

His lifeless body falls to the floor.

"Should have taken my offer of being friends." I sigh as I drop the towel and hurry over to Taylor, yanking her gag down. "Miss me?"

"Idiot, free me now!" she yells, her eyes red from tears.

"So mean to me, even after I saved you," I mutter as I untie her. "Did you see me? Was I badass? Like a female John Wick? You could be my dog." I sit back, and she throws her arms around me. Grunting under her weight, I pat her back awkwardly. "You're fine. You knew I would come."

"I know," she whispers, sniffling. "I just don't like the interior design of this house. That's why I'm crying."

"Don't worry, it will burn down soon, which reminds me. We should definitely go." After I help her to her feet, we head to the door, but I stop and hurry back to the kitchen.

"Bex!" Taylor hisses, but I grab my towel and throw it over my shoulder as she gapes at me.

"What? It came in handy. I might start a new weapon line and call it 'Cooking with Murder.'"

I hear her sigh even over the flames.

I help Taylor into our house, but she freezes at the door. "Ignore the mess and bodies," I mutter as I sit her down on the couch and hurry to the bathroom. I grab one of the many first-aid kits we keep scattered around the house. Kneeling in front of her, I lift her hands. Her wrists are bruised, but not bad, thank goodness. I carefully apply some bruise gel as she looks around, her eyes narrowed.

She's pissed. I'm definitely going to get screamed at, so I stay quiet as I clean the cut on her head where they knocked her out and cover it. I sit back when I'm done, waiting to be scolded, but she surprises me when she covers my hand. "Thank you, Bex, for coming for me," she says softly, staring into my eyes.

"Always. We're family," I reply like it's obvious, which, to me, it is. I will always protect her. We're sisters. I can't help but smile as I look around though. "I love you, but I'm not cleaning this up."

She laughs, which in turns sets me off until we are sprawled on the messy sofa. "So who were they?" she asks as we quiet down. "They didn't say much. It was obvious I was just bait."

"Nobody important." I don't want to worry her, and it's been dealt with anyway. I try to keep her from this life as much as I can. It isn't working well, but I really am trying my best. "Lauren is fine, by the way. I made sure. She'll be back tomorrow, so I guess we should move the bodies."

"I'm tired," Taylor whines, "and it's your turn for grave duty."

"Nuh-uh, I did it last time with that idiot who followed you home, remember?" I grouse as I glare at her, and she sits up.

"I was taken prisoner this evening, Bexley." Her eyes narrow, and I glare back.

"I had to save you. I hurt my wrist," I retort.

"They knocked me out."

"I had to kill people."

We both glare, neither of us winning the usual game. "Rock, paper, scissors?" she finally suggests, and I nod. We both yell it before revealing our hand, and I groan when she wins.

Smirking, she stands. "Make sure to scrub all the floors. We can't have Lauren seeing even a drop of blood. The mop is in the hallway closet. I'm going to bed. Have fun." Chuckling to herself, she heads upstairs as I look around at the mess.

"I save a bitch and still have to clean." I look at my new best friend, the towel. "You wouldn't make me do this. I wonder if I could pay someone. They should start a body removal service. Hell, I should as well, and now I'm just talking to myself." I haul myself to my feet and prop my hands on my hips. "Okay, which one of you assholes is farting, though, because it stinks in here?"

No one answers.

10

NEO

Sipping detox juice, I watch the news while scrolling on my phone.

"The fire was finally put out around 5AM. The police believe there are no survivors, and law enforcement isn't saying whether it was an accident or intentional, but locals believe the man who owned this once beautiful mansion was heavily involved in trafficking drugs." That piques my interest, and I scan the screen displaying the cinders of a house. It isn't one I recognize, so it isn't anyone we know or work with.

Whoever it is clearly had a very bad night.

"Do we know them?" I ask the guards in the room.

"No, sir," one replies. "I can look into it if you wish."

"It doesn't concern us. Leave it be, just keep your eye on it. If someone is roasting crime bosses alive, then we need to make sure they aren't coming for us," I command.

"Yes, sir," he responds, and I focus on my phone. Just then, Zayn strolls in, wearing nothing but a silk robe, and sits at the head of the table, grabbing coffee as he meets my eyes. I scan the numbers on the latest email, the update for the casino we are building, as I wait for him to speak. He was out late, wining and dining some CEOs for us after reading contracts. I don't miss the scratch marks on his chest, but I don't comment.

We all make sacrifices for the family.

No more than Kane. Speaking of . . . "Dodge, where is Kane, and why aren't you with him?" I ask when he enters the room.

"He had an early meeting. He wanted me to take the young master to school," Dodge answers.

"Right on. Dodge, can you delete the door footage from last night?" Zayn asks.

We both turn to him, and he grins. "I might have had a bit too much to drink. Father will kill me."

"What did you do this time?" I grumble.

"I might have fallen into the pond and then maybe his new Rolls Royce did as well." He toasts me with his coffee. "Don't worry, I'd already be dead if Kane saw."

"He saw. They are pulling it out right now," Dodge informs him as he pours himself a coffee and leans against the table. "You're dead. Sorry."

Zayn groans, pinching his nose. "What if I tell him I sealed those three deals last night?"

"With your dick?" I say, nodding at his gaping robe. He smirks as he leans back, showing whoever's handiwork.

"One of them took some persuading, and Kane said any means necessary."

"And I bet you enjoyed the hell out of that." I scribble on the email's signature line for the new apartments before giving him my full attention. "You need to be more careful, Zayn. I know you're the youngest and still in your wild phase, but we have enemies everywhere. The birthday party should prove that."

He pouts. "It's been quiet."

"I know, but that doesn't mean it's safe," I reply, but I frown as I process his words. It *is* quiet, too quiet.

"Dodge, do you know what's going on? We usually deal with at least four threats a day, and there hasn't been anything for a few days," I ask.

"I'm not sure, sir. Kane was discussing it this morning as well. It seems most of our usuals have stepped back, and I am looking into why," he explains, but he seems troubled by it too.

"It could be to lull us into a false sense of security. Let's triple our staff and patrols—"

"Already done, sir. Kane suggested the same. Either they are planning something or someone is out there protecting us. The first is more likely. I have your guards on extended shifts. That's why I took the young master to school, and Kane wants everyone to lie low for a few weeks until whatever it is occurs."

Zayn groans but doesn't argue. The last time something like this happened, someone tried to blow up our house with a missile. He's still picking dust off his suits, so he knows better than to argue when it comes to this. "I'll poke around and see if any of our men in prison have heard anything. The vines inside are quicker to spill than out here," he mutters as he pulls his phone from the pocket of his robe and heads out of the room to make those calls.

I watch him go before glancing at Dodge. "Whatever the cost of the car, take it from my account. I'll cover it and the damages before Kane gets back. He might not kill him then."

"Yes, sir." Dodge smirks. "You can't keep covering for him though."

"He's my brother." I shrug. "Besides, we all did stupid shit when we were young. I still remember that day you ran butt naked through the hotel—"

"Nope, no, no." Dodge holds up his hands. "Don't make me relive that."

"It was funny," I say as I down the rest of my detox juice.

"It was humiliating, and you'll never let me live it down," he grumbles as he checks his watch. "I'll go check on Kane. Call me if you need anything."

I salute him as he leaves and get back to the mountains of emails I have.

Everyone thinks being a mafia family must be so easy, just murder and mayhem, but the paperwork is killer.

"Okay," Zayn says as he walks into my room without knocking and throws himself across my bed, his ridiculous robe parting and showing me everything. Rolling my eyes, I turn back to the mirror and deftly knot the black and gold tie before tugging down my waistcoat. Turning to face him, I raise an impatient eyebrow as I button my sleeves.

"Okay?" I prompt when he says nothing.

"Sorry, forgot how comfy your bed is. Why is it better than mine?" he complains.

"Because you're an animal that breaks yours all the time. Okay, what?" I press as I grab my suit jacket and pull it on, straightening the front. I glance at the mirror to check out the black and gold design I chose today.

"I managed to get some answers, though I don't think you'll like them." My eyes narrow as I turn back to him. "Apparently, that fire was set by our new bestie, Karma. Seems someone pissed her off. Word is she's on the warpath, and most people think it's in protection of us thanks to the party and Kane being at the bar. People are backing off because of her." I blink, and he grins. "I knew you'd like that."

"Wait, our enemies think this random woman, Karma, is on our side, so now they are taking a step back because they are . . . scared of her?"

"She killed fifty people in that fire." He shrugs. "My men inside tell me she's fair but crazy and not to piss her off. Evidently, she's a legend with a lot of pull. I think they are waiting to see what our connection to her is and what she'll do before they act again. I suppose it buys us a little peace."

"And her a lot of enemies," I mutter. "If they think she's with us, then they'll go for her too."

"They already did. The owner of that house, Mr. Merchant, has been trying to make a move on us for years, wanting our southside land. Seems he thought he could get to us through her. He was wrong and turned into an overcooked ham."

I sneer at the reference, making a mental note not to eat ham for a while. "We should tell Kane and then speak to her. She might be angry if they assume she is with us, and we don't want her turning on us as well. We can't fight a war on every front."

"We should just adopt her, since everyone thinks she's with us. She's hot and crazy enough to be one of us," Zayn says as he gets even more comfortable, his robe riding up so his bare ass is on my Egyptian cotton.

"You really think she'll be mad?" he asks conversationally.

"If someone came after you over someone you barely know, wouldn't you be pissed? Worse, wouldn't you hate them? We can't afford to make an enemy out of her. We will need to rectify this situation and clear the air. We'll wait to see what Kane says, but we'll try to set a meeting again, this one formal so nobody gets any ideas."

"And so she doesn't kill us," he adds helpfully. "Although, I don't think the location would stop her. She took down all those men on her own. What a woman." He sighs wistfully, and I gag when I see his cock hardening.

"I fear for your sanity."

"I would too. I lost it a long time ago." He grins.

Sighing, I run my eyes over my brother and genuinely do not understand how we are related. "Please get your naked ass off my bedspread." With an evil look, he slings the rest of the robe off and rolls across my bed, wrapping my comforter around him as he goes.

Snarling, I pull my phone out and call downstairs. "Yes, Ms. Hedge, please burn my bed when my ass of a brother gets out of it."

Zayn laughs as I hang up. "Where are you going?"

"A meeting. Don't forget about court this afternoon. See you tonight." I stalk out, shaking my head when I hear him getting comfortable.

He's such an idiot.

11

KANE

I was stupid, and now it might get me killed.

I should have taken more guards with me. I knew it didn't feel right. I'm almost thankful Dodge wasn't with me to get killed like the others who were cut down in broad daylight. The parking garage under the hotel I was supposed to have my meeting at was empty, until it wasn't. Gunfire lit up the area and screams filled the air as my guards dove at me, trying to get me to safety.

They lost their lives as they tried to protect me with their bodies.

I managed to kill a few of our assailants, but there were so many of them pouring from black SUVs and blocking our car, I wasn't able to do much. The last thing I remember is running back to our vehicle before an explosion of fire engulfed it, and I was thrown backwards. I hit the ground hard, tasting blood, and then . . . nothing.

Until I woke up here.

I must be underground somewhere because the air is stale and slightly damp. The room is small, more of a cell than anything else. There are no bars on the door, but the door itself is thick metal. There's a stained mattress I woke up on and quickly rolled off of, and now I sit with my back to the back wall with my knees up, my arms resting on them. My chains clank with every movement, the collar I'm wearing feeding into the shackles on my wrists then bolted to the back wall. I tugged on it until my wrists bled, my strength no match for my bindings. I need the key or I'm not getting out of here.

The room is maybe the size of my bathroom, and I don't know where I am or who took me. It could be any of our numerous enemies. The list is long, after all, but one that's brave and well connected enough to do this? It reduces the list of suspects.

With nothing but time, I go through those names, trying to figure out why. Knowledge is power, especially in this situation. I'll get out of here, I have to, but in the meantime, I need to be strong enough to withstand whatever they will do to me.

By the time I hear a noise at the door, I've narrowed it down to four possible families, and I'm almost eager to face them when the door opens. Five burly men step inside, clearly guards or workers. They are covered in ink and dressed in a mix of street clothes.

That rules out Grant, since his men exclusively wear suits, and Polly's men usually wear sparkles, so that leaves two. It could be either of them. I refuse to ask, though, because I won't show an inch of weakness.

I lean back into the wall, a cocky smirk on my lips as I watch them like they've stepped into my kingdom.

It isn't the first time I've been captured and tortured, and it won't be the last, but one thing always happens.

Everyone who touches me dies.

The idiots.

By now, Zayn and Nero will know that I was taken, and our people will trace what happened and find me. There is nowhere in this city they can hide me where I won't be found. It will just take time—time I need to stay alive for.

One on the left cracks his knuckles. He has a square, menacing face with tattoos covering every inch of visible skin, his hair styled up in a bright mohawk. He has madness in his gaze, but I always find that those who make themselves look menacing like that aren't the ones you need to fear.

It's the ones in sheep's clothing who are the scariest. I know from experience.

I look like any other businessman, yet I have so much blood on my hands, they will never be clean.

The one on the right, who is dressed in all black, looks too calm. He's definitely the one I need to watch out for. The other two are low-level thugs, all brawn and no brains. They are used for torture and protection. Every organization has them. They are replaceable but essential.

"Let me guess," I drawl as I eye the four guards, "you aren't here for a tea party."

They remain silent, and I climb to my feet, tilting my head back. "Let's begin, shall we?"

No matter what anyone tells you about being tortured, there is a moment when any man or woman will break—either from physical pain, mental agony, or outside factors. I know that moment will come, so I need to hold out as long as I can to give my brothers time to find me. Besides, there is a reason I am the head of the family.

My shirt is long gone, exposing my old wounds, which they take great care in cutting open. I was right. The silent man in black is the true wolf, especially when he heats up a poker and repeatedly slams it against my back. I hold in my howls of pain, refusing to make a sound.

Once they split my back open, they step over to their table of tools, debating which one to use next. I watch as mohawk picks up a whip and coils it, a split tongue slipping from his mouth and caressing his lips in a creepy manner. He definitely has that psychopathic trait down to a T, that's for sure.

"Lovely," I joke.

His fist slams into my face, wrapped with the whip, and snarls as he steps back. "Shut it."

Spitting my blood on his polished boots, I grin up at him. "I don't want to tell you how to do your job, but torture works better when you tell the victim what you want first."

"We don't need to tell you—"

"Oh, I'm sorry," I interrupt mohawk. "I was talking to your boss, not you." I glance at the silent man. I am still deciding between two families, and the more I know, the better. They took me for a reason. Usually when I'm taken, they want money or land—hell, revenge is a possibility too.

The silent man steps forward, rolling his sleeves back, and I get my first look at the tattoos that cover his arms from his wrists up. Interesting. It means he either feels the need to hide who he is or he is in a position where he must. It's something to take note of just in case it comes in handy later.

"We are just having fun until he arrives."

"Ah, so he does speak." I grin. "You were better when you were silent. I can smell your breath from here. Have you visited a—" The breath whooshes out of me as he punches me in the gut. Grabbing my hair, he yanks my head up and snarls in my face.

"Keep up your jokes, they'll eventually fade. All that bravado will flee and you'll beg," he sneers.

"Begging? Not really my style." I smirk. "But feel free to try. Many have attempted the same, but they were much bigger and scarier than you, little boy."

His elbow slams into my face. I feel my nose burst, filling my mouth with blood, but again, it isn't the first time it's been broken. "You'll have to be much more creative than that," I say as I cough up the blood. "You're letting our side down, giving us all a bad name. It's very disappointing. Give me those tools and let me show you how it's really done."

It only enrages him further, and he wraps his hand around my neck, squeezing until I have no air. I smile, knowing he won't kill me, not yet. If they wanted me dead, they would have killed me in the parking lot with my men. No, they want something, which means they will keep me alive for now.

I tap his hand. "Can't kill me yet," I force out, and he snarls as he lets go. "Good dog," I sputter, and mohawk has to drag him back as I grin and suck in rough breaths.

The door opens, and I lean back in my chains. "Ah, well, this just got interesting," I admit out loud, my voice rough as I get my first look at the person who captured me.

12

BEXLEY

I t took us all night to clean the house. There were some things we couldn't salvage, and I hated seeing Taylor upset about that. We have both worked hard to make this a safe place, and it was ruined because of me. I don't sleep due to guilt, so instead I make sure Taylor gets to work safely and then check on Lauren before I get started for the day.

They came after me because of the Sai brothers, which means I owe them a visit. I climb onto my bike, tugging my helmet down and shooting off into the city. It wasn't hard to find out where they live.

I park my bike a couple of streets away and use the back gardens of the rich ass mansions for cover as I survey their house for the next hour. I note the guards' patterns and access points. There is a reduced number of them, which makes me think the Sais aren't home, but that doesn't mean they won't be back. They are supposed to be the most protected family in the city, but nothing can protect them from me.

My family was hurt because of them, and they need to answer for it. When I'm sure of my path, I make my way around the back wall and hop over it, hiding in the bushes. As soon as the guards pass on their patrol, I dart across the grass, around the house and pool, and scale the posts that hold up the second-floor balcony. I've just rolled over the lip of the veranda when the guards walk under me. Smirking, I crouch walk to the glass door and pull out my pin, picking the lock before slipping inside. The carpet muffles my steps, but I'm still careful, moving as silently as possible down the hall. The art and decor scream of wealth, and I almost scoff at the family portrait that hangs over the top of the double stairs. Swearing under my breath when I hear a guard heading my way, I duck into a room, hiding behind the door.

"Those fucking tacos have gone through me," the guard snaps. "Give me a break." The door I'm behind suddenly opens, and I look around as he rushes inside and slams it closed. He doesn't even notice me as he rips out an earpiece and shoves his pants down.

"Well, this is awkward," I remark, and he spins, his pants falling to the floor. Unluckily for him, he chose to go commando today.

"What the fuck?" He scrambles for his gun, while I grab the closest object, which happens to be the bottle of soap from the sink. I rush him, knocking the Ruger out of his hand, and he gapes at me again as I toss the bottle in my palm. "Question. Aren't you worried about shitting your pants when you go commando? Does it chafe?"

He stares at me, and I sigh. "You're going to scream, aren't you?" I mutter.

I see him debate it, and then he opens his mouth to yell for help, which I can't let happen, so I slam the bottle into his face.

"Congrats, by the way." I nod at his cock before I swing the soap bottle into his head again. It takes a few hits for him to go down cold, then I drop it into the sink. "Fucking rich people. Can't they have better weapons on hand?" I grumble as I prop my hands on my hips and look down at him. "Now, what do I do with you?"

An evil thought comes to mind. Grinning to myself, I get to work. He's a heavy fucker, but I manage to strip him easily enough. I pull his uniform shirt over my head and leave my own pants on since I don't want his ass germs. I add the tie and push it up into place, then I shove my hair up into a high ponytail.

Slipping his blazer on, which is a little big, I button it then add the earpiece. "Southside clear," I hear, and I look down at him.

"We can't have you waking up and ruining my plan. Sorry, but hopefully you don't shit yourself while you're out. That would be embarrassing," I say as I glance around and grab one of the long towels. I spin it to create a rope and bind his arms and legs, hog-tying him before grabbing a smaller towel and shoving it into his mouth.

Grabbing his phone, I unlock it with his finger and navigate to his browser, raising my eyebrows. "Damn, you're just out here watching porn, and not even in private. You are bold, but nice choice though," I tell him as I load the video and press it to his chest. The sounds of groaning and farting fill the air—you know, just in case. Stepping back, I inspect myself in the mirror before slipping out of the door and shutting it behind me. Anyone who comes to investigate will hear that eight-hour loop of a man struggling to shit, so they shouldn't look—at least for now.

With more confidence, I wander back to the stairs to wait for them when a guard rounds the top and stops. He's a big bastard and mean looking, with a scar intersecting one eye that twitches as he runs his eyes over my sloppy uniform. "Why aren't you at your post?" he snaps.

Ah shit. Think, Bex, think. He grows increasingly annoyed at my lack of an answer, though, and steps closer.

"Are you new?" He frowns, and I nod. "Figures. Find Pat downstairs and get your position," he orders as he barges past me. "Fucking newbies. Why do they keep bringing them on?"

Flipping him off when he isn't looking, I head down the stairs. I mean, seriously, who needs this big of a staircase? What are they doing, having sliding contests? It's excessive, but then again, everything about this mansion is.

I peek into a few rooms before I find the one I want, and I shut the door behind me. I pour myself a drink and hop up onto the dining table and wait. I'll stay all day if I have to.

Luckily for me, it doesn't take long before I hear engines and the front door opening. Several footsteps head this way, which means I got lucky again. It would have been really awkward if we had to play a game of hide-and-seek.

The double doors open dramatically, admitting Neo and Zayn Sai.

"Sir, sir! We found one of our guards bound and gagged upstairs —" They stop in the doorway as I lounge on the dining table. The blazer is folded to my side and the tie is hanging loosely down my unbuttoned shirt.

"That would be my handiwork. Sorry about that, but he got in my way. At least he's still alive." Leaning forward, I grin at their shocked faces. "Hello again."

Guns are instantly aimed at me, and I roll my eyes. "That's not a nice way to greet a guest," I tease.

"A guest usually knocks or is invited," Neo comments idly as he stalks to the bar and takes a seat on a stool. "They don't break in and knock out the help."

"I'm a bad guest. Spank me." I shrug as I slide to the edge, swinging my legs back and forth, but my smile drops and my expression turns deadly. "We need to talk."

"I figured," Neo replies as he pours a drink. "If you wanted to kill us, you wouldn't do it like this."

"True. Smart boy." Taking a sip of my own drink, I eye them. "My house was broken into and raided, and someone important was kidnapped. I, of course, dealt with it, but the issue is, they felt safe coming after me because of you. They thought I was in bed with you, which put me in their sights. I'm giving you two days to rectify this or I'll have to prove I am not working with you."

Neo stares at me, and I arch an eyebrow, showing how serious I am. I have a reputation to uphold. No one fucked with me, but since they came into my life, everything has gone tits up. "Unless, of course, you would prefer for me to make your lives a living hell."

"Usually, I'd enjoy playing with you, but not right now," Zayn comments, and his eyes are tight with stress. I tilt my head.

"What happened?" I ask curiously. I should be the only one stressing them right now. I don't like having my thunder stolen.

They share a look, and it's clear they are considering not speaking before Neo sighs. "Kane, our older brother, is missing. His guards are dead, and he's been captured. You wouldn't know anything about that, would you?" The look he gives me would terrify anyone else.

"Wish I did, but not my style. If I wanted your brother dead, I would have slit his throat in his sleep, not made a sloppy mess. Shame, though, because he was really pretty. Well, good luck with that." I hop down and head to the bar. Reaching over, I grab the bottle of whiskey I was drinking. It's good, though I'm betting expensive since it was locked in a glass box.

"Call this payment for my gas." I shrug as I walk to the door. Guards step into my path, aiming their guns at me. I touch the top of the closest one and push it away. "Don't be ridiculous. You'll die before you pull the trigger."

"If it wasn't you, then maybe you can help us," Neo says, and I glance over my shoulder to see him on his feet. He nods at his people, and they lower their guns. "You take contracts, don't you? We pay well. Help us get my brother back and you'll be richer than you could ever imagine."

It pisses me off that they think they can buy me so easily. I mean, he's not wrong, but it's the principle. "No thanks," I reply, toasting him with the bottle. "You couldn't pay me enough to get involved in your shit. Word of advice—deal with my issue before getting your brother or there won't be a place in this world where you can hide from me. See you." I barge through their guards and into the foyer. The man I knocked out is sitting on the bottom step with a towel around his waist, and when he sees me, he falls back with a yelp.

"Sorry about that," I tell him before I wave at the others and walk out the front door. They let me go, which is smart of them.

13

T he door shuts, our guards stepping out to give us privacy, except for Dodge. I grab a drink from the bar and down it, the alcohol burning my throat but not washing away my panic.

"What are we going to do?" I throw my empty glass, watching it shatter before I round on Neo. "Kane is gone, and his guards are dead. Who knows who has him and what they are doing to him. We need to tell Father."

"Not yet," Neo says calmly, but I see the tightness around his eyes. "We'll handle this ourselves. If we don't, he'll take control back and never trust us again. Dodge, did you get the footage from the surrounding area? We need to figure out who would be bold enough to take him, and then we'll find and kill them."

"It should be here any second, sir," Dodge replies. He's quiet and withdrawn. I know he's blaming himself for not being with Kane, but the truth is, he only would have died with the others. He's like family to us, so it's a good thing he wasn't there. "I'm very sorry." He bends into a deep bow, and Neo slaps his back.

"It isn't your fault. We'll get Kane back. He's counting on us and tallying up how long it takes us, so let's focus on that, okay? Keep it as quiet as we can. We don't need anyone else figuring it out and coming after us while we are weak."

I pour myself another drink, but Neo's hand covers it. "I need you to be sober," he snaps. "Kane is counting on us."

"What if he's already dead?" The words escape me, and I glance up at Neo, begging him to tell me I'm wrong. I might act tough, but the truth is, my brothers are my security. They've always been my shield. I couldn't imagine . . . Even the thought scares me.

"If they wanted him dead, then they would have killed him in the parking garage. That means they want him for something and he's alive—for now," Neo says, and it helps me relax a little. "I don't know how long, though, so I need you with me, brother."

"I'm here." I take a deep breath. "Tell me what I can do."

"Reach out to your contacts in the police department. I want every eye on it. They might find something we can't. Get the information on the bodies Kane took down—IDs, addresses, known associates, everything. We need information stat."

Nodding in understanding, I pull my phone out and get started, knowing he's right. Every minute we waste is another Kane will be suffering. It's up to us to save our brother, the way he has saved us his entire life.

NEO

Zayn leaves, talking on his phone, and when he's gone, I slump and scrub at my face.

"Neo—" Dodge starts.

"Don't apologize again." I raise my eyes to him. "No one disobeys Kane's orders. We know that. Just help me find him, okay?"

Weight presses down on my shoulders, and I realize for the first time how much my older brother suffers to keep this family safe at all times. He does so silently and selflessly, but with him gone, it's all on me. We need to present a united front so no one suspects anything is wrong, including our father and younger brother, all while we look for Kane before it's too late.

"Of course, sir," he responds, and I watch him depart before taking a sip of my drink. The alcohol soothes my nerves, if only slightly, but I will only be able to breathe properly when Kane is back. Whoever took him . . . they have plans. They knew where he would be and how many guards he had, which means I can't discount someone on the inside helping them. It makes me feel angry and downright confused.

"The cameras at the scene were disabled beforehand," Dodge tells me when he steps back into the room, "but we managed to capture some vehicles speeding on cameras as they left the area. Our team is tracing the plates as we speak."

"They disabled the cameras, which means it was planned," I mutter as he hands over the tablet, and I watch the footage as four black SUVs roll out of the garage across the street. "They will either be unregistered or stolen, unless they are stupid."

"My thoughts as well, sir, but we might get lucky," Dodge replies. I nod as I pull my phone out, checking if any of my contacts have gotten back to me yet, but there's nothing. Kane has been missing for half a day, yet we still don't even know who took him. I need to make a move.

I call the person most likely behind it, one of the other leading males in our sector. Grant answers on the second ring.

"Well, to what do I owe this pleasure?" His voice is dark and unwelcoming. "Is this about that stupid land suit again?"

"Not this time," I reply as I swirl my glass, watching the liquid whirl. Someone took Kane, then it has to be one of the men wanting to snatch our title. Grant hates us, and he stands to gain the most from our downfall.

He won't just admit if he took Kane, but word games are my strong suit.

"I wish to set up a meeting. Kane's orders for tomorrow." If he took Kane, he'll be surprised, and if not, then he'll be happy, thinking I'm giving him a shot at that land.

"Of course. Does ten work? I can bring the lawyers," he answers quickly, betraying his interest, and at that moment, I know it isn't him.

Fuck.

"I will check and get back to you." I hang up, lowering my head. "It isn't Grant," I tell Dodge. I kind of hoped it would be. He's powerful and rich, but we also know how to deal with him. Not knowing is worse.

"What about Polly?" Dodge asks.

"No, he isn't smart enough to make that move," I admit. "Which leaves the other two." And they are far more dangerous and unpredictable. Compared to us and Grant, they are street rats grabbing for power and territory. They couldn't have done this alone.

My thoughts come back to the same conclusion—someone on the inside helped them, which means . . .

I need someone who isn't on the inside to help find him.

There's only one person who comes to mind.

14

BEXLEY

"U se your fists, not your feet, dumbass!" I call to the ring where the newbie is training. Turning with a scoff to Reacher, I shake my head. "These young ones."

"I remember when you were that eager," he teases as he leans back, his tracksuit crinkling.

I sigh dramatically. "Now I'm all old and washed up."

"You aren't even thirty," he scoffs.

"Physically." I nod. "Mentally, I'm ninety. I like naps, comfy beds, and watching hot men on TV."

He blinks, and my grin grows. Muttering to himself, he looks back at the newbies. "Was the fire you?"

"You have to ask?" I gasp, offended as I uncap my beer and take a sip. He spares me a look, and I shrug. "They fucked with mine."

"Fair." He nods. "There are rumors going around."

"When isn't there?" I groan. "I swear, Reacher, you love gossip more than Tay."

"I'm worried about you, kid." I meet his eyes and see he means it. "You're in bed with some very powerful, bad people, and it's putting a target on your back."

"Not in bed with them, trust me. I might as well get the perks at this rate, though, if people are going to think I am," I quip before sighing. "I'm not with them. It was a mix-up, one I will guarantee they make certain everyone knows. You know my rules."

"I do." He nods. "Do they?"

"They'll find out," I mutter as I take another sip. "You have a lot of new blood here."

"Gotta make money somehow," he comments. "I'm getting too old to run around on these streets, so this is all I'm good for anymore. Besides, it stops them from running guns and drugs if they are in here. You're moving too slow!" His yell is sudden, and I follow his gaze to a boxer beating the bag. "Even Bex could kick your ass with her eyes closed."

"Her?" The big bastard chuckles as he cracks his knuckles, trying to appear intimidating as I watch him. "She looks like I could break her in a second. How about it? Show me how tough you are."

"I'm so scared." I feign a shiver. "Sure, but I don't play fair." He stalks my way, and I press my hand to the table until he moves close enough.

Flicking the cap, I watch it smash into his face, and he goes down hard, making Reacher sigh. "The one you just blinded is my best fighter."

"Oops. He had a big mouth." I shrug. "He has another eye. It's just greedy to think he needs both."

"Bexley," he admonishes as the boxer is dragged away. "There are other rumors."

"Tell me." Information is power, and he might be a gossip, but he also knows more than anyone else around here. It's how he has survived so long.

"Apparently, the eldest Sai is missing—an inside job, I hear." This piques my interest. I didn't tell anyone about Kane missing, and I doubt they would either, but it's reached the streets. "I even heard who might be behind it."

"Well? Don't keep me waiting," I drawl, but he looks far too serious as his eyes dart around.

"Butcher," he murmurs, and I freeze, hardening all over.

"How sure are you?" I ask, my voice callous.

"Almost a hundred percent. His men were bragging in a bar outside Mai," he admits. "Are you okay, kid?"

I nod as I breathe through my anger and panic. If Butcher went for them, then I don't stand a chance. If he thinks I'm in bed with them, he'll come after me again. This peace I've had will dissolve, but worst of all, it means he's back. I've been waiting for this for a while, but now that I'm faced with his return, all the old fear and pain return. I drink the beer and slam it down.

"He's back then?" I ask.

"Looks that way. I guess he's stopped lying low. He's probably trying to get his name and land back, thinks going after a big dog like Sai will get him that, or he's just batshit crazy."

"A bit of both," I murmur, knowing him far better than I wish. "If it's true, Kane—Sai is in big trouble."

"Why do you care?" He eyes me, and I force my expression to blank.

"I don't. Just saying." I shrug.

"Kid, don't do it." He leans over. "You got out. You aren't that scared girl anymore. Don't go back there."

"If he finds out I'm here and alive, he'll never let me go," I explain. "I need to strike him first."

"Damn it, kid." He slams his fist onto the table. "You barely escaped, and now you want to go back?"

I cover his hand. "I survived because of you. If he finds out, you'll pay too. You're right. I'm not that scared girl anymore. I'm a weapon, his karma. I'll remind him of that."

Sighing, he takes my hand. "Don't die, kid, alright?"

"Me? Never. I'm living forever, remember?" I tease, and we're both quiet for a moment before he pulls away and opens another beer with his teeth.

"Enough of this touchy-feely shit," he dismisses. "I expect you'll need some supplies."

"Probably, but for now let's just watch them kick each other's asses." I toast him with another beer, kicking my legs up on the table. I appear casual and calm, but inside is a raging storm.

Past and present collide as everything I escaped, everything I ran from, catches up to me. Nothing really stays secret or dead in this world, not for long, and it seems my time just ran out.

I'm distracted, which is why I don't notice the commotion at first. Fighters stop, confusion filling the air, and I glance around with a frown.

"Remember what you said about not being in bed with them?" Reacher nods, and I turn my head to see Neo and Zayn with their guards standing in the open gym doors. "Might want to remind them of that."

Sipping my beer, I watch them as they look around before finding me, and then they walk my way like they own the place. They wear designer brands and drip with wealth, yet they move like they are as comfortable here as they are in a mansion. It's surprising.

When they reach me, I hold up my hand. "I know why you're here. The answer is still no. You wasted a trip." Draining my beer, I put the bottle down and nod at Reacher. "I'm going to work off some energy on your new fighters and test them like you wanted."

"Don't kill them," he grouses.

"I won't. I will just hurt them really, really badly." I smile as I remove my overshirt and climb into the ring, wearing nothing but my cargos and sports bra.

The three fighters hesitate as I roll my shoulders and bounce on my toes, loosening up my body before I look at them. It's obvious they don't want to do this, but they know the rules. To train here, they have to do as they are told.

They aren't completely useless though, and they come at me together. I don't bother raising my guard as I duck and weave under them, having fun, but their wild swings go wide and they can't keep up, so I get bored. Leaping toward the ropes, I flip over the first and drive my fist into the back of one's head, making him go down, hard. Spinning, I duck under the next's swing and plow my fist up into his chin. I hear the click of his jaw, and then he's down as well. The last fighter steps back, eyeing me cautiously.

He's smarter than the others. I could wait for him to come at me, but where would be the fun in that? I advance on him, even as he retreats, positioning him exactly where I want, and when he has no choice but to lift his arms to protect his face, thinking I'm aiming for it, I slam my knee into his balls. His guard breaks as he roars, and I slam my fist into his face until he goes down.

Looking around, I eye the groaning fighters and search for my next match. There is this antsy, angry feeling inside me that I need to let out.

Butcher's name repeats in my head, bringing back old horrors, and this is the only way I can get rid of it. I ignore the Sai brothers as much as I can, but it's clear they won't extend me the same courtesy.

"You call this burning off energy?" I glance over to see Neo leaning against the ropes. "You aren't even breaking a sweat. You aren't the type to waste time on those who are weaker than you."

"You have no idea what type I am," I retort as I sip my water.

"No? You like a challenge, you like to win, and you like to be the strongest in the room. I hate to tell you this, but you aren't."

"No?" I arch an eyebrow as everyone looks between us. "Then who is?"

He smirks. "Me."

I laugh loudly, and his smile only grows. "You? Did your daddy tell you that every night, pretty boy? You couldn't stand one minute in this ring with me, never mind land a single hit. Go back to your designer stores and parties, little boy. You aren't welcome here."

"If I land one hit on you, then you have to accept my contract," Neo snaps, clearly offended. "If I land a hit, then you have to find him."

Heading over, I crouch before him, cupping his chin through the ropes. I tug him close until our lips nearly touch. "No," I whisper when it looks like I'm going to kiss him, then I thrust him away, laughing. I turn, but I feel movement behind me. I duck and turn to see his arm stretched out to grab me. He got into the ring silently. I'll give him that.

"Scared?" he calls loud enough for the others to hear, and the crowd says, "Ooh!" Someone even laughs, and I narrow my eyes, knowing what he's doing. "I think you're scared to lose."

Tugging off his coat, he folds it and hands it to a guard. "Like you said, it's designer. Now, are you going to accept or run with your tail tucked between your legs? If you do, you aren't who we thought you were."

The bastard backed me into a corner, and he knows it, but that's when I'm most dangerous.

"Fine, rich boy," I scoff as I step back. "Show me what you've got."

The crowd grows, their cheering intensifying, but I ignore them as I stand casually with my arms at my sides. "Well, are you waiting for written consent?" I sass as he stares.

Smirking, he slowly rolls back his sleeves, exposing tan, muscular forearms, and my mouth goes dry as his veins only seem to bulge. The prick. He doesn't know it's a weakness of mine, but when I meet his eyes, he's watching me carefully.

"Some time today," I call out of annoyance and embarrassment. "Do you need your brother to hold your hand?" I duck under his punch, coming up next to him and driving my fist into his side with all my strength. "That was slow and weak. You can't hurt me, rich boy, so don't hold back on my account." I dance away as he covers his side before shaking it off.

He watches me move around him, and then he dives at me. He has good control of his body. Neo doesn't give away his moves before he makes them, but he fights too clean, and I use that to my advantage. I hop over his leg and under his swing, dancing around and driving my foot into the back of his knee. He goes down, then I bring my knee up into his face twice. He groans as he falls forward, blood dripping from his nose as he flops to his back. His pretty, perfect face is covered in rivulets of red. Most fighters would back away, but I'm not most. You need to make sure they don't get back up—a lesson I learned the hard way.

I slam my foot into his face and then step back as he covers his bleeding nose.

"Stay down," I scoff, looking at him, but the idiot climbs back to his feet. He's stubborn and stronger than I expected. I even hear the crowd muttering in respect.

Shrugging, I pivot and dance around the ring to avoid his wild, angry hits. He's not holding back now, which is good. His teeth are stained with his blood, and his eyes are bright and furious. He exudes power, even in a suit. He's brutal, but I can't let myself get distracted. Using the ropes when I hit them, I launch myself at him, wrapping my legs around his neck and spinning us so he hits the mat. Keeping my legs tight, I choke him out, even as he slaps me and rolls us, lifting me into the air and slamming me back onto the mat. The blow loosens my legs, and he launches at me, but I drive my fist into his face, and he falls back with a groan as I climb to my feet above him.

"Are you stupid?" I ask as I crouch in front of him as he coughs, spitting blood into the ring.

"No, just determined," he replies as he lifts his head and eyes me. "I'd do anything for my brother, and right now, we need you."

Grudging respect and understanding fill me. I'd also do anything for my sister.

"Go home before you get yourself killed," I tell him softly. "This isn't the place for you."

"No, but it is for you, and we need you." He climbs to his feet once more, lifting his fists.

Sighing, I stand and shrug. "Okay."

This time, I don't hold back, and neither does he. He dives at me with a viciousness born from training and survival, but he's not as fast as I am. No matter how much he has trained, there is a difference. I had to adapt to survive, while he did it for protection, and that means I always fight to win because losing meant pain or death. I always fight dirtier and faster because I had to. I learned the hard way how to win and what happened if I lost. Most fighters spend their lives in gyms, trying to learn what I have, but I would give it all up if I could forget the memories. It serves me well now, though, as I weave under a jab that would have rendered anyone else unconscious.

His eyebrow splits as I drive my fist up, and when he jerks back, I bring my knee up into his stomach. Neo bends over, and I ram his face into it before spinning behind him, where I wrap my arms around his throat and jerk him back to the floor. I go down with him as I wrap my arms and legs around him. He wheezes in my grip, slapping me and the mat, twisting his body to try and get free. Once he realizes he can't break it, he does the only thing he can—he rolls us and lifts, slamming me down until I release him, and then his fists come for me. I roll out of the way, flipping to my feet and meeting him head-on again.

His reach is longer than mine, so I need to get under his guard, which isn't hard. He's blinking a lot since blood drips into his eyes, and I duck under it and kick out, my foot connecting with his face, causing him to spin and hit the ropes. Yet again, he gets back up, spitting his blood over the side before turning to face me.

He has the same look in his eyes I used to have in mine when I fought—desperation.

He will do whatever it takes to win this because he feels like he has to.

My respect for him only grows. I thought the Sais were posh, rich boys playing gangsters, but his eyes tell me differently. I know they love their family, since I've learned enough about them, but being willing to die in this ring for Kane? That surprises me.

Besides, what he doesn't know is that I'm involved in this now too.

I should walk away, but I've built a life here.

A family and a community.

I'm not leaving it now, so I'm going to strike first.

I consider their offer, but the truth is, it gives me a chance to go after Butcher. I would get what I've always wanted with their help, which means I might just be able to handle it without dying.

Butcher is the reason I am who I am. He's the reason I became Karma.

We spar back and forth, getting more and more brutal until Neo's panting and dripping in blood, but I'm slowing as well. After all, I can't make this too easy.

He throws wild jabs at me, driving me back into the ropes, his teeth clenched and coated in blood.

His fist comes at me again.

At the last second, I move my face ever so slightly so it's in the path of his swing. No one else would ever notice I did it, but it's the excuse I need as his punch lands, marking him as the winner.

My head swings around, and everyone freezes, falling silent. Poking my aching jaw, I turn back to see his wide eyes. Licking my teeth, I glance from him to his brother. "I guess that means you win."

Nodding at him, I duck out of the ring, ignoring the shock and confusion, and slip my shirt and coat on as I nod at Reacher. "See you later, old man." I don't look too closely. Seeing his knowing smirk already has my hackles up.

Outside of the gym, Zayn and Neo catch up with me. Their guards surround me, with more waiting at a blacked out SUV, and I stop.

"So you're going to help us?" Zayn asks, sounding confused.

"A deal is a deal. I'll help you find your brother," I reply.

"You agreed to it easily," Neo states, watching me as he shoves a handkerchief into his nose, making his voice muffled. I wonder if anyone has ever landed as many hits on one of the Sai brothers before. "Why?"

I run my eyes over him, letting my smirk grow. "You call that easy? You got your ass kicked." His brother chuckles as Neo's eyes narrow, and I roll my own. "Let's just say we have a mutual interest," I admit as I look from him to his brother. "Let's do this, shall we?" I spin on my heel and walk away, letting them choose to follow me.

Climbing on my bike, I grab my helmet as I look at them. "Keep up if you can." I shove it on and take off, leaving them to scramble after me.

15

ZAYN

S wearing, we dive into the SUV, our guards piling in after us. "Follow her!" I order as I'm thrown back into my seat. We speed after her as I hurry to put my seat belt on, her already ahead as we pull out onto the street, weaving through traffic like a mad woman.

"I swear she's trying to kill us," I mutter, and then I glance at my bleeding brother. "I mean, she definitely tried to kill you."

His eyes narrow as he pulls the rag from his nose. "She let me win. It didn't look like it, but she did." His gaze goes to the window. "I want to know why."

"Someone like her? She doesn't let people win," I scoff. Even I know that.

"Exactly, and she said she had an interest. There's more to this than we know, and I don't like being in the dark," Neo responds, and I nod. "Follow her closely. Don't lose her or you're dead."

The guards know we are serious, and they speed up, racing through red lights to keep up as she effortlessly moves through the streets like she owns them, which I guess she technically does. We found her, but it was fucking hard. No one wanted to betray her trust. The only reason someone told us in the end was because, I think, they wanted to see us get our asses kicked by her, and Neo did, but desperate times call for desperate measures.

We lapse into silence after that, focused on following her. We seem to be going in circles, and on the next road, we lose her. Swearing, I lean forward. "Go back and search for her bike." It takes us five minutes until we see it parked outside of a restaurant. "There." We stop behind it. Neo and I get out, our guards falling into step behind us as we open the door to find the restaurant's empty bar. Karma sits in a booth at the back with a menu in front of her.

Heading her way, I slide onto the opposite bench, Neo squeezing in beside me as he drops his bloodstained cloth on the table.

"I thought we were finding my brother," he snarls.

"Well, I'm hungry," she says as she drops her menu. "Besides, you have questions, and so do I, so we'll talk as we eat. Did you think I was going to somehow magically find him in the city in one second? Please tell me you're smarter than that, boys, or is Kane the only smart one?"

"Bexley," I warn, "we are a little impatient right now, as I'm sure you can understand. Don't fuck with us."

"It's my favorite game." She shrugs idly as a waiter appears. "Ah, I'll have the burger. Well done, please, I've seen enough blood for today."

"Just water for me," I order.

Neo says nothing, and the waiter disappears. I look between Neo and Bexley, who are having a silent staring contest. "You look a lot better a little messed up," she blurts without blinking, and Neo jerks his head back, confused, making her smile because she wins.

"Sir." A guard kneels at Neo's side, sparing Bexley a worried glance. "Do you need me to call the doctor?"

I bite down on my smile as Bexley grins. Neo looks at her worriedly. "Do you need a doctor?"

She rubs at the slight bruise on her jaw with her middle finger. "No, you hit like a wimp, but you definitely need one. You look like you just survived a zombie apocalypse."

Neo's eyes narrow, and he dismisses the guard, not taking him up on his offer, which only makes me fight my smile harder despite the situation.

"Why do you have an interest?" Neo asks, and it's like cold water is thrown over me, reminding me that Kane is probably being tortured. We need to find him, and if she can help us, then we'll do what it takes, but Neo is right. She wants this . . . . Why? If Bexley didn't want to help, she wouldn't. She flat-out turned us down before, so why the change of heart? If she truly did lose on purpose, then it means there's definitely a reason.

"You are ruining my appetite," Bexley says as she leans back, eyeing us. Neither of us speaks, and she sighs. "Fine, I need to confirm something before I speak, but if the person behind your brother's kidnapping is who I think it is, let's just say we both want to find him."

"And if it is that person and you find him?" I ask.

"Then I'll kill him." Her expression is cold, her eyes dead as she stares at me. Her countenance changed so quickly, it makes me hesitate. She blinks, and some life returns to her eyes, but not much. "Tell me everything you know about your brother's disappearance."

Neo nods, and a guard passes her a tablet, cueing up the video. She watches it repeatedly. "They were waiting for him, which means you suspect someone on the inside. I'm betting they are the only people who had his schedule. He was taken alive, so he's most likely still alive now. They probably need him for something. Those men who attacked are trained, but not professionals."

"And what does that tell us?"

"They are from the streets, not military or militia. It's most likely who I think it is." She zooms in, and we let her take her time with the video before she hands it back. "Any luck IDing them?"

"We traced the plates, but it was a dead end. They were false," I admit.

"There's only one place they would go for that kind of job here." Food is placed before her, and she smiles at the waiter before digging in. We watch her eat in confusion and silence. She devours the burger and fries before downing her drink and standing, wiping her mouth. "Meal's on these guys," she announces before walking away.

Neo and I share a look before I shove him from the booth. "Hurry up and pay."

Grumbling, he does as he's told, and when we get outside, she's waiting on her bike. "This time, I'll go alone. They won't speak to suits like you. I'll call you when I know something."

"You don't even have our numbers," I scoff.

"Want to bet?" She grins as she shoves her helmet on. "Oh, and don't try following me. It won't end well for you."

With no other choice, we watch her leave. "Do you think we can trust her?"

"No, but we have no choice. We'll keep digging into it ourselves from different angles as well. Let's get back. Dodge might have found something on the cameras."

16

BEXLEY

I don't know how I get myself in these messes, but I can't deny that I need answers. One mention of that bastard's name and I'm right back to being a terrified teenager, not the survivor I made myself into after him. Besides, what fun would it be if someone else got to kill Kane Sai? If anyone is going to it's me. That's my duty, no one else's. I'm not saving him for his brothers or even for him, if I'm being honest, but it's a good excuse.

I promised myself I'd never return, that I'd never once look back, but years have passed and I'm still haunted by what he did. It's why I pull up outside of Auto's Chop Shop, the one place in the city where we go for information like this. Street rats to bosses alike, Auto's is the place to get rid of cars and have them replated. He's so good, even the police can't tell the difference, and he's been in this game a long fucking time.

Propping my helmet on my bike, I head toward the warehouse that takes up most of this corner. Half disassembled cars line the lot as well as brand-new ones—a mix of old and broken, just like this joint. The building looks like it's ready to come down at any minute, with its old and weathered wood sign hanging low on one side. The lights out front have long since blown, and the sliding shutter door doesn't even lock anymore. I duck under it, and the sound of grinding metal meets my ears. Eyes land on me, and a few of the workers hesitate. I know someone will have gone to tell the boss, so I don't bother introducing myself.

Wandering through the oil-stained garage, I move around the cars until I reach the area at the back. The office door is open, and I know it leads to a private area, a place no one is allowed to go, ever. Auto is hunched over a bench with plates spread out before him. A lamp is directed at them as he works.

The TV he keeps glancing at is playing the repeat of last night's game, and he has an open beer to his left, which he reaches for blindly. Buddy, his fat, snoring, and farting Labrador, doesn't even move from his feet. I once asked Auto why he got him, and he told me it was for protection, but I think he just likes having the dog around since he doesn't even wake up when someone comes close to his master.

I move silently, creeping up on him with a wicked smile, wanting to catch him off guard, but I should have known better.

"And what brings the bitch of the West to my door?" he greets without looking at me. "Karma, it's been a while."

"Damn it, how do you always know?" I grumble as I move to his side and hop up on the bench, grabbing another beer from the box. I hit the top into the side, popping the cap and flicking it toward the bin. He glances up from the game, his bright eyes locking on me—one is unseeing now, though it doesn't stop him.

He smirks. "You're too loud."

"I'm fucking silent, and you know it. I swear you aren't human," I dismiss.

"Everyone has a weakness if you look hard enough," he replies mysteriously as he leans back, grabbing his own beer as he spins around on his stool. "I'm betting this lovely visit isn't a social call."

"Not quite," I hedge.

"You know I don't give away customers, Karma, so don't ask me to," he warns.

"This is different," I counter.

"Why?" His words echo in my soul, and despite my best efforts to remain impartial and cool-headed, the truth slips out.

"It's personal." He sits upright. Out of all the jobs I do, some do get personal, but nothing close to this one, and he must sense it.

"Well, shit, looks like you do have a heart after all. It's just a black one. Fine, who are you trying to find through me?" he grumbles.

"The oldest Sai brother is missing." He probably already knows, and if he doesn't, I need the information he has more than protecting their secret. They'll be considered weak while he's gone and become a bigger target, but the need for information outweighs that, and if they can't protect themselves, then that's their issue. "The people who took him were in black SUVs with your plates."

"The Sai brothers? That's personal? Why are you involved with them? Don't be a fool, Karma. They are wild. They use people and then discard them. They aren't someone to play with, and you can't control them like you do everyone else. The only people they care about is their family, and you aren't family, girl."

"I have my own reasons," I answer idly.

He scoffs as he looks back at the game. "Everyone has my plates."

"Five SUVs, top of the line, recently done, and probably used once. I already know. I just need you to confirm."

His eyes are glued to the game as he sips his beer, and I shuffle closer, lowering my voice. "If it's who I think it is, then you know better than most why I'm doing this."

He glances at me, his gaze hard and sad. "Don't, kid. You're going to end up dead. Let it go. Leave the past where it belongs."

"I can't," I admit, my voice choked. "I . . . can't. If he's back, I'm not safe, and neither is anyone I care about. I can't run and hide this time. Please, Auto, I know I have no right to ask this of you. You took one look at a scared kid and gave me a fresh start." I wouldn't be here without him. He found me half dead outside of his garage just before dawn, took me in, and nursed me back to health, even when I was a total psycho to him and wouldn't let him get close without freaking out. He fed me, clothed me, and gave me a job when I told him I had no home. When the time came, he gave me a year's salary after one month of work, a ride, and new papers to get free. I didn't go far. After all, this city is all I know, but without Auto, I would have died. "I have no right to ask any more of you than you've already done. You risked everything to help me, but I'm asking."

"You know I don't fuck with what those bastards do," he snaps. When I first met him, he terrified me so much, I lashed out before I realized his anger covered his horror. "I'm too old, and I know too many secrets about them, but what they did to you . . ." His face pales as he remembers. "I don't want them to do it again. Do what you should have back then. Go far, far away and forget."

"I can't. I can't forget the taste of my blood. I can't forget everything they took from me and did to me. I have nothing else, Auto, just my family and need for revenge." My voice is cold, but memories flash deep inside of the horrors I survived and tried so hard to forget, until I heard his name again.

His sigh is deep, and he drains his beer as he looks at his game. My shoulders slump. "Thanks anyway—"

"The file is upstairs on my desk." I sit stoically as his words sink in. "The ones who ordered the plates, it's upstairs." He gives me a meaningful look. "I can't tell you or give it to you, but if you were to happen to take it . . . well, what's an old man to do?" My smile is slow but bright. "Don't look so pleased, kid. I can't do anything, but the gang members in the garage will have to. The code, you know that. You'll have to get past them."

"That I can do." Standing, I go to turn when his hand catches mine, greasy and rough but familiar.

"Don't kill them, kid. They are just doing their jobs," he implores.

"Sure thing, old man." I head to the office door, and it sticks like usual. I have to ram my shoulder into it for it to open, and then I take an immediate right and head upstairs, knowing I don't have long. They creak under my weight, and old memories of dragging my tired feet up them after cleaning the garage make me smile wistfully. I was so young back then, no muscle or know-how, and Auto wouldn't go easy on me no matter what. I learned after a while it was his way of showing he liked me. He pushed me harder than I've ever been. Most people would have broken, but I'd been broken a long time before. There was nothing left to destroy, and when you're at rock bottom, the only way is up.

I worked my ass off for my freedom with greasy, broken nails and sore muscles, and then I worked some fucking more to get where I am.

Nobody is taking that from me again.

Nobody.

At the top of the stairs, the wooden door is already open. I step into the small office space to the left instead of the living quarters to the right. The smell of tobacco and whiskey hits me, calming my nerves and making me feel at home, for as short of a time as it was.

Sad but true, even sadder is that it was the safest home I ever had until Taylor.

The ancient computer is off, and I don't bother booting it up. Auto is an old-school man, all handwritten and memorized in his brain. The curtains are partially shut, the lamp on the desk is on, and his chair is kicked back from lounging. I hurry through his notes, reading his chicken scratch in ways most probably couldn't until I find the order I need. As I scan the paperwork, my stomach sinks as I see the billing information.

I was right.

The head of whoever orders has to pay. It creates a paper trail to protect Auto, and right there is the one name I never wanted to see again—Butcher.

My hands crinkle the edges of the paper as my eyes close. It's him. It's really him, and that means there is no more hiding, not that I have been. I've been waiting for this moment.

Swallowing hard, I open my eyes as I hear a clank downstairs.

"Come on, Karma. Don't make this harder than it needs to be!" someone calls. "Rules are rules."

Blowing out a breath, I carefully fold the paper and pocket it before I stomp down the stairs and head out of the office to see the workers waiting for me. Some have pipes in their hands; others have wrenches or rags. None look happy.

"We don't want to do this," one says, an older guy. Most gang members start or end up here. They all owe Auto and their employers. Breaking the code is a punishable offence. They have to do this, no matter how much they don't want to.

"Don't worry, I won't kill any of you. It will just hurt a lot," I promise as I slide my leather jacket off and drape it across the bench next to the door. Auto gave it to me, and I don't want it to get ruined. Cracking my neck, I step forward and wait. A few of them hesitate, but they have a job to do, and so do I.

Sharing looks, two men lunge at me. I duck under the first and bring my knee up into the second's groin, grabbing his head and throwing him at his friend. There is no such thing as a clean fight when it's for your life. They stumble into the door, and I kick again so they smash through it, and then I turn to find another running at me.

I sprint his way and drop to my knees at the last second, sliding through the oil patch until I can spin and come up behind him. I wrap my arm around his throat and yank him back, clenching until he's out cold. Dropping him into the oil, I narrow my eyes when a dirty cloth smacks into my face.

"Rude," I snap, pointing at the one who did it. Grabbing the rag, I leap at him as he scrambles back. He slips and falls, and I ride him down, pressing the material into his mouth as he kicks and screams, choking on it, but it's too slow, so I grab his head and slam it into the concrete floor twice until he stops moving. Before climbing off him, I turn his head so he doesn't choke and die, and then I turn to see the others heading my way. I know the garage like the back of my hand, so as I duck under their wild punches, I lead them where I need them to be. Grabbing one by the back of his mangy brown hair, I shove his face into an oil barrel and hold it there as he flails. I kick out at another that gets too close, holding the first man until he stops moving, then I let go and turn to the others.

Glancing at Auto, I find him cracking open another beer as he watches the game, not even looking at us, and that makes me grin as I kick the worker running at me. He flies back and hits the closest car, and I leap at him, slamming the open hood down on his hand. His face contorts as he shouts as something hard hits my back, making me grunt and stumble. Turning, I grab the wrench heading for me again and yank him forward before smashing my head into his. The guy goes down hard, and when I turn back, the man with his hand still trapped in the car is pulling out a knife. Rolling my eyes, I lift the hood, and he slips deeper into the car as he stares at his ruined hand. I bring the hood down again. This time, it hits his head. I make it hard, but not hard enough to kill, and he slumps to the floor, his fingers mangled and pointed in different directions.

A whistle cuts through the air, and I turn in time to dodge a rag being tossed at my face. Hoisting the stolen wrench up, I toss it. It spins through the air and slams into the man's face, knocking him out.

Someone grabs me from behind, and I'm tossed over the roof of a car, hitting the ground hard. My side starts to ache, but I ignore it as he leaps over the top. Turning onto my back, I use both feet to kick him in the balls, then I open the passenger door, climb through the middle, and hop out of the driver's side. When he follows, I slam the door in his face. His scream fills the car as he drops back, and I kneel and crawl under it as I feel the others converging on me. After dragging my ass out from underneath it, I pop up on the other side to see them stalking around the vehicle. Walking backwards, I eye them. There are four of them—two big fuckers and two younger dudes, but they are all mean looking.

Every street kid has this certain look to them, so it's one I know well and understand.

"I don't want to hurt you," I tell them.

"I want to hurt you, girl," one of the bigger ones calls. "Karma under my boot? I'll be a god."

"You're a dumbass, but I suppose Auto doesn't hire based on intelligence." I sigh. "Come on then, big boy."

With a shout, he lunges at me, but I meet him halfway, flinging myself up into the air. I wrap my legs around his throat and swing up and around, driving my elbow into his head and riding him to the floor until he's out cold. I roll from his body and block the swing of a pipe with my arm. It instantly goes dead, but I ignore that for now. I've fought with much worse. I once had to slide my leg bone back into the skin so I could win a fight. I'll do whatever it takes, just like they will.

Grabbing the discarded pipe, I swing up and around. I keep swinging as I stand until the man is down, and then I turn to the last two. Flipping the pipe in the air, I wave it at them, not even panting. "Don't suppose you want a two-for-one special? I'm getting hungry."

"Fuck you! You broke the rules!"

"Yeah, yeah . . ." I spin and kick the pipe midair, and it smacks into his face. Down he goes. "I know the drill. Alright, as the last one standing, you win a prize. You get to pick how I knock you out. Think carefully or I'll choose for you."

The man looks confused, glancing between me and his downed friends before he drops the pipe. "Boring." I sigh. "Alright, I'll pick." I walk over to him, even as he backpedals. Grabbing the bottom of his shirt, I rip it up, exposing his muscles as I wrap it around his neck and tighten it. He coughs and chokes, struggling against me, but it's useless, and when he drops, I wipe off my hands and look around. Some of them are waking up, and I really am hungry, so I head over to Auto, who's on his third beer. I down mine then wipe my mouth as I pull my jacket on.

Leaning in, I kiss his wrinkled cheek. "Thanks, old man," I murmur before I head out, my heart heavy and stomach empty.

17

KANE

"Long time no see, Kane," Butcher says as he steps into the room. I know him by his ugly fucking face from the folders we keep on potential threats. It's my job to know everyone, but Butcher? He's a ghost.

"I don't think I've actually ever met you in person, but you obviously know me. Lucky me." I grin as his men step back. "We certainly don't run in the same circles, and we've never fucked with you, so that begs the question . . . why were you foolish enough to kidnap me? I'm still alive, so it's for a reason."

"Bait." He smirks. "This isn't about you, Sai. Well, not totally. Two birds, one stone."

Bait? That confuses me, but I don't show it.

Butcher disappeared years ago, just completely went off grid. He had been piquing our interest before, growing in power and money from running guns, drugs, and women, uncaring whose turf he was on. We identified him as a problem, and then one day, nothing. Almost everyone thought he was dead, but not me. I captured a picture through one of my sources. I knew he was off hiding, licking his wounds, and I can see why.

His face is a mess. There's a huge scar all the way from his temple to his chin. It's like someone tried to split him in two. One of his eyes is jacked up, and his lips are mutilated too. He looks horrifying. He's still tall and large, if only a few years older, but that face . . .

"How do you go outside with that ugly ass face? Do you wear a mask?" The knife slams into my outstretched arm, and I bite back my shout as it tears through muscle and skin.

"Still a smart-ass, I see. I thought this world would have broken you of that. No problem, I still can. I'm very good at breaking people." He hums as he walks over to the table and picks up a small dagger. "I know exactly what people fear the most. Oh, it took a few years, but I figured it out after much trial and error. You know, you remind me of a pet that I first learned this all on. She refused to scream as well . . . at first." He drives the dagger into my ear. My hearing explodes. and a yell escapes my lips. I shake my head, trying to dislodge it as he twists and turns before pulling it out. I feel blood dripping down my face.

He deafened me.

Horror fills me, and I stare at him in shock. No one would dare do this to us, so why does he feel like he can?

What does he want?

Pressing the bloodstained knife to my face, he taps my cheek with the blade. "Told you that you would scream. Let's see how loud, shall we? The great Sai leader . . . I'm really going to enjoy this. I might even record it to send to your little family."

The idea of my brothers seeing what's to come . . . no. I can't scream. I can't give in. I will not do that to them.

Despite the pain I am in, I aim my usual telltale smirk at Butcher. Years of having to control my expressions is coming in handy now. "Do your best."

His smile drops, and a macabre growl twists his rotten face as he drags the bloody knife down mine. "Before I'm through, I'm going to carve up your face so badly, not even your own family will recognize you."

I don't let my reaction show. I can't. If he's recording like he said he is, then I won't give my brothers any regrets. I need to find a way out of here. Others would keep me alive, but he doesn't care if I live or die, not really. He needs me for something, but his bloodlust is starting to outweigh that need.

"But first, let's start with some oldies but goodies." He whistles as he surveys the tools to the right, enjoying this.

"You said two birds . . . Who are you trapping and what do I have to do with it?" I ask, figuring I have nothing left to lose and knowledge is power.

"Ah, that would be telling. You'll know soon enough, but until then, let's have some fun," he taunts as he turns to me with pliers in hand. "That's a pretty smile you have."

I clamp my jaw shut, but he just laughs, opening and closing the pliers repeatedly. "Force his mouth open," he orders, and his men hurry to do his bidding. One holds my head in a viselike grip despite how much I fight, and the other digs his thumbs into my jaw until my mouth is forced open. Butcher shoves the pliers in, and I taste metal and rust, which makes me gag as he clamps something, and then red-hot pain fills my mouth along with the taste of copper as he yanks the pliers free, showing me one of my wisdom teeth.

They hold me like that, with blood dripping down my throat and chin, until I'm choking as he removes four more. When he steps back and sits on a chair one of his men pulled up, they finally release me. Jerking my head away, I turn and spit my blood at them as they recoil. My entire mouth is on fire, but I don't let it show as I keep my mouth partially open and breathe through my nose, ignoring the taste of blood on my tongue.

I watch in disgust as he licks my teeth before pocketing them. "You know, I used to look up to you. You were my idol growing up. I told myself I'd be just like you—powerful, rich, and running these streets— but as I got older, I realized it was all a facade. Oh, you dip your toe in this world with fear, guns, and money, but never the really deep stuff, like drugs and people. It's like you think you're too good for it, but that's where true power and fear lie. You act all high and mighty, like everyone should be scared of you, but the truth is, they should fear me more. You have rules and standards, but I have none. There is no length I wouldn't go to get what I want, but you . . . You have a weakness—your family." He sneers the word with a chuckle as he drags the pliers across his face, coating his skin in my blood. "Family is overrated. They just get in the way and make you weak, so I killed mine."

"Great story. You sound like a fanboy, like you still look up to me and want me to know how truly badass you are," I taunt as I reveal my bloody mouth in a sick smile. "Want the bitter truth, Butcher?" I drag out his name. "You will never be like me. No matter what you do or how far you go, you'll always be this, hiding in the dark, scared and fighting for scraps."

My head jerks as the pliers smash into my cheek, no doubt fracturing it, but I just smile as I turn my head, licking my bloody lips. "Hit a nerve, did I? What, no long-winded story now? Come on, you're so proud of who you are. Was your family your first kill?"

I can see him fighting himself, but in the end, he wants them to know how sick he is. He thrives on shock and fear, and he wants that from me, like a child begging for his father's attention.

"My first human," he corrects as he leans back. "I killed animals before—cats, dogs, birds. I found it intriguing watching the light die from their eyes. I was always curious if it was the same with humans. I killed my little sister first, because she was easier to handle. Smaller, you see. Then I worked up to my parents. She cried so much, begging me and asking why, saying she loved me. Idiot. Like it would save her. I watched her choke on her own blood, and then the light left her eyes. I enjoyed it a lot. I was going to pace myself, but I couldn't stop, so I went to my parents' bedroom next."

Jesus fucking Christ, what the fuck is wrong with this guy?

"My mother barely fought, but my father was a big man. He got a few good punches in, even gave me this." He rubs a faint scar along his neck. "But in the end, he hesitated because he was sentimental and I was his son, but I didn't hesitate." He tilts his head as he stares at me. "I wonder if you would if I made you choose between your brothers."

I feel my face tighten, anger building at the mention of my family, and he chuckles. "There it is, that look, the one that tells me you're plotting my death." His eyes widen as he moves closer. "What if I dragged them in here and executed them one by one? What would you do?"

I don't speak, and I try to control my reaction as much as I can, knowing that's what he's looking for. I must not succeed, though, because he grins.

"You're like me," he murmurs as he presses his face to mine. "You just hide it better."

"I don't kill innocents," I correct.

"No? I think you have, though, and I think if you had to, you would." Standing, he goes to choose another tool when the door opens.

"Sorry, sir," a man interrupts, ducking his head in fear. It's clear he's terrified. Butcher's men aren't loyal out of sacrifice or love, but pure fright, and it shows. "You're going to want to see this."

"If this isn't good, I'm going to do to you what I was doing to him," Butcher warns as he stands, throwing the pliers on the table before looking at me. "To be continued, Kane."

He follows his man out and leaves me alone with the taste of my blood in my mouth. A horrible feeling for my family grows in my gut.

18

BEXLEY

I head home in a daze. Now that I'm out of there, the truth of what I found sinks in, and I know what I have to do, but I drag my feet as I stare up at our house. Music blasts from inside, and I can hear Taylor and Lauren singing from the porch. Their out-of-tune voices join in together, and my lips twitch despite the situation. When I open the door, the smell of baking hits me, which lets me know Taylor had a good day. It's the only time she bakes.

"Hey, Bex!" they both call, turning to see me. They are covered in flour and wearing matching aprons. Sometimes, it's easy to forget they are sisters, with Taylor acting more like a mom, but in times like this, I remember how young she is. "Hey, what are you making?" I ask as I sit on the sofa and lean forward, my hands wringing nervously between my parted legs.

"A cake." Lauren giggles. "Then we are going to binge watch that new show. Taylor said I could. We figured it's a girls' night."

"Sounds fun," I say, trying to keep my tone normal, but Taylor frowns and turns off the music.

"Everything okay?" she asks as she wipes her hands and leans against the doorframe, leaving Lauren stirring their batter.

"Sure," I reply, but it must not be convincing because she frowns, and I know I need to get this over with. I just wanted one more minute with them. It might be the last time I hear their laughter and I wanted to enjoy it. I need it to get me through what will come next. I don't want to lose myself like I did before, but I probably will before this is over. Last time, Taylor and Lauren saved me. They brought me back and gave me a reason to keep going. I need this to be the same, so I need them to be safe. "Can we talk for a minute, both of you?"

I don't know what Taylor sees in my face, but she sits heavily. Lauren joins us, smiling before it fades as she looks between us. "What's wrong, Bexley?" Taylor asks.

"I need you to listen, and I need you to do as I say, okay?" I begin.

"Aunt Bex, you're freaking me out," Lauren whispers, her big eyes filling with tears.

"I'm sorry. I just . . . I need you to understand." I look at Taylor. "I need you to pack and head to Shelly's at the beach, okay? You need to leave tonight and turn off your phones. Don't turn them back on no matter what until I come for you."

"Bexley, what's going on? Are you in danger?" Taylor asks as Lauren starts to cry.

"I need to do something that might put you in danger," I admit. "Go pack, please."

"I don't want to go!" Lauren yells as she leaps to her feet, and I stare at her sadly. "I'm sorry if I did something wrong. I'll be better. I promise. I won't cause any trouble."

My heart cracks.

"Listen to me." I grip her hips and tug her into my arms as she sniffles. "You could never do anything wrong, and even if you did, I would fix it." I hold her tightly as I look at Taylor.

"Let us help," she pleads, leaning forward. "Whatever is happening, Bex, let me help."

"Taylor, listen to me. Everything I do is to keep you both safe. I need you to trust me. I can't be who I need to be if I'm worried about you two. Please, I can't lose you," I say as I hold Lauren tighter.

"Is it him?" Taylor asks softly. I never told her everything that happened, but she knows enough.

"Yes." I won't lie to her. "It's him. I need to finish this or we'll never be safe. He's the only person who could ever take our lives and home from us."

A tear slides down her cheek as she reaches over and takes my hand, sitting straighter. "Then finish it, and you make that bastard pay."

"I plan to," I promise as I force a smile.

She wipes her face with her other hand, looking up through her lashes at the ceiling for a moment. "Okay then." Slapping her thighs, she stands. "Lauren, let's go get packed, okay? It's road trip time."

She whines and cuddles closer to me. It's the hardest thing I've ever had to do, but I pull her gently away from me and push her to Taylor. "Go." I grin. "A road trip will be fun. Besides, you love Shelly and the beach."

Lauren is still crying, but Taylor turns her away and heads upstairs, and I finally slump, burying my face in my hands. This is for the best, but it doesn't stop the pain. They are my family, the only reason I still live.

It doesn't take them long, Taylor sensing the urgency of the situation, and when she comes down, I have the go bag ready. I hand it to her, and she slips it over her shoulder. "It has enough money to start over in case something happens to me. It also has the deed to this house, passports, IDs, Lauren's school information, and all of the favors I'm owed. Call them in, you hear me? Get them to look after you and get out safely."

"Promise me, Bexley, that you are coming back," she demands as she grips Lauren's hand.

"I'll meet you at the beach," I promise, even though it might be a lie.

She nods, and I help her to the car I bought her and load it up before assisting Lauren into her seat. "I can do it myself," she grumbles, still sniffling.

"I know you can," I murmur. "Just let me one last time, okay?"

She nods, and I buckle her belt before grabbing her face. "Look after Taylor for me? I'm depending on you."

"I will," she replies seriously.

"I love you. You are the best thing to ever happen to me, kid, even when you're a pain in the ass. No matter what happens, I'll always be there."

"Bexley, don't talk like you'll never see me again," she begs.

"I will. I'll help you learn to dive when I get there, okay?"

"Okay." She nods, and I tug her into a hug before stepping back and shutting the door. As I round the car, Taylor rolls down her window, her eyes misty with tears she's trying her best not to let fall.

"Don't stop until you get there, understood?" I tell her.

"I know the drill. Don't worry about us, just take care of yourself." She grabs my hand. "You better get your ass to that beach."

"I will. I wouldn't miss it for the world," I insist as I squeeze her hand. "Stay safe."

"You stay safe," she retorts. "Remember, Bexley, you're so much stronger than anyone else. End this and find us."

Nodding, I step back and force a smile onto my face as I wave. I haven't warned Shelly that they are coming. She's an ex-prostitute I helped save years ago. I don't want to leave a trail to them, but she'll know what to do. She'll take care of them for me.

Their headlights splash over me, and I keep waving until they are out of sight. When they are gone, I let one tear drop, and my smile fades.

I don't know if I'll ever see them again, but I would do anything to keep them safe. I promised I would meet them there, so I won't stop until I do, unless I'm dead.

I turn back to the now empty house and blow out a breath.

It's time to get to work.

Honestly, it's becoming way too easy to break into the Sai mansion. Lounging back on the silk bed, I wait with my boots purposely messing up the perfect sheets before I start to wonder what terrible things Neo has done in them. Probably nothing nastier than I have, so I watch the porn I charged to his card, opening all his fancy creams and slathering them over my hands and face. I also stole a couple of twenties because why not?

I hear the shower cut off and get comfy. Luckily, it doesn't take long before the door opens. Steam wafts in before he steps into the room, wearing a loosely tied blue robe with his name embroidered on it. His hair is pushed back, and his skin is still damp. He looks good enough to eat.

"Hello, Neo," I drawl.

"Motherfucker!" he shouts, clutching his robe as he stares at me in shock.

"Wrong, I prefer fathers," I retort. He blinks at my comment as the door flies open. Guards rush in, aiming their guns at me, followed by Zayn, who's wearing unbuttoned suit pants.

Zayn chuckles. "You know how to make an entrance. Honestly, why do we have locked doors?" he asks as he looks at the guards. "A bit late now. Fuck off." He kicks them out and shuts the door as he walks my way.

"How did you even get in here? Can we turn off the porn?" Neo mutters as he glances at the TV.

"It's just getting to the good part." I sigh as Zayn chuckles and climbs onto Neo's bed next to me, both of us watching the TV as she reaches her big finale. "A bit fake, but it did the job."

"I'd fuck it." Zayn shrugs.

"Me too." The TV shuts off, and we both turn to Neo.

"Why are you here?" he asks, his robe tied tightly now.

"Don't feel the need to close it up on my account. I liked the show. There's something very slutty about a man in a loose silk robe," I tease before I become serious. "I know where your brother is."

"Where?" they both ask.

"Well, I know who has him, and I plan to find out where he is. I just came to let you know so you don't get in my way." I shrug as I lift the stolen face cream. "I'm taking this, by the way."

"Focus. Our brother," Neo demands.

"There's no point in telling you since you won't get to him, but I can." I shrug as I lean back into the bed. "This shit is really comfortable."

"How?" Zayn asks, ignoring my other comment for once.

My expression becomes cold as I look between them. "By giving him what he wants—me."

19

NEO

We have been asking her all night, but she refuses to tell us who has our brother or where he is. It's irritating me, but she says she has a plan, and we need to go along with it. I don't trust anyone but my family, but I don't seem to have another choice. We aren't getting far in our investigation when she clearly is. My brother's life is on the line, so we'll go along with it.

She eventually got tired of our questions and took a nap before waking up and demanding to be fed. I watch her demolish the food our chef made. Father is away on business, which is the only reason he doesn't know about Kane yet, and I want to keep it that way. We need to get him back before Father finds out.

"Another serving?" Zayn asks, watching her closely. He has a weird smile on his face. "It's so hot watching you eat."

"You have issues," she says as she shoves another bite of omelet into her mouth. "Kinky, but I'm into it."

"At least let us know how we can help your plan," I tell her, and she sighs, shooting me an irritated glare as she cleans the last of her plate and drains her mug before standing.

"Come on then, let's get moving before you piss me off so much I hurt your pretty face again."

"Wait, we're going now?" I leap to my feet.

"Yup. Unless you have yoga or some shit," she scoffs as she stalks out of the room, expecting us to follow, and we do after we grab our boots and jackets. She's leaning into one of our cars when we find her, wearing sunglasses on her face, and I frown, wondering where she got them before I see one of our guards clutching his nuts and leaning into the pillar.

"Where are we going?" I ask, but she just climbs into the car.

"With us," I tell Dodge and our guards. He nods and climbs in the driver's seat as we get in the back, Zayn squished between us.

The radio comes on, and she hums. "I love this song. Turn it up."

"Karma!" I snap. "Where are we going?"

"So rude. Drive toward the Meatpacking District." She hums along with the tune, and Dodge looks at me. I nod, and we set off. She ignores us the entire way, singing with the radio until she randomly shouts, "Stop here!"

Dodge slams on his brakes, and we hear cars honking behind us, but we ignore them as she turns to us.

"Okay then, let's do this." She rips her jacket off, and we just gape as she starts piling weapons on our laps, pulling them from places I didn't even know you could hide them.

"What are you doing? Not that I'm not enjoying the show," Zayn mutters.

"I can't take anything with me. I don't want to give them a reason to touch me more than they have to." She shrugs as she puts her jacket on and looks at us. "It's your lucky day because the man that has Kane hates me just as much as he hates your family, so I'm going to walk into one of those shops where I know his men are and let them take me. He'll keep me close to your brother, and I'll get him out."

"That's fucking insane. You're going to let yourself be kidnapped?" I hiss.

"It's the fastest way." She shrugs. "Your brother is still alive for now."

"How do you know?" I whisper.

"Trust me. He likes to keep his victims alive, but we don't have

116

long. We need to find them quickly, and this is the easiest way," she explains.

"This is a trap."

"Well, duh," she mutters. "I want it to be a trap, but he only has one day left."

"What do you mean?" Zayn asks.

She considers something for a moment before blowing out a breath. "My uncle raised me after my parents died. He was a good man, at least to me, but he worked in this . . . industry, providing services, and the man who took your brother didn't like that. He thought he was a threat, so he kidnapped my uncle and me as insurance. He tortured my uncle for five days before executing him on the sixth. It's his habit. Always the sixth day. I have no idea why; it's just who he is. Tomorrow is the sixth day, so if he doesn't have whatever he wants from Kane, then your brother is dead, so I'm going in there, and I'll get him out."

I stare at her, unable to process what she said until it clicks. "The guy who has my brother, he . . . had you too?"

Her face closes down, going so cold I swear I shiver. "For many years. Nobody knows him better than I do, and luckily for you, he's been looking for me for a long time."

"Why?" I ask.

Her smile is evil. "Because I'm the only one who ever escaped him alive. He can't have that."

Jesus Christ.

ZAYN

"This man, he'll hurt you," I state.

"Nothing I haven't survived before." She shrugs, but I see her body tightening. What has this woman been through to have that kind of reaction? "Besides, it's the only way. Before I could even get close any other way, he would know, and we'd lose our only advantage. This is the only way. Trust me, if there was another, I would take it. I escaped that hell once before, and I'm not too happy about walking back in."

"Then don't. We'll find another way," I offer. "Right?" I glance at Neo, but his face is twisted.

"Are you sure you can do this?" is all he asks.

"Neo!" I snap.

He ignores me, and I stare incredulously. Is he really willing to let her walk into who knows what? Are we really that kind of people?

"I'm the only one who can. One way or another, one of us dies. I'd bet on him."

"I'd always bet on you," Neo murmurs. "Okay."

"But what if you don't come back?" I whisper.

"Then your brother and I are both dead." She softens as she looks at me. "I can do this. I know this man better than anybody. I'll finish what I started back then and kill him, and you'll get Kane back."

"At least tell us who it is," I whisper.

"No," she protests. "You'll go at them like a force of nature, and it won't solve anything. If a time comes when we need you, I'll get word to you. You're just going to have to trust me."

I share a look with Neo and Dodge, but both see no other option. "This is crazy!" I argue. "Bexley, don't do this."

"This man took everything from me," she tells me, letting me under her guard for a moment. "I thought I killed him, but I didn't, and because of that, I don't know how many people have suffered. This is my fight more than yours or your brother's." Taking a deep breath, she forces a smile onto her face and looks between us.

"See you on the other side. Is there a code word for me to tell your brother so he knows I'm with you?" she asks.

"Whiskers," I tell her softly, and she blinks.

"Okay then, whiskers." Opening the door, she climbs out and looks back at us. "See you soon, or maybe I won't." She leaves.

"She can do it," Dodge murmurs. "If not, we'll keep looking."

"If she's right, it won't matter because he'll be dead," Neo retorts. "She's our only hope."

We watch as she crosses the road and, without a hint of hesitation, plunges past the gang members at the door and into the butcher shop, something about it all niggles at the back of my head but I re-focus on her. She doesn't look backwards even once.

"What the fuck do we do now?" I ask.

"We wait and hope she's as good as everyone says she is," Neo responds as he glances at me. "And we hope she and Kane make it out alive."

"That's an awful lot of hope," I sneer, hating everything about this.

"Sometimes it's all you have," he replies.

20

KANE

I don't know how long I'm out before the cell door opens. I sit up as much as the chains will allow, bracing for the next round of torture, but instead the guards come in and throw something on the filthy mattress—not something, someone. They step out of the room, leaving me with the person. Their back is to me, and it's hard to see much in the dim room, but they are breathing so they are alive.

They look too small to be one of my brothers, which is my only saving grace.

A little while later, there's a groan, and the person rolls onto their back. I try to make out their features. They have long hair, which is odd, and a small face, and when they turn, I realize why I know it.

Karma.

She blinks at me and then looks down at the mattress. "Tell me you didn't shit yourself on this. Piss, fine, but not shit."

Luckily, she's on the side where Butcher didn't ruin my ear, but I tilt my head a little to hear her better. Sounds are strange now, but I'm trying my best to grow accustomed to it.

"Why is piss fine?" I ask before I realize what is going on. "What the fuck are you doing here?"

Grunting, she sits up and pushes her hair back, exposing a wicked bump on her forehead where they must have knocked her out.

"To rescue you, of course," she explains as she stands, cracking her back and looking around.

"Oh, well, you're doing a great job," I deadpan, and she glares at me with an annoyed frown.

"Rude. Do you think I want to be here? I did this on purpose," she grumbles.

"What do you mean?" I frown in confusion. "Wait, you got kidnapped on purpose? That's insane."

"Thank you." She bows as she squints at me. "You look like shit."

"Thanks," I mutter.

"No, like really bad, like the old you was fucked by a lawnmower, and not a small one either, one of those industrial ones." I stare, and she stares back.

"Right," I grunt. "Could you commence with the rescue maybe?"

"So impatient. You're such a bad damsel in distress." She looks around. "It isn't the worst cell I've been in."

"Great, maybe we could rank them later. Your damsel is in distress." My lips twist despite the situation. I want to chuckle. I don't know how she does it. She makes even the worst situations better. I shouldn't be happy she's here, but I am. I'm glad to see her.

The door opens, and her humor fades, her expression locking down. The transformation is scary, and I realize just how much she was letting me see. Karma also drops into a fighting stance, which surprises me, when Butcher steps into the room. He isn't looking at me, however. He's glaring at her with possessive intent. There's a gleam in his eyes that raises the hair on my arms, and I jangle my chains to get his attention, but he doesn't look away from her.

"Hello, Bexy, it's been a long time. I've missed you." He looks at me then, as she pales. "Didn't I tell you about my pet? Well, that was our dear Bexy here, though she goes by Karma now." He grins at her. "Quite the ironic name."

"I see your face healed well." She smirks, and his eyes narrow. "I should have cut deeper."

"You should have if you wanted me dead," he agrees.

"I won't make that mistake again," she vows as he moves closer. She doesn't back up, but I can tell she wants to. He thrives on fear and intimidation.

"Look at you. I remember when you used to hide and cry anytime I came near, like a scared kitten. One move and you would flinch. I guess your time on the streets has been good to you. The years made you stronger. Want to know what the years did to me? They made me angrier, made me sit and think of all the things I would do to you when I got you back. It's all I thought about."

"You need a hobby," she sneers.

"I have one—you, my little pet. Don't you remember? You were always my favorite toy." He strokes her face, and she glares up at him. "You grew up well, so beautiful and strong . . . I can't wait to break that again."

"I'm going to carve the rest of your face off," she retorts as she leans into him. "I'm not scared of you anymore."

"Sure thing, pet." He smirks as he steps back. "Shall we get started? I was going to do it privately, but not now. I think he should watch, don't you? He's why you're here, right? You're working for those Sai brothers. That's low for you, but I'll show you what loyalty gets you. He won't do anything to save you, not even when you're being tortured for him."

"I'm the one you want. Leave her alone," I snap.

"That's where you're wrong, Kane. I want you for other reasons, but she was my target all along. Like I said, you were bait, and it worked." He moves to the table, and I look between him and the tools, but the door opens again and his men rush in, out of breath.

"Sir, we have a problem!"

His growl fills the air, and he hesitates. Turning back to her, he grabs her throat and yanks her close, swiping his tongue down her face to her ear. "I'll be back soon, and it will be just like old times. You are never getting away from me, pet. I have plans." He leaves, the door slamming shut.

The silence is tense as I look at her. Her hands are fisted as she glares at the door before she turns her head and meets my gaze. "Don't feel sorry for me, Kane, or I'll kill you myself."

"You did that to his face?" I ask instead.

She blinks before nodding.

"Good work." She smiles, and I return it with one of my own.

She sits with her back to the wall. She tried to free me, but it didn't work, so now she's planning, but I think she's just bored.

"So, Butcher—"

"No," she interrupts, not even looking at me. "I know what you're going to say or ask, and no, I'm not going there. Not with you."

"We have nothing else to do until he gets back," I say softly.

"So what? I should share my past with you? Not a chance, Sai," she snaps like a feral creature backed into a corner, but I see the truth in her eyes.

"You're scared." It's not something I ever thought I would say about her. She seems fearless, but it's in her eyes, as much as she tries to hide it.

"Fuck off, Sai. I'm not—" Her eyes flash.

"Not of this situation, but of him," I muse as I look at her. "That's why you did this. Not to save me or for money. You did it because you are still scared of him, and you can't have that."

Her nostrils flare as she looks at me. "You have to kill fear," she explains. "No matter what it is. Yes, I'm still scared of him. He's the very last thing in this world I fear, and that is a weakness I won't tolerate."

"He's just a man," I say. "Men can be killed."

"To a god, he's a man, but to a little girl, he was the devil," she replies, her head falling back to the wall as she looks at me. "He's the only thing left that can hurt me and those I love, so yes, I'm not just here for you or the contract I have with your brothers. I have my own reasons, but don't worry. It will serve you well."

"I wasn't worried about me," I admit, and it's the truth. Despite what I've endured, I can tell it's nothing compared to what she has been through and whatever else he has planned for her. "So what's the plan?"

She looks at me, and her eyes are completely fucking dead. "I'm going to kill them."

"Then I'll help you," I resolve. "I don't suppose you have an idea about how to get me free?"

"I do, but you won't like it." She smirks, and the look is downright terrifying.

21

KARMA

I did tell him he wouldn't like it. His jaw pops as his eyes harden, and he jerks his head at me in a nod, waiting for me to start. Lifting the blade from the table, I wink at him as I move closer. It has to look real.

He's right, I'm still scared of Butcher, but I meant what I said. Fear has to be killed. I have no intention of sitting around and waiting for him to come back and torture me again, and he would. No, I'm not the scared little pet I was then, so this time, I'm taking the fight to him.

He told me I should have made sure he was dead. The truth is, he should have made sure I was because I've had years to stew on my fury, hatred, and bloodlust, and it's all aimed at him.

I run the blade teasingly over Kane's lips, and they part as his eyes heat and lock on me. Grinning, I drag it down his chin then slice his chest. He hisses in pain as blood wells, but he isn't loud enough. I need the guards to hear him, who are no doubt nearby.

"Scream for me," I tell him.

His eyes tighten and his lips flatten, so I trail my hand down his torso and grab his cock, making him jerk. "I said scream, Kane."

"Make me," he retorts, but there's something other than pain in his eyes—desire. He hardens in my hand, and I can't help but grin.

"Oh, you are really fucked up, Sai," I tease as I sink the blade into his shoulder. The shock is what makes him finally cave. His cry echoes around the room before he cuts it off, panting as the knife protrudes from his shoulder.

He's still hard in my other hand, and that makes my eyebrows rise. The smirk he gives me is bloody and evil. "Never said I wouldn't enjoy it, Bexley."

The way he caresses my name sends a shiver through me before I remember our situation. The sound of footsteps snaps me back to the present, followed by the door unlocking. "Leave them to me," I whisper. "I have some aggression to get out anyway."

"You better leave me some." He frowns just as the door is opened behind me. I know what they see—me, a bloody knife, and Kane pretending to be weak. They probably think I got myself in here to kill him, or I just took my opportunity.

"Shit, she's killing him!" they shout as they rush in. With a wink at Kane, I wait until they are close enough, and then I turn. There are three of them, and I throw myself at them, knocking them back as I yank the wrench from the back of my jeans and hammer it into one of their heads. He goes down as arms wrap around me and lift me into the air. Using the momentum, I flip over him and bring the wrench down across the back of his head. He stumbles forward, waving his arms, and I bring it down again as the other tries to get around them and at me.

Kane wraps the man up in his chains, holding him as I finish off the others. I turn back to them and walk over. Yanking the blade from Kane's shoulder, I slam it into the man's chest and twist it as he grunts from the pain. "You can let go," I say, and Kane does. The man drops dead to the floor, and I smile. "See? My plan is working great."

"Amazing. Could you free your damsel?" he asks, eyeing his shoulder then me.

Rolling my eyes, I scan the room. The idiots even left the door open in their haste.

"Bexley," he prompts, jangling his chains.

"Don't be such a baby. It's just a flesh wound. There's nothing vital there. I made sure." I search the bodies until I find the keys, and then I skip over and start undoing his chains. They fall away, and he climbs to his feet, rolling his bad shoulder.

"It still hurts like a son of a bitch," he responds, eyeing me darkly.

"Good, I needed it to. Now, if you've finished whining, let's go kill some bitches." Heading to the table, I pick out some toys and slip them into my pockets. I watch as Kane wraps a chain around one of his arms, and the sight of it is hot as fuck. He catches me looking and grins, so I turn away and search the bodies. I find three guns, so I pocket two and offer the other to Kane.

"Why do you get two?" he grumbles as he checks the chamber and clip.

"I found them. Finders keepers." I shrug as I head to the door and peek out.

He presses against my back, and lips brush my ear. "I found you. Does that mean I get to keep you?"

I elbow him, and he steps back with a grunt. "Babe, I found you, not the other way around."

"Then are you going to keep me?" he flirts.

"How about we save this until we're free?" I retort as I step behind the door just as another man rushes in. Kane throws his chain out, smacking the guard under his chin and snapping his neck. He drops to the floor, and Kane winds the chain back up. He barely even looked at the man, keeping his eyes on me.

"I can multitask. Want to see?" His gaze sweeps down my body.

Walking out the door, I palm an electric prod as I go, my stolen toy. "You know, if I didn't know better, I'd say getting stabbed was fore-play for you, but I heard the great Sai older brother is as sane as they come."

"Or so everyone thinks," he teases as he follows me, letting me take the lead.

Two men yell as they rush around the corner at us. Kane throws one at me and grabs the other, effortlessly breaking his neck. Ducking under the knife my guard is wielding, I stab the electric prod into his balls. His scream cuts off as he jerks and pisses himself. When he falls, I shove it into his eye, watching the skin burn as his body writhes, and then he's dead. Blowing my hair back from my face, I glance at Kane to see him leaning against the wall, watching me.

"I wear sanity well, don't I?" He tilts his head, grinning. "Always have. Nobody apart from my family knows how truly insane I am, especially when it comes to things I consider mine."

I aim the prod at him. "I am not yours, Sai. Keep that in mind. I belong to no man."

"No?" His tongue sweeps across his lips as he steps toward me. "How about belonging to three instead?" My eyes narrow, and he smirks. "Fine, hellion, how about I belong to you? You did rescue me, after all, so I have to thank you." He steps closer as he speaks, and I don't back down, not even as he presses against me. He's injured, yet the sick bastard is still determined.

His brothers shouldn't have been worried about him. Kane Sai is like a cockroach, impossible to kill or keep down. No wonder they are as powerful as they are. I have no idea what game he's playing now, but I don't want any part of it. I have a feeling getting tangled with him would cause me nothing but misery and death, no matter how pretty his face is or how much I want to find out just how much he really enjoys pain.

"Stop right there!" someone calls, and without looking, we both pull out guns and shoot. There is a muffled yell then a thud as we lower our arms. "What do you say, hellion? Want to find out what it means to own the Sai family?"

"You wish," I scoff as I lift my gun and press it against his chin. He leans into it, his eyes locked on me. "After I save your ass and get my revenge, you won't ever see me again. Now, let's go kill them."

Turning, I keep my pistol out as I step over the bodies and around the corner. "Never say never, hellion. Nobody escapes me, not when I have them in my sights."

I ignore his words, even as they send a slow roll of pleasure through me. Everyone is scared of me, and even the men I date are careful with their words and treatment of me, yet here is Kane mother-fucking Sai, threatening to stalk me. It should annoy me, but I find it endearing.

Taylor was right. I am messed up in the head.

22

KARMA

There's a trail of bodies leading out of the basement we were kept in. We linger at the top of the stairs, trying to figure out the layout and people above. I have no idea where we are, but from the size of the labyrinth below, it has to be some sort of industrial area and building. What of, I have no idea. Considering the police didn't arrive after the barrage of gunshots and screams, I'd say we are outside of the city. Butcher always did like to stay off grid, since it's easier to do his work. He likes the freedom seclusion brings him.

"You go first." I nod at the door. "Age before beauty and all that."

"You're my rescuer. You go first," he counters with a cocky smile.

"Pussy," I mutter as I reach for the handle, but he knocks my hand away and opens the door, creeping out. I follow behind him. We are in another corridor, with horrible lime-green walls and a swinging door at the end. We move silently together. Putting our backs to the walls, we count down and nod, bursting out, only to freeze.

The place is fucking huge. There are two floors, with metal railings surrounding the second floor above, showcasing private offices and rooms. Down here, there is old machinery and crates that are being moved, most likely filled with drugs and guns. I spy some guards milling about, but that's not what has horror gripping my heart.

133

It's familiar.

As I spin around, I realize I know this place. I never saw the basement, but up here? I remember it all too well.

"Bexley?" Kane mutters as he drags me down behind a crate and peeks around to see if we were spotted, but I'm frozen. "What is it?"

"I know where we are," I grit out, tightening my hold on the gun, needing that lifeline now more than ever.

"Great. Where?"

Licking my teeth, I take a deep breath. "It's an old power plant outside of the city. It's heavily guarded, and they use it for their films," I tell him.

"Films?" He frowns as he looks at me in confusion.

I meet his eyes. "Snuff films, that kind of thing. He used to bring me here to show me what would happen if I didn't behave. There are cages in the back filled with women. They also sell them here for an hour, a day, a night, or forever. I don't see the setup for auctions, so it must not be happening right now. I came back to this place after I thought I killed Butcher, but it was empty. I guess they moved in right under my nose." I hate this place. It's filled with nothing but horrible memories I would rather forget, which is precisely why he brought us here. He thinks reminding me of the broken woman I was when I was here before will hurt me. He's wrong, it just infuriates me.

"These films . . . Did he make you perform in them?" he asks, anger etched into his features.

"Sometimes, but not the snuff films. He made me watch the deaths, knowing I couldn't do anything." I meet his anger with my own. "I want to burn this place to the fucking ground."

"Then let's do it." He nods. "You know the layout?"

He doesn't offer sympathy or pity, simply accepts it and offers to help me, and in that moment, I realize I trust Kane, which is odd since I trust no one.

Peeking over the crate, I debate our options. "If Butcher is here, he'll be in his office. We need a distraction to set the fire and get up there. There are too many guards for us to take down. If we circle around, we can get to the holding area at the back. There are usually only a few guys there. We can take them out quietly and let the girls out, cause a distraction, and give them a chance, then we'll set the fire and let Butcher and his men burn in it."

I know my face is cold and my voice is deadly, but he nods. "Lead the way."

Putting my gun away, I pull out two knives, holding one in each hand as I crouch walk to the next crate, and then I wait before darting to the next. It's slow-going, but we move like that until we circle around the room, and the railing offers protection from above. Behind the wall of crates, I open the door that leads to the back and the holding cells.

The smell is the first thing that hits me—unwashed body, excrement, and piss. It's a smell I used to be blind to, having been around it so much, but now it's as unfamiliar as the chains that lock the cells. "Shit, I thought you meant cells like the one we were kept in. These are fucking cages," Kane grumbles in horror.

I look around, seeing what he does. Rows upon rows of animal cages are stacked on top of each other, reaching the ceiling. Some are empty, but most are filled with women of all ages, and they are all naked except for the collar around their neck with Butcher's initial on it.

"Yeah, well, cell always felt better than admitting we were kept like dogs," I snap as I head down the aisle in the middle. Some of the older ones have probably been here the longest, but they don't even bother looking up. They don't expect anyone to save them, so they don't call out. There are a few gazes that track us, unsure and hostile. I can tell who's new. They reach through the bars, begging as hope flashes in their eyes. Eventually, they would be punished, and hope would be beat out of them, but for the moment, they still have it.

"Keep quiet or the guards will come," I admonish. "We are getting you out." That gets their attention. When I reach the end, I find the button that controls the electronic locks. The panel is unmanned, which is odd, but I guess sometimes luck is on our side. "When the doors open, run out and right to the back door. Don't stop for anyone. Keep running and don't look back, and don't accept help. Get to the nearest police station and demand protection," I order. That's all I can do for them right now. I have no way of contacting anyone on the outside to pick them up, so I have to hope they can save themselves. It's more important we end this and kill Butcher for good. Otherwise, he will never let them or me go.

Slamming my hand into the button, I hear a buzz fill the air just before all the cage doors swing outward. For a moment, nobody moves. "Go!" I yell, and they scramble from their cages, falling over each other. Some help others down, but most rush to the door, hesitating before taking their chances then making a run for it. While they do, we move through their midst and go left, heading behind more crates as shouts ring out. Guards forget their posts as they sprint for the girls and the door they are escaping out of.

The front is completely abandoned, so I take a chance, stand up, and rip open the lids of a few crates. Straw lines the tops with drugs hidden underneath in chopping boards. Rolling my eyes, I open the next few and pile the straw up, hoping like hell it ignites.

"I don't suppose you have a lighter, do you?" I ask as I look at Kane.

"Fresh out, hellion, but I have a gun." He covers my face and fires into the stack I made. It lights, and we hurry away, crouching behind other crates near the stairs as the fire begins to spread, engulfing that crate and crawling to the next, eating everything in its path as the fire alarm blazes. Guards hesitate, torn between their merchandise and the fire, and it's the distraction we need. No one notices us silently climbing the stairs in the chaos. My throat tightens from the smoke rapidly filling the warehouse, but I keep my burning eyes wide open.

I can feel Kane close behind me as we take the stairs two at a time, our steps loud on the metal, but it's drowned out by the whooshing of the flames and shouts. We get halfway down the walkway when a guard comes running toward us. "This one is mine. You get his friend," I tell Kane as another appears.

Grabbing the railing, I throw myself over it and land on the other side of the frozen guards. Leaving the first to Kane, I grab the second and slam my knee into his balls before throwing him over the railing.

He lands with a thud below, and by the time I've turned, the other guard is sprawled on the walkway behind me, his stomach and throat ripped open. Kane stands above him, running his eyes down me as his tongue darts out to lick his lips.

"I don't know about you, but killing together has got me feeling some kind of way."

Rolling my eyes, I stomp down the platform toward the door at the end where Butcher's office is. He wouldn't move it because he likes to look down on people. It's why he chose it. My eyes scan the glass window that looks into the room next to it, showing his bedroom and the dog bed he keeps there—the one he used to force me to sleep on. He's nowhere to be seen, and when I reach the door, I realize why. He's on the phone, not even looking our way as he heads toward the door to see what the hell is going on. I debate going in, since it would be satisfying to kill him with my own hands, but I can think of something much worse. Turning, I grab Kane's chain and wrap it through the door to the railing, linking it shut just as he looks up. His eyes widen for a moment as he peers at me through the glass, and his phone falls to the floor.

He tries the door, and it rattles, only making my smile grow as heat swells around us. The whole place is filling with flames and smoke. "Pet," he warns.

"Don't mind if I stick around this time just to make sure, right?" I sneer, and he releases a full belly laugh before the sound turns into an angry roar as he yanks on the door. It rattles in its frame but doesn't budge.

"Little pet," he drawls, "when I get my hands on you, you'll beg for death."

"Seems unlikely since you're behind that door. You'll burn to death in the very place you wielded your power. Ironic, isn't it?" I grin as I move closer. "You always were too cocky, and look where it got you. You really thought you could control someone like me? Dumb move. You should have killed me when you had the chance," I tell him before pressing my lips to the glass and stepping back with a grin.

"Let's go." Kane coughs. "The fire is growing."

Laughing, I turn away, leaving Butcher roaring and rattling the door that will become his coffin.

I hear it the moment before it happens—a smash and a pop. My head turns in time to see Butcher bursting the door from its frame before he throws it out of the way. I flatten myself against the window with no time to warn a wide-eyed Kane as it soars straight for him.

It slams into Kane, knocking him back and over the railing, and I turn my head to see Butcher in the open doorway, his muscles heaving as he glares at me. He'll kill me if he gets his hands on me, so I take the first shot.

After all, sometimes you just need to fight a man and beat the shit out of him to show him who's really boss.

Rushing him, I grab the discarded chain on the way and tackle him back. He catches me as we fall, his hands going to my waist to throw me off, but I'm faster. I wrap the chain around his thick neck and through the grates of the walkway underneath.

I yank it tighter and lock it in place as he roars and bucks below me. His neck bulges as he pulls on it, but the metal doesn't budge because it's now attached to the bottom of the walkway, pinning him like a bug.

"Pet!" he roars as I spit on him.

"Now who's the pet?" I growl before I turn and walk away, leaving him screaming after me. I thought I would feel more satisfaction, but the fact that I won't get to watch him burn is irritating me. Self-preservation tells me to get my ass out of here, since I don't want to be a kebab.

Leaping down the stairs, I cover my nose and mouth as I scan the building until I find Kane.

He's just getting to his knees, coughing and rubbing his head. Rolling my eyes, I run his way and help him up as he leans into me, disoriented and hurt.

"How many times do I have to save your heavy ass?" I grouse as we stumble to the door.

"However many you want. It seems to be your kink," he teases, coughing as we suck in fresh air and fall through the open door. We turn to see the warehouse engulfed in flames and share a look. His eyes darken before he grabs my neck and pulls me close, his lips finding mine.

He tastes of blood and ash, and for a moment, I lose myself in the softness of his lips as he demands entrance to my mouth. He kisses me like he can't stand living another second without it, like I'm the air he needs to breathe.

Still, he didn't ask.

My fist slams into his gut, and he drops to his knees, coughing as I let him go. His watering eyes meet mine as I smirk and reach down, tilting his chin up as he heaves and coughs. "If I wanted to kiss you, Sai, I would have. Now, be a good boy, and let's get our asses out of here."

"If I'm good, will I get to kiss you again?" he rasps.

"Try it and see."

Kane takes me by surprise when he yanks me down and presses his lips to mine again. I don't move for a second before I ram my knee into his balls. He falls away with a cry of agony.

"Worth it," he wheezes as he rolls on the ground while I turn and walk away, leaving him groaning in pain.

He eventually catches up to me, and we wander to the road and keep walking. Neither of us have a phone. It's going to be a long walk.

23

KANE

I can still taste her. My thumb tugs at my lip as I remember our kiss, and I know I'd gladly die for another taste of her. I probably would, knowing her, but I felt it. For a moment, she kissed me back. She's not as unaffected as she tries to appear, and I'll wield it like a weapon until Bexley is mine.

I meant it when I asked her earlier if she wanted to belong to us. I want her. I'll have her.

The street is abandoned and dark, with just a road and not much else. She was right, it's outside of the city with no traffic around for miles, so we simply walk on the side of the road, hoping it will lead somewhere.

She's quiet, and I shoot her a look she ignores. "Bexley—"

"I've had enough of men tonight. Don't make me kill you too," she warns.

Well, shit, you bet I shut my ass up, leaving her to her thoughts. I have no doubt being there brought back a lot of shit for her. I can't even imagine it, so instead, I walk by her side until lights hit me. A car goes past us, and I realize it's a fucking taxi.

She must notice at the same time.

She lets out an impressive whistle, and the cabbie, despite my expectations, stops. He doesn't even look surprised as he runs his eyes over us. "You have money?"

"Shit." She glances down at herself and then to me. "You have money, right?"

I can't help but laugh. "For the first time in my life, I actually don't."

"No money, no ride." He rolls the window up and speeds off, leaving us gawking after him, but when our eyes meet, we burst into laughter.

"I guess we'll walk," I say.

"Looks like it." She shakes her head. "Next time, remind me to plan the post rescue better. I hate walking and running. The only time you should be running is if someone is chasing you."

"You have a weird life," I grumble as our hands swing so close they almost touch. I have the insane urge to grab her hand, even though that's stupid. We need them free for weapons. I've never been tempted to touch anyone else like that, not for pleasure or death, but just to touch.

"And you don't, Sai?" she teases, arching an eyebrow. "You really have to admit, neither of us are normal."

"I've never been normal," I concede. I've lived a privileged life. "But I'm usually the one doing the chasing. So, will you run if I chase you?"

"No, I'll beat your ass," she retorts, teasing me even though I'm serious. "Knowing you, you'd probably like it though."

"Probably," I agree. "Look." I point ahead when a building comes into view. We both speed up until we draw close and realize it's a gas station, but it's boarded up.

"There," she says as she crosses the road and approaches an old payphone. "Let's hope it works." She picks up the phone and nods.

She does something to it, and it rings suddenly. "Call your brothers."

I input their numbers and listen to it ring. "Who is this?" Neo hisses when he finally answers.

"Is that any way to greet your brother?" I taunt.

It's quiet for a moment, and then I hear a shaky breath. "Kane, is that really you?"

"No, I'm fucking with you," I quip. "It's me."

"I thought you were fucking dead," he exclaims before he recovers. "Where are you?"

I glance around us. "Who the fuck knows? There's a closed gas station opposite us. Hellion, do you see any road signs?"

"It's I-80, near Widow's Peak," she replies without even opening her eyes as she leans into the pavement. She must feel my gaze because she cracks one eyelid. "I escaped before."

I repeat it to Neo, who I hear scrambling and shouting orders. "We're coming. Don't move."

"Not a chance. My balls hurt too much to walk anyway," I reply as I hang up and sit down next to her, wincing as I spread my legs wider.

"Your balls deserved it," she mutters without looking at me.

"Did you really hate kissing me that much?" I ask. It won't stop me from pursuing her, but it will change my tactics. Bexley is unlike anyone else I've ever met. She doesn't react how I expect her to, but that's what's interesting. My life has always been carefully controlled, but she is wild chaos, and I can't seem to stop craving it.

She blows out a breath and looks at me, seemingly annoyed by my question, but I don't back down. Her eyes narrow on me as I wait. "Do you know how many men forced themselves on me, Kane? How many stole kisses like they belonged to them and used them against me? You did the same tonight. You might not have meant to, but that's what you did. You took my choice away."

Sickness washes over me at the realization.

"I didn't mean it like that," I whisper in horror, but even that feels like a pathetic excuse.

"They never do." She shakes her head, laughing bitterly as she leans back. "Men think we are just something to use for their own pleasure. It doesn't matter if that's in the situation I was in or out here in normal life. They always want something, always want to control. You didn't even bother to ask. You wanted to kiss me, so you took it, just like they did."

She's right, she's completely fucking right, and I hate the fact that I reminded her of her past in any way, shape, or form.

"I will not touch or kiss you again, not until you ask. If you want to kiss me, you can start it or ask," I tell her, and her eyes widen as she stares at me.

"Like I ever would." She tries to tease me to lighten the mood, but I lean forward, forcing her to look at me again.

"I mean it. Never again. I want to kiss you, touch you, and fuck you more than I have ever wanted anybody else, but I won't act on it until you ask me to."

"So sure I'll ask," she brushes off.

"I see the way you look at me. You might not want to admit it, but you want me too, hellion. I can wait for the day when you figure that out and come to me," I promised.

"It will never happen."

"We'll see." I smile, and she glares at me as we lapse into silence again.

"At least it's over. Butcher is dead, and you're free. We don't have to see each other again," she explains.

"I told you that you aren't getting rid of me. I plan to invade every aspect of your life—"

"Like a disease," she sneers.

"Besides, you had a contract with my brothers. If you try to disappear, we'll just withhold payment until you come back." I shrug.

When she doesn't respond, I lean back on my hands. "They could be a while. Feel free to nap if you want. I can wake you."

"Like I'd do that. We could be attacked at any moment," she snaps, but within minutes, she slumps to the side. Shaking my head with a soft chuckle, I catch her and guide her so she leans into my shoulder. The adrenaline has drained from her body, and she hasn't slept. She breathes softly, and I keep a sharp eye out, unwilling to let anyone hurt her.

Thirty minutes later, a caravan of cars heads our way. I stroke her hair softly, knowing she would hate to be caught vulnerable like this. "Hellion," I purr, "they are here. Wake up."

She snaps to attention quickly, looking at me and the road before she clears her throat and gets to her feet just as they pull up. Guards stream out and surround us. Dodge runs his eyes over me before sighing and slumping in relief as Zayn and Neo fly from the car and tackle me in a hug. She steps away, but my eyes lock on her, even as I hug my brothers.

"I'm okay," I promise as they step back. "But we need to get out of here before the fire is reported."

Zayn frowns. "Fire?"

"I was annoyed," Bexley mutters, drawing their gazes, "and I got your brother back, so you owe me." She climbs into the car, ignoring their wide-eyed looks that swing to me.

"She did save me," I tell him. "Come on." Clapping their shoulders, I climb in after her, ignoring their silent questions.

When we reach our house, I expect her to disappear, but she heads through the front doors like she owns the place. Stopping in the foyer, she looks down at the trail she is leaving. I'm leaving one as well. "We should clean up, and then we can discuss your payment," I suggest, using it as an excuse to keep her around.

"I don't know . . . . The whole bloodstained look works for you," Zayn teases as he looks at her. "Not you, brother."

Neo is quiet, glancing between us, as are our guards, but I don't care. My attention is on her as I try to think of a million ways I can keep her here.

I stink, though, and I'm covered in blood and ash. I don't want to track it through the house to my room, so I strip.

I let my clothes fall to the floor in a stained, smoky heap and step free, naked, but my eyes are for her. I wait for her reaction, since she never does what I expect. Bexley arches an eyebrow and simply meets my gaze, removing her clothes and leaving them on top of my pile as she looks me over. I snap my fingers, and all the guards turn, averting their gazes. "I've seen better," she remarks before she turns away. "I hope you have some good showers in this ridiculously large house with a million bathrooms."

I watch her go, unable to contain my smile or my body's reaction.

"We're happy to see you too, big brother, but not like that," Zayn taunts, and when I spare him a look, he's glancing at my dick, which is hard.

Rolling my eyes, I flip them off as I go upstairs to clean up, my brothers trailing after me. They don't give me an inch of space as I step into the shower and turn on the four jets. Agony spirals through me as the water hits my wounds, but I'd rather be clean than without pain. I try to ignore the ringing in my ear as best as I can. I have no idea what damage Butcher did with that delightful torture, but it's clear it's something bad. I got used to the disorientation down in the cell, but now, moving around? It's a lot worse.

"So, tell us everything," Zayn goads as he hops up on the counter. "How was your romantic getaway?"

"Too bloody for you?" Neo scoffs, joining in, but I sense his worry.

"Just bloody enough." I grin as I scrub my hair. "Call the doctor. I have a wound that needs to be stitched. How's Dad? He doesn't know, does he? And our brother?"

"You think we're dumb? We managed to keep it a secret," Neo replies.

"Good. Did you close the contract for the plaza?" I ask, racking my brain for everything I was doing before this happened. "And did you speak to the commissioner about the new shipments? What about—"

"Brother," Neo interrupts, and his serious tone is what makes me look over my shoulder. "Calm down. We took care of everything. I'm glad you're back, though, because I hate paperwork, but it can rest for the night." He pulls his phone out and lowers his head, but I swear I saw tears there before he moved. "I'll call the doctor." He leaves, and I'm left staring after him.

"He took it all on when you . . . disappeared," Zayn reveals, sounding uncharacteristically somber. "It was a lot. He was worried, and Karma kicked his ass before she agreed to work with us, so go easy on him, big brother."

"It's what it takes to stay alive in this world," I murmur as I stare at the empty spot he vacated. "We all have to grow up sometime."

"Not me." Zayn laughs as he hops down. "I'm staying young forever."

He follows after Neo, leaving me alone. Bowing my head, I press my hands to the wall and watch the dirt and blood drain with the water. I could have died this time. I want to go easy on my brothers, but they need to be prepared for the day when I might not be here anymore. Our family depends on it.

I'm the head, it's where the bullets go, not the heart like they are.

One day, someone will get the better of me. It's the way our lives work. And when that happens, they will need to be equipped to deal with it, like it or not.

The reminder of my mortality is not something new, but it does make me more determined to take what I want.

And my little hellion?

I want her.

24

BEXLEY

I pick one of the rooms upstairs at random, seeing the suits in the immaculate walk-in closet. It has to belong to one of the brothers, and from the style, I'm guessing Zayn. Feeling extremely petty yet happy, I hide all his ties and underwear before heading to his bathroom and making a mess of it. I use his shower, scrubbing every inch of my skin with his fancy loofah and shower gel until I smell better than I ever have, and my hair is silky and falling over my shoulders in wet waves from their fancy shampoo. Wrapped in one of his extremely fluffy towels, I stare at the bottles of skincare on his counter and decide to pick them at random, then I start slapping them on my face. They must cost thousands of dollars, but I use them like they are water— again, petty happiness. All the while, I try not to think about what happened tonight.

Butcher is really dead this time. It's over.

I should feel relieved, and I do, but there's this sense of bleakness at the same time, as if everything I endured now means nothing. It's bullshit, though, so I stroll into the dressing room again and rifle through Zayn's extremely organized drawers. Grabbing a designer T-shirt, I slip it on. It drowns me, the hem falling to my knees, then I find some sweatpants and tie them tightly to stop them from falling. I even take his socks, since I have no shoes, and grab a particularly fancy leather jacket from the back of the dressing room. The leather is supple and rich, and there are patches up the arms and a skull on the back. It's epic, and I plan to keep it as a part of my payment.

Once I'm done messing up his room, I head out to the landing and follow the voices downstairs, leaning against the doorway in a formal sitting room. There's a fire burning at the back, casting the room in a warm hue. The overhead lights are off, but I see floor-to-ceiling windows and a set of leather couches facing a coffee table. Perched on one is Kane, who is shirtless and has wet hair. A man wearing a suit kneels in front of him with a bright light aimed towards Kane as he patches him up.

That must be a doctor. Of course Kane has his own private physician.

"Hey, that jacket is custom!" Zayn complains. "It looks so much better on you though. Could you take everything else off and leave it on so I can take a picture?"

I give him the bird, ignoring Neo and his battered face as he leans into the fire, watching me. Kane's eyes lock on me, dark and cold, as if he's waiting for me to speak. He assesses me, no doubt coming up with plan after plan on how to deal with me, his fingers dancing across his knee in a strange rhythm, one I saw him doing a few times before.

"Dodge, everyone, leave us," he orders, and a man I didn't even notice in the back corner steps forward.

"Yes, sir." He hustles the guards out so the room is empty, bar us and the doctor.

"They really did a number on you here, maybe even worse than the ear," the doc grumbles, interrupting the silence as he cleans Kane's shoulder wound. I can't contain my smile.

"Oh no, that one was me. Make sure to leave a pretty scar on him," I tell him as I walk farther into the room and grab a tumbler from the bar. I fill it to the brim with whatever fancy ass liquor they have.

"There will be no scar, sir," the doctor says, shooting me a scared look.

I simply watch Kane, and his lips twitch. "It's fine, let it scar. That way I'll always remember the way the hellion here likes to play."

Touché.

He's laying it on thick. I thought his flirting game would be over when we got back, but evidently not. Even his brothers seem surprised, though they control their facial expressions well. "My payment." I nod at Neo. "Wire it. I also want extra. I had to haul his big ass outside, and I broke a nail." I hold it up to show him. "My nail girl is going to kill me."

"How much did you agree on?" Kane asks casually.

"Five mil." I shrug. "Pocket change for you, but me? I'm going to buy a boat."

"A boat?" Zayn scoffs. "Where will you keep it? Do you even like boats?"

"No, but all rich bastards have boats. I want a boat to say I have one." I smirk. "So make it seven mil."

"Seven?" Neo groans. "Bexley, we agreed—"

"Seven is fine," Kane interrupts, still eyeing me. "Give her whatever she wants."

"Brother," Neo hisses, "what has gotten into you? Did she do something to you?"

"Yeah, I stabbed him," I drawl as I take a sip. "Apparently, for him that is considered flirting. Who knew?"

"You didn't kill me, so I'd call it flirting." He rolls his shoulder as the doctor finishes. "Check her wounds."

"No," I snap as I drain my drink.

"Hellion," Kane starts, and I narrow my eyes, but I know he won't back down, so I have no choice but to explain why, even if it feels like eating glass.

"No," I state tightly. "Butcher's doctors were as bad as he was. No one but someone I trust touches me."

His face tightens, but he nods. I sense Zayn's and Neo's confusion, but they don't speak until Neo breaks the silence.

"Wired," he murmurs softly.

"I'll check it once I'm home. It better all be there, or I'll come back here and kidnap your brother myself," I warn, pointing at him.

"I'm starting to think he'd like it." Zayn chuckles as he throws himself onto the couch. "Feel free to kidnap me any day. I'm not into stabbing though. Oh, and my safeword is apples."

Walking closer, I lean over the back so I'm in his face. His eyes widen, and all that bravado fades as he glances at my lips. "I don't do safewords, little boy," I tease before I stand up, leaving him staring at me. "Now, this was lovely and all, but I'm going home. I never want to see your faces again."

Kane stands and steps into my path. "What about the issue regarding the others thinking we are linked together? All our enemies will come for you."

"Let them. I can take care of myself." I sidestep him, but he moves into my path again, and I bite back my irritated sigh. "Move, Sai."

"What about the insider?" he asks, and my eyes narrow. "To get to me like that, someone on the inside had to help. That means your contract isn't finished yet."

"I was only asked to rescue you," I remind him as I pull out a gun I stole from Zayn's room and press it to his chin. His brothers freeze, and the temperature in the room drops. "So either move or I'll drop you and step over your dead body. I just showered, don't make me have to take another one."

"Neo, what was her contract?" he asks, not backing down despite the gun aimed at him.

"To rescue you and eliminate those behind it," he replies, and my nostrils flare as Kane smirks victoriously.

"That means Butcher and anyone who helped him. Your contact is still in play, and from what I know, Karma, you always complete a contact." His smile is smug. "I'll arrange a bedroom for you. You'll have to be close and part of our organization to figure out who the mole is."

"I'll kill them, you know that, and anyone else who gets in my way," I growl, annoyed that he's right, but I'm bound by my duty and contract as much as I'd like to be far away from Kane and his lustful eyes that do things to me.

He presses his lips to the barrel of my stolen gun, kissing it. We both know he wants it to be me instead. "Then kill them. Anyone who dared to betray my family deserves worse. You have free rein."

"You'll regret saying that," I warn him as I pull my gun away and step back. "Fine, I'll find your mole, and when I do, we are done forever, understand?" I glance at them. "You'll stay away from my life and business. Don't make me your enemy, Sai. You have enough already."

As I move past him and walk out the door, I feel them fall into step next to me. "Where are you going? Starting now?" Zayn asks excitedly, and I throw him a glare.

"No, I'm going to eat, I'm fucking starving, then I'm going to sleep and probably ruin one of your fancy as shit guest rooms."

"I'm hungry too." He skips at my side. "Kitchen's this way."

I'm going to end up killing them. I can tell.

I had to take a fucking elevator to their kitchen. It spans half of the bottom floor. The industrial space is big enough to feed an army, but I suppose they have one. Sitting opposite Neo, I continue my sullen glare as Zayn bustles around. Kane is sitting at my side on his phone.

"Can you even cook?" I ask Zayn.

"Of course. I took some lessons from a Michelin-star chef," he boasts as he ties an apron around his waist.

"Why?" I ask curiously.

"She was hot." He winks. "Unluckily for me, she liked playing with food more than me, so I stopped the lessons, but it means I can cook something, so don't worry."

"Of course she was." I shake my head. "You're a scoundrel, just like they say."

"What else do they say?" he asks, looking at me. "That I have a big dick? I can show you if you want to prove the rumors right."

"If you get your meat and tackle out before I get food, I will chop it off," I warn.

"So after." He nods before he turns and gets back to cooking. Yep, I'm definitely going to end up killing them before I find the mole.

Shuffling in the chair, I try to get comfortable, but my feet ache, and it makes me cranky, plus I'm tired. After a bit of killing and torture, I like to be alone, not surrounded by hot idiots. At least with their mouths shut, they are something to look at. It's when they start talking that I want to commit another murder.

"Why are you moving so much?" Kane asks, and I glance at him, realizing he was paying more attention than I thought.

"My legs ache," I grumble, shooting him a glare. "I told you I hate walking."

Without warning, he scoops up my legs and lays them across his lap, spinning me in my chair, and his hands cover my feet and start to massage.

"I'll kill you later," I say around a moan as he digs his fingers in.

"So Butcher is dead?" Neo asks, and my mood sours. I glare at him, and his eyes widen.

"Your face is really pretty, but I enjoyed hitting it. Remember that," I growl.

"Fuck, feed her. She's even worse when she's hungry," Neo tells Zayn, who moves swiftly around the kitchen like he does it a lot, which is surprising. I expected he'd have staff to cook and wait on his every need, even with his skills. Hell, I bet he doesn't even bathe himself, the spoiled fucker.

Kane hits a particularly sore spot, and I swear I nearly come. "Do you make these noises during sex?" he asks.

"You'll never know," I retort, and Neo and Zayn laugh.

"Want to bet, hellion?" he flirts as he makes me moan again. "Because I'd risk it all to find out."

"It would be the last thing you do," I whisper as my eyes close in bliss.

"I'd die happy," he scoffs, and I refrain from flipping him off since he's working my feet and legs so well. There's a bang, and I open my eyes to see a grinning Zayn staring at me and a plate in front of me. It's a sandwich, but it has shit on top, and I raise my eyebrows.

"The quickest thing I could think of—croque monsieur—but I can make more," he tells me happily . . . too happily.

"Are you on drugs?" I ask. "No one smiles that much. It's weird."

His smile dims for a moment before he perks up. "Try it."

He looks so hopeful that I pick up the fork and knife, cut off a bite, and shove it in my mouth so he'll stop.

"It's like you've adopted a kitten or some shit with the way you're all watching and fussing," I grumble around a mouthful. Flavors explode in my mouth, and I swear I do orgasm. "Fuck me, that's good."

Zayn looks ecstatic as he hurries back into the kitchen as I start to devour the plate of food.

"A spicy kitten maybe," Neo scoffs, "who dislikes people."

"Only men," I correct as I swallow and cut another bite.

"Only men?" Neo asks, tilting his head.

"I hate men," I say.

"So you prefer women?" Neo asks.

"No, I like to fuck men, but do I like men? No. You're all idiots and annoying as hell. Just because I like dick doesn't mean I'm happy about it." I turn my head to eye Kane, who's on his phone. "Did I say you could stop rubbing my feet?"

His crooked smile makes my heart flutter as he puts his phone down and carries on. "Sorry, hellion."

"Fuck me, what magic do you have? I once had to physically pry his phone from his hand." Neo gapes. "Brother, you're under a spell!"

"So?" Kane replies. "Finish your sandwich." He nods at me. "You need to sleep. We'll start work tomorrow."

I shovel the rest in my mouth, and when Zayn appears with another plate, I grab it and stand, still chewing. "I'm out of here. Peace out, motherfuckers." I head to the elevator to find a room before I become too comfortable in their midst.

I remind myself that I hate them and they are trouble.

Yet . . . Fuck.

They are fun.

25

BEXLEY

I did, in fact, sleep like the dead. Damn them and their thousand-thread-count sheets and comfy fucking pillows that smell like lavender. No wonder the rich are so happy all the time. How could they not be?

I follow my nose downstairs, smelling food and coffee. I wander around until I find the dining room. They are already seated, suited, and booted, with an older man sitting at the head of the table, a newspaper before him. I didn't know people still read them. I use it to bag dog shit left in front of our house and set it on fire when I track down who did it.

Still, I meander in and take a seat, grabbing a mug and pouring coffee as Zayn waves at me and Neo smiles. Kane is frowning, looking at an iPad, seemingly lost in whatever work men like him have to do.

I bet he's really watching porn or playing cards.

"Who is this?" the older man asks, politely giving me a confused smile. He looks similar to the guys, just gray. Maybe he's their dad.

"Name's Bexley." I nod as I sip the hot coffee, but I need the burn to feel alive in the morning. Honestly, I need an IV of it, even after sleeping.

"Bexley will be consulting with us on a problem," Kane explains as he looks up, his features seeming to soften as he looks at me. "Hellion, this is my father."

"Oh, the original Sai." I nod as I sip. "Sup? You're not as old as I thought you would be. I don't suppose you're into being a sugar daddy, are you? I have a lot of bills piling up. Kids are so expensive."

"You have a kid?" Zayn spits out his juice as I frown.

"What did we discuss? You're pretty but not too smart, so don't speak," I reply sweetly. "No, it's my niece, Lauren. You met her at the party."

"Oh, when you sliced the man's hands off." Zayn nods. "She was funny."

"So, Sai OG, sugar daddy?" I turn back to him.

He laughs as he sits back. "Ah, you're the hand thief. My sons have told me a lot about you. Sorry, I don't like my women young, but I'm sure one of my children would be more than happy to help with the way they are watching you."

"They are too vanilla for me." I shrug. "I prefer my men more experienced. What a shame." Reaching over, I steal Zayn's plate of food and start to eat as he pouts. I can feel all the Sais watching me, but I don't care.

"Karma," Dodge calls, appearing at my side. "There is a message for you."

"Karma?" Their dad's eyes widen. "As in Karma of the streets?"

"So you've heard of me. You're reconsidering the sugar baby thing now, aren't you?" I tease as I look at Dodge. "From whom?"

"Wait, you two know each other?" Neo frowns, clearly annoyed.

"Before I went to sleep last night, I tracked down your head of security—"

"While I was showering," Dodge mutters.

"There wasn't a damn thing you needed to be shy about." I wink, and he blushes. "I asked for some messages to be passed along since I don't have my phone and information. I take my contracts seriously. The quicker I deal with this, the quicker I don't have to see the three piggies again." I take the phone from Dodge and read the text, scoffing before deleting it then handing it back. "Thanks, cutie."

"Well, what was it?" Kane drawls like he's uninterested, but his focus is entirely on me and my answer.

"Oh, I was asking if they knew the best way to castrate someone," I taunt, and his eyes narrow. "Chill, old man, nothing important yet, just an acceptance. Once I finish eating, I need to review all your staff."

"There are a lot," Daddy Sai says. "Is there a reason you need to review staff?"

"Don't worry about it, Dad," Kane murmurs, covering his father's hand. "Just business."

"You're a lousy liar, boy, but I'll pretend I believe you. I also won't ask what happened or why the doctor was here so late." Oh shit, Sai Sr. is more in the know than they want.

"It's nothing to worry about. I'm handling it," Kane promises and shoots me a glare that clearly tells me to zip it.

Out of the corner of my eye, I see Zayn reaching for his plate, so I stab my fork into the fleshy part of his hand. He howls as he pulls away, but I continue eating. "Fucking hell, hellion," Kane yells. "You can't stab my brothers like that."

"Why? That's two out of three." I look at Neo and grin. "Only you're left, chosen one."

His eyes widen, and he stands. "I have court to get to, bye." He flees, making me laugh.

"You stabbed Kane?" Daddy Sai asks, more curious and unsure how to take me than mad. I know who he is. He might look calm and welcoming, but he built this empire. His hands are covered in blood, and he's the most dangerous person here, so I have to be careful . . . or, I should be.

"He deserved it," I answer as I shovel the rest of the food down and stand, nodding at Kane and Zayn, who's cradling his bleeding hand. "I'll get to work. I'll find you if I need you. Make your people aware that they will either work with me or end up in a grave."

"Understood. They won't get in the way. Dodge, make it happen,"

Kane calls as he eyes me. "Try not to kill anyone after four. My little brother will be home."

"If I do, I'll hide the body," I compromise as I turn to Dodge. "Let's go, hottie."

I follow Dodge to finish this contract and get the hell out of here, their father's voice following me.

"I like her."

26

ZAYN

My hand hurts like a son of a bitch. It's been cleaned and bandaged, but I'm in a mood as I slump into the chair opposite my father, the chessboard between us. I don't usually play with him, since it takes more patience than I have, but I have nothing better to do. My work is finished, and I don't want to follow Bexley around.

I'm mad at her.

She stole my food.

"So why is Bexley really here?" my dad asks as he moves.

I debate my answer as I move my piece. "Like Kane said, just boring work stuff."

"Boy, I taught you to lie better than that," my dad scoffs as he makes his next move, and I glower at the board, knowing I will lose. I stay silent, and he grins as he leans back. "That's better. If you can't lie well, stay silent. "

"I'm an adult. When will you stop giving me lessons?" I grumble.

"When you've learned them. I gave you and your brothers our business for a reason. It needs all three of you. Take Kane, for example. He leads well. He's smart and calculating."

I roll my eyes. I've heard this speech a million times. I will never be as good as Kane in my father's eyes. It's something I've grown to accept, unlike Neo, whom my father seems to forget about most times. He doesn't mean to. It's just who he is.

He raised us in a brutal world to be brutal men. He didn't admit he was proud of us until he handed the business over and retired. He's softened as much as a man like him can over the years, but I still find it strange.

I know my father loves us. He just wants us to survive long enough to find happiness.

"I didn't mean it like that," he adds when he reads my face—something I wish he couldn't do, but no matter how old I get, he always knows what I'm thinking. "I'm proud of how far you have come, Zayn. You're just still so young sometimes, I forget."

"It's fine, Father. I understand," I murmur as I make my move, and he wins, as usual.

I turn my eyes to the garden, but I feel him watching me. "You like Karma."

I glance at him before quickly looking back. "She's interesting."

"She is, but she's also deadly, so be careful," he replies. "Don't let your dick get you killed. No woman is worth your life."

"One day one will be," I correct. "One day, I'll love someone so much, I would die for her if that's what it took." I'm a romantic. I want love. I want marriage. I want the whole nine yards. I want kids with united parents, not like us.

I hear him sigh, but he says nothing, just resets the board.

"Ah, Karma, Dodge, how is your work going?" I whirl around to see Bexley heading our way, Dodge behind her. She grins at me, and I glare before averting my gaze.

"Well, thanks. Are you guys busy?"

"Not really. There isn't much to do when you're retired," my father complains.

"I'm sure someone with as much money as you can find a way to fill your time," she replies impartially. "I was going to check your perimeter guards, but they are busy."

"Indeed, you have time to kill then," my father says. "Bexley, do you know how to play?" my father asks, and I sit up. It's his way of assessing people.

"A little," she responds. "Would you like a match while we wait?"

She's being too polite. I track her, knowing something is up. She's probably planning to stab me again.

"Please, sit." I stand and move out of her way, and she throws me a look, which I ignore, as she sinks into my seat, eyeing the board and making her first move.

"You're younger than I expected from your reputation," my father comments as they play, trying to dig out dirt.

"Old enough to know when someone is fishing for information," she responds as she takes one of his pawns. "Just like you're old enough to know how to play word games."

"I practically invented them," he replies as he counters.

I watch their back and forth with Dodge, curious who will win, my ire forgotten for a moment.

"Indeed, you mentioned a sister?" He watches her move before analyzing the board, taking his time. "Is she well?"

"I presume so," she answers carefully. "She is not biologically related to me, but she's as close as. You have four kids? Your first three have a different mother, yes?"

Oh, she's playing him at his own game.

He smiles like he knows it as he makes his move, sacrificing a piece. She takes it and moves like he wants her to. "Different mothers. Neither are in the picture." He gives her the information like he did the player to get what he wants. "Your parents?"

"Who knows? Well, I do, of course," she admits, falling into his trap, but then she flips it and takes another piece, putting it back on him. "You control nothing in name anymore, they simply come to you for advice, yet I see you have your own security detail."

"Some see me as a threat."

"Smart, since you are the power behind the throne. Your details are loyal? Do you trust them?"

"Yes," he answers as he makes a move. "Why?"

"Just curious. You said you were bored. Maybe you're jealous of your son's success?"

My eyes widen as she implicates my father. "Bexley."

She ignores me as she makes her move, playing quickly now, as if she were only testing him.

"Never. I want this for them and more. Why?" he asks, trying to keep up on both fronts. She has him on defense now, which I've never seen. Usually, he's the aggressor.

"Just making sure you wouldn't risk Kane's life out of petty jealousy or desire for the return of your empire. If your guards are loyal to you, then it makes me wonder if it's only you," she retorts as she moves again. I watch my father's mouth part in shock as she smirks, holding his queen. "Checkmate."

She beat my father.

She actually beat him.

I tense, but he suddenly starts to laugh so loudly, I see tears forming in his eyes. "I'm guessing my sons are in danger, which is why you are here."

"Your sons are in constant danger, but you know that," she remarks as she stands. "Thanks for the game. I'll get back to work."

We both watch her go, and I sink into her vacated chair. "She's good," I murmur.

"She is. She might be the best, but none of it matters if she goes at it alone." He looks at me. "Nobody can survive this world alone, no matter how strong they are. I think I'll go for a walk. See you later." He departs, his guards following him as I look at the board, trying to figure out how and when she flipped it on him.

Is he right? Is she the best?

She's on our side right now, but what would happen if she wasn't?

I don't think any of us would be safe.

27

BEXLEY

I want to call Taylor so badly, but I know as soon as I do, she'll come home, and it's not safe yet. The mole knows I'm hunting him, and they are lying low. Anyone willing to betray their employers to Butcher could have other connections, and desperate men do desperate things.

I need to stay focused and catch the leak in the Sai house before I bring my family back.

It's also very obvious that Butcher knew I was coming, which means they tipped him off about me. It must be someone close to the brothers, someone who was around when Kane wasn't. They have a lot of staff. I start with the obvious, running over their financials with Dodge for any suspicious payments or new investments. It takes a while.

And I mean *a while*, and I get bored and have to take breaks. I much prefer hunting someone down on the streets. Whoever this mole is, they are smart and hiding well, so I have to play their game. Leaving Dodge to compile more paperwork, I wander the house aimlessly. It was more fun when I had to sneak in. Either way, I find myself by a bedroom where the loudest blasting of *Howl's Moving Castle* is coming from. Peeking inside, I find Lauren's little buddy sitting before a TV. Neo is on a couch behind him. His head is back at an awkward angle, his eyes are closed, his suit is messed up, and he has glitter all over his hands.

The kid must hear me because he turns his head and smiles. Sneaking a look at Neo, he grins and puts his finger to his lips before climbing to his feet and heading my way. "You're Lauren's aunt, aren't you?"

"I am," I murmur as I lean into the door. "I'm working with your brothers for a little bit."

"Does that mean Lauren's here?" He looks so hopeful that I feel shitty dashing it.

"Sorry, buddy, she's with her sister on vacation right now." Glancing around his room, I find it stuffed with all the latest tech as well as toys, yet he looks so sad that I sigh. "Don't you have other friends?"

"I do, but my brothers don't like me playing out of the house a lot." He spares Neo a look. "It's weird when I have to take guards with me. The other kids laugh at me and call me names, so I just stay in and play with my brothers instead, but they've been tired and busy lately."

The kid is probably Lauren's age, which means dear old Daddy got his freak on not too long ago. Having a kid when you're older must be odd, especially since his others are fully grown.

"How about I play with you for a bit?" I offer. "I play with Lauren all the time, and she doesn't complain much."

"Would you?" He looks happy for a moment before his expression turns crestfallen. "You're working. I'm sorry. I shouldn't bother guests."

"You aren't bothering me. Honestly, I was bored and looking for some trouble to get into. Want to help me?" I wiggle my eyebrows, making him giggle, and he looks back at his brother before nodding. He shuts the door to his room and steps into the hallway with me.

"I know of some places I'm not supposed to go," he admits.

"That sounds perfect. Lead the way. If we get caught, we'll use your age as an excuse."

"Hey, you should take the blame," he grumbles as we walk.

"Nah, kids get away with more," I tease, and he shakes his head but keeps walking. He seems like a serious child, but I guess growing up as the youngest son of Sai might do that to you. It's clear he's loved and spoiled, but I wonder if he might miss some normalcy—not that I can say shit, since Lauren sees way more dead bodies than she should.

We take the elevator down to the basement floor, and he looks around nervously. "The key to getting into trouble, kid, is doing it with confidence," I explain. "Watch." Stepping out, I nod at the guards and just keep walking. He hurries to keep up, and not one of them says anything, mainly because I'm allowed to be here, but he doesn't know that. He seems excited, looking around at everything until he points out a sliding door. My eyebrows rise when I realize it's a shooting range.

"Shit, look at the guns." There's a whole wall full of them. "Do you know how to shoot?"

"Only pistols." I blink, and he nods. "It's important to be able to protect myself. Guns are not toys."

Fuck, this kid is an old soul.

"Okay then, let's shoot some guns." Rubbing my hands together, I select the biggest bastard I can for me and get set up.

Two hours later, the kid can't stop smiling. I don't let him shoot alone, I'm not insane, but he's having a great time. After pulling off his earmuffs and glasses, I carefully put the gun away and lean against the booth's wall, whistling at his target.

"You're showing me up, kid. Your aim is amazing!"

"I'm a Sai. It has to be," he replies, voicing what seems like a recited line.

"Bexley, are you shooting guns with my eleven-year-old brother?" Zayn drawls, and we both turn to find him leaning against the wall behind us. I have no idea how long he's been there, but he seems amused.

I grab the kid and push him in front of me as a shield, even as I grin. "Quick, do your duty, small child, protect me."

"Best day ever!" he yells. "Bex is so much fun."

"Bex?" Zayn raises his eyebrow.

"She said I could call her that, not you." He sticks his tongue out, making me chuckle as Zayn grins.

"Dad's looking for you," Zayn says as he rubs his brother's head fondly. "Run along."

"Fine," the kid mutters before looking at me. "You'll play with me again?"

"Anytime," I promise, and he skips away as we watch.

"Thank you," Zayn tells me as I look at him. "He has a good life, but we are overprotective. I worry sometimes he feels lonely here."

"He's a great kid." I shrug as I choose a rifle, shove my earmuffs on, aim, and fire. The kick isn't too bad, but I check the sight again, recalibrating it before squeezing the trigger. Once the clip is empty, I put it down and glance back to find Zayn still there.

"Need anything?" I ask.

"Was just looking for you." He steps closer. "Should have known you'd find trouble or weapons."

"Always both," I tease as I stow my earmuffs and glasses. "What's up?"

"Kane wants to meet for an update, and it's mealtime. Come on."

I reluctantly leave the guns behind and follow him upstairs to the formal dining room. This place has three because, you know, one isn't enough. I bet these weirdos never eat in front of the TV, but I sure as shit am going to, and get crumbs everywhere while I do it. Like it's a nightly occurrence, the entire family is in attendance and dressed to the nines with a feast spread across the table.

"Found her," Zayn says as he takes his seat. "She was in the shooting range with Tommy."

"Tommy . . . as in our eleven-year-old brother?" Kane gapes, his head swinging up to see me.

"No, Tommy the stripper," I deadpan.

Standing, he buttons his suit as he walks around the table. "This isn't funny, hellion."

"No? It's at least as funny as the look on your maids' faces when they find the giant dildo collection I set up in your room."

His eye twitches as he stops in front of me, ignoring my quip.

"Bexley, you may have free rein, but my brother is off-limits. You don't have power here. Remember—" I silence Kane's rant by picking up the pan from the server's tray and slamming it across his head. Kane goes down with a grunt, and I hand the pan back, stepping over his prone form. I walk to the seat next to his father and sit. "This is what happens when you don't discipline them growing up. No respect. Don't worry, I'll do it for you," I say as I open my napkin and place it on my lap. "Would you like some coffee?" I ask sweetly.

His bark of laughter is loud in the silent room, and he shakes his head, his eyes glistening. "No doubt my son deserved that and worse. Kane, get your ass up, boy. You're embarrassing me."

"Bexley," Neo hisses, "didn't your parents ever teach you to solve things with words?"

"They didn't teach me much on the account of them being dead," I retort with a blank face, and the horror in his widening eyes makes me giggle. "The dead parents shit always works."

"Fuck, Bexley," Zayn grumbles. "You can't make jokes like that. It's not funny."

"It wasn't when they both died either." I wink as they continue to stare at me while Kane stumbles to his feet, throwing off the guard helping him and glaring at me. He sinks into his chair, a trail of blood running down his scalp.

"I thought pain was your foreplay," I coo. "Oops, my bad."

"Do you like chicken, Bexley?" their father asks as he continues eating like we are the best entertainment ever.

"Uh, who doesn't? Well, I suppose vegetarians." I dig in. At the first bite, I nearly orgasm. The noise that leaves my mouth is inherently sexual, but I can't contain it. "This might be the best chicken I've ever tasted."

His dad grins as he cuts off a section of his and slides it onto my plate. "Family recipe. I asked them to make it especially for you. If you want it again, you'll have to, I don't know . . . marry into the family."

"Good one, Pops, or I'll just torture one of your sons for it," I reply as I eat, his laughter reaching my ears.

The rest of the meal is spent in silence—well, my silence as I gorge. They discuss boring business shit I have no interest in.

When their dad excuses himself, I sit back in my chair and wait. "So, did you find anything?" Neo asks.

"You mean have I found your mole and killed them? Not yet." I shrug as I spear a bite of the incredible chicken from Zayn's plate. He rolls his eyes as I steal it.

"You find anything at all, hellion, or are you too busy corrupting my kid brother?" Kane grumbles.

"Bit of both. Dodge is running financials," I answer idly.

"You don't sound convinced," Zayn says. "I figured you would help him dig through the financial records of our entire staff with the way you were both talking."

"I figured you would want to be out of here as quickly as possible, hellion," Kane teases, "or maybe you're considering my offer."

"The only thing I'm considering is which brother to kill first." I take a drink. "And I'm not helping him because I know it won't work out."

"What do you mean?" Neo asks, outwardly the most normal and calm, which is odd since he let me beat his ass.

"Well, Butcher doesn't work that way. It's a nice idea, so I'm letting Dodge do it, but most of the time he uses . . . different ways of persuading people. Are you going to eat that?" I ask Kane, who rolls his eyes and pushes his half untouched chicken over to me. I don't know what kind of magic or money they put into this shit, but I'm going to have to kidnap their cook so I can have it all the time.

"What do you mean?" Kane asks, pulling my attention away from my kidnapping plans. We could keep a cook. We have a spare room.

Sighing, I sit back. "Fear, pain, love . . . that's Butcher's trifecta. If he wants to turn someone, and I'm guessing most of your soldiers are loyal, he would use one of those, so that's what I'm looking for. People with missing family members. People who are acting out of the ordinary. People who are terrified because that's what he does. Why waste money when fear works faster? I'll let Dodge keep searching just in case, but I'm going a different direction as well."

"Jesus," Zayn whispers.

"Nope, just Karma," I taunt as I finish off Kane's plate. "Now, if you'll excuse me, I have a card game with your soldiers to attend. What better way to learn their secrets than take all their money?"

"Are you sure it's not just for their money?" Neo drawls.

"Two birds, one stone, and a whole lot of bills. Isn't that the phrase? Or kill the bird or some shit. Either way, Mama's going to be rich tonight." I rub my hands together. Throwing them a peace sign, I head back to the elevator and take it down to the bottom floor, where their soldiers' living quarters are.

It's time to steal some bills and secrets.

28

NEO

I leave my brothers to it as I take the stairs down to the first sub level and claim a seat in the bar area that overlooks the gaming room below. Most of the guards' rooms are on that floor, so the living area was made into a game room. It's equipped with virtual golf, darts, pool, bowling, and casino tables. It's where I find her, sitting at the high-stakes game with a beer at her side and a cigarette dangling from her mouth as she inspects her cards.

She went from annoying us to sliding into our guards' midst. It's strange, but she seems to fit quite easily in both. There is no way our staff would be this relaxed if we were down there. They'd be on alert, refusing to drink or have fun, but around her, they don't seem to care, which is exactly what she wants.

They laugh and joke around her. I can't hear what they are saying, but she smiles as she lays a card down and takes another. "Sir, would you like another drink?" I tilt my head up to see one of the guards who was sitting in the bar when I arrived. It's a small area but stocked with every-thing they could need. As long as they don't drink and work, we don't care. We offer them the very best in money, cars, and a good lifestyle. It's why they are so loyal, and the notion that one of them has betrayed us sits sour in my stomach. I search his flat brown eyes, wondering if it's him. His hands shake slightly as he lifts the bottle of bourbon to show me. It's good, not as expensive as what I usually drink, but it will do.

"Sir?" he asks nervously, shooting his companions in a rear corner booth a worried glance. The lights are low in here, the red and gold accents tastefully done and reminiscent of a speakeasy, which is what they were going for.

"Of course, thank you," I murmur, shaking off my stupor. It's not like they will poison me. The only person who probably would is sitting at the table down there, and she would do it for fun. "You don't have to serve me though. I'm invading your time off, so please, enjoy yourselves."

"It's no trouble at all," he says as he tops off his drink. "Are you here to keep an eye on Karma?"

"You know her?" I ask as I take a sip and smile as much as I can to get him to relax. The mention of her name makes me curious.

"I met her today. She's cool. Some of the others know her reputation, and others even know her . . . well, as much as she lets them," he admits and glances at the marble table before me. I incline my head in invitation at his obvious question. He sits carefully on the maroon velvet seat and watches her through the window like I was. "I heard there are only two people she cares about in this entire world, and they are off-limits. Someone tried to hurt them once, and she killed their entire family, going back two generations. She's not someone to mess with."

"I know," I say as I watch her. "Keep an eye on her for me, will you? If she does anything you are worried about, report to me."

"Not Kane, sir?" he asks, even as his eyes sparkle in interest. It's something I realized a few years ago. The guards are bigger gossips than my father.

My eyes find him, and he jumps to his feet, bowing his head. "I meant no disrespect, sir."

"Not Kane, me," I assert as I turn away, dismissing him. I hear him leave, but my eyes are for Karma. Kane doesn't know I'm watching her, but it's for his own good.

There are no secrets between us brothers, none but her. Kane has been tight-lipped about whatever happened between him and Bexley when they were kidnapped. It worries me. She can look after herself, she's made that very clear, but when it comes to her, Kane seems to have a soft spot.

She is a weakness he doesn't know how to handle. It's my job to make sure it doesn't implode his life or wreck his heart.

Karma doesn't seem like the type to stick around forever, and when she leaves, I don't want her to take what is left of my brother's happiness with her.

She moves around the room, playing cards and drinking games. She laughs and smiles, but her eyes are cold as she scans everything. If I wasn't looking for it, I wouldn't notice. She blends in well, but she's like a predator stalking her prey. She's getting them exactly where she wants them, and she knows it.

The man was right. She's dangerous. If she spends more time here, she could probably bring down our entire empire on the secrets she learns alone. We need to be careful.

Two hours after she came downstairs, she's whistling her way back to the elevator, counting her winnings. I rise and button my suit jacket, leaving my half empty drink on the table. The guards in the bar leap to their feet and bow. I have long since given up trying to make them stop. When I was younger, their fear and respect made me uncomfortable, but Father wore me down over the years. They are here to keep us safe, and their respect is part of that and who I am. I shouldn't deny it, but embrace it.

Heading to the stairs, I watch the glass elevator pass and hurry up, sweat trickling down my back as I take the many flights until I reach the main floor. When I get there, though, the door is open, and Karma isn't in sight. Frowning, I step into the elevator, searching it before turning and stepping out, only to freeze as something sharp presses against my neck. I feel her heat behind me, a trickle of my blood gracing my neck from the sharp edge of whatever blade she is holding against my skin.

How did she even know I was following her? Did someone tip her off, or is she that good?

"Following me, pretty boy? Are you aching for a round two?" she whispers into my ear. A shiver runs through me, and desire I try to ignore pools in my gut. It's just another of her weapons, but it doesn't seem to stop my lust for her. "You think I didn't see you watching me all night? You aren't very inconspicuous. You don't blend."

"I'll take that as a compliment," I murmur, not moving in case she decides to slit my throat for fun. "I was just keeping an eye on you. I'd be a fool not to with an assassin like you in our house."

"I prefer the term homicidal cleaner. Besides, you invited me to stay," she teases as she moves silently around me. Despite facing me in the ring, she still thinks I'm weak. They all do. The second brother, never quite comparing to Kane. I like to be underestimated, especially in court, but for some reason, the idea of her thinking I'm powerless irritates me, and I make a rare impulsive decision.

Swinging my hand up in a quick movement she doesn't even see coming, I catch the dagger as it knocks free from her hand without cutting me. I catch it midair and spin it, pressing it to her neck. "I guess I win round two."

"Do you?" She smirks and looks down. Following her gaze, I see her gun pressed to my balls. I didn't even see her move. Laughing for real, I shake my head even as I keep the dagger against her throat before I remember why I'm keeping my eye on her.

"What offer did my brother make you?" I ask. Kane mentioned something about it earlier.

Her head tilts as she watches me, her smile fading to something entirely different. Goose bumps erupt on my arms, and the breath in my chest catches as she leans into me. My eyes widen as she moves so close, I can smell the beer on her breath. "To own all three of you, to belong to you . . . to be yours." My mouth drops open as she chuckles. "Your brother is insane. Don't worry, I have no inclination of taking it. I will never belong to another, and I certainly don't want three prickly Sai brothers as my own." Removing her gun, she steps back as she winks before she turns to walk away.

I watch her go, swallowing hard, and before I know it, the question slips free. "Why?" I call, and she stops with her back to me. I hurry to catch up until I'm right behind her, and I can't seem to control myself. I should be careful because Karma is a walking weapon, but it seems like I'd be willing to cut myself on her for just a taste. Sliding my hand around her throat, I feel her there, steady and strong, as I slide my other hand to her hip, slipping her dagger back into place. "Why wouldn't you want all three of us? It's something every woman in the world dreams of."

My voice is huskier than I wanted it to be. Being this close is muddling all my intentions, and desire leads my actions despite my intentions. My cock is hard in my pants, so I pull my hips away so she doesn't feel it.

"I'm not every woman," she responds, and despite her steady heart rate, I hear the breathlessness in her tone. She's not as unaffected as she wants to appear.

"No, you're not. That's why he offered." I lean down and inhale her scent. My eyes close in bliss at the sweetness that is all her. No perfume, just her, and it drives me crazy. She'd kill me and not think about it after. I should protect my family, but one word from her and that was all it took for my desire to roar to the forefront of my brain.

It's clear Kane feels the same way and is trying to tie her to us. That in itself is surprising, not to mention the fact that he clearly knows we all want her. Zayn has made it obvious, and Kane tried not to, but he knew I wanted her. Instead of stealing her away, he tried to give us what we wanted.

"You three are really not all that," she snaps as she spins and glares at me. "If I want something, I take it, so clearly I don't want you."

"That's the first time I've seen you lie." I smirk as I lean closer, copying what she did. Her eyes widen before she can control it, and I feel her heartbeat speed up under my hand. "Your heart gives you away, Bexley."

"And your heart . . . or your dick, will be the reason you die if you continue," she warns. Grabbing my hand, she twists it and me and slams me into the closest wall. I relax into her grip, grinning as her mouth brushes my ear. Her warm breath blows across the sensitive shell. "This is the closest you will ever get to having me, so think about it when you get off later."

"Oh, I will," I promise as she releases me, and by the time I turn, she's gone.

Banging my head back to the wall, I take a deep breath and frown.

So much for trying to keep my family safe. One look and I was no better than my brother.

What kind of black-magic hold does Karma have over us?

29

BEXLEY

Marching into the room I commandeered, I remove my shoes and stolen coat, throwing them onto the bed as I pace. That was not how I expected that conversation to go. I could feel Neo watching me all night, my neck burning from his intense gaze. I expected him to threaten me or attack, not flirt!

These brothers all have issues. I mean, Neo's pretty . . . . Okay, he's beautiful. They all are, with bodies that would even make a god weep, but they know it. They use their beauty as a weapon. I just never thought it would work on me.

He's right. I want him. I lied.

I want them all, even that annoying fucker Kane, and they are determined to push my buttons. I need to finish this contract and get the hell out of here, yet I can't calm down.

It's just been too long since I had sex. That's all. I'll find someone and have a quickie. I'm in their house, so the available options are vast if I include their guards, but I don't know who I can trust, and it would take sleeping with the enemy to a new level. What if it were the mole? No, that rules out the guards and leaves me with three options—four if you include their father, but I have a feeling they would be pissed about me sleeping with their dad. It's never been my kink either.

"No, this is dumb," I mutter as I stop pacing and cross my arms. "I don't need sex. I have hands. I can get off." I head to the bathroom before pivoting and turning around. "Then again, it would mean nothing—no." Turning back, I head to the bathroom before freezing. I throw my hands in the air. "Fuck it."

Before I can second-guess what the fuck I'm doing, I'm out of my room and striding down the corridor. I move fast up to the next level so I don't turn around, and when I reach the door at the end, I storm inside without knocking. Kane leaps to his feet, his eyes widening in surprise.

"What's wrong—" Before he can finish, I grab his neck and push him back to his bed. His shirt is gone and his pants are undone, as if he were just getting dressed.

"Hellion." The wound on his chest is covered, and the sight of his golden muscles only solidifies my decision. I want Kane, and it's clear he wants me. He also understands my past, even a little, and the limits. He's a safe option—well, as safe as fucking any of the most dangerous men in the world can get, not that I plan to fully fuck him. I just need to get off.

"Don't think this means anything," I order, and his brows furrow as he frowns. "Kiss me."

His eyes widen before they smolder, and he reaches for me, his lips curling in happiness until I block them with my hand. "Uh-uh. I said you could kiss me, but I didn't say where. Not my mouth, Mr. Sai," I purr. "You wanted to taste me, so taste me."

His eyes burn with understanding. Smirking, I step back and shed my pants, waiting. He lowers to his knees, and I stroll closer, dragging my hand up his perfect chest to his chin, which I tilt up so he's looking at me. "Let's see if this arrogant mouth can do more than talk."

Stepping back, I wait to see what he'll do. He climbs to his feet and reaches for me, and I tut.

I press my foot to his shoulder, my leg stretched high, and push him down until he's on his knees in front of me again. "This is the only way you'll get me. Take it or leave it." I groan as he grips my hips and pulls me to his mouth.

He eats my cunt in a hungry attack, forcing my thighs wider apart and burying his tongue inside me. My head drops back as pleasure spirals through me, an urgent need demanding more. Grabbing his hair, I grind into his mouth as his tongue pulls out of my channel and slides up, circling my clit until he finds a rhythm that has me groaning and pressing against his face. He uses it against me, slowing his strokes around my clit as I feel his thick fingers press against my entrance and slip into my wet core. My head lowers, and I meet his eyes between my thighs as he licks me faster and harder. His fingers spear deeper and crook until he rubs my G-spot. I gasp his name and clench around him, my pleasure continuing to grow until I can't hold back.

I need this so badly, and his mouth is so good. I shatter with a scream before I bite my lip to swallow the sound. My thighs clench around him as he licks me through my release until I push him away, too sensitive.

His smirk is cocky as hell, his lips glistening with my cum. "I'll make you crave me, hellion, until you sneak in here every night and beg me to make you scream."

"You wish, Sai. This is a one-time thing," I tell him, stepping away. I got what I needed, but I should have known he wouldn't let me go so easily. I stepped into the devil's lair, and he's determined to have his way with me.

He pushes to his feet and grabs me, throwing me down onto the bed. He crawls between my legs as I drape them over his shoulders. Narrowing my eyes at the smug look on his face, I grab my gun and aim it at his head. "Don't get cocky."

He doesn't seem bothered by the threat as he presses between my thighs again. "Shoot me. It's the only thing that will stop me, hellion. Otherwise, I'm not finished eating yet."

His mouth is on me again. I'm surprised he didn't push me further and try to fuck me, but if anything, he seems determined to get me to come to him for that as well. Instead, he eats me like a starving man, his hands sliding up my sides to grip my breasts. My back arches in ecstasy as his large, rough palms cover my tits before he rubs and pinches my nipples. Pleasure arcs between them and my abused clit as he sucks it with the same intensity. I drop the gun as I roll my hips, riding his face shamelessly. My pleasure is already growing again, consuming me, until I forget why this is a bad idea. I shatter again with a scream, writhing beneath him, but he still doesn't stop. I'm flipped, my face pressed to his bedding, as his hand slips between my thighs and strokes me as he places kisses and nips down my back and ass. I shake below him, my cunt clenching with aftershocks, but he doesn't relent. He shoves three fingers into me, forcing me to take them, and his mouth sweeps over my ass and down, licking me again until I push back.

"Fuck, don't stop," I beg, hating that I am.

"Never," he murmurs against my flesh. His warm breath has me groaning as I drop my head and push back, taking his fingers harder. It's too much. My skin is too hot and my clit aches, yet I can't stop, and he doesn't let me slow down. He fucks me straight through my orgasm and toward another before his tongue circles my ass. "One day, I'm going to be buried in this tight channel while you scream for me just like this," he warns. "I'll fuck every inch of you, hellion, and we both know you'll love it. I can wait, but for now, I want to see you come again. I want you to drench my bed so I can sleep in your scent."

Fuck, fuck, fuck.

His depravity should scare me, but if anything, it gets me off, driving me higher as I rock back into him. His tongue slides into my ass, and an orgasm tears through me, taking me by surprise since I've never come this much.

It hurts, and I feel myself dripping down his fingers as I fall forward. All my energy is sapped for a moment as I shake in pleasure. His fingers stroke me gently before pulling free. Kane's body presses against mine, and I have the insane urge to turn over and demand he fuck me.

That is what gets me moving, despite the shakiness of my legs.

Rolling from the bed, I hit the floor and scoot back before getting to my feet. The need to pounce on him and finish this consumes me. He smirks like he knows my thoughts, and he licks the wet spot on the bed. "Delicious."

Sliding from the mattress, he kneels before me, a hurricane of devastating hunger in his gaze as he watches me. One word and he would be on me.

Swaying slightly, I lick my dry lips and ignore the shaking of my legs as he kneels, his eyes wild with lust. I need to regain control. I can't lose myself with him. It would be more dangerous than just killing him.

He's a Sai brother. I'm a street rat.

Fun is all we can have, and we both need to remember that before we return to our lives. "You can finish yourself off. I'm nice like that."

Lifting onto his knees, he reaches for his pants as he smirks. "Why, you want to watch?"

Rolling my eyes, I turn and flee from his room. My pulse is hammering because the truth is, I did want to stay.

After Butcher, sex was fucked up for me. But I've never wanted someone as badly as I want Kane or his brothers, and that's dangerous. I can't allow myself to want someone like them.

The only people I can depend on are Taylor and myself.

I walk away, even as every part of me wants to go back into the room and finish what we started.

30

BEXLEY

I slept well last night, probably due to multiple orgasms, so when I come downstairs, I expect the Sais to be busy doing whatever evil overlords do, but I find them seated at the dining table, their plates set but empty.

I slide into my seat and look around, ignoring Kane's lust-filled gaze. "Have you guys eaten already?"

"I know I did late last night," Kane quips, and I narrow my eyes in warning. "We were waiting for you. You can serve breakfast now."

They waited for me to eat? Why?

"What are everyone's plans today?" Kane asks as he leans back in his seat, his open laptop to the side as he focuses on his brothers.

"I have a site walkaround today for the new hotel," Neo replies. "I might need to head upstate after for a few meetings. We'll see how it goes."

"Make sure to get that new contract signed if you do. Take Mr. Henderson out, wine and dine him, and compliment his wife. It will do the trick," Kane suggests, and Neo nods, pulling his phone out and making notes. It's strange watching their dynamic. Kane is their brother, but sometimes he acts like their boss, which I guess he technically is, and it's clear they defer to him a lot and look to him for approval and guidance. It's almost cute.

"Zayn?" Kane asks as he takes another sip.

Zayn blinks, chewing and wiping his mouth before he speaks. "I have marathon training this morning. I need to up my speed if we want to come in first."

"Wait . . . marathon training?" I ask incredulously.

Like . . . running? No murder, mayhem, or torture, but running?

"Even criminals need hobbies, Bexy," Zayn mutters, and I glare at him even though he's right. "It's for charity. One of us competes every year. It's tradition. This year is my turn."

"Oh," is all I say, and then I lean back as breakfast is served. Once the staff leaves, I add some sauce to my plate as Zayn leans across and grins at me.

"Want to join me on my run?" He looks so hopeful, so happy, it's almost too much fun to ruin his joy.

Sometimes you just need to remind a man of his place and dash all his hopes and dreams.

It's my favorite hobby.

"I'm going to stop you right there. That sounds horrendous, and it isn't something I want to do at all. Why are you running? Who's chasing you?" I chew as I watch him. "I could help you keep your time if you want?" I manage to hide my evil smile . . . but only just.

"Sure, that would be great. We'll go after breakfast." He nods, smiling.

Oh, this will be so much fun.

"This juice is nasty," Neo comments, oblivious as he sniffs it and makes a face.

"I don't know. I think it's delicious and sweet," Kane says as he eyes me, licking his lips, and I roll my eyes.

Subtle.

I hurry to finish my breakfast, and then I get to my feet since I need to prepare. "I'm going to get dressed. I'll meet you outside." I skip away as I giggle.

"Why is she so excited?" Neo asks curiously.

"Maybe she's just happy," Kane replies with masculine pride in his voice.

"It scares me when she's happy," Neo admits.

I always knew he was the clever one. It should scare him. It really should.

As I roll the car down the driveway, Zayn stops stretching and lifts his hand to cover his forehead as he peers at me. He looks fucking good in his shorts, but I'm practically giggling with glee as I lower the window and grin at him.

"This is Kane's, right?" It's nice, a Bugatti Centodieci, if I'm not mistaken. I've only ever seen them in magazines back in Auto's shop. "I'll follow you and keep time."

"Oh." He looks at me. "Uh, sure, but be careful. That's his pride and joy."

"I'll be very, very careful. Go on then, get running, hottie." He grins at me as he steps back and flexes.

"You like this outfit? I could take the shorts off if you want, and we could try a very different workout." He gapes when I blare the horn and ruin his flirting. I see all the guards staring, but I ignore them.

"Sorry, I was cutting you off before I threw up in my mouth. Start running before I get bored." I rev the engine. Sparing me a frown, he turns and starts to jog. I follow him out of the gates and onto the private street. Once there, he speeds up, and I do as well. He keeps looking at me then forward before he's forced to swerve onto the road when his footpath ends.

I speed up, and he glances back, his eyes widening as he has to run faster to avoid being hit by me. Grinning, I settle into the leather seat and hit the radio, singing along to Chappell Roan.

Taking a donut out of the bag the cook handed to me, I nibble on it. Sheila is a lovely lady. She has three kids. Who knew? We bonded over our annoyance of men after she caught me running from Kane's guards with his keys in hand.

Eight miles in, Zayn is slowing down and clearly needs some motivation.

"Speed up!" I yell out of the window, still eating donuts. "You need to beat your time. Hurry your ass up or I'll hit you with the car."

"I'm trying," he wheezes, glancing back at me. He is covered in sweat and glistens in the sun, and I consider appreciating his pretty body, but when he slows again, I have no choice.

I don't make idle threats.

I rev the engine and tap him with the bumper. It's a little love tap, really, but he flies forward, rolls, and jumps back to his feet. At least I didn't break anything. It would be a shame for all those muscles to go to waste.

Gasping, he turns to me where I wait. "You hit me!" he yells.

Leaning out of the window, I push my shades up and wink. "A threat is only a threat if you're willing to follow through, and I always am. You should have run faster. Now move."

His eyes widen as he rubs his ass, and I rev, creeping forward until he spins and starts to sprint away from me.

By the time he's on the home stretch, he's sprinting and screaming as I laugh manically, and when we reach the driveway, he collapses into a guard's arms. Turning the engine off, I wipe my sticky hands and climb out, whistling at the dent in the bumper.

"You must have a hard ass. You dented his car," I remark as I lean into the hood.

"You hit me with it four times!" he yells as he shakes off his guard and glares at me.

"Did you not beat your time?" I retort, and he glances at his watch before gawking at me. "See? I helped. You're welcome." Turning away, I head toward the front door, and he follows me into the foyer.

"You're so mean, but I still want to fuck the shit out of you. I have issues," he grumbles, and with another glare, he limps to the stairs, rubbing his ass and legs.

I watch him go as Kane stops by my side. "Do I want to know?" he asks curiously.

"Motivation and positive reinforcement." I shrug as I hold up his keys. "Your car is nice. I hope you don't mind crumbs everywhere. Oh, and your bumper is dented." I head to the elevator and grin at him as he holds his keys, his eyes snapping to me.

"Hellion!" he roars, shaking the house, and I burst into laughter.

Oh, it was so worth it.

Mole hunting is surprisingly boring. I took two naps this afternoon while Dodge scanned personnel files. Honestly, I just want to round them all up and beat the truth out of them.

Wait, not a bad idea.

Leaping to my feet, I ignore Dodge, who calls my name, and head to the main area where the off-duty guards hang out. If Butcher can turn them with fear, then I can get the truth with it.

Clapping my hands, I climb up onto one of the tables, kicking glasses aside as I prop my hands on my hips. "Listen up, minions. Everyone is to meet me at the pool. Five minutes. No longer." Pointing my finger, I scan the crowd before I land on someone. "You, get me coffee." I turn and go to leave before stopping. "Wait, remind me where the pool is."

A commotion of voices respond, and I wave at them, ignoring their grousing. Some of them don't like me being here, some are scared of me, and others are following orders. I simply don't care.

When I get to the pool after a small diversion, I find them gathered, and all eyes turn to me as I glance around. There are a bunch of lounges and beds, and the pool is Olympic sized. Bulletproof glass lines one wall, looking into the garden.

"Okay, here is how it's going to go. I'm going to line you up in front of the pool and ask you questions. If you lie to me, you'll die. You all know by now what I'm searching for, but if you don't, let me make it clear. There is an informant in your ranks who betrayed your employer, and it's my job to find you. I will do just that, so let's begin. One line. Go."

"You can't be fucking serious. If they suspect us, then they should ask us!" one yells. There's some agreement, and my eyes narrow as I pull the stolen crossbow around for them to see. Their armory really does have everything.

"You can't do this!" a man shouts as he steps forward, going toe-to-toe with me. "Who are you to question us? I've been with this family for two years—"

"And yet you're still stupid," I retort. "No one is irreplaceable, not even you. Someone betrayed their employers. You should want to help me find them, unless it's you?" I tilt my head as I watch him. "Is it?"

"You're a crazy bitch. I'll show you who's stupid here!" He advances on me. Rolling my eyes, I lift the bow and fire.

I didn't aim, and honestly, I've never really used one of these since I'm not in *Mad Max*, so when the bolt slams into his eye and he hits the ground, my eyes widen. Oops, I just meant it to be a warning shot, but the others' fear can only help my cause.

"He had kids!" one of his friends yells from the side of the fresh corpse.

"Why does everyone always say that like it's a reason for me not to kill you? I just did them a favor. He was a total ass." I shrug. "Now, line your asses up!"

Some of them glare at me, but most fall into line, and I wait. Those who linger stand before me.

Lifting the bow to my eye, I grin. "Make sure not to move too much. I don't have much practice with this, so I'd hate to miss." They fall into line, and I drop the crossbow and pace. At least forty men, all in their telltale black suits with the Sai logo on the crests.

One of these men betrayed them.

"Okay then, let's start here." I pick a guard at random and step closer. "Have you ever cheated on your partner?"

He gapes at me and looks around for help. "I thought this was business."

"Fine, ruin my fun," I grumble. "Did you betray the brothers?"

"No. Never," he spits vehemently. I watch his eyes as they tighten slightly—nerves. A bead of sweat rolls down his forehead, but I know he's telling the truth. Taylor always said I was a truth machine, amongst other not so nice things. "Do you know who did?" I ask.

"No," he says, fisting his hands as he looks straight ahead.

Truth.

Stepping to the next man, I repeat the process, watching his shifty eyes before moving on to the next. This one simply looks pissed off as I ask, "I said, do you know who did?"

"No," he responds, but he looks left, his body tightening.

He's lying to me.

Stepping closer, I press the sharp bolt tip to his chin. "You're lying to me. Last chance. Who betrayed the brothers?"

"I don't know," he grits out, "and if I did, I would never tell you, so do your worst."

Stepping back, I take aim and fire. He plunges backwards into the pool with a huge splash. The water quickly turns red. "Make no mistake, I'm not here to be your friend. I don't care if you live or die. If I have to kill all of you to find the mole, I will, so do not test me."

"You think whoever it is will just admit it?" someone snaps, and I search the line until he steps forward, nodding at me. "With all due respect, no one would admit it."

"Very true," I agree. "It was worth a shot. I hate paperwork. Fine, let's try something else."

They might as well entertain me as I think through another idea since he's right. "Suits off, shirts off, get in the water."

"With the body?" a younger guy asks.

"It's just a dead guy. He isn't going to bite. Get in," I tell him as I turn and lie on the lounger, crossbow still in hand. I can tell they don't want to, but they've been ordered to listen to me. Ignoring my command would mean ignoring the Sais' orders. I watch as they strip, exposing so many chests that I sit back happily.

They splash into the pool, standing stiffly as they wait for further instructions, but I just check them out, enjoying my view while I think.

It's always good to have something pretty to stare at while contemplating how best to torture people.

I could follow the paperwork, but like I told the Sais, whoever betrayed them wouldn't do it because of money. My bet is fear or love, but how do you track that? Trace their entire family? Too tedious. I prefer torture. Unless . . . What if we set a trap?

"Hellion, what are you doing?" I glance up to see Kane there. His eyebrows are raised, and two men in suits stand behind him. I've never seen them before, but I ignore them and focus on Kane.

"Well, it started as a murder and answer session, but I got distracted, so now I'm just watching them swim and glare while I check them out," I admit. "I'm weak, and there are so many muscles. I'll get back to killing them soon."

"Alright, everyone back to their posts." He turns to me as I lean around him to watch them get out. Why is it always slower in *Baywatch*? I don't have enough time to look at all of them. Kane's eyes narrow as he moves close to block the view until I slump back. "I lost all of my guards, leaving us unprotected. If you need something beautiful to look at, hellion, then you just need to find me."

"You think too highly of yourself," I scoff as his hand grips my chin, forcing me to look at him.

"You didn't think so last night when you were screaming for me." That makes my eyes narrow. "How about I remind you?"

Standing, I leave the crossbow behind, otherwise I might use it on him, as I poke his chest. "Don't test me, Kane."

"Why, hellion?" He captures my finger. "It's so much fun to play with you."

I kick out, my foot hitting the center of his chest, and I watch as he hits the water and goes under before surfacing and gasping. His guards dive in after him as he drips in his fancy ass suit. "Serves you right. That's the only wet thing you'll be getting today," I warn before picking up my crossbow and heading back to Dodge, since apparently I can't just torture his entire staff.

How boring.

31

KANE

A s I stare at the foil invitation before me, a wicked idea comes to mind, and I look up at Dodge. "Get my hellion for me."

"Sir . . ." Dodge sighs, eyeing the open door. "You're letting an assassin wander around our house and poke through our business. What if she betrays you?"

For a moment, the ringing in my bad ear intensifies. It comes and goes, and after a few tests from the doctor, he's confident it will heal on its own, though he doesn't know if it will ever truly be the same. Most of the time, I can ignore it, but then suddenly it will cut through the noise like now. Blinking slowly, I try to reorientate myself while it lessens so as not to give my weakness away. I steeple my hands under my chin and watch him, knowing he means well, but he doesn't understand this like I do. Anyone who wasn't there with us won't comprehend. I saw another side to my hellion in Butcher's dungeon, one she wants nobody to know about. For all her strength, determination, and power, she is still a person who is inundated with trauma and damage, just like us.

She's one of us, so no matter how hard she pushes, I will push back.

"I'll take responsibility," I assure him. "She won't anyway. It isn't her style. She's a blunt weapon, the type to shoot and stab when annoyed, not play the long game. If she wants us dead, then she will just kill us. It's simple. She's just having fun with us now."

"She killed staff—"

"Playing." I shrug. "Let her. She's welcome to. Our home is hers now."

"You're so sure about her. Why? You're never that open or trusting of anyone but your brothers." Dodge sighs as he sits. "I don't mean to question you."

"Yes, you do." I chuckle. "But you've earned the right. The truth is, I don't know. From the moment I laid eyes on her, it was like I was struck by lightning. I'm not just thinking with my dick, but with my soul. It recognizes hers. Besides, she saved my life. She earned my loyalty, and I expect you to treat her as such."

He nods and stands. "I'll get her."

"And remind my brothers about our party tonight. Call Neo back no matter how late it is." After inclining his head in acknowledgement, he leaves my office, and I look at the invitation and smile, excited for her reaction.

It doesn't take her long to arrive, and she storms into my office, ready to fight. She's so fucking magnificent. I get hard just seeing the fire in her gaze. "You don't summon me like one of your staff," she hisses as she stops in front of my desk.

"It got your attention, didn't it?" I rub my jaw to hide my smile.

"I have three guns on me," she warns. "Choose your next words carefully because I might decide your ability to eat pussy is no longer worth keeping you alive."

My lips twist in amusement as I slowly run my eyes down her body. "Still thinking about last night? I know I am. Want me to remind you?"

"Kane," she growls, but my dick is hard.

"I didn't call you here just to flirt—"

She smirks. "You call this flirting? Your skills are getting rusty, old man."

Narrowing my eyes, I yank her onto my lap, but I grin when I feel a gun press against my cock in warning. "I was simply going to show you I'm not that old."

"Try it, I dare you," she retorts.

Grinning, I release her, and she leans back on my desk, gun still in hand. "Fine, I'll stop teasing you. I was just given an invite. There's an event tonight we need to attend. You will come with us."

"And why the fuck would I do that? I don't want to spend my evening around rich pricks," she scoffs.

"You'll come with us in case we find out any information. They might be rich pricks, but they are a fount of gossip and information. Besides, I need to show my face. By now, word has hit the streets of my kidnapping. We need a show of force to remind them of our control."

"Control is an illusion men like you tell themselves to feel superior. The truth is, whoever has money always wins."

"Very true," I concede. "Most power comes from the idea of strength rather than actual strength. A few well-placed actions and the entire city fears us without us having to keep up the act. Like last night. All you had to do was order me and I was yours."

"The next time—"

"So there will be a next time?" My smirk is victorious as she rounds my desk. She aims her gun at me, and my grin widens. "Fine, but you still need to attend the event. It's black tie, so let me know if you need one of our stores to send you something."

"I'm not going. I would rather shove a hot poker up my pussy," she scoffs.

"And what if we are attacked? What if the mole follows us? It's a chance to observe and fulfill your contract." I shrug. It's a stretch, and we both know it. "You know I'm right. I'll see you at six sharp. You can go back to terrorizing my household now."

"Me? I'm a sweet angel. Martha, your house manager, said so."

"Martha?" I frown. "That's a woman, right?" My jealousy still flares.

"Seriously? You don't even know who works for you?" she snaps.

"Hellion, I employ over forty thousand staff members throughout the city. I don't know their names," I reply.

"You should at least know the ones in your house." She stands. "They live with you. They serve your family in your safe space. Don't ever think you are too big for that, Mr. Sai." Ah, shit, I'm back to Mr. Sai. "No amount of money can change that." She leaves, and I sit back in my chair.

I feel well and truly reprimanded, even worse than when my father used to scold me.

Is she right? Have I overlooked things like that? Yes, I'm busy, but they are in my house and serving my family. Turning to my computer, I click through the files and open them, determined to learn their names.

It's definitely not for her.

I should have known she wouldn't do as I expected.

I was prepared for her to be in a killer dress after Dodge contacted one of our boutiques at her request, but as she descends the stairs, I can't help but grin. She looks incredible, even better than in a dress, but I want to laugh at what she chose to wear.

Her suit is matte black, with a silk trim around the collar. The jacket has a low V-neckline, showing her impressive cleavage since she has no shirt on underneath. There's a long necklace dangling between her breasts that makes me salivate before I look at the rest of her. Her hair is pulled back away from her face, and her makeup is dark and sexy. She's a mix of temptress and elegance, and my mouth goes dry as she gracefully prowls toward us.

How does she always look so good?

Whether she is covered in blood in a dungeon or wearing black-tie attire, both suit her, and it drives me crazy. I can't even speak, and her red lips tilt up like she knows it.

"Why does she look better in a suit than I do?" Zayn grumbles.

She stops in front of him, straightening his tie as he leans into her.

"I don't know. You look pretty good. I might even let you strip it off later so I can see what's under it."

"Why later? Why not now?" He reaches for his jacket as she laughs and steps back.

"Well then, let's get this fucking thing over with. Don't worry, I only brought two guns."

"Where are they hidden?" Zayn asks. "Let me feel—" He steps back, holding his hands up as she flicks a dagger at him.

One of our maids appears silently at my side with my coat in her hand. Her head is lowered respectfully, and I quickly scan my brain for the files I memorized earlier when I should have been reviewing new contracts.

"Your coat, sir." I take it from her and slip it on over my suit. The long black fabric drapes around me, sweeping against the floor.

"Thank you, Helen," I murmur, and the maid's eyes widen before she drops to her knees, pressing her forehead to the floor.

"Mr. Sai, whatever I did to displease you, please forgive me." Panic courses through me, and I urge her to her feet. "I'm so sorry. Please, I have kids—"

"I—no, I was thanking you," I say, fumbling over my response. "Your kids, Jem and William, are getting close to their next birthday, correct?"

She cries harder, and I look at the others for help. "Jesus, Kane, stop scaring the poor staff." Bexley sighs as she guides Helen away.

"What the fuck, brother?" Neo scoffs.

"I was trying to show I care. I don't know what I did wrong," I defend, rubbing my head.

"You said her name. The only time you use someone's name is when you're about to kill them. The poor woman." Zayn slaps my side. "Stick to your job and leave us to be the nice ones."

They walk outside to the cars, but I keep my eyes on Helen until she disappears. When Bexley returns, she shakes her head. "I changed my mind. Don't try to get to know them. That poor woman nearly had a heart attack. Come on, Kane, let's get this over with."

"I was trying to be nice," I tell her as I follow her outside. She turns to me, her eyes sparkling with amusement.

"Maybe leave that to others. Nice doesn't suit you. Besides, I like the cruel, cold asshole . . . sometimes." She disappears into the back of the SUV, leaving me frozen.

She . . . likes me?

I dive in after her as gracefully as I can.

32

BEXLEY

The event is in the heart of the city, at one of the top five-star hotels. Politicians and royalty stay here, but when we pull up, there is a red carpet with security and cameras eagerly waiting to capture the arrivals.

"If I'm pictured with you, I will personally kill each and every person you love," I warn them as the door opens. I slide out first, ignoring the Sai brothers, and step up onto the pavement just before the red carpet begins. I feel them hurry out behind me, and when I glance back, they have formed a triangle. For a moment, I feel small, which is odd since I'm tall. It's not the first time I've noticed how they tower over me or how attractive they are, especially all dressed up, but part of me prefers the messy, just been fucked look, especially if blood and bruises are involved.

Their pretty faces look better with my marks.

Every single eye turns to us as we step from the car. I don't know if it's because the three Sai brothers are a force to be reckoned with or if it's the fact that they look like movie stars, but I'm choosing to believe it's because I look so damn good, not them.

They look flawless and untouchable. The power they exclude is sexy as hell, and they know it, which means I have to knock them down a peg.

I glance back, my meaning clear as I step up onto the carpet.

Kane simply snaps his fingers, and Dodge leans in. I watch as Kane whispers something, and their guards pour from the other SUVs, surrounding the paparazzi and snatching their cameras as Kane looks at me. "Is that better?"

A hand slides across my back, and I turn my head, expecting Zayn to have taken a liberty, but it's Neo, which confuses me. He looks down at me as I stumble. A knowing little smile tugs at his lips as the warmth of his palm burns through the fabric of my suit as he walks by my side. I hear whispers and questions, but I ignore them as I keep my focus straight ahead.

"All their eyes are on us, but ours are on you," he whispers in my ear. "I know you went to my brother the other night. Tonight, you'll come to me."

"Keep wishing," I retort as we walk up the steps toward the grand entrance where security is tight.

"Not wishing, preparing. It's going to happen. You can't avoid us forever. You want me, Bexley," he murmurs. "Just admit it." He hands the invitation to a staff member on the right.

I scan the area, remembering my instincts while trying to ignore his cocky remarks. All three have been handsy and flirtatious since Kane announced he wants to make me theirs, and they aren't holding back. Ignoring Neo and the feeling of his hand still burning into my skin, I eye the metal detectors and a security guard who heads my way.

"Miss, you must be searched," he says idly as he starts to pat my arms.

"Easy there, handsy," I tease as the guard pats me down.

"Fire him," comes a sharp voice, and I turn my head, expecting Kane, but it's Neo again. He takes my arm and tugs me from the man's grip. "She is with us. Nobody touches her."

A different man in a suit hurries over with an earpiece in. "Mr. Sai, it is so good to see all of you. We are happy you accepted our invitation. Any guest of yours is welcome. Let them through," he barks at the guards, his voice turning from sickly sweet to angry in a blink

Rolling my eyes, I move away from them and walk through the metal detectors. They go off, and security looks at the man who stares at me. "Bra," I say, "or it could be the three guns I'm carrying."

His eyes widen as Kane chuckles and follows me through, setting it off as he takes my arm and leads me forward, ignoring everyone else. There are groups of people in suits and dresses lingering about before the stairs. They nurse drinks as they talk, but the area falls silent as they turn to us. We head through the reception to a set of carpeted stairs, and Kane leads me up them and into a ballroom.

Diamond chandeliers sparkle as the lighting gives the space a club-like effect, but more high end. There's a large bar where bartenders are showing off, throwing drinks and earning cheers from guests. Tables are placed throughout the entire floor below, with a small space for dancing and a screen naming a charity.

As soon as we walk down the stairs, every single person turns to look at us. "You sure know how to make an entrance," I tease.

Kane leans closer, making me shiver. "They are all looking at you, wondering how I got to be so lucky to have you on my arm," he flatters, and when we reach the bottom, he nods at a burly man watching me from the closest table. "An Arabian prince. If you let him, he'd quickly make you his wife. The man over there is running for the presidency next year. That woman in blue is the head of the Supreme Court."

"Jesus, it's like a room filled with all the types of people I hate, including you," I note, and he laughs loudly, drawing shocked gazes his way.

"Mr. Sai." A woman in a tight emerald dress hurries over, clutching a board. Her eyes are wide with awe as she looks us over. "We are so delighted to have you. We received your confirmation this morning and arranged your table and everything how you like it. Please, follow me." Turning away, she wanders through the tables, swaying her hips deliberately, and when she glances back, she makes sure Kane is behind her, but she seems disappointed when he isn't checking her out.

"Look at the woman's ass, damn it. She must have worked hard on it. It's a nice ass," I tell him.

He gapes at me and stumbles. "You're telling me to look at her?"

"Duh," I reply. "It's just offensive if you don't. That ass is incredible."

"I can't win," he grumbles as she stops by a booth higher than the others in the back. There are already two wine buckets there with chilled bottles protruding above the rim, and I grab one as I slide in, pop the cork, and start to pour it.

"Ah, the two bottles you requested," she whispers, watching me. "We ensured it was the correct year you wanted. We had to scour the world for them. At five million a bottle—"

I spurt the wine across the table and look at the bottle and then the three brothers. "Five mil a bottle? What, is it going to marry me then fuck me until the day I die? Why the fuck would you spend five mil on wine that tastes the same as the one I buy for five dollars at Joe's?"

"It doesn't taste the same," Zayn says as he slides in and grabs my glass, drinking from it. His eyes sparkle with mirth as he licks the wine from my skin where I spilled it. "Definitely worth the ten mil."

"You're all insane." I top off my glass, and Neo laughs as he slides in on my other side, forcing Kane in last, opposite me.

"Yet you drink it," Neo teases.

"It's your money. If you want to waste it on stupid shit, then go right ahead." I shrug as I down the glass and pour another, only to look up and find the green-dress hottie gaping. Glancing at the brothers then her, I offer her the glass. "You want to try it?"

Her hands automatically come up, and she actually steps back. "No, I couldn't—"

"Ah, come on. I bet you've never tasted something so ridiculously expensive. Ignore them, they don't care. It's pocket change." I pour her a glass and shove it into her unwilling hand. Lifting it carefully, she sips it and eyes it then me. "So?"

"It tastes like normal wine," she admits, and we share a smile.

"By the way, congrats on your ass. Is it real?" I ask, and she nods shyly. "Damn, it's incredible. What's your secret?"

"Pilates," she answers brightly. "You have an incredible body too. Do you work out?"

"Ah, yeah, I have to chase down idiots and kill them. It helps keep me fit." Her eyes widen and her face pales, but she nods and tries to put her glass down.

Zayn chuckles at my side, his arm across the back of the booth as he plays with my hair. "Take it. If you don't, she'll be offended."

Green-dress woman smiles but takes it and hurries away. "Pilates, huh? Who knew."

"Your ass is amazing too, but I can double-check. Stand up—" I smack Zayn without looking and sip my wine, eyeing the room.

"So, how often do you get attacked at events like this? I can't imagine much happens, other than spending money and rubbing shoulders with snobs," I remark.

"You never know," Kane answers idly, looking at his phone, but when I speak, his attention seems to zero in on me. "That's why you're here."

I smirk. "Or you wanted arm candy."

"More like I'm your arm candy," he responds before Dodge appears. I leave him to his business.

A fit, middle-aged man with salt-and-pepper hair joins us, and Kane sighs. Zayn sits up, and the transformation of his usually smirking face has my eyebrows rising. It's like a mask slides into place, his smile small and mocking, his eyes cold. "Sarinto, didn't expect to see you here. How's your son doing?"

"You mean after you sued us for billions and ruined his life?" he retorts. "Good, we'll bounce back. We always do."

"I'm sure," Zayn drawls, taking a sip of his wine. "You wouldn't have lost if you spent more money on good lawyers and less on whores."

Sarinto snarls, growing angry, as Zayn chuckles. "I warned you not to insult me, but you did it anyway." Zayn's expression is ice cold. "Now, move along before I decide ruining your company and his inheritance isn't enough and I need a pound of flesh in retribution."

Sarinto's face pales, but he glares at Zayn before disappearing, and I whistle.

"You know, you're cute when you get all angry and powerful," I tease.

Zayn rips his jacket off, making my eyes widen as he reaches for his shirt. Life seems to seep back into him, his eyes crinkling in amusement as he flashes straight white teeth in a smile that makes me grin.

"What the fuck are you doing, brother?" Neo snaps.

Zayn freezes, glancing from Neo to me. "She said I was cute."

"So?" Neo grumbles, clearly not following the logic.

He looks back at me for help, but I just tilt my head, waiting. "I thought that meant she was finally giving in and wanted to fuck me."

"Jesus fucking Christ. I compliment you one time and you're ready to strip?"

"Do you need a ring first? I'm not the type to commit, but for you, I can make an exception," Zayn murmurs as he slides closer.

Pressing my hand to his chest, I trail my fingers up before fisting his tie and using it to drag him closer. "I told you that you couldn't handle me."

"What about all three of us?" I turn my head to see Neo smirking as he looks me over. "I think between the three of us, we could."

"You've been spending too much time with your brother."

"Don't blame me," Kane says as Dodge walks away. "It's your fault for making us obsessed with you."

"Oh yeah, blame me. All I did was threaten and beat all of you continually. Who knew you three sickos would find that attractive?"

"You should take responsibility," Neo retorts.

"For what?" I ask, swinging my gaze to him. All their focus is entirely on me. It's almost too much.

"For the way you made us fall for you. It's all your fault, and now we are ruined men." He nods. "You should take responsibility and make us yours so we don't go insane."

"You're already insane," I reply. "No wonder everyone is afraid of you. It's because you're sexual deviants."

"And you aren't?" Zayn teases, his face becoming my entire focus.

I don't like the way my stomach twists or how my heartbeat speeds up at his nearness. I don't want him. I don't. "You're at fault for our ways now. We never even looked at women more than once before, and now we are all thinking about you all the time, going out of our way to impress you."

"You call this impressing me?" I retort.

"What do you want then? A city? A country? Millions? How about every enemy of yours dead at your feet?" Zayn asks.

"They already are," I reply sweetly. "I'll accept money, but it doesn't mean I'll accept you."

"Cruel," he purrs, trailing his fingers up my arm to my neck, which he grips to tug me closer until our noses touch. "Name it. It's yours as long as you are ours as well."

The intensity in his eyes is nearly my undoing. For a moment, I almost believe that men like them could be serious about someone like me, but a sweet voice pulls my attention from him, and I lean away, turning to find a young woman at our table. She watches us with big doe eyes before focusing on Kane. She's young, probably in her early twenties, wearing a butter-yellow silk dress. Her stunning face is made up to perfection, and her nails and jewelry indicate she comes from money, as does the air about her.

"Hi, Mr. Sai. Do you remember me? I'm Rebecca Tinns. We met at an event before," she says sweetly, leaning into the booth and Kane while placing her hand on his sleeve. Long, perfect, French tip nails press into the material, and she flutters her lashes in nervousness.

Kane looks at the hand on his arm, appearing annoyed for a moment before he meets my eyes and grins, leaning into the woman so her breasts press against his side.

I drink my wine as I look at her, knowing exactly what he's doing. I'll admit, a twinge of something I don't want to name flows through me, but I also know if I snapped my fingers, he would be on his knees, begging for me. "I like your dress," I murmur, and her eyes flutter to mine as I stare at her chest purposely, eyeing her cleavage. "Are you here alone?"

Her eyes widen as she glances between Kane and me. "I'm with my older brother."

"He must be very handsome, since his sister is so beautiful," I purr, and her cheeks flame red, her nails digging into Kane's arm, but interest flashes in her eyes, especially as I lean over and finger a stray curl of her perfect blonde hair.

"Oh shit, I bet the Bugatti she wins," Zayn whispers.

"You're on," Neo responds.

I ignore them as I smile at her softly, pressing my chin onto my other hand as I continue to play with her hair as she sways forward. "You should play with me instead of him. I'm a lot more fun."

"I-I . . ."

I drop my hand and take hers, turning it over softly and running my nails across her racing pulse. I lower my head to kiss the same area when a hand comes between my lips and her skin, and I end up kissing the back of it.

"Enough," Kane barks, and he cruelly pushes the woman away. "Leave now before I kill you."

She drags her eyes from me to Kane, nodding jerkily before glancing at me as I wave my fingers at her.

"Fuck," he grumbles, pinching his nose. "I tried to make you jealous, but in the end, it backfired."

"Never play games with me, Kane. You'll always lose."

"How far would you have taken it to win that?" he asks, looking irritated.

"As far as it took. I never lose." I shrug.

The music seems to grow louder, and I turn and watch as couples take to the floor. Zayn slides from the booth, buttoning his jacket, then he holds out his hand. "Would you do me the honor of dancing with me?"

"No," I rebuff as I sip my wine.

His eyes turn sad for a moment before his smile becomes mean. "Is it because you don't know how?"

I know he's goading me on purpose, and dammit, it works. Downing my wine, I slide from the booth, grab his hand, and drag him to the dance floor as he chuckles, and when we turn, I clutch his arm. "I lead."

"Whatever you want." He shrugs, sliding one hand down my back, but I drag it up, and he grins mischievously as it settles on my waist. His other hand is in mine as I turn and start to dance with the music, leading him. His feet move effortlessly, like he's floating across the dance floor.

"Let me guess, you were forced to take lessons?" I ask, my voice low since we are so close.

"Since I was young," Zayn replies. "Our dad wanted to give us the best opportunities in life, but you surprise me. You dance well."

"One of my neighbors used to teach ballroom," I admit. "He was this sassy, old jerk that no one else could stand. He taught me when I was bored. When I realized it made him happy and he was just miserable and alone, I always came back."

"And now?" he asks curiously.

"He died from an illness. I miss his lessons," I reply, and Zayn sighs, but it turns into a burst of laughter when I dip him back like the others do to their women. The sound is so bright and loud, it seems to startle him. When I lift him, his eyes are sparkling.

"You're a constant surprise, Bexy."

I can't help but return his smile. It's so addictive, happy, and carefree. Despite the world Zayn lives in, he still retains his almost childlike innocence and happiness that I haven't seen in forever. It reminds me of the person I was before everything happened, and part of me craves the sunshine that seems to follow him around.

"Can I join?" a dark, seductive voice murmurs, and I glance over to see Neo. I frown, not understanding as we stop and he steps behind me. His hands find my hips, and then we're moving again. This time, both of them lead as they guide me around the dance floor. They spin and whirl me effortlessly.

Being trapped between them makes my hackles rise, but I force my fear and memories away, refusing to let them ruin this moment. I relax into their hold, letting their warmth and strength surround me as I experience how it would feel to simply be normal and enjoy the touch of men without wondering how quickly I could slit their throats. I lose myself in it and the music as it turns to a slow song. Neo's hands tighten on my hips, gripping them tighter, and we slow until we sway in the middle of the dance floor. My arms are draped around Zayn's neck, his eyes darkened with lust and happiness as he watches me lean back into his brother.

"You're going to cause a scandal," I warn as I dance between them.

"Do you think we care?" Zayn whispers in my ear before biting my neck. Gasping, I elbow him, an automatic response, and he chuckles breathlessly. "Worth it."

"Why the fuck are you biting me? Are you a dog?" I hiss, turning to see him as Neo's hands grip my hips and keep me moving.

"If you want me to be. I'm just marking my territory. Besides, your skin is so soft and creamy, I couldn't resist," he confesses as I feel Neo's nose run down the other side of my neck.

"And you smell so good," he growls before his teeth dig in too.

Splitting from them, I point my finger in warning. "I'll bite the next person who bites me."

"You think we wouldn't like that?" Zayn teases as Neo turns, both of them facing me.

"If you bite us, baby, you'll be getting fucked right here in front of all the richest men and women in the world. That would definitely cause a scandal, but I have a feeling you would like it."

"You two are insatiable," I snap before I spin on my heel and stride off the dance floor to the bathroom, needing a minute. Pretending to be annoyed, I push inside, pressing my back to the door and closing my eyes.

My heart is pounding so hard it hurts, and I press my hand to my sternum, encouraging it to calm down. It's not like I haven't been flirted with before, and this is just a game, so why am I reacting like this? Heat flashes through me, making my knees weak and my skin clammy.

I'm so distracted by my inner issues, I almost miss it—*almost*. I duck at the very last second as I feel the air change above me, and when I open my eyes, I find three men standing there. Embedded in the door where my neck just was is a sharp blade.

"Dude, what the fuck? Do you know how long it took to do my hair!" I complain as the three big men exchange looks. Sighing, I glance down at my suit. "This is designer. If you get blood on it when you die, I'm going to be really annoyed," I threaten, then I reach behind me and lock the door.

I notice the guns at their hips and the hard glints in their eyes. They are mercs, and it's clear I'm their target. They must have been waiting here for me. I was so distracted by those damn Sai brothers, I didn't even notice.

Ducking under the first's arm, I slide to my knees and punch the second man in the dick, then I spin behind the third, grab his arm, and throw him over my shoulder. He lands in a stall, the door splintering under his weight and the toilet bursting when he hits it. Spinning, I bring my arm up and knock away the gun aimed at me. The pistol hits the floor with a clack and spins away as I duck under his punch, grabbing his arm once more. I yank him forward and slam my knee into his balls before crushing his head into the wall. He stumbles, disoriented, so I step around him to the third man, who has two blades in his hands.

"Nice, I'll take those when I'm done," I predict as he comes at me. I move fast, but I feel the side of my suit split, and it pisses me off so much that I dive at him. Grabbing a hand, I bite it until I taste blood, and he drops one knife before trying to gut me with the second. I block him with my arm, the resounding hit making my bones vibrate and ache, but then I punch him, and he stumbles back. His nose gushes blood as he blinks in shock, and I advance on him again.

Slamming him into the door with a kick, I watch in satisfaction as he impales himself on the blade he left there, meant for my neck, just as arms grab me from behind. I lift my legs as I struggle, but a meaty arm wraps around my neck, dragging me backward and cutting off my oxygen supply as I lean forward.

There's a knock at the door as I struggle in the man's headlock. "*Ocupado!*" I call as I heave us back into the wall, hearing the tiles crack, and his grip loosens. Whirling, I grab his head and crush it into the dryer next to us until it falls from the wall, then I pick it up and smash him with it as the knocking comes again. I look up to find the last man climbing to his feet from the stall.

Reaching down, I pull one of my blades free, not wanting to risk a gun. The noise might draw trouble, and I don't need that. My heart thumps with adrenaline, and I take all my mixed, confused feelings out on them. I watch him eye my blade before he reaches for his gun on the floor.

"Nuh-uh." I wag the dagger before throwing it. It embeds in his forehead, and he falls to his knees, blinking as blood drips around the blade. Whistling, I stroll closer, press my hand to his shoulder, and ram my knee into the blade until it splits his head open.

The knocking gets louder. Huffing, I step over the bodies to the door and rip it open. I breathe heavily as I blow the hair from my face and smile at three worried Sai brothers. Their concerned expressions turn into looks of shock as they glance behind me. "Sorry, line was huge," I say as I step over an arm that flops out into the hallway. "Has the food been served yet? I'm starving."

"Dodge," Kane calls, and he appears. "Clean this up."

Kane offers me his arm, shaking his head with this amused glint in his eyes. I let him lead me away and leave his men to deal with the bodies.

Maybe tonight won't be as boring as I thought.

33

ZAYN

When we get back to the table, we look to Bexley for answers. We need to be free of the area, but we trust Dodge to handle it. When she didn't come back from the bathroom, I was worried we'd pushed her too far, so I grabbed my brothers and went after her.

I honestly never expected there to be dead bodies, but I guess I should have.

"What happened?" Kane asks, looking at her with concern rather than annoyance. The last time I killed someone in public, he beat my ass black and blue, but when she does it, he looks like she went off to war without him.

Favoritism, but I suppose I can understand it.

"Hired mercs." She shrugs like it's an everyday occurrence. With her, it might be. "I didn't have time to ask who hired them before they tried to kill me, but I can guess. The mole is trying to cover their tracks. They are desperate, which means we are getting close."

"Damn it," I grumble as I gulp my drink. I'm antsy, and there is this tight feeling in my chest. I don't like that she's in danger because of us, not that I would dare speak those words out loud to her. I don't have a death wish. "Are you okay?"

"Like they could even touch me." She chuckles as she looks around. "It was a bold choice. It means they knew you were coming. They are someone close, but getting rid of me wouldn't have been enough. No, something else is happening." She frowns as she plays with her glass before grabbing the bottle of liquor that turned up while she was gone. I needed something to take the edge off after dancing with her. Having her rub up on me like that was the best kind of torture.

I grab it and glare at her. "Not this. It's mine," I tell her. "I got you the wine."

"You won't even share? What a prick," she grouses.

Neo chuckles as he plays with a strand of her hair, but I see his finger shaking. It seems we were all worried about her. "It's his favorite. He doesn't share it with anyone."

Something in her eyes tightens as she watches me. "Is that common knowledge?"

Is she jealous? How cute. I guess I could give her some.

"Yeah, why?" I respond as I take a big gulp.

She shakes her head and looks around, but her eyes seem to catch on something. When I follow her gaze, I notice her staring at the pale bartender who quickly turns when he's caught watching us.

"How many of those have you had?" she demands briskly.

"A few. He pounded a couple after you danced. Why?" Kane responds, his eyes sharp as he sits up.

Frowning, I lift my glass as I look between them, not following the logic.

"Don't." She deftly snatches it from me, eyeing me anxiously. "How do you feel?"

"Fine," I reply, reaching for it, but my hand misses it, making my lips tilt down in a confused frown. Reaching over with furrowed eyebrows, she presses her hand to my forehead and hisses. "Shit, he's burning up. He's been drugged."

"Drugged?" My voice sounds odd, and I giggle. "You drugged me? I knew you were flirting with me!"

She turns to Kane, ignoring me, which makes me pout. "The

bartender. Stop him and lock the rest of this place down. We need to get Zayn upstairs, cool him down, and find out what he ingested," she orders. She looks so pretty when she's angry. I reach for her to feel her soft cheeks, but then everyone moves swiftly, too fast for me to track. Ignoring the hive of activity, I reach for her, sighing as I nuzzle into her fragrant neck. My dick hardens as I try to pull her closer. I want to climb inside of her so we can be together forever.

"Zayn, focus, okay?" She grabs my face. Giggling, I poke her cheek.

"So soft. Is all of you soft?" I whisper, and she blinks. I press my nose to her cheek and inhale again. "You smell so good."

"Hold on." She pushes me away, turning to talk to someone, but she's all I can focus on as I fall into her. The heat inside swells until I burn. What was once comfortable warmth is now setting me alight. I can't catch my breath, and my cock is so hard, I tremble.

"It hurts," I whisper, lifting my hips to relieve pressure as my pants dig into my hard-on. "Baby, it hurts," I whine as I reach for her, looking for comfort.

Turning back to me, she smiles softly, even as her eyes are tight. Is she mad at me? I don't like that.

"I know. Come on." I'm up, stumbling on my feet, and the world spins around me, so I close my eyes. My stomach rebels as the world whirls until her scent reaches me. I bury my face in that softness, and everything is alright until there's a ding, and then we are moving again. I focus on her scent, ignoring the voices around me as I hear another beep, and then I'm tossed down on something soft.

I open my eyes, but the lights are too bright, making them water. It's hot, so hot. We're in a room. A hotel room? Good, I need her. I reach for her, but she dances away, watching me worriedly.

"Baby," I beg as I fall backward. The heat becomes unbearable, until my brain won't work. My cock presses against my pants, throbbing for release, my heart beats so fast, I feel like I will die, and my skin is too tight.

I rip at my clothes until my jacket and shirt are off. My pants are too tight, so I tear them open as my back arches off the bed. Even the brush of the air against my skin is too much to handle. I grab my dick, needing relief. It's the only thought I have now.

"Jesus, brother!" Neo yells, but it fades as I pump my length.

"Wait, did you roofie him? I thought it was poison," Bexley scoffs, but her voice is far away. "Yo, asshole, what drug is this?" I hear a slap, but I'm lost in the heat burning me alive.

"A new one. I don't know much about it. It's supposed to incapacitate your opponent, and they lose impulse control. It's like Viagra on crack," an unfamiliar voice replies, but the rest is swallowed by a pain so deep, I bellow and writhe in the bed, my hand falling from my aching dick.

"We need to help him," Kane mutters as my eyes open. They swim above me as I reach for Bexley.

"So help him," she says, slapping my hands away, and I roll with a whine, grinding my hips into the bed for relief.

"He's my brother," someone mutters. "Please, please help him."

"Get a guard too," she snaps.

"I can't let them see him like this. Bexley, he's suffering."

"Damn it, get a hooker," she responds.

"Baby," I whine, reaching for her again, and her face softens as she looks at me.

"I won't force you, hellion. We can figure something else out," Kane responds, and she looks from me to him as the wave of heat engulfs me again.

"Shh, okay," she murmurs. I didn't even know I was making a noise, but her hands cradle my face. They feel like ice, and the relief is instantaneous. "It's okay. I've got you." She hardens her voice. "Clear the room."

There's a scuffle then a bang, and she smiles at me as she slides her hands down my overheated neck. I stretch it out and lift my hips, needing more. "It hurts," I whimper.

"Goddamn it!" I hear her yell, and I'm flipped. Hands grab mine and press them down above me. I turn my head up to see a stern-faced Kane there before someone kicks my legs open, with Bexley standing between them.

"I know. I'll make it better;" she promises, sliding her hands down my chest until her fingers circle my cock. Her icy touch makes me yell, and pleasure explodes through me, draining me until I slump, but the heat doesn't stay gone for long and I whine, lifting my hips into her hand, still hard and hurting.

"Shh, it's okay," she assures me, then she presses her mouth to mine before gliding her lips down my neck. She licks and kisses a trail of heat, and my desire increases.

Her tongue flicks my nipple, and even that slight pressure is enough for me to explode up from the bed. Kane grunts, holding me down. Humming, she sucks my nipple into her mouth before licking over my chest, and that has my balls drawing up, my hips lifting as I urge her to give me more. Her lips curve against my skin as she kisses down my chest to my dick. The moment her hand wraps around the base, my back arches in ecstasy. Pleasure consumes me, and then her lips slip around my cock.

Panting, I look down, trying to regain control, but the heat swallows me as she envelops me down to her hand, her cheeks hollow. The light, wet heat of her mouth is so incredible, my eyes roll back in my head, and I can't hold back. I pump into her mouth, moving my hips hard and fast. I force her to take it as I thrust down her throat. My balls draw up as acid drips down my spine, and then it explodes out of me and into her.

Grunting, she swallows my release as I slump, whining as my cock slips from her mouth. Her lips are swollen as she stares down at me, but the heat is still there, and my dick is hardening again.

"Fuck," Neo growls. "Does he need pussy or sedation?"

"No, I won't fuck him, not while he's drugged. I won't do that to him, even if he wants me when he's sober. He can't consent. I'll help, but I won't take that from him," she explains as she strokes my chest softly.

"Baby," I beg, and she grips my cock, pumping me again. Pleasure obliterates everything else but her touch.

Driven by need and madness, I rip my hands away from Kane and grab her. She yelps in surprise as I toss her above me and pin her to the bed, grinding my hips into her ass as her face is pressed into the bedding.

I feel hands trying to haul me back, but I snarl and fight them as she manages to roll and glare at me. The glint of something sharp presses against my neck. "No." It's one word, but it invades my desire-riddled brain, and I sag, letting them haul me off her. I hang between my brother's hands, my hard cock dripping with her saliva. My chest heaves as I eye her hungrily as she sits up before sliding to the end of the bed.

"I'm sorry. It hurts," I whisper as some sanity returns, but the heat and pain remain.

"I know. It's okay." She slips from the bed and drops to her knees, cupping my face and kissing me. It starts soft, my lips numb and unmoving because I'm scared of hurting her, but she grips my face and forces my jaw open. Her tongue slides inside and wraps around mine, tasting every inch of my mouth and forcing me to kiss her back. She groans into my mouth, pressing closer, and I kiss her so hard, I taste blood, then my arms are free, but I don't reach for her. She, however, pushes me backward.

My back hits the carpet, and she moves away for a second. Before my eyes can open, I feel hot, warm, naked skin against mine, and my eyes widen as I look down to see her removing her blazer and pressing her naked chest to mine. Trailing her fingers down my arm, she grabs my hand and lifts it, pressing it to her breast. I squeeze the perfect handful as my hips lift, grinding into her stomach as she kisses me. I groan in ecstasy as she straddles me, pressing my dick to her cunt through her pants. I feel her heat, and I can't take it.

I grind into her. It's all I can do to stop myself, even as I moan into her mouth as I pinch her nipples and squeeze her breasts as I let the heat flow from me to her.

I buck below her, groaning into her mouth like an animal until I explode. I feel my release blast through me, but the heat still doesn't abate, and I whine. Soothing me with her kiss, she rocks above me, sliding my hands down her skin. Before I know it, I cry out her name and come again. It hurts this time, and when the pleasure floats away, I'm exhausted.

Slumping down, she lies on my chest and strokes my face before moving away. I reach for her, and I'm lifted and carefully placed back on the bed. She lies next to me, caressing my head and cheeks as I pant. I still feel feverish and strange, but exhaustion consumes me now.

When my body finally cools, I bury my head into the bed and let the darkness claim me.

34

BEXLEY

I watch Zayn sleep. The lights in the room have been long since turned off, and the skyline outside the window glitters beautifully, but he's all I see. He clings to me, nuzzling closer and sighing happily, so I let him as I stroke his back and hair. It took him hours to cool down enough to rest. I wiped him down with cold towels, but before I could get dressed, he was pressed against me. I'm sure it's due to the remnants of the drug, but he seems to want to feel my skin against his, and I don't protest.

We had to keep wetting his body, and tomorrow, he'll need to be checked by a doctor, but for now, we let him rest. I left Neo and Kane to deal with the bartender. I could hear him screaming as they questioned him before they came out and told me he was dead. Kane's jacket was off, and there was blood speckled on his shirt. The bartender didn't know who hired him. It had been done through a burner phone and cash drop, but the brothers will keep looking. Between the mercs and the bartender, there are more trails to follow.

I should rest, but I lean back against the headboard, my chest still bare, and goose bumps rise on my skin since we turned the air conditioner down low to help Zayn.

I'm thinking out loud when my voice interrupts the silence. "What was their plan? Why drug him like this? Why not poison?"

I turn my head, meeting Kane's sharp eyes. He's seated in an armchair next to the bed, the shadows giving him a menacing aura, but I know he's awake. I can feel his gaze, which never leaves me and his brother. His fingers are the only part of him moving, tapping away on his thigh again, like I've seen before.

"They couldn't risk killing him. Fear, I suspect. They knew if they did, we would never stop, but putting him in a compromising position and filming it? Blackmail. Whoever the mole is knows we would do anything for our family." His voice is a rumble, dark and dangerous.

"Assholes," I grumble as I look down, remembering what the man whose body currently lies in the tub said—no impulse control. Yet, as soon as I said no, Zayn stopped. My heart melts at that when Kane suddenly leans forward into the light, his eyes hard.

"You didn't get a release. Are you okay?" he asks, his head tilting like I've noticed he does sometimes now after his ear injury from Butcher.

I blink, and my cheeks heat for a moment. "I'm fine," I mutter. "I'm not an animal."

"He wound you up and didn't get you off. Come here." He pats his thick thighs, but I ignore him. "Don't make me come over there. If we wake my brother, I will be annoyed."

Snarling, I get to my feet, and Zayn sighs, hugging a pillow. I freeze, but then he snores quietly again. When I'm close enough, Kane yanks me down into his lap so I'm straddling him. "Use me, Bexley. Get the release you need. You helped my brother, now let me help you."

I glance at Neo, who's asleep on the couch with his hand over his face, and then Zayn, but Kane grabs my chin and forcefully turns me back to him. "Only look at me. Use me." Grabbing my hand, he places it over his fabric-clad cock. I can feel how hard he is, and I shiver from it. My eyes drop to his lips, and desire burns within me, just like before. I tried to ignore it, focusing on Zayn, but his hands and the feel of him below me had me on the verge of coming. I was so close, and somehow, Kane knew. "I've already told you this body is yours."

Licking my dry lips, I try to stay focused, removing my hand. "We should have Dodge check the cameras." My eyes flare wide when his hand covers my mouth.

"Enough," he orders. "No work right now. Don't focus on anything but me and this."

"Kane—" I begin, but his hand slides down between my breasts, stoking my desire. I didn't put my blazer back on, Zayn wouldn't let me, and now his brother takes advantage, caressing my skin until I arch up into his touch. His lips tilt in a cocky smirk, and I try to move away, but his hand slides down my back, keeping me there. He leans in and sucks one of my sore, tight nipples into his mouth, soothing the ache from his brother's rough hands.

"Kane."

His lips tilt up against my skin. "Shh, hellion, I've got you. If you wake them up, I'll have to share, and I don't feel like sharing right now," he warns, biting my breast until I gasp. His words are possessive. I shouldn't let them go, but I do because I need this too much. I need to come, and he's here. I know I shouldn't, but all the lines have already been crossed. What's one more? Grabbing his hair, I pull his head up until his dark eyes lock on me. I reach down and tear his shirt open. The pang of buttons hitting the floor is loud, but he doesn't react. "Hands on the arms of the chair. If you move, I'll wake your brother and fuck him instead."

His eyes narrow, but he does as he's told. When I'm sure he won't move, I release his hair and lower to my knees in front of the chair, licking down his neck. I stop to suck the sensitive skin on the curve of his shoulder until his breath comes out in a shaky exhale. Biting down, I wait until he hisses then soothe it with a swipe of my tongue and move on. I follow this pattern over every inch of skin I can reach. I wish the room were brighter, since I want to see his golden muscles, but I can feel them, and that will have to do.

His fingers curl into the wood, gripping as his head falls back. His heavy-lidded eyes remain on me, burning with desire, and I lick and suck my way across his chest, leaving my marks as I wind him up until he's just as needy as I am. It's all a power game between us, neither wanting to lose, but it's also fun.

I tease him, running my tongue along the top of his pants. "Hellion," he growls, and I know he's close to snapping. I wonder how far I can push him . . . .

Opening the top of his pants, I slide my tongue inside, and that's when I get my answer.

I'm yanked up onto his lap, straddling him again, and he rips off my pants so I'm naked, and then he frees himself. The low light lets me get a look at him, and I swallow hard. My pussy tightens at the idea of him being inside me. He's huge, slightly bent at the tip, and so wide, it's going to hurt in the best way.

"Where do you even get underwear that fits?" I mutter, and he chuckles, using his finger to press my chin up until I meet his gaze.

"I'm glad you like me. I look good, but I feel better. Let me show you, hellion." It's his way of asking for permission, and that causes my last shred of control to disintegrate. There's no room for hesitation or old memories between us. This is Kane. He would never take away my choice.

I lift and grab him with my hand, then I lower down until his wide tip is pressed against my entrance, making him grunt. "Then show me, or are you all talk, Sai?"

He doesn't waste another second, grabbing my hips and impaling me on his length. When I would have screamed from the sudden intrusion, he slaps a palm across my mouth. I wiggle, trying to get away. He's too big, too thick. It feels so good, but it hurts, and he doesn't let flee. His eyes lock on mine as he drops his hand from my mouth, and those elegant fingers find my clit and attack. He uses his knowledge of my body to make me whimper.

I'm still unable to move, feeling every hard inch of him and his fingers until the orgasm that Zayn began shatters me. I cry out, and Kane drinks it down, watching me come as I shake on top of him, my cunt clenching his dick, and then he moves. His hand is still between our bodies, so each hard thrust of his hips pushes my clit into his fingers.

The pleasure that was ebbing grows, spreading through me until I move with him. I meet his hard thrusts with my own, refusing to let him have all the control. We don't speak, our faces so close our breaths mingle, yet we don't kiss. We just stare at each other, the eye contact more intimate than anything we are doing, and I am the one who looks away first.

I kiss him, tasting blood mingled with his flavor, then I deepen the kiss when we speed up, finding a fast, hard rhythm. The chair rocks from our movements, a creak of warning reaching my ears, but I don't stop, and neither does he. Both of us have needed this for too long. Sliding my hands up his chest, I twist his nipples before digging my nails into his shoulders as I ride him, wanting to come again. The intensity of this fire between us should scare me, but I'm too far gone now.

It's never been like this, this all-consuming need. Even the warmth of his hand on my ass drives me wild. Every sensation is heightened, until I feel like I'm the one who's been drugged.

Breaking the kiss so I can suck in desperate breaths, I feel the need to regain control and put some distance between us. I lean back so far, my arms stretch to their full length as I grip his shoulders. He places messy, open-mouthed kisses down my neck then my chest as I gasp. Our pleasure-filled noises are the only sounds in the quiet room. I should have known he wouldn't let me have control. His hand grips my ass, urging me to move faster, as his mouth trails over every inch of skin he can reach. Desire grows within me, becoming so overwhelming, I know it will swallow me whole. It terrifies me, but I can't stop.

"Kane." I try to slow us down, to give me a second to contain it, but he doesn't let me. He bites my chest, right above my heart, as his fingers press against my oversensitive clit and his cock hits my G-spot. I detonate, losing my vision and hearing, coming harder than I ever have until I float away. When I come back to the present, I'm limp in his arms.

"Good girl, hellion," he praises, kissing my head as I shiver and shake. "You did so well. You looked so beautiful when you came for me."

He's still hard inside me, and then he stands, lifting me effortlessly as I cling to him, and my back is pressed to the bed. He rolls his hips, burying his length deep inside me as one of his hands presses onto the mattress inches away from his brother.

His fingers stroke down my face and then cover my mouth when I would speak, since Zayn is so close. My breathing is choppy, my skin is slicked with sweat, and his brothers' breathing fills the air over the slap of our bodies. There's a sigh, and someone turns. I freeze, but Kane smirks above me, rolling his hips until I bite his hand to contain my whine.

The bastard did it on purpose.

He does it again and again. I draw blood, my whimper of pleasure filling the air despite his hand muffling it, and I hear the moment someone wakes up. A creak lets me know they are on the sofa.

Neo.

Kane must hear it too, but he doesn't stop driving into me with slow, deep, maddening thrusts that have me writhing below him.

"Bex, is everything okay?" Neo asks sleepily. I can't see past Kane, so I shove his shoulder. He's hard and heavy above me, refusing to move. Instead, he leans down, his lips close to my ear.

"Yes, hellion, is everything okay?" He punctuates his words with a thrust so deep, it makes me ache.

"Fine, everything's fine!" I reply loudly, and he stills. We both wait, and when Neo's breathing evens out, Kane chuckles quietly.

"Good girl. I'd be annoyed if I had to kill my brother for interrupting." He lifts up, the shadows wrapping around him. The sight makes me clench, and he must feel it because he lifts my hips and fills me again.

Speeding up, he uses my body before pulling out and flipping me. My head is pressed to the bedding and something hard—Zayn. My face is against his leg, but I can't protest because Kane is filling me again. He thrusts into me from behind, the new angle hitting those nerves that have me biting into the bedding to stop a scream.

One of his hands slides down my back to my ass, parting it. He circles my hole as his free hand grips my hip. Clawing at the duvet, I lose it when his fingers slip into my ass. I bite back my howl of pleasure as I come. He grunts behind me, unable to pull from my body, and then I feel his release flooding me, buried so deep I feel like I'll never get him out of me.

Waves of pleasure trap me until they finally ebb away, leaving me in the afterglow.

Saliva drips from my mouth to the bedding as I gasp, exhausted and so sated I float. I don't even make a noise when he pulls from my body or cups my cunt, preventing his cum from leaving me.

When he picks me up, I let him move me around, too exhausted to protest, and when I feel Zayn, I bury my face into his back, throwing my arm over him as he sighs. Then, unexpectedly, I feel Kane slide in behind me, pressing me into his arms as he holds us both.

"Sleep, hellion," he whispers into my ear. "Sleep and dream of us."

35

NEO

Well, fuck, that's unexpected.

Blinking down at the wide bed, I watch Kane sigh and tug Bexley closer. I know he's sweet on her, but seeing my big brother, the man who never lets anyone close when he's asleep since he's vulnerable, curl her into his chest and sigh while deeply asleep lets me know just how fucked he truly is. Let's not even talk about Zayn, who is snuggled into her back like she's a teddy bear, naked and snoring, but alive and drugless—or at least, I think he is.

Taking a quick picture of all three of them, I prop my hands on my hips as Bexley's eyes snap open. She goes from dead asleep to awake, her gaze locked on me before she relaxes. It makes me think of what Kane hinted at, that she has a bad past.

Just how bad was it to elicit that kind of reaction?

"That isn't fair," I whine as she lifts her head, and Kane looks at me groggily. "You all had a cuddle party and didn't invite me."

Kane closes his eyes once more and buries his head into Bexley's neck, even as she slaps him. He just pulls her closer as Zayn groans and burrows under the quilt. "Too loud, too bright."

"Not just a cuddle party, a fuck party," she replies between fighting off my two brothers.

"You had an orgy, and I had to sleep on the sofa." I point in her face teasingly. "Double standards." The door buzzes just as I glare at them. "Don't get up. Your least favorite brother will do it."

"Get a coffee for Bexley while you're at it," Kane orders, his eyes still shut.

Unbelievable.

Opening the door, I find a waiter with a cart and Dodge behind him. "I ordered breakfast for all of you."

"Thank you," I say before raising my voice. "At least some people care about me." As I step back, letting them both in, Dodge's eyebrow rises, but he doesn't question it, just like last night when he and our crew handled the bartender's body. I didn't ask how, and I don't care. I'm more worried about how someone was brave enough to drug a Sai brother and try to get away with it. Bexley is right. Whoever helped Butcher is scared and lashing out. It means they are dangerous, and I hate that they are inside our house. If this carries on much longer, I might just kill all of our staff and start over.

Dodge nods at me respectfully as he follows the butler, who quickly sets up breakfast. "I have the doctor coming in ten minutes. Do you need anything else?"

"New brothers?" I murmur as I sign the bill and the guards stationed outside allow him to leave. "Anything on the cameras or the bartender?"

"Not yet. We checked financials, family, and friends. No connection to anyone in our organization, but there has to be one. We'll find it, don't worry," Dodge reports.

"You should look at the drug." The yelp I let out is not sexy or manly as I whirl to find Bexley right behind me. A mug of coffee is already in her hand, and she's completely fucking naked. There isn't an ounce of embarrassment on her face as Dodge's eyes widen before averting to the ceiling out of respect.

"What do you mean?" I ask, covering my pounding heart due to fright.

"If it' new, it will be limited and hard to come by. It's definitely a street drug. Don't worry, I'll make some calls, find out where and how he got it and if anyone else was there with him."

"Out," I tell Dodge when his eyes drop without meaning to. The only reason I don't pluck them out for looking at her is the fact that he's been with us for a very long time and is like a brother to us. He turns and shuts the door. Glaring at Bexley, I strip my shirt off and drape it around her shoulders before buttoning it. I ignore the feeling of her skin brushing against my knuckles as I kneel to fasten the final buttons before taking her arms, one at a time, and rolling the sleeves back.

When I'm done, I stand but freeze when her finger trails down my ribs and side. "Nice ink. What is it?"

Every thought flees my head at her soft, probing touch, and when her eyes roll up to mine, I fall into them. I understand why my brothers are so enamored. I'm worried she will destroy our family when she leaves, but I'm starting to care less and less. "Neo?" she prods.

"I just thought it looked hot," I admit, and she grins, moving her finger back and forth over the dark ink until I shiver, my cock hardening in my pants. I want Bexley, always have. She likes to tease. It's a game between us to see who will give in first, and after watching her with both brothers, I know I need to taste her, but I won't beg. I won't force her. I'll wait for her to come to me.

"Do you have any more?" she asks with a mocking grin that tells me she knows exactly what she's doing to me. Her hand drifts down to my Adonis belt, stroking my skin above my pants. "Maybe hidden away?"

"You'll have to find out," I retort, daring her.

Her hand moves to my pants as if she's going to undo them. She leans in as my breathing quickens from hope and hunger. "You wish. Maybe next time."

I slump in both relief and disappointment, because once I get Bexley where I want her, it won't be a quick ten minutes, which is all we have before the doctor arrives. I'm going to spend all night fucking her brains out until she forgets why she hates all three of us.

"Is your coffee good?" I ask, trying to cover my speechlessness.

"Want to try it?"

I nod for lack of better options, and I expect her to offer me her mug, but she takes a gulp, pinches my chin, yanks my head down, then presses her lips to mine, forcing the hot coffee into my mouth. Her hands grip my neck, feeling me swallow, and then I hit the wall behind me as her lips move against mine in a hard, brutal kiss. The warmth and taste of the coffee linger and mix with her sweetness.

I shouldn't, but my hand slips down her side and grabs her thigh, feeling the softness of her skin over her hard muscle as I pull her close and deepen the kiss. Her moan makes me harder than ever, and I debate how fast I can get naked just as there is a knock at the door. It breaks us apart, her lips swollen from the kiss.

"Doctor is here," Dodge calls through the door, knowing better than to open it since he still thinks Bexley is naked.

Bexley bites my lip then steps back and sips her coffee. She turns around and takes a seat at the dining table like nothing happened. Meanwhile, I'm pinned against the wall, my dick so hard it hurts, and when she leans back in her chair and crosses her long, perfect legs and arches a brow at me, I nearly drop to my knees and crawl to her for a taste.

"Come in," I order unsteadily, and the door opens. Our usual doctor looks around. "He's still in bed. He was drugged last night."

"I heard." He nods at Bexley as he walks past her, and I follow him into the room, finding Kane sitting in the chair next to the bed on his phone. He's completely dressed and put together, like he was never any different.

"Zayn, the doctor is here. Wake up," Kane commands as he looks up. "Zayn."

Bexley strolls in and stands by my side. "Zayn." He's instantly awake, sitting up although still half asleep, his hair sticking up at all angles. Smirking, she gestures at Kane.

"Okay, first things first, we need to take some blood. It looks like it's out of your system, but I want to check, then we need to give you an IV, but I think you should be okay." The doctor moves fast, checking his vitals before setting up to draw blood, which makes Zayn antsy. He's always hated having his blood drawn, the wimp. He looks to me for help, since I usually have to force him to do it, and I eye Kane with a sigh, knowing we are probably going to have to pin him down. A coffee mug hits my chest, and then Bexley crawls into the bed with Zayn, no doubt seeing him growing infinitely more upset as the doctor prepares.

Grabbing his head, she turns him until he's facing away from the doctor. "Just look at me, not him." Her voice is gentle and coaxing, and it's obvious she has a soft spot for Zayn, especially right now. When the doctor pulls his arm to lie flat, however, he lets out a little whine. "Shh, it's okay. You're doing well. Just keep looking at me, okay?"

"I can't . . . Just give me the IV." He starts to panic, pulling away, when she slaps him hard. His head jerks, and she looks at the doctor.

"Now," she orders before she grabs him while he's distracted and kisses him. He's so shocked, he doesn't react as the doctor slides the needle in.

By the time it's done, Zayn is bewildered and still leaning into Bexley as she breaks the kiss and sits back.

"Wait, I think I need more blood taken. Don't you, doc?" he calls as he grabs Bexley, but she slaps him away.

"Behave," she scolds as the doctor sets up the IV. We all watch him. We trust him, but we can never be too careful—that much is evident after last night.

When he's done, I call Dodge, and when the door is shut, we talk again.

"Was I really drugged?" Zayn asks as he leans back in the bed, his arm with the IV stretched out like he doesn't want to look at it. "Wait, was it you?" He looks at Bexley. "If so, you didn't need to drug me— ow!" Kane slaps the back of his head as he walks past to make coffee.

"You're lucky she noticed. She probably saved your life. She definitely saved your dignity," he snaps.

"Dignity? Never had any," Zayn says, making me grin, which I cover when Kane glares at us.

"Do you remember last night?" Bexley asks, looking a little distant.

"Not really, but I'll try." Zayn sighs as he closes his eyes. "Right after I take a nap. Wake me up when the IV is done."

Leaving him to it, since he has an excuse, I head to the table and take the coffee Kane's stirring and hand it to Bexley as I walk to the bathroom. "Clothes are being delivered soon. I'll wash up first. We'll leave as soon as Zayn is good to go," I call.

"Look at you, taking charge," Kane teases as he starts making another coffee without complaint.

"Someone had to since you were both too busy fucking," I grumble as I shut the door in their faces, not at all feeling left out.

Not one bit.

The organizer and hotel manager apologized profusely before we could get in our cars and drive home. I think they were just scared of what Kane would do. They should be. I know he's already making plans, since he's been on his phone all morning. If there's one thing you don't do, it's fuck with his family.

When we are back, Bexley heads off to do who knows what, but she finds us twenty minutes later in the security office with a glass in her hand. She thrusts it at Zayn, who looks confused. "It's good for you, trust me. I accidentally took LSD, and this shit saved me the next day."

"How do you accidentally take LSD?" I ask.

"You don't want to know," she dismisses as she sits in a chair and starts to spin before the screens. "What are we doing?"

"Reviewing security footage from the hotel, hoping to see who the bartender met," I admit as I load up the next hour and start scrolling through it, looking for a familiar face. She wheels closer, resting her head on my shoulder. My attention is split between her and the screen, so I almost miss him.

"There," she says, so I rewind it and press play. She's right. It's of the loading bay yesterday afternoon. The bartender is there with someone else. Their hood is up, covering their face, but they hand over a vial. "That has to be the drug. Is there a clear shot of his face?"

I scroll through the other cameras until we get lucky, and when he lifts his head to cross the street, we get a look at him. "Of course." Bexley laughs, and we turn to her.

"You know him?" Kane asks, and she wheels back. I instantly miss her warmth and want to drag her closer.

"Who doesn't know Fletch? He's . . . an appropriator of all things weird and wacky. The weirder the better. He'll do anything for money. I once heard he stole a monkey for someone, but when I asked, he wouldn't free the lions from the zoo for me. Asshole. Let me make some calls and see where he is, and we can find him later and ask who employed him."

I watch her call until someone answers, and she puts it on speaker, still spinning in the chair. "Fletcher, you weasel," she greets, but her voice sounds amused.

"Goddamn it. It's been quiet. I thought we got lucky and you were dead," a grumbling voice responds.

"You aren't that lucky. I need help." She stops spinning for a moment as we watch her.

"I already told you, I'm not breaking into the president's office and setting up deep fake nudes of him. I don't want to be sent to unknown places for life. Just give it up."

She laughs. "Not what I want this time, but good to know you're still a pussy. You gave a man a drug yesterday at Hotel Opulence, a new fancy street drug. Who paid you?" she asks.

"Shit, Karma, you know my clients are confidential. I didn't go spilling when you tweaked out that entire law office just because they called you and Taylor an unfit guardian." My eyebrow rises, and she mutes him as she looks at me.

"Don't judge me. They were being condescending assholes by trying to take Lauren from us. I just taught those limp-dick fuckers not to mess around." She unmutes him. "Yeah, well, I also didn't let the cops get you that time you crashed our car into a police horse, so spill.

Don't make me find you. We both know you wouldn't last through one minute of torture."

"I bruise easily." He sighs. "Fine. If they find out, my cred is gone—"

"Fletcher," she warns.

"Alright, alright, Jesus, hold your tits," he concedes. "I don't know his name. He had a distinctive face though. Blue eyes and a scar on his neck under a tattoo of a moth. Scary looking motherfucker on a Harley. He told me where and what he needed. He wanted something that wouldn't kill but would be embarrassing as hell. For blackmail, I think. That's all I have."

"Good boy, go back to playing chemist." She hangs up and looks at us, but I'm already thinking. "You know him?" she asks.

"We have a lot of staff," I say as I turn to the computer and load the files, scanning through them. "But he doesn't seem to be here."

Another dead end. Great.

"If there's no one here who looks like that, he could be a paid middleman. Your staff can't leave at the moment, it would raise too much suspicion, which means they would have to come here somehow to get the order and money. They wouldn't risk this over the phone or online, not even on a burner. They would be paranoid since we are looking for them," she reasons. "We need to investigate everyone from the last two days and see who came and went." Sitting back, she stares at the screens showing outside. "Wait, that van . . . it was here the last time I snuck in."

"Oh, those are the cops. They've been watching us for years. It's their mobile unit," I explain, and she grins as she stands.

"Wait, where are you going? Bexley!" I call. I have a bad feeling, and when I look at my brothers, I know they share it.

"She's definitely going to need a lawyer," Zayn teases, toasting us with the green smoothie he was forced to have.

36

BEXLEY

rossing the street before the van can leave, I open the door and grin at the shocked faces of the techs and cops inside. "Hey." Climbing in, I shut the door and look around. "Nice setup. Wait, where do you pee if you need to go?"

They just keep staring, so I sigh. "Fine, I was just making conversation. Don't worry, I'm not here to kill you or anything. I just need your footage, thanks." I slap the seat of one guy, and he glances at who must be in charge before standing. Sitting, I look at the screens and cameras. "Damn, you've got a lot of angles, but none inside."

The big guy in charge says, "It's illegal, but if you were to help us—"

"I'm going to stop you there, badge boy. I'm not about to be an informant. Like I said, I need footage." I scan the screen. "Your setup is good, but the quality of your cameras is shit. I guess being in the public sector doesn't give you a lot of access to cool toys. No wonder you don't have anything on them to make an arrest."

"We think the Sai brothers are involved in multiple crimes," badge boy says as he moves closer.

"I have no doubt." I shrug, turning to the tech. "I have no idea how to use this shit. I'm looking for a dude with a scar on his neck under a moth tattoo, and he drives a Harley. It would be during the last two days. I can't be bothered to look through all the footage, but you must have been watching. Ring any bells?"

"Why would we help you?" badge boy snaps. "We should arrest you right now—"

"Yeah, yeah, I don't have a lot of time for dick measuring. Tell you what, show me what I need, and I'll give you whatever you want."

"If we help you, you have to help us," badge boy agrees, no doubt seeing a way in. It's obvious he's been stuck with this shitty job for a while and is getting nowhere. "If we show you, then you have to give us something we need on the Sais to arrest them."

"Sure, sure, show me," I reply.

He watches me, analyzing my expression, and I wait, but honestly, he has nothing to lose and he knows it. He nods at the tech, who leans over me, doing something on the screen. "There was someone like that the other day. I flagged him for review, thinking he might be a link to someone from the Sai brothers' shadier business. He met with a guard at the side of the house down the street. Here." He leans back and plays the footage. Pulling my phone out, I record it as I eye the guard. I don't know him, but they have a lot. "When we looked into him, we found he's a paid merc. Is that what you needed?"

Makes sense. He paid someone to get and deliver what he needed. No doubt he was desperate and was going to blackmail Zayn and the brothers for money or protection and then get the hell out. He's scared, which makes him stupid. It's Butcher's specialty, breaking someone so much they do things out of the ordinary.

"Cool, thanks. That's it." I stand and gesture at the chair, and the tech sits hesitantly. "I'm out. Keep up the good work."

"Wait, you said you'd help us with them," badge boy snaps.

I lift my fingers to show him. "I had them crossed. Sorry. Thanks again!" I duck out of the van door and shut it before hurrying across the road to find all three brothers standing at the front door, waiting for me.

Kane sighs. "What the fuck, hellion?"

"I was asking the cops for help. Don't worry, they did." I hit send.

"That's the guard. It's up to you to find him now. I'm going to take a shower and a nap. See you later, hotties." Walking past them, I sing to myself as I head upstairs. This is almost over. Then, I can get Lauren and Taylor, we can go home, and everything will go back to normal.

No Sai brothers or trouble, just home. Nice and simple.

Why does something inside me twinge with that thought?

I won't . . . miss them, will I?

I don't *like* the Sai brothers, do I?

That thought stops me cold.

I must ask myself some very serious questions before I decide.

Do I actually like them, or are they just tall?

Am I attracted to their money or them?

Do I appreciate that they can kill a man in under three seconds without breaking a sweat? Is that why I'm like this? Or do I actually . . . *like* them?

A shudder of horror rolls through me at the notion that I might actually be into them, so I shake it off and hurry to my room before I throw myself over the stairs at the thought. There's no way. I just like their dicks and money.

That's all.

I nearly shoot Neo when I come out of the bathroom in nothing but a towel and find him waiting. He looks up from his phone, and his smile instantly drops. His eyes heat with hunger as they drag down my body.

"What's up?" I ask. "Or do you just want to perv on me?" He usually rises to the bait, but when his eyes meet mine again, they are hard and demanding, and I stiffen.

Standing silently, he prowls toward me, stopping when he's close enough to touch. "I came to tell you we found who it is, but he's in the wind, so your contract isn't done yet. He must have figured out we were onto him."

"Okay, well, you told me." I try to step around him, but he hooks his finger in the top of my towel and tugs, pulling it down to reveal more of my chest. Neo leans down and licks a drop of water from the swell of my breasts, his warm tongue making me shiver.

I want to fuck him, but he's fun to play with so I've been doing that, but he looks like he's sick of playing and now wants to just throw me down and ravish me. I wouldn't mind that, to be honest. I want to try them all before I go, even with the horrifying thought that I might actually . . . like them still haunting me, or maybe it's so I can prove to myself I don't.

"We need to finish what we started this morning," he murmurs, his lips pressing against mine in a featherlight kiss.

"Fine, why not? I've had two out of three anyway. I might as well collect you all." I push him back, and he stumbles, hitting the bed and sitting heavily as he watches me. I undo the towel and let it fall to the floor, then I saunter toward him, ready to take what I want, but when I'm close enough, he grabs me and throws me down.

"Collect us all you want," he taunts as he licks my chin before nipping it. "But you can also say no. You can tease me for the rest of our lives if that's what you want. I want you, but I want you to want me more."

His words make my breath catch, and when he lifts, I see he's serious. Was I agreeing because I felt like I had to? I search myself and realize I wasn't. I want this. When I grab his hand and press it to my pussy, my thighs tight around it, I meet his gaze. "Does that feel like I don't want you?"

His fingers twist, stroking my wet folds. "I need your words. Tell me what you want."

God fucking damn it. Wrapping my thigh around his waist, I flip us so he's below me, then I lean down until my face is near his. "I want this. I want you. I want you to fuck me until I can't walk. Is that good enough for you?"

His hands grip my hips so hard it hurts, and I grunt. "Your wish is my command, Bex." He lifts me effortlessly, his muscles flexing, and places my knees on either side of his head, then he buries his face between my thighs.

I gasp in surprise, but the sound soon turns into a moan of ecstasy as his tongue slips inside me and curls. He holds me prisoner above him as he eats me leisurely, like he has all the time in the world. His tongue alternates between thrusting inside me and curling around my clit in a way that has me grinding down. My desire only grows until I'm riding his face, needing to come, but he doesn't relent. He keeps that slow, maddening pace that drives me higher, but it isn't enough to get me off.

"Neo," I hiss. "Hurry up, I need to come."

He lifts me like I weigh nothing until I can see his smug face. "It's like a good bottle of wine. You don't down it, baby. You savor it," he flirts, licking his glistening lips.

Before I can retort, he drops me, and I moan as his lips seal around my clit. Despite his taunting words, he sucks me hard and fast until I splinter. The release takes me by surprise as I rock on him. I would fall, but he keeps me in place, licking me through my orgasm until I struggle to get away. He finally lets me go, and I fall to the side and slump in the bed next to him, breathing heavily.

I hear him moving, but I don't open my eyes as I enjoy the aftershocks until bare skin presses against mine. He's straddling me, now naked as he leans back.

"What are you doing?"

"Letting you get a good look at what's yours." He smirks before he lunges at me, kissing me hard and fast until I'm meeting his fervor. I suck on his tongue as I slide my hands from his wide shoulders, down his tapered waist, and over the globes of his ass, urging him to give me more.

Rolling us once more, I sit up and sweep my eyes down his impressive chest. He has less definition than Kane, but his waist is tiny, and that V is so deep, I lick my lips. His cock is thinner but longer, and I know I'm going to feel every inch.

"Are you just going to look?" he taunts, stretched out below me. He acts like he has no cares in the world, but I see his cock jerking as precum beads on the tip. I wrap my hand around him, his hiss making me grin in triumph. Leaning down, I suck the tip into my mouth, tasting him. I lick and suck until his hips lift, but I never take him deep enough for him to get off, and when he's practically snarling below me, I chuckle and sit up.

"You're right. Savoring it is better," I purr, licking my lips. His eyes narrow and he yanks me, pressing me against his dick. My breath hitches as his hard length rubs along my core, coating him in my release as he moves me.

Despite being brothers, fucking Neo is nothing like having sex with Kane, yet it feels just as good. I expected to feel a little guilty, but there's nothing but satisfaction as I press down onto his cock.

Our gazes never break apart as I sink farther down, guided by his hands. I take every single inch of him until I'm fully seated on him. I was right, he's so long it hurts, but I've always liked a little pain with sex, so I move, slowly riding him. Neo watches me adjust to him, and there's something so hot about that, so I slide my hands up his muscles, feeling every dip and groove before leaning down. It causes him to slide deeper inside me, and I shudder at the bloom of pain, but I still bite his ridiculously gorgeous waist before my hands find his and I straighten.

I speed up slowly, riding him with our hands twined. The momentum builds between us as he observes me with dark, obsessive eyes.

My hands press to his, pinning them above his head as I roll my hips. My eyes sweep over every inch of his hard, perfect body. It's no wonder the Sai brothers are worshiped as gods. He looks like a lost god below me, all hard edges, and yet I'm in full control. The power I feel has me moving faster, using my knees for leverage until I'm fucking him hard. Releasing his hands, I reach back and grab his solid thighs, feeling them harden under my touch as I roll my body. My head falls back as I use him to get what I want.

"Bex, look at me," he demands, but I ignore him, chasing pleasure until he snarls.

He slides his hands up my back to my shoulders and presses me closer until there's no room between us, his lips finding mine in a scorching kiss. Pulling away, I look at him. His face is soft despite the hunger in his gaze as we come together like we were made to do this.

My heart thumps, and not because of what we are doing, but because of the look in his eyes.

I turn away, burying my head against his neck to hide. It's too intense. It feels a little too much like love for me.

I can't fight the pleasure, however, and when I come to after an all-consuming orgasm, he soothes me through it, his hips never stopping as he lowers me to the bed.

I open my eyes once more, my gaze clashing with his. He keeps my hands prisoner, trapping them above me as he moves. I wrap my legs around his waist, taking him deeper and raising my hips to meet his wild thrusts. Gone is the soft, savoring sex, and in its place is fucking. Sweat slicks our bodies that slap together. My wetness is so loud, it makes me more needy, and the feel of his hard chest pressing against my nipples drives me crazy. I scratch and claw at his hands, but he doesn't release me, so I bite every inch of him I can get, but he still doesn't stop. His teeth are clenched as he fucks me brutally, and I can't do anything but follow along.

"Come for me again. I want to feel it," he orders, his voice thick with need. His hips move faster, hurting mine as they hit, but neither of us complain. "Now, Bex, let me feel it."

Like his words unlock my release, I let go, drowning in his eyes as pleasure swallows me whole. My body jerks in ecstasy as my hips stutter and stop, my thighs clenching him. The pleasure is so intense, I feel my toes and fingers curl.

My eyes shut as I float away with my release. I still feel him fighting my fluttering pussy to push deeper. His movements are sharp and wild, so I know he's close, yet he doesn't let go. I can feel how much he needs to. It must hurt.

"Please, baby, I need your eyes on me," he begs, and I finally blink them open, and as soon as I do, he groans and explodes inside me.

The whine that leaves my throat is animalistic, but he shakes above me, his hands clenching mine before he slumps against me. Our hearts thunder between us before he's up, my brows furrowing as I wonder what he's doing. I'm not exactly a cuddler, but disappointment fills me. I wanted him to touch me more. There's something comforting about his warm hardness pinning me down.

Pulling his cock from my pussy, he flips me and presses it against my lips, shoving inside, and my disappointment changes to shock and then need. "Taste yourself on me. Taste how hard you just came for me. All that bratty attitude, yet you're this wet for me. Taste how badly you want me." Sucking him deeper, I savor both of us mixed together. His eyes are narrowed as he hisses, trying to pull from my mouth, but I suck him clean until he groans, and only then do I let go.

"I taste good," I murmur as I press closer. "So do you. Next time, I want you to finish in my mouth."

"Next time?" His smirk is smug. "You said it, baby, so you can't take it back now."

I go to move away since he doesn't seem like the type to linger, but his arms wrap around me and drag me down to the bed. "Where do you think you're going?" he says into my ear, every inch of him pressed to my back.

"To wash up then sleep," I respond in confusion.

"Sleep first," he murmurs with a soft kiss against my pulse. Despite everything we did, this feels more . . . intimate and dangerous. "Sleep, baby. I've got you."

I fight it, trying to get free, but he doesn't let me, and eventually, I relax back and let the soft tiredness claim me.

When I wake up, Neo is still there, his arm and leg tossed over me, and I swallow as I reach up and trace his cheek.

I can't actually like them, can I?

Liking a Sai brother, never mind all three, would be bad. Sex is one thing, but emotions are another. Kane offered for the three of them to belong to me, but I know what that means for men like them—sex, money, and power. Never emotions, and never forever.

They don't do forever, and neither do I.

The thought of walking away when this contract is done still makes my heart ache.

37

ZAYN

I manage to avoid Bexley the entire next day. When I was going to sleep the night before, what I did and how she helped me all came back to me.

I can't let it go.

It was the best night of my life, or at least it should have been. She's everything I've wanted with a woman, and yet she was forced. She had no choice, and I almost took something I wasn't supposed to. I know enough about her past to understand that's something she would never forgive. I don't want to make her uncomfortable, so I lock myself in the guesthouse after telling Kane. He tried to talk me out of it and told me just to speak to her, but I can't.

I'm so ashamed of myself.

She'll leave once we catch the mole. I won't make her even more uncomfortable until then, and I don't think I can look at her without wanting to vomit. I took what she didn't offer. I'm no better than the men before me. I always thought I was a good guy deep down. Yes, I'm involved in shady shit with my family and I'm happy to kill people, but they always deserve it. I don't hurt women, and I don't take what's not offered, but I was wrong, and I can't live with it.

What I didn't expect was for her to hunt me down. I sit upright on

243

the lounge chair in my swim shorts as she stops in front of me. "This shit stops now. Why are you hiding? Are you embarrassed about being drugged?"

"How did you—"

"I'm a hunter, Zayn. It's my job. Now spill," she demands, sitting on the edge of the lounger. She's so close, my foot touches her leg. I lift it and spin around, putting space between us. Even now, I want to kiss her so I can taste her without drugs in my system. I'm a sick bastard.

"I just wanted some space," I mutter and stand when she reaches for me. I don't deserve her touch or comfort. Stalking over to the water, I stare down into the still blue depths, wishing it could swallow me whole. How could she stand to be near me?

Why did she come?

"Zayn." I feel her at my side. "Talk to me." When I don't, she sighs. "Look at me." I can't. I stare at the water until she yanks me around, but I quickly look away, feeling sick to my core.

Before that night, we could tease and flirt. It was fun, but now it is a reminder of what I did to her. The drugs took away my consent, but they also took hers.

"Zayn, what's wrong?" She won't let me escape, so I meet her eyes, allowing myself one last look. Even if she doesn't hate me, I hate me. "Zayn, I can't help you if you don't tell me. Whatever it is, I can solve it. You know I can."

"You can't fix this, Bexley. No one can. You stand for justice, your name is literally Karma," I scoff bitterly, "and yet I forced you."

"Forced me?" She frowns. "What do you mean—" Her eyes widen. "Oh, you think you made me help you when you were drugged."

"Of course I did! You didn't want to, but you had no choice. I didn't remember until last night, but when I did . . . God, I feel sick. I'm so sorry, Bexley, so fucking sorry. I know that doesn't change anything."

"Zayn." She stops my rant, touching my arm, and I look at it, hating and loving it at the same time. I wish she would never let go, but I know she should. "You were drugged. It wasn't your fault."

"Even if you don't blame me, I blame me," I admit, turning away and plunging into the pool, sinking to the bottom in punishment. She appears in front of me, fully dressed, and yanks me up, but I fight her off so she sinks with me. When she continues to sit there, I panic and yank her to the surface.

"What are you thinking?" I roar in her face as I cup her cheeks. "Are you okay?"

"I'm fine," she answers, slicking her hair back, so I let go and swim backwards. When I can touch the bottom, I turn and start to walk away, needing space. If I'm close to her, everything gets hazy and all my good intentions turn to dust. I want her so badly, even now. I want to believe her and remind her how good we could be together, so I walk away, but I should have known Bexley would follow.

"Zayn, I wanted it too. It's fine. Besides, we didn't have sex," she reasons, splashing water as she follows me.

"They had to hold me back!" I roar, and she stops. The water splashes as I hit it with my hands, my heart clenching. "They had to pin me down."

"Zayn, you were drugged—"

"You said no. I remember you saying no." I sink to my knees, looking up at her as a tear falls. "You said no because of me."

She sinks to hers before me and cups my face, wiping away my tears as I break. "I said no, and you stopped, even when you were drugged out of your mind. I said no, and you stopped because you're a good man, Zayn."

"I forced you," I croak.

"Damn it, Zayn. I know what force feels like. I know what it means to have my choice taken away. What we did wasn't rape. I wanted it. You don't think I feel guilty about wanting you, even in that state? Because I do. If you're a bad person, then I'm even worse. You didn't take advantage of me. I took advantage of you because I care about you and couldn't stand to see you suffer. You didn't hold me down until I choked and passed out. You didn't chain me up and send all of your men in. You didn't set up a camera and laugh while I was crying and screaming. You are nothing like those men who hurt me. Even in the heightened state of being drugged, with no thoughts and impulse control, you stopped. You are a good man, Zayn, and I don't blame you."

"Please forgive me," I whisper, tears falling from my eyes. I want to find all those men and kill them, but right now, I need her absolution.

"Only if you forgive me," she replies gently, softly wiping my tears away.

Pressing my head to hers, I close my eyes. "There's nothing to forgive."

"Not for me either, so stop overthinking," she says, sliding her hand into my hair. I copy her movement, gripping her hair and pressing her tighter against me.

When I open my eyes, I find her watching me, and I see something soft in her gaze that makes me melt into her. Bexley doesn't look at anyone that way. Ever since we met, she's been as sharp and unyielding as a blade, but she's watching me like I'm something special, and my heart races at that one look that tells me everything and nothing all at once.

Does she feel how I do?

This started as fun for us, especially since Kane claimed her, but it turned into so much more. I like having her around. She fits in with my brothers and family. She's brought joy and happiness into our hard, demanding lives. She plays with me, lightens Kane, and keeps Neo on his toes.

She's perfect, and I know we all want her as ours.

Does she know? It's not a game, and when we decide something, it's done, especially Kane.

"I want you," she whispers, shocking me to my core. "Do you still want me? Even knowing all this?"

"I've always wanted you. I don't think I can stop wanting you," I murmur.

Her eyes drop to my lips, and I heat under her gaze. "Then what are you waiting for? Let's erase the other night and replace it with this, both of us wanting each other."

Dragging her close, I kiss her, tasting the water as our tongues tangle. My hand slides into her wet hair and grips it, pulling her closer until I feel her hot body against mine. As I swallow her small noise of pleasure, I can't help but feel victorious. I know she's had my brothers, but I don't care. This isn't about them. This is about us, always has been. Kane might have brought her to us, but I've wanted her since the first moment she stormed into our party. I've wanted to see her hard eyes melt with desire for me.

This isn't just sex. I've had plenty in the past to fill a need and boredom, but it never meant anything, not like this. We are worth fighting for, and I show her that.

Nobody has ever cared about me or my family as much as she does. I've never met anyone as strong yet pure, and I want to belong to her. I want her to stay in my arms forever, kissing me like nothing else exists, but desire demands to be fed and she hops up. The water splashes as I catch her, her giggle making me grin against her lips as she wraps her legs around my waist.

"Fuck me, Zayn," she whispers. "I need you like you need me."

Desperation takes hold, but I know I can't do what I want in the water. I want to taste her skin and have every inch of her.

Her legs tighten around me as I walk from the pool, carrying her. I open my eyes so we don't fall and stumble toward a place where I can take my time with her. She kisses me aggressively, biting and sucking until I'm throbbing and bleeding, and the flames of need only grow. I look around until I feel the sun change to shade and know I'm there. I could take her out in the open, but what if someone flies over? What if there's someone with a camera watching nearby? I will never let her be seen like that, not like those assholes from her past. No, this is for us, and I want her to feel safe with me.

The door of the guesthouse crashes open, and neither of us bother to shut it or go farther. She rips at my shorts as I tear at her clothes until we are both naked, dripping and needy.

She tugs me, and before I know it, I'm inside her. Both of us are desperate for this, but the feel of her tight heat makes me drop back with a groan of pleasure.

She feels too good. I want to touch and taste her, but she has other ideas, her body arching below me to take me deeper. I slow us down. This means something to me, and I hope it means something to her as well. I want her badly, but this is more than sex. There's a bond between us, an understanding, and it's real and raw, and I show her that. I refuse to let her retreat from it.

It's not wild fucking, despite us being on the floor and covered in pool water. It's so much more real. There's no need for anything else, just our bodies and our lips meeting in desperation that drives us both.

Stroking my hands across her skin, I drop my head as she whines and suck on her nipples. She clenches around me, and feeling her body's reaction makes me smirk as I take my time.

"Zayn." She tugs my hair, trying to get me to move, but I stay right where I want to be. My hand slides between us to pet her wet cunt until she rolls her hips, trying to get off. "Zayn, fuck, please. I want it hard and fast. Please, fuck." I bite her nipple as I circle her clit, finding the rhythm she likes. I don't like the way her head drops back and hits the floor. Frowning, I look up, and she uses my distraction to spin us. She starts to ride me, but I throw her back down so I'm on top, slowing her again as she snarls below me.

"If you want me, then you get me like this," I tell her. "Look at you . . . You look so damn sexy when you're angry." Her eyes flash at me in warning, and her fingernails scratch my chest. The hint of pain makes me harder, but I don't relent. I fuck her slowly, caressing her skin and teasing her.

I feel the moment right before she comes. Her thighs tighten, quaking around me, her eyes flare, and her mouth parts, then she cries out loudly and clenches so firmly around me, I grunt. The pleasure is so strong, I have to turn my head and bite my arm to stop myself from coming, but that pain is what splinters me, and I can't hold back.

I've never lost control before, but with her, I do.

I rise and pull her to her feet, then I bend her over the couch. I place one hand in her hair, the other on her hip, as I snarl and hammer into her. Kicking her legs wider apart, I take her hard and fast like she wanted. Her cries of pleasure mix with my grunts.

"Yes, like that!" she screams, her hand hitting a lamp on the side table, which crashes to the floor. Neither of us care as I lift her until her toes barely touch the floor, tilting her hips so I can be deeper inside her. I let her feel the piercings along my cock. I wanted to show her, but the impatient little thing will see them next time. Instead, I let her feel them, and if the noises leaving her throat are anything to go by, she likes them a lot.

Something else crashes to the floor, but we are too lost in the hurricane of desire to care.

"Sir, is everything okay? We heard a crash—" Before whoever it is can enter the door, I bend over her without stopping and find the blade hidden between the cushions, then I throw it. There's a yelp, and I hear him duck. "Sorry, sir!"

"Zayn!" she screams, pressing back. "Fuck, I'm so close. Please—" She whines as I smack her ass before cuffing her neck. I press deeper and take it out on her body until she can't speak. Pleasure claims us both, rolling through her to me, and her yell matches mine as I explode inside her. Her pussy clenches so hard on my length, I see stars as she comes. My legs give out, so I throw myself across her as our slick skin sticks together. Both of us are lost in the ecstasy, and I swear I'll never be able to move right again. When it finally lessens and flows away, I'm left smiling and pressing kisses to her bare shoulder.

"You still alive, Bex?" I tease, but my voice is hoarse.

"Uh-huh, yup, totally fine. Just give me a minute," she rasps, and that makes me chuckle. "Wait, is your dick pierced?"

I press my softening cock deeper so she can feel it, and she shudders. "I thought you might like that."

"Perverts, all of you," she mutters, but she relaxes into me. "When I can walk, we're going for a swim, or maybe a nap or food."

"Whatever you want, Bex," I murmur, kissing her again as I cuddle closer. "In five minutes."

"Maybe ten," she says. Only she can take it all away and leave me truly happy. For the first time in my life, my smile is real.

I'm so happy that it scares me.

Does it scare her?

38

BEXLEY

I might have spread the word about Oliver Cooper, the guard who was Butcher's mole, to my contacts on the street so we can find him faster. Part of me wants to end this, but the other part wants this to last forever. The longer he's free, though, the more dangerous he is, and I don't want the Sais to be hurt. Fuck, I can't even admit that without feeling sick, but seeing Zayn's reaction to being drugged has made me realize I want this over now.

When word comes of his location, I load up and step into the dining room, where they are all working.

Their eyes drag down my body, which is strapped with weapons, and Kane's eyebrow arches. "Either you're about to flirt with us or someone is going to die."

"Silly man, I can do both." I smirk as I toss a bag on the table. "Your weapons. Let's go, hotties. Team Murder Bros, roll out."

"Did she just try to quote *Transformers*?" Zayn asks, and I'm happy to see the light back in his eyes. I warned him that if he avoided me again, I would tie him up in my bedroom and force him to watch every single Barbie movie ever created.

Neo simply grins as he looks in the bag, his eyes widening. "Are we going to war?"

"I like to be prepared. There is no such thing as too many weapons. Chop-chop, children." Turning away, I whistle as I head out to the car where Dodge is waiting, his sunglasses in place.

"It's a fifteen-minute drive to his current location," he says, his eyes rising to the setting sun. "We'll be there just after dark. I'll make sure we cut the lights and engines so you can go on foot to have the element of surprise."

"I love it when hot men are also smart." I pat his cheek, and he recoils, his head dropping in a bow. I turn, expecting Kane, but Neo is behind me. His eyes are colder than I have ever seen, and his face is twisted into an expression like he's facing an enemy as he glares at Dodge. He slows his walk until he's behind me, and I can feel his heat. Everyone around us drops to their knees, rounding their shoulders in fear. The world is silent, even the birds quieting their songs.

Sometimes, I forget they are Sais. Neo always seems so calm and, well, normal for this family, but one look at him now and there is no mistaking what he is—a predator.

Instead of fear like it produces in the others, my stomach clenches and my cunt flutters in memory as his deadly eyes land on me and lock me in place. "Do not flirt with our staff, Bexy, unless you want their deaths on your hands."

"He's been with you for years," I scoff, turning to him.

His hand darts out and grabs my throat. I let him. I could have moved, we both know it, but I didn't. His nostrils flare as he tips my head back. His voice is quiet and so fucking lethal when he says, "And I would miss him, but I would still kill him. Remember that next time. You do not play with what is ours, and you are ours." Letting me go, he goes to step past me, and my irritation flares.

I won't let them walk all over me. I will never belong to another person again. I have to remind him of that, so I kick the backs of his legs out, taking him by surprise. I hear his guards gasp, but none move to stop me. I've heard whispers, but now I know it's true. They were warned that if any of them harm me or even look at me wrong, they will die a horrible death. It seems the Sais are determined to protect me, but they forget I don't need protection.

Grabbing Neo's hair, I yank his head back until his cold eyes are on me as I tower above him now. Fire burns in their icy depths, which are alight with desire and obsession. It's a look no man should ever wear because of it's devastating effects, but he doesn't seem to care who's watching. He eyes me like he's waiting for me to devour him and would enjoy every second.

My hackles are up. How many times did Butcher call me his pet and claim me like that? Maybe that's why I do it, or maybe I just like pushing them as far as they can go.

Leaning down, I tighten my hold on his hair and watch his eyes widen, his lips parting in a pant. "Bex," he rasps, and the shortened, familiar version of my name only makes my eyes narrow more.

"I think you need to be reminded of who really belongs to whom." I let go, and he jerks forward before spinning to me as I step back a couple of feet. I cross my arms. "Why don't you show them? I'm not yours, Sai, but you're mine. Crawl to me and I'll accept that. Crawl to me and I'll let you into my bed for however long I want before I get bored. If you get up and storm away, I will never touch you again."

I wait as he observes me, thoughts passing through his eyes. He knows I'm serious. I don't make idle threats. I can feel his brothers behind me, but I ignore them. It's his choice. Either he concedes and completes the humiliating task I've set or he will never have me again.

He starts toward me but freezes when I snap in irritation.

"I said crawl, not walk," I order as I step back and wait.

He's a Sai brother. He might not be the family leader, but he runs this city, and everyone knows it. He's one of the three most powerful and dangerous men in the area. People have disappeared for a simple look or word, and I am ordering him to crawl to me. Anyone else would die, but I'm not anyone else.

I tap my foot impatiently. "Now," I snap.

His eyes lock on me, making this something intimate. When he sinks to his knees, I fight my shock, but he knows, his lips kicking up at the edges in satisfaction as he drops to his hands and starts to crawl toward me. Despite him there on his knees, we both know who's in charge, and it irritates me more.

"Look away!" Kane barks sharply, and I hear the guards turn away, but neither Neo nor I spare them a look. We are locked in a battle of wills until he reaches me. His hands slide up my legs as he kneels, his head level with my stomach, and then he releases me from his gaze, purposely submitting and losing.

For me.

It's silent.

No one else would know, but I do.

He just relented his control to me.

"Well?" he murmurs, burying his head in my stomach so it raises my shirt. He licks my bare skin, making me gasp. He doesn't seem to care about the guns and knives strapped to me as he rubs against me like an overgrown cat. "Looks like you can't get rid of me now."

His eyes meet mine again, and I know he's right. I won, but at what cost?

"I'll crawl too!" Zayn cuts in, his voice chipper and teasing, and the tension breaks. A guard chuckles before coughing to cover it, and I know he did it on purpose. Kane leads this family, and Neo is the backbone, but Zayn is the heart. He keeps everyone together and happy. I wonder if he chose that or if he feels pressure to be the calmer, funnier brother to keep the peace.

I'll have to check.

Grabbing Neo's chin, I drag him up to his feet and pat his cheek. "Fine, your choice. You look good when you crawl. I'll remember that for later." I step around him and into Kane. I expect anger and retribution. Nobody humiliates his family, not even someone he is sleeping with. I've heard rumors of the last person he was fucking. She ordered Zayn to do something, thinking she was the woman of the house, and before her sentence was even finished, she was on her ass outside, and he tore her life apart until she had nothing left.

He wants me, but when it comes to his family, he is a completely different animal. Is that why I did it? Was I hoping he would turn on me so I could escape and push these feelings down without consequence?

I wait like a soldier going to battle. I feel Neo and Zayn step to my side as if ready to leap in front of me and take the words like bullets.

"Brother," Neo begins.

He slices his hand through the air, and Neo falls silent. Kane and I stare each other down, but then his lips tilt in a smile. "Remember what you just said, hellion, and remember what I told you. What one has, we all have. That means we're yours now." Stepping closer, he caresses my cheek softly, but the deadly knowledge of how easily he can kill with that hand turns me on, and he knows it. "Remember, you will protect this family as if you were me, including my brother's dignity." It's a small reprimand, but not what I was expecting.

"Only until I'm bored, remember?" I snap, feeling like I lost this round.

"If you say so, hellion, though we all know what you claim, you claim for good." He turns and heads to the car, looking back at me. "Weren't we in a hurry?" He holds the door and waits. Tossing him a glare, I stomp past him and slip inside, wishing like hell I'd never slept with any of these crazy bastards.

I should know better than to feed the animals.

I try to focus on business and where we are going, ignoring their looks. Zayn's leg is pressed against mine, but his other bounces restlessly. Kane is checking his gun across from me, and Neo is still watching me hungrily.

"So, where are we going? Who are we killing?" Zayn asks, breaking the silence. "Is it war? Are we your little assassin slaves tonight?"

"Would you kill my enemies without me asking?" I ask.

"Sure." No hesitation in sight. "Where you go, we go. So who is it?"

"Not my enemy, yours," I admit. "I found the mole and got his location. He's been lingering there for about an hour, hence the speeding."

"What's his name?" Kane rumbles, our previous interaction forgotten in the face of business.

I meet his gaze head-on, almost falling into the darkness of those orbs. "Would it matter if I told you? Would you know it?"

"Try me," he demands.

"Oliver Cooper," I say, and there's no recognition in his gaze. "Just as I thought. He's a lower guard and pretty new. No money troubles, wife, or girlfriend, but they got to him somehow."

"Are you sure?" Neo asks, but he doesn't seem to be questioning me, more like he's sad to confirm one of their own betrayed them.

"I'm sure. We found a link, but I'll let you question him."

"I suppose that means your job is done then," Zayn reasons, and his eyes are downturned. I shouldn't stay. I should accept the money and get the hell out, never looking back, but for some fucking reason, I can't say any of that when he looks so sad.

"I think I'll stick around for the fireworks. Besides, my house isn't exactly far." His head jerks up, his eyes gleeful, and I realize he was manipulating me.

We jerk to a stop, and that's the only thing that saves his life.

"We are here," Dodge announces. "He won't see us from here."

"Good, stay back. If he spooks and runs, I'll be pissed as hell if I have to chase him," I threaten as I get out of the car.

Rounding the corner of the parking lot, I step over the concrete blocks and through the trees, and then I see him. He's framed by the city lights behind him as he leans into the metal railing in front of the river. It's dark now, and not many people are out here walking at this time of night, but it's like he hasn't realized the sun has set.

Guilt? Fear?

Maybe he feels us closing in and came here for one last look at freedom. Either way, it doesn't matter. I start toward him, my footsteps light and silent. There's a crack behind me, and I turn as Zayn winces, mouthing, "Sorry," as he steps on a tree branch. Whirling forward, I expect Oliver to have moved, but he's oblivious. Shit, he really is a new guard if he didn't hear that.

When I step up behind him and press my gun to his head, he doesn't stiffen like I expect. "I knew you'd find me." When he turns slowly, his eyes widen. "I thought it would be Kane."

"I'm here." They fade out of the darkness behind me, spreading out like an execution squad.

"Why, Oliver? Money? You know we look after our own," Kane asks, needing to understand.

"No," he whispers as he sinks to his knees, tears filling his blue eyes. He's young, but right now, he looks ten years older and ripped apart, as if the betrayal has ruined him, yet he doesn't try to run or defend himself. "Not money."

"Then what?" Kane presses angrily.

"Tell them," I murmur. "They need to know."

"Please, I'm sorry, sir. I had no choice. He took my sister," he sputters and cries, bowing his head in shame.

Fear. Loved one. I knew it.

What would I do for my sister? Anything.

"I understand." His head lifts at my words. "If someone took my sister, I would burn the world for her. You did what you thought was right, but it won't save you. You betrayed your people and almost cost us our lives, but I promise I will find your sister and save her if I can." She has to be kept somewhere. I can find her. I'm good at that.

"Thank you," he whispers in relief. "I didn't know what else to do."

I glance at Kane, waiting. It's his choice, but I know what I would do.

"I'm sorry, Oliver. We can't let this stand. We'll make it quick." He nods at me and moves me aside, pulling out his own gun. "He is one of mine. It's my duty."

I'm just putting my gun away, Oliver's quiet sobs filling the air, when I hear engines. It's the only thing that saves our lives. I throw myself at the brothers, knocking them all to the ground as lights flood the area and bullets whiz over us. Instantly, I hear Dodge and their guards shoot back. Risking a look, I tighten my hold on my Glock.

"Stay down," I bark at them as I get to my knees, ignoring their insistent voices and tugging. When I don't die, I scramble to my feet and rush toward the gunfire.

They, of course, do not listen, the stubborn idiots. I hear them running after me, but I'm faster and I get there first. I scan the area as I use a tree for cover. Some of the Sai guards are down, having clearly been taken by surprise. The rest have spread out, using cars and doors for cover. To the right are three trucks, their lights so bright I can't see who's firing, but they are aiming at the brothers' men now.

Semi-automatics, at least fifteen of them.

I calculate it all in the time it takes to blink, and then I shoot. My aim is better than the guards', who are firing wildly to suppress the assailants, and I take them by surprise. I shoot out their headlights, giving us better vision before they realize I'm here. I spin and press my back to the trunk as they fire at me, but then they have to switch back to the guards.

Kane ducks in at my side, his gun out, and when we nod, we both slip around each side of the tree and fire. I hear shouts as bodies drop. I step from behind the trunk, ignoring the guys' calls. I'm not letting these assholes get away. I skinned my fucking elbows, and they will pay for that.

Dropping my pistols when they are empty, I swing my shotgun around and start to fire as I advance on the trucks, reloading as quickly as I can. When I reach the first, I kick the passenger door shut, knocking the man inside back. He raises his hands, but I fire then turn and shoot the man who rushes toward me around the back of the car. He flies back from the wound, and I drop to my knees as glass from the back window explodes across me. Lying on my side, I shoot under the car when I see the man's feet, and he screams as he crumples. Sliding through the open back door and out the other side, I kick him in the face and shoot him in the back before reloading. I just duck behind the car as it explodes with gunfire from the others.

I hear screams, and I look out to see Zayn and Neo taking care of one man, and Kane and Dodge the other. Huh. I guess it's easier when there are a few of you. Keeping my gun out just in case, I step out as the night falls silent.

As I walk their way, I fire into a man's face as he groans, reaching for his gun. I step over him and join the brothers. Dodge and his team set out, checking the dead, and I finally relax my hold as I run my eyes over Kane, Zayn, and Neo.

They are doing the same to me, but they seem satisfied I'm not hurt. "Was it a trap?" Kane snaps.

"That or they followed us. We need to find out. Where's Oliver?"

"Here," he whispers, appearing around the truck, the back of his jacket held by one of the Sai guards.

Sirens tear through the stillness of the night, and I curse. How the fuck are we going to explain this? We aren't in my neighborhood. I have no contacts and no time.

"Clear," Dodge calls, kicking one of the downed men.

"This is why I always come prepared," I mutter as I run my eyes over them.

"We should get going, sir, and leave the police to deal with this. I will get their information later," Dodge advises worriedly as the sirens grow closer.

"It's not safe," Kane counters, dragging me away, but I'm staring at the dead men.

Who is trying to kill the Sais now?

Is it a new enemy or an old one?

They were right. They really do have a lot of people trying to kill them. I should switch sides, since it would probably be safer, but then again, I never did like boring safety.

39

BEXLEY

We get back in record time. After securing Oliver in what seems to be their prisoner holding area, which in reality is just a room on one of the lower floors, Dodge heads back out to clear up the mess and find out what he can.

The other guards watched as Oliver walked through their midst. Everyone was disgusted, and he hung his head in shame. I watch him now as he sits docilely in his bindings. He's already broken.

Shrugging out of my jacket, I toss it back into the corridor and lean into the wall. This is their show, it seems, as Kane paces before the man. I glance at Neo to see him stripping from his suit jacket, and I freeze. I step before him, and his eyes widen. Lifting his arm, I meet his eyes when he notices it. The fabric on his bicep is ripped and bloody.

Tearing it open, I check the wound. "It grazed you," I mutter.

"Guess I didn't duck quickly enough," he says, but I keep my narrowed eyes on him. "Next time, I'll be faster." Dropping his arm now that I'm sure he's not dying, I retake my position as Zayn leans next to me. It seems a gun fight puts him in a good mood, which it usually does for me as well, but this time, I just have this odd feeling that not even killing a bunch of people can take away.

Strange. It's usually a good stress reliever.

"I can be injured too," Zayn offers, nudging me. "Want to check every inch of me?"

When I don't respond, he sobers. "What is it?"

"I don't know," I admit, but Kane hears and turns to me, his brow arched, demanding I carry on. He trusts my instincts. "Something isn't right. I trust my contact, so unless they were tracking us or Oliver, they wouldn't have known. Who would want him silenced or us killed?"

"Maybe someone was just taking their chance," Kane suggests, trying to reassure me. "We have other enemies, hellion, and some like to pounce when they think we are weak, knowing it's the only time they would win. We'll find out."

I nod, but I still feel wrong. Something is niggling at my brain, but when I try to grasp it, it floats away.

"It was Butcher," Oliver comments, and all eyes go to him.

"Butcher is dead," Kane snaps.

The world crumbles under my feet, my stomach dropping. "I killed him. I watched him burn," I say, my voice a shaky whisper.

Oliver's eyes land on me, filled with sadness and hopelessness. "Did you watch him burn to death? Did you stick around until the end? Because I spoke to him yesterday. Butcher is alive, and he's determined to kill the Sais now. More so now than ever. He's . . . feral. He's wounded but more deadly than I've ever seen him. Whatever humanity was holding him back before isn't now. All he cares about is their deaths."

And no doubt mine.

"How? How did he survive?" Kane roars.

"I don't know. I think Alexis found him before it was too late and got him out. He's burnt but alive. He was howling your name while they patched him up and dragged me out to him. I'm sorry. I'm *so* sorry. I couldn't tell you. They would have killed my sister."

The guard . . . the one I shot last . . . that's what's bugging me. I knew him.

"He's right," I croak before clearing my voice. "I didn't realize until now what was bothering me. That last guard, he was loyal to

Butcher to a fault. He wasn't at the warehouse, but he was there tonight, and we killed him. He wouldn't have thought of this alone. This was ordered, and there's only one person who could control Alexis, and that is Butcher."

The sick feeling only triples, and the room suddenly closes in on me. My skin is too hot, I'm sweating, and I feel faint.

I was so sure . . .

"Do you know where he is?" Kane asks Oliver.

I feel his eyes on me, his roared promise as I left him there to burn. He won't stop, especially not now. If he was angry before, well, now he'll be furious. I can barely breathe, and I can't even hear Kane's words anymore. I slip out of the room, ignoring them, and before I know it, I'm running up the stairs and breaking out into the back garden, gulping in air.

A hand soothes over my back. "Breathe in and out, just like that. It's just a panic attack. That's it. Follow my breathing, nice and slow."

I can't even tell who it is because my senses are dull. Blood rushes in my ears, and my vision blurs. I screw my eyelids shut, trusting whoever it is to keep me safe as I try to copy his breathing. His soft murmurs are more of a sound than words, but I hold onto them like a lifeline, and when I can finally breathe enough to straighten, I find Zayn.

He smiles sadly at me and opens his arms. Before I know it, I bury myself in his embrace. I don't scream or sob, but silent tears slide down my cheeks, wetting his shirt. He says nothing, just holds me tighter.

I don't know how long we linger, but he kisses my head as I settle down. "We'll find and kill him," he promises, but it's not enough.

Butcher has escaped death twice, and both times, I thought I was free. I'm so fucking tired, scared, and exhausted.

When I can't take it anymore, I step back, unable to meet Zayn's eyes as I wipe my face in shame. "Find out what you can from Oliver." I walk away.

He calls after me, but I don't answer.

I can't reply over the lump in my throat.

I hide from them. I'll admit that's what I'm doing. It's a big house, but they could find me if they wanted to. They are giving me time.

I take a sip, letting the alcohol soothe my frayed nerves and fear. I shouldn't drink because he could come for us again, but I can't seem to stop. I clutch the bottle as I walk, finding myself in a part of their mansion I haven't been in before. It's down some steps, but the door buzzes when I get closer, opening for me.

Once inside, I dangle the bottle from my fingers in shock. There are three floors with a giant electron in the middle, all open. Every single brand of bike and car stretches as far as the eye can see. It's like a car dealership, but of the most elite vehicles in existence, and it's one of a kind.

Jesus, how much money do these assholes have? I should have asked for more.

It's an idle thought as I wander through the space.

The rage that helped me survive Butcher is present, but the old fear is back—the one from a child who believed he was immortal and unstoppable. I'd die before I ever let him take me again, but that terror is hard to fight against, and behind it all is sadness.

I thought this was over. I let myself forget and enjoy life.

I was stupid.

I hear the door open and know it's them. It seems they are done giving me space. I don't turn to look. I don't want them or anyone else to see me like this, but especially them. I need to be strong, to be the Karma they know, but all that's here right now is a broken Bexley.

Taking another swig, I look around at the cars, wishing I could escape, but I know they would find me.

They would find me anywhere.

40

KANE

Her back is to me, and she clutches a bottle in her grasp like she's worried we will take it from her or she's planning to kill us with it. Either one wouldn't surprise me. Moving silently to the side, I see her profile, and my heart aches.

She looks so lost and alone, not like my usual little hellion. Part of me hates seeing her like this, while the other part cracks and tightens, my protective instincts roaring to the forefront. Her weakness is a pain in my soul. I like it when she's strong and happy, and seeing her like this . . .

God, I lose the last piece of myself to her.

She glances at me for a moment, searching my gaze, and I let her see whatever she wants. When she's done, she turns away, and I almost stagger from the loss of her attention. Everyone else knows, even our guards, the power she has over us, but she seems oblivious, trying to push us away.

I let her think she's in control and that she could walk away if she wanted, but if she tried . . . well, she'd end up right back here where she belongs.

She claimed us as hers, and she doesn't get to walk away from that, not when she has stolen our hearts.

It is obvious she hates being vulnerable, especially in front of us, but I won't let her go through this alone. We tried to give her space, but it wasn't working, so now I'm going to be here, with my brothers, until she's okay.

Her voice is thick with unshed tears when she speaks. "Which car is the most expensive?"

We share a look before I point at the Bugatti in the corner, and she walks toward it, swaying as she opens the door and climbs into the driver's seat, then a sob echoes around the garage.

We tread closer as she sips the bottle and cries against the leather, smacking the wheel with her other hand.

"If you're going to cry, it's better to do it in a fancy sports car, right?" she murmurs, wiping her eyes as she leans back, taking a swig of the alcohol.

Kneeling near the open door, I reach for my handkerchief, but she beats me to it, grabbing my wallet from my pocket. My eyebrows rise as she opens it, chucks it back at me, and dabs her eyes with wads of cash.

"Even baddies get the saddies sometimes," she rasps, and I can't stop my soft chuckle. Even hurting, she is still able to make jokes, and I know she's going to be okay.

If killing Butcher will help, I will hunt him down and tear him to pieces and give her his head on a platter, but I know she needs to be part of it. Bexley needs to know he's truly dead, so I won't do that. She doesn't need us to protect her as much as I wish she would. She needs us to trust and help her, and that's exactly what we will do.

"You don't need to entertain us," Zayn murmurs as he stands behind me. "You don't have to feel anything except what you feel right now. You don't have to be strong here, *cariño*." The endearment makes me look at him. It's what my father called our mother, and Zayn once told us the only woman he would say it to was the love of his life, the one he knew he would marry. If that doesn't solidify us never letting her go, then I don't know what would.

She looks at us with big, tear-filled eyes.

"Let go," Neo encourages as my bad ear starts to ring, making me wince as I do my best to ignore it. "We'll catch you. You're not weak for it, and no one else will ever know. I promise." We create a barrier between her and the world, and tears slide down her cheeks. She's so fucking beautiful.

"Let go, hellion," I murmur, and it's like it gives her permission.

Bexley screams, hitting the steering wheel as she begins to sob.

We are her silent guardians, knowing how much of an honor it is to protect her in this moment.

We don't speak, not even when she leans back and wipes her face again. Her chest heaves, the bottle of booze forgotten. "We need to find him and end this," she states, her voice hoarse and low. "I need your help."

"It's yours," I reply instantly. "Everything we have is yours."

"We'll find him," Neo promises.

"And then we'll watch you kill him for good. He doesn't get nine lives. He's nothing special, just a cockroach," Zayn adds.

Nodding, she looks out of the front windshield. "Keep Oliver alive if he isn't already dead. We might need him. We need to go to the street to get the word out and discover what's happening. If he's lying low, he can't hide forever. He was hurt and needed help, and there aren't many places to go for that, but he forgets they are my streets now, not his. I will remind him of that."

Some of her spark is returning, the blazing anger chasing away her fear and sadness.

"We'll go with you and find him," I tell her. Nodding, she slips from the car, and we back up. If she doesn't get some of her anger out, it might cause her to react too quickly.

"Let it out," I say once more. "I see the rage in your eyes. We need Karma, who is smart, calculating, and just crazy enough. Get it all out here, and let's end this."

She frowns for a moment before blowing out a breath, knowing I'm right. Turning, she walks over to the wall where we keep tools to maintain our cars—we have our own team of mechanics, but none are here now. We kicked them out when we saw her heading this way.

Gripping a tire iron, she stalks back to the Bugatti and smashes a back window and then a tire. Her muscles easily swing the iron bar. "Feel better?"

"Yes, actually," she says, and then she swings again. We let her.

She smashes the Bugatti and then moves on, ranting as she wrecks the cars. "Fucking useless piece of trash. He dares to live? He dares to attack me? I'll tear him to fucking pieces. I'll make him beg for death!" she screams as she lands a particularly hard blow onto a hood of my newest Rolls-Royce. I flinch, not at the car, but at the way her hands lose their grip on the iron.

It must hurt, and I can't have that.

41

BEXLEY

Panting, I rest the tire iron against the floor like a crutch as my muscles burn. I work out, but I've been going for a while.

"Here." Kane offers me his gun. "Don't hurt your hands with the tire iron."

He steps back, watching me as I make my way through their precious cars. I shoot out lights and windows, and I even create a smiley face on a mint-green Lamborghini. My anger guides me as I work my way through the garage with the brothers behind me. When I'm finally panting, unable to move any further, I collapse to the concrete, but I'm smiling.

I lie like this for a while as my heartbeat slows, and then I blink up at them.

"Why? I whisper. "Why did you let me wreck all this?"

"Because it means you trust us," Zayn replies, and I swing my eyes to him. "You've been taught to cry silently because of your past. The fact that you are crying and lashing out means the world to me. You trust us enough to do that."

Shock sets in when I realize he's right. Butcher taught me to cry quietly. If I cried loudly, he either got angry and punished me or thought it was the funniest thing and would do something worse to make me sob harder. It had only been years later when I realized it had stuck, and even when I was bawling, there wasn't a sound, but today I let out years' worth of agony, and they are watching me with nothing but longing and happiness.

Neo grins. "Besides, now we can bill you for them, and there's no way you can afford them, so you'll have to stay with us, which means we get to keep you."

"Asshole," I grumble, and he grins.

"I'm a lawyer, baby. I'm always two steps ahead, especially when the prize is you."

Laughing, I wipe my face, trying to get back on track. "Is Oliver alive?"

"For now."

I nod and blow out a breath, holding my hands out. "Help me up. I'm going to get changed. If we are heading to my streets, then I can't go looking like a kept woman."

I feel so much better in my own clothes. I sent Dodge to get some of my stuff, and dressing how I normally do brings back the edge and confidence I earned.

Okay, I might have dressed up more than normal, not just for the Sai brothers, but for me as well.

My makeup is dark, my hair falls to my waist in long, black tendrils, and my fingers are covered in rings over my tattoos. My long legs are encased in my favorite pair of black, knee-high leather boots. They are a pain to get on, but so worth it. My skirt is black with a frilly edge, barely reaching the tops of my thighs, and my crop top is tight and high-necked, with snakes and daggers over the hem, showing off my stomach and ink. Shrugging into the leather jacket I stole from Zayn, I walk down to the car and slip inside, feeling all their eyes on me. Smiling, I lean forward and steal Kane's sunglasses, then I sit back as I slide them on.

"Let's go, Dodge." We set off instantly, but they haven't stopped staring, so I lift my left leg and place it on Neo's thigh, flashing my black lace thong. "I missed some of the zipper. Help a girl, won't you?"

Leaning down, Neo slides his hand up the boot and grabs the slider. He holds my gaze as he raises it until it's fully zipped, but his hand slides higher, caressing the ink on my thighs. "I want these on later."

"Kane?" Zayn asks, his voice filled with amusement.

"Huh?" Kane blinks and looks around. "What?"

"Finished gawking?" Zayn teases.

Kane gestures at me and pinches his nose as if he's in pain. "Look at her. How can I concentrate?" Grabbing my other leg, he lifts it so I'm stretched across them, my legs parted in a V. "Dodge, take the long route," he calls, and then he's on me, kissing my boots and thigh.

Laughing, I lift my leg and press the heel against his chest, my knee bent, and shove him back. His eyes are wild with hunger as I lean back in my seat and drop my heel to his cock, where I press slightly, making him hiss, but he arches his hips up for more. "Behave," I warn.

"You come dressed like that and expect us to behave, *cariño*?" Zayn whispers in my ear, and I realize I made a mistake. I have Neo and Kane trapped with my feet, but they were a distraction.

Zayn's hand lands on my thigh and slides up under my skirt, and before I can protest, my thong is pushed aside and his fingers sink into me. My head falls back unbidden, and I'm brave enough to admit I was wet as I teased them, but as he twists his fingers and rubs my clit, my eyelids flutter shut in ecstasy.

"Look at them, *cariño*. Look at my strong, unmovable brothers. They are wild, wishing they were touching you. They would kill me right now to take my place." My eyes open, clashing with Neo's and Kane's. Both are still . . . too still, like predators ready to strike.

Zayn's expert fingers play with me until I slide down in the seat, widening my legs to give him better access. I should focus, but my good intentions fade as his tongue drags along my neck before he bites it.

We don't have time, we need to focus, but I can't help but give into them, and he feels it.

"Good girl, *cariño*. Come for me while they watch," he whispers in my ear, his fingers twisting until his palm presses to my clit, and when I meet Neo's and Kane's eyes, I fall into the release building within me, my back arching.

My eyes close as I shiver for him. He pulls his fingers free, but I don't bother looking until Kane's voice fills the silence. "Get her on her knees. I want her mouth. It's time I shut the great Karma up."

Before I can protest, I'm manhandled between all three of them until I'm on my knees, my skirt hiked up. Kane's hand is in my hair, stroking me as he frees his hard dick and drags it along my lips.

"We don't have long, hellion. I'm going to come down your throat so I'm the only thing you'll taste all day." The thought shouldn't excite me, but it does, and when I feel Zayn behind me, my pussy clenches. "You like having him behind you, don't you, hellion? You like the idea of him fucking you while I claim your perfect mouth."

"Yes," I admit without shame, leaning forward to lick him as his eyes narrow. "Stop talking and fuck me."

His hand moves down, clenching my jaw and forcing it open, and then he shoves his dick into my mouth. I gag before I breathe through my nose, trying to hold onto his pants, but I fall forward as Zayn pushes inside me, burying himself in one smooth thrust.

It's cramped, but they make it work, setting a hard pace.

This should be degrading, but the obsession in Kane's gaze and the hunger in Zayn's wild touch tell me this is all about me, and I'm the one who's really in control.

I groan around Kane's length as his hand fists my hair as he drives into my mouth. My eyes roll up, meeting Kane's dark gaze, as his brother thrusts into me from behind, his grunts filling the air. My pleasure grows from his feral touch, which hits just the right place, and the control Kane has on me. I love the way he throbs in my mouth, how his eyes tighten, and his jaw jumps, the veins in his neck standing out as he fights his own need.

I suck him deeper as I clench around Zayn, their moans of pleasure making me want to laugh. "Hellion," Kane growls as his hips lose their careful control until he just fucks my mouth, chasing his release. "Brother, I'm close."

"Me too," Zayn rasps, and then he pinches my clit. "Come for me, *cariño*. Let me feel it."

His fingers increase their pressure, and I have no choice but to give in, even though I want to drag it out. I fall into a hard release, and he groans as I tighten around him. His hips fight my cunt to get deeper, then I feel the warm splash of his release while Kane drags my head farther back, and then with a snarl, he fills my mouth with his cum. I choke on it, but he strokes my neck, making me take it all, and only then does he release me.

I sputter and gasp, leaning into him, while Zayn leans into me from behind. "Good girl, hellion," Kane praises, stroking my hair as I shiver and recover.

A noise draws my attention to Neo. He looks away when I notice him, his face pained, and I see why—his pants are tented—but he says nothing.

Licking my sore lips, I slide up the seat, pulling from his brothers, and straddle Neo's lap. "You didn't think I was done, did you?" I lick his chin and then his neck as he grunts.

"Bexley, you don't need to—"

"I want to," I whisper in his ear. "I want your cum inside me. I came twice, but I want more. I want to ride you while they watch."

"Fuck." He slides his hands up my skirt and exposes my thong, which he rips off, and then he's inside me. Neo is so hard and long, my eyes close as I moan.

I'm so wet, it drips down on him, but he doesn't seem to care as he forces me to ride him.

I lean back, digging my nails into the leather headrest as I roll my body and ride him hard. I could kill them all right now and they wouldn't stop me. They are that lost in me, and it's a powerful thought.

I ride Neo harder as he groans my name, and we both lose ourselves in the pleasure claiming us. His cum fills me alongside his brother's as I curl against him, riding my own release.

Neo strokes my back and kisses my head. "You're so beautiful, Bex," he murmurs. "Do you know how much we—I need you?" I have no idea what he was going to say, but I don't care. I'm sated and happy.

"Come here, baby." I don't bother looking. I let them lay me out between them. Something wipes between my thighs, and something else cleans my mouth. I let them fix me up as I relax into their soft, caring hands. I should object, but it's nice to be looked after. Eventually, my determination returns, and I pull away and sit back in my seat, trying to focus on what is to come. We have things to do. I can't be sex muddled. Instead, I look out of the window, trying not to get caught up in my feelings. There's something wrong with my heart, too, but I ignore it as best as I can.

By the time we reach my neighborhood, my skirt is fixed and I'm put together, smirking as the car stops.

"Welcome to my kingdom, boys." I grin as I get out of the car, only wobbling slightly.

42

BEXLEY

I can still feel them inside me, and the well-used feeling makes me even more relaxed and confident as I step onto the familiar street. It's the heart of where we live, a meeting place of sorts. The car has drawn attention, and people drift over until a call goes up.

"It's Karma!"

"Yo, Sanchez, I need information," I say, but he glares at me, the car, and the men getting out behind me.

"You sold out, Karma?" he hisses.

My eyes narrow as a crowd gathers. People who were loyal, people who were afraid of me, are whispering. Butcher wants me to believe they have abandoned me.

He always wanted me to feel like I had nobody but him.

"You left!"

"She's with the Sais!"

I hear questions I never would have faced before, and irritation courses through me, but so does anger when they look at me like I'm an enemy. I've fought at these people's sides, I've been to BBQs, Christmases, and parties galore with them, yet they look at me like I'm an outsider. Maybe it was wrong to bring the Sais, but this is their fight as much as it's mine, and honestly, I don't want to do this alone anymore. They promised to help, and I'm going to let them, and nobody, not even the people I live with, get to question that.

"I live here," I yell, and the crowd quiets down. "Did you forget that I watch your kids? That I protect your businesses? Who stopped the serial killer running around on our streets? Not the cops or Butcher. Me!" I roar loudly, and I see some nod, their eyes dropping in shame. "Me! I am one of you, and right now, I'm asking for help for an enemy we all have."

It's quiet, but no one makes a move, and that, more than anything, destroys me. This place is my home.

Has Butcher taken that too?

"You fucking morons!" Reacher snaps as he pushes through the crowd. "Don't make me kick all your asses. That's Karma, our Karma. Who cares who she's riding with or why? She earned her name before some of you were even born, you idiots."

Someone laughs, and the tension breaks.

Reacher stops in front of me, lowering his voice. "I don't know what you got yourself into, girl, but you better sort it out quickly. Rumors have been spreading, turning friends against neighbors."

"It's him. He's trying to make my home unsafe and cause chaos for him to hide in," I mutter.

"Sorry, Bexley." Sanchez offers me his fist, and I bump it. "We had to be sure. We've been hearing shit."

"Shit you shouldn't be listening to," I scoff. "You think I'd sell out? When your mama hears, she's going to kick your ass."

"Ah, shit, don't. She's still mad at me for last month's arrest," he grumbles, but he's grinning. "What do you need, *chica*?"

Sanchez was low on the totem pole, just a kid, when Butcher was around previously, but he'll remember him.

"Information. Butcher is alive and hiding somewhere. He needs medical attention. Obviously, he or his people have been stirring up trouble here. Have you heard anything?"

He nods, looking at his gang members. "There are rumors of someone holed up in Dr. Willow's place. He forced his way in, but when we checked, she said she was fine. We saw a man all burnt to hell in the background. We saw the fire. Was that you?"

"It was." I raise my voice. "Know this—anyone who aids or gives him or his men sanctuary are dead to me and mine. Stay off the streets for the next few weeks, it's going to get bloody."

"You need backup?" Reacher asks, and others call out in support.

"Not this time, but if anyone hears or sees anything, let me know, okay?"

"You got it," Sanchez says. "Stay safe, and don't forget it's Mama's sixtieth at the end of the month."

"Like I would. Her food is the best," I tease, nudging him before I wave and walk toward the Sai brothers, Reacher following.

"What are you thinking, girl?" he asks as I reach the brothers. "Let us help."

"Never." I pat his shoulder. "I'd never risk my family."

"Taylor and Lauren are safe. I checked." My eyes widen, and he chuckles. "I have my ways, girl. Go do what you need to do, but we are here if you need us. Remember where you come from and who your friends are." He glares at the Sais. "Are they your friends?"

"We are hers," Kane states.

Reacher's eyebrows rise, and he scoffs. "Always liked them crazy. Be gentle on Willow. You know she's been struggling since her husband's death."

I watch him walk away with a small smile, knowing he would ride with me, even into death. Most of them would, but this isn't their fight.

"Why do I feel like I just got quizzed by your dad?" Zayn asks.

"Reacher? Nah, he's more like my fun drunk uncle. Auto, now, he's more like my father. If he saw you, he'd shoot you on sight," I say sweetly as I climb in and reel off Willow's address.

We arrive there in ten minutes and park around the corner so we don't spook any lookouts. Sneaking through gardens, I observe from three houses away. Her white three-story house is beautifully kept, if slightly old. Her parents lived in it until they retired and moved away, then she took it over with her husband. Lovely people, even when she got money from her career.

"I don't see any cars," Kane comments.

"Me either, but still." Keeping low, I cross the road and use the side gate, then I open the cellar door and head down. I don't need light to see as I make my way across the basement, since I know my way well. Taking the stairs to the top, I press my ear to the door as someone falls behind me, grunting. When I hear nothing, I pull my gun out, crack the door, and step through.

Willow whirls around in the middle of cleaning her surgery table. "Jesus, Bexley, you scared the shit out of me." I drop the gun, but the Sais step around me and search the house.

"Where is he?"

"Who?" She frowns, but her eyes tell me she knows. "Hey, this is my house. Stay out of there!" she yells at the brothers as they search.

"Willow," I bark, and she looks at me as they join me again.

"No one is here," Neo says softly.

"Bexley, what's going on? This is my house. You know the rules. I don't talk about what happens here," Willow snaps. She's lithe, tall, blonde, and in her late forties now. I always wondered why she never remarried, and when I asked one day, she said there was no one else for her. She and her husband were soul mates, the kind who meet when they are young and plan their lives together.

"There was a man here, Butcher, burnt. Where is he?" I demand, trying to stay friendly. She's helped me a lot over the years, so I don't want to piss her off. Also, you should never annoy a woman who has access to drugs and scalpels.

"I did. I patched him up and sent him on his way," Willow replies, not backing down.

"Do you know who he was, Willow?" I ask, trying to be nice. She's still fragile after her husband's unexpected death.

"I didn't at first, but I'm a doctor, Bexley." She hesitates over the word. She doesn't practice at the hospital anymore. She was a big surgeon there, but after what happened, she couldn't do it. She had no idea the man she saved one night had been the one who'd mugged and shot her husband, and she couldn't live with it after. Now she takes care of us. "I help people. I don't ask what they've done, just like when you come here with bullet wounds."

Nodding, I relax. "I know that. I'm sorry, Willow. Let's go, he isn't here."

"Hellion," Kane begins.

"No. Willow is a friend. She won't be dragged into this. If he knows she spoke, he'll kill her. We're leaving now," I snap, and he nods in understanding. I won't endanger anyone on my path to revenge. I will find Butcher. He can't hide forever.

"Bexley." I turn, and she licks her lips. "I didn't know. I'm a doctor, but if I knew who he was to you . . . I'd have let him die slowly and painfully." She smiles. "A doctor has her ways, after all."

I know that too well.

We share a knowing look. I was the one who found the murderer after he'd been acquitted due to lack of evidence. I was the one who brought him here, gagged and bound him, and kept watch. I never asked what she did, but I heard his screams, and when she came out shaking and stripping off bloody gloves, I remained silent. I got rid of the body, and we've all protected her since.

"I don't know where he went, but he had five men with him. They spoke about the Sai brothers and a woman, which I'm guessing was you. Be careful. Men like him are dangerous, Bexley."

"So am I," I reply. "Stay safe, Willow."

"I never thanked you for what you did for me and my husband," she murmurs. "For protecting me after."

"You don't need to thank me. We have each other's back. You know that," I tell her.

"I do, and that's why I'm telling you this. He has a contact here, someone he was going to. I don't know who, but someone here has betrayed you. He'll be coming for you. You better get ready."

The words make my heart ache, but it makes sense. Someone is covering for him, and I have no idea who. "Then I'll be waiting." I kiss her cheek and take the same route out just in case they are watching.

Back in the car, Zayn looks at me. "What now?"

"We could chase rumors all over. He's hiding, but that won't last long. He wants us dead too much for that. She's right. He'll come for us, so let's allow him to." I smirk.

I can tell Kane is worried. He sent his father and brother away on a "vacation." His father was angry but accepted it after a lot of bribery. The guards are all on high alert, and everyone is strapped, even the Sai brothers.

I watch them as I recline on the couch, the fire burning in front of Kane, who is leaning against the mantel, talking on his phone. Neo is pacing as he looks at his screen, and even Zayn seems cold for a moment as he stares out of the window before blinking and bringing his gaze back to me.

Sighing, I throw my legs up and stretch out. "You're all way too tense. If this carries on, you'll give yourselves heart attacks before he even comes for us."

Neo glances at me and then Kane before texting. "Keep me posted," Kane says as he hangs up and turns to look at me. "And what do you suggest? We are preparing for an impending attack."

"Doesn't mean you can't have fun while you wait. He won't care about what you're doing. In fact, being stressed and tiring yourselves and your guards out is what he wants. He wants you to be afraid."

"I am not afraid," he snarls.

"Fine, he wants you to be worried," I correct with a roll of my eyes as I cross my legs. He watches the movement hungrily.

"Then what do you suggest we do?" Zayn asks, sounding uncharacteristically serious, which I don't like.

"Me." I grin, and the room falls into silence. "He could come tonight, tomorrow, or next month, but I know one thing for certain—I plan on coming tonight either way, so take your pants off. You can keep your guns if it makes you feel better."

"You're demanding sex?" Neo asks, a smile curling his lips.

"Might as well enjoy ourselves. Besides, a good fuck puts me in the mood for murder."

"What if we are attacked?" Kane asks, though he doesn't seem bothered. He slowly removes his suit jacket, folding it carefully over the edge of the chair before starting on his cufflinks.

"I can multitask. Can't you?" I flirt.

"Not when I'm deep inside you."

"I'll take that as a compliment," I purr as Kane starts to unbutton his shirt with deliberate care, and when I glance up, he's smirking, knowing exactly what he's doing to me.

"We can't have him beating us, brother, can we?" Zayn asks, and when I glance over at him, he rips his shirt off, making my eyes widen.

"Very true," Neo agrees, and when I drag my eyes from Zayn's inked chest to Neo, he is stroking his bare torso and wearing a smirk on his lips. Desire explodes through me. I was partially teasing, but I should have known better when it comes to the Sai brothers.

Kane steps up to their side so I can view all of them at once, his lips tilted in a cocky grin. "Lost for words, little hellion?"

When I don't respond, too busy gawking, he prowls my way, tipping my chin up with one finger. "Keep those pretty eyes on us. Tonight, we are going to show you what it means to be owned by the Sais, because we treasure and protect what is ours, and we also share."

He steps back and sits opposite me. His shirt is undone to expose his chest, and his pants are unbuttoned and zipped, but he leans back casually with one arm stretched across the back of the chair. "Show her what I mean, brothers."

The firelight sweeps over solid muscle and ink in a beautiful display of soft light, making my mouth dry and my cunt clench as Neo and Zayn head my way, prepared to attack.

I glance at Kane for a moment to see him watching, and I shudder at his hungry, possessive expression.

The Sai brothers are the most beautiful creatures I've ever laid eyes on—not that I would ever tell them that, since someone has to keep them humble—but for tonight, I'm going to pretend they are mine.

Who knows when Butcher will attack? When he does, we might die. I'm not afraid of death, but I would regret not having them again.

We have our own lives, so I'm not stupid enough to think we will work out in the long run. This is sex, nothing more. We have been thrown together and baptized by blood and betrayal, but when that is gone, there will be nothing tying us together, so for one night, I'm going to pretend.

Neo and Zayn reach for me, and I let them tug me to my knees on the carpet. They keep me facing Kane, even as I'm pushed forward and hands slide across my skin. I can't tell who is who, but I keep my eyes locked on their brother as they stroke every inch of me, except where I need to be touched. I grow impatient and shoot a glare over my shoulder.

"Eyes this way, hellion," Kane orders, and for some reason, I obey. When he nods, a mouth wraps around my pussy, licking and sucking. Then Neo's fingers slide inside me . . . which means Zayn's mouth is on me. Shivering, I push back to take more, wanting all of them like this. I'm theirs, and they are mine, and tonight, we are making sure we know it no matter what happens.

Before I can come, however, Neo and Zayn move away, leaving me whining, unsatisfied, and annoyed, and then a dick presses into me. It's only because of the piercing that I know it belongs to Zayn.

He fucks me shallowly as his and Neo's hands continue sliding across my skin. Two cup my breasts as another rubs my clit. A moan erupts from my lips and I press back, begging to be fucked harder, but then he pulls away again.

Snarling, I go to fight them, but Kane leans forward, his eyebrows raised. "Move and we stop."

I settle back down, planning to get my own back another night, but for now, I do as I'm told. As I'm lifted, I look down for a moment to find a hungry Neo below me, his hands gripping my sides, and then he's inside me. He buries himself deep and just waits, lifting his head and sucking on my skin. Zayn's hands stroke my sides and ass, and I know then what he's going to do.

"We are going to fill every hole," Kane explains as Zayn's wet cock presses against my ass. "Only when you're dripping and going crazy will you get me in your mouth." He nods at his brother, and Zayn slowly pushes into me. I try to relax, but he's big, and so is Neo who's already inside me. I'm stretched to the point of pain, so I try to wiggle away, but Neo's mouth presses to mine in a kiss. Hands stroke my pussy and body until I relax, and Zayn slowly rocks until he's buried deep inside me, and they both kiss and touch me until I'm the one moving. I feel so full, like I could burst, but each shift sends one of them rubbing against me in a way that has me crying into Neo's mouth and tearing away to pant. My eyes find Kane's again as they start to move—one pulling out, one pushing in.

They set a gradually growing pace until I writhe between them. The pleasure is more than I've ever felt. It overwhelms me, and they know it. They push me harder between them.

"So beautiful, baby," Neo whispers. "You feel so good."

"Does he feel good inside you with me?" Zayn asks darkly.

Their words send me spiraling toward that precipice, but it's the curve of Kane's lips that sends me over that edge. I scream, locking up between them.

They fuck me through my orgasm, using me, and I love the way that ache turns into nothing but pleasure. They set a pace like they could do this forever, and it drives me wild. I'm sweating, moaning, and dripping while they are almost too calm.

Kane watches his brothers fuck me like he doesn't have a care in the world, and my eyes stay locked on his as I come again. He drinks down my pleasure as he orchestrates us, but when I whisper his name and hold out my hand, he rises and comes to me, lowering to his knees before me.

The great Sai is bending to my will.

I reach for his dick, keeping my eyes on him as I suck him into my mouth. Kane grunts, weaving his hand in my hair as he forces me to take him all the way into my throat, and then he holds me there, his brothers stopping from some silent signal. They are all buried deep inside me. There isn't an inch of me that's unfucked or touched by them.

"Hellion," Kane whispers, "you're ours now."

I couldn't speak if I wanted to, and he knows it. He slips from my mouth then thrusts back in, easily matching his brothers' rhythm, which speeds up. I close my eyes and focus on the sensations.

Neo's lips on my skin.

Zayn's hands.

Kane's filthy, whispered words.

I let it flow through me and into them, and when I come this time, I drag them with me. Neo yells my name as he plunges so deep, it hurts, and explodes inside me, lashing me with hot cum. Zayn groans, fighting my tightening ass before filling me.

Only Kane holds out, but when I meet his eyes, his thrusts push into the back of my throat and he shoots his release there.

I must black out because when I come to, they are curled around me on the rug, all stroking my body and whispering sweet words.

I might have done this as a last hurrah, but for them, this was so much more.

I have a terrible feeling I'm never getting away from the Sai brothers, but that thought doesn't scare me as much as it used to.

43

BEXLEY

Three days later, I'm spray-painting Kane's bathroom when it finally happens. The bright pink paint drips down his perfect white walls, forming hearts, stars, snakes, juice boxes, and quotes. I can't wait for him to see it, but as soon as I feel it, I drop the can and turn. I'm eager for this to be over. I'm not the type to sit around and wait, so it's been hell.

Three days of being locked in the house with increasingly paranoid Sai brothers and their guards was enough to drive anyone crazy, so I'm almost gleeful when the house rocks from an explosion.

I have no idea what took Butcher so long, maybe he was licking his wounds or trying to wait us out so he could pick us off one by one, but it seems he's finally run out of patience.

Removing my gun from my holster, I grab one of my blades from my thighs. Like the brothers, I've taken to being armed at all hours of the day just in case. I refuse to be taken alive again by Butcher or let him win. It ends tonight. Lightning flashes outside the big windows as I kick off my shoes and pad silently across Kane's bedroom. Rain lashes the windows, making it hard to see outside as I open the door. I shouldn't have worried about being quiet, however, because I hear

285

coughing and yelling, then another explosion followed by gunfire. My heart races, and I want to throw myself over the railing to the three floors below and make sure they are okay, but I need to be smart about this. Being stupid gets you killed, and besides, they can look after themselves.

Peering out into the top floor hallway, I step over the threshold, carefully shutting the door, and head to the banister, where I look down. I can't see much, but I can hear fighting from up here. I know by now Zayn will have triggered his contact to keep the police and fire departments at bay for as long as possible to give us time to finish this without Butcher being spooked.

I turn off the safety on my pistol and head to the weapons' cache on the second floor. Dodge showed me all of them yesterday. They are planted all over the house.

I just reach the stairs when the giant, supposedly bulletproof glass of the arched window explodes inwards. Throwing myself backwards in a roll, I duck behind a potted plant and glance around, my gun lifted.

My heartbeat slows as my adrenaline centers me. When a man swings in through the window on a rope, I'm already firing. He drops dead onto the carpet, the rope hanging through the opening. When no one follows, I tiptoe closer and around the body to cut it loose. I hear more smashing and crashing downstairs, and I know they are probably doing it on every level. Kneeling next to the guy, I tug his mask off and check his pulse to ensure he's dead. He has no ID, the weapons he carries have no serial numbers, and his gear is tactical.

Mercs. They are paid muscle—good but not as good as I am. It means Butcher has more firepower and men than we thought. I need to get to that weapons' stash. I'm good in a fight, but you don't bring a knife or knuckles to a gun fight.

Ripping off my hoodie, I toss it down over the broken glass and hurry over, still crouched, then descend the stairs. Halfway down, I stop and aim. Two men in similar tactical gear are sweeping the hallway from the broken window they climbed through.

There's no point being quiet, since the gunfire will cover anything anyway, so I fire in rapid succession, and they are both dead before they can turn. Covering the distance between us, I check to make sure they are gone and then clear the floor as swiftly as I can. I find three more men toward the back of the house, and they meet the same fate before I head back to the main stairs, frowning at the glass everywhere. It's going to be a bitch to clean up, but it's also slowing me down. Glancing at one of the dead bodies, I check his feet before inspecting his friend. His are smaller, so I unlace his combat boots and try them on.

"Why are your feet so fucking big?" I hiss before sparing him a sad look. "You know what they say about big feet. What a shame you're an asshole . . . and dead. Sorry to all the future pussy you could have had." I slide his boots on, giving up on stealth. It's more important that I don't cut myself up and leave a blood trail.

Climbing back to my feet, I pick up my gun just as I feel one press to the back of my head. "Don't fucking move."

"Does that ever work?" I ask curiously before I drop my head to the left to avoid the shot of surprise he gets off, then I spin, sweeping out his legs. He goes down hard, and I clamber over him, sliding my knife into his eye. His scream echoes around the floor, and I wince as he thrashes.

"Oh my god, get it out!" he roars as he bucks, and I struggle with the slippery blade, trying to free it from his eye socket.

"I'm trying," I say as I twist the handle, the sound and sight making me gag as I try to get it free. "Shit, sorry, it's stuck." I keep twisting as he yells until he finally passes out, and when I get my weapon free, I look down. "Sorry about that." I pat his face before picking up his gun and standing above him. I shoot him three times in the chest then stare in awe at his semi-automatic.

"My precious," I whisper as I holster my pistol and keep his instead. Finders keepers. Swinging the strap over my shoulder, I head to the stash. The wall looks the same all the way down, but I move three steps from the painting and press my hand into the pot Dodge showed me. There's a light and then a click as the safe pops open. I stuff my pockets with knives and grenades, then I swing a shotgun over my shoulder before heading down the next set of stairs to the first floor.

Sparing a look outside, I see the Sais' men fighting more men, using cars for cover, but I leave them to it, knowing it's a distraction. They are trying to split our forces, which means Butcher will be here.

I don't have time to worry about Kane, Neo, and Zayn. I'm trusting them to hold their own as I stumble to a stop with a wince. Eight men turn to look at me where they were trooping toward the stairs to come up.

"Hey," I say slowly, trying to think of a way out of this that doesn't involve me looking like Swiss cheese. I'm too pretty to die that way. If I'm going to connect with the afterlife, then I want it to happen in some hilarious, grand way. "Funny story."

"That's the one, grab her!" someone commands.

Yeah, fuck that. Reaching into my pocket, I clutch a grenade, pull the pin, and throw it. I've always wanted to try one, and since I won't have to clean up the mess, I might as well.

The man at the front looks at the grenade that rolls between his feet and then me before he picks it up and throws it at me. Yelping, I catch it. "The fuck? Finders keepers!" I toss it back.

"Happy birthday," he responds and throws it to me.

Snarling, I deftly turn the gun around, grip the barrel like a bat, and swing it at the grenade. It flies through the air at them before exploding.

"Merry Christmas." I grin as the man groans on the floor. "I can't believe that shit worked." I gape down at the gun I just used as a bat before I swing it around and step over their bodies.

The gunfire suddenly stops on the first floor, and I hesitate before I hear Kane's voice, which brings some relief. "Stand down!" he yells.

I try to peer over into the foyer to see what is happening, but a crunch of glass has me spinning around to see a man sneaking up on me. By the time I turn, though, he's already throwing a knife.

Grabbing a metal serving tray from the table to my left, I yank it up just as the blade hits it. It stabs through the platter but saves my life, and the merc charges at me. Twisting the tray, I slam it over his head and then down onto his neck. The tip of the blade finds its home there.

He drops to the floor, and I crouch next to the plant and table and peer below to see what is happening. My heart stops when I get a good look. Neo, Zayn, and Kane are on their knees with guns against the backs of their heads from more mercs. Their guards are pressed against the wall with their hands above their heads.

Why did they surrender? The Sai brothers would rather fight to the death.

Butcher steps into my line of sight, and I have to bite back my snarl. My hand inches toward my gun when three bodies are thrown down, and I freeze in shock and horror.

Taylor, Lauren, and another woman.

Lauren is sobbing, curling into Taylor, who's glaring at Butcher defiantly. The left side of her face is swollen, her lip is bloody, and there is a gun to her head.

Kane glances up and sees me, shaking his head before looking away.

They surrendered to keep Taylor and Lauren safe.

"Where is she?" Butcher asks, and I glance back in time to see Neo's head jerk to the side from the backhand delivered with Butcher's gun.

"Little pet, come out, come out, wherever you are. I brought you some presents. Come and play!" he shouts, his arms wide open as if to present the scene to me. The left side of his face is completely covered in gauze, but I see burns extending across his skin, making half his face dip, and his left hand looks shaky and unusable.

He has my family down there, however, and when I don't respond, he chuckles and lifts Lauren. Taylor screams, reaching for her sister, and my heart explodes from my chest in fear. I always wanted to keep them safe from this part of my life so they could have a better one than me, but I failed. "Don't you touch her!" Taylor's head smacks against the floor from the force of a blow.

Lauren struggles and cries before spitting in Butcher's face. "My aunt is going to kill you."

"I see she's been training more little pets for me," he remarks as he gets into Lauren's face. "Did your aunt tell you I like them young? She was a lot prettier than you and a lot more important, but I think it might hurt her to watch me do to you what I did to her."

Bile claws at my throat, and I close my eyes for a moment. "Did you hear that, pet? You have ten seconds or this one here becomes your replacement. You did well trying to hide them from me, but you should know better. There are no secrets between us, and you can't have any family but me!"

He's going to kill them, and he will make it hurt, all to get to me.

Dropping my gun and some of my other weapons, I hesitate before I see it. I strip the rod from the plant, and then I stand and head downstairs with my hands out to my sides. I keep one knife partially on display and a few others hidden just because they would never believe I don't have weapons otherwise.

"No!" Zayn yells when he sees me before his head jerks back, his nose spraying blood when someone slams their gun into his face.

"Quiet," the merc orders.

Dragging my gaze from them, I look at Butcher as I step down into the foyer. There are bodies everywhere, but it's Taylor and Lauren I look at. Shame fills me as I fight to swallow my nausea when I see them surrounded by so much death. "Let her go."

"Of course." He drops Lauren, and Taylor yanks her back, her eyes wide as she stares at me. "I'm glad to see you, pet." His hand lifts self-consciously to his face. "I have some repayment to be made, don't you think? Why would you hide from me? You are mine!" he roars before laughing maniacally. "Come to me, pet."

Grinding my teeth, I start toward him, hearing the Sai brothers struggling, but I ignore them.

"Wait, wait. Check her for weapons." Butcher chuckles, wagging his finger at me like I'm a disobedient dog. "My pet has teeth."

Two men step forward, and my eyes narrow when I recognize one. "Really, Corey, you're on his payroll?" Now I know how he got around the streets and hid from me. Willow was right. One of our own betrayed us. Corey is a lowlife, but he was one of ours.

"Sorry, Karma," he mutters, not meeting my eyes. "I had no choice. I needed the money. I had no idea he would touch Taylor and Lauren."

Fury fills me. "They are innocents."

He meets my gaze, and before he can check me for weapons, I slide the knife down my arm and slice his throat. He falls back, gasping. I look at Butcher, ignoring all the guns now aimed at me. "He betrayed me, and as soon as he did, he signed his death warrant." I look at the other merc who was coming to check me for weapons. I turn the knife and hand it to him handle first. "You can check me now."

Butcher chuckles and claps his hands. "That's my little pet, always so bloodthirsty." He looks at Taylor stroking Lauren's head idly. "She wasn't always like this. She was so sweet once. She used to cry and beg me to protect her, but I broke her of that quickly, and now look at how magnificent she is."

"Don't touch her." Kane beats me to it, and Butcher turns his attention to them as I'm patted down.

Butcher's amusement swiftly turns to anger, and he crosses the floor and slams his fist into Kane's face. He sways, and Butcher does it again as Kane crumples to the side, spitting out blood as he gets back to his knees.

"You'll have to do better than that," he taunts.

"Butcher," I snap, regaining his attention. I eye the Sai brothers coolly, like they are nothing to me. "Don't play with the help."

Butcher stalks closer to me. "You were using them, weren't you? I knew I was right."

"Of course, why else would I be here? I needed bait." I shrug. "You can kill them if you want, but I'm tired of standing here."

I make my voice as cold and uncaring as I can. I hear some of the brothers' guards yell and struggle, thinking I've betrayed them, but if Butcher thinks I care, he'll torture and kill them. If he believes they are nothing to me, then he'll leave them alone long enough for them to get away.

"I knew it." He smiles brightly at me, and I notice he's acting more crazed than normal. Whatever sanity he held onto is long gone, which makes him infinitely more dangerous. "I knew my pet wouldn't slum it with the likes of them."

"She's clear, sir," the merc says as he steps away.

"Pat her down thoroughly, she likes to hide things." Butcher chuckles. The merc eyes me then checks me again, adding two more knives to the rapidly growing pile of weapons he found on me. He eyes me worriedly as it grows.

I remain silent, glancing at Taylor and Lauren to reassure them as I pull the wire forward in my mouth.

"Okay, now she's clear." Grabbing my neck, he throws me toward Butcher.

"My pet." Butcher pats my cheek before gripping my neck hard enough to cut off my air. "That wasn't very nice, leaving me in the fire." For a moment, I feel his need to kill me before he relaxes. "I'll make sure you understand the pain you caused me though. I have missed you, and even though you don't care for them, I think keeping you will hurt the Sai brothers. Two birds, one prisoner, you see. Come willingly and I'll leave those two alive." He nods at Taylor and Lauren. "They are nothing to me, but I know they mean something to you. That's why you sent them away, like you could save them from me. What do you say, pet? Want to come home?"

I aim a macabre grin at him, showing the wire there, and then I slash it across Butcher's throat. The only thing that saves his life is one of his men yanking him back.

His hand covers the thin cut, even as I try to hide my disappointment. I had one chance.

"You'll pay for that, pet." He turns to Taylor, and panic fills me.

"No!" I step in front of her. "I'll pay the price."

He looks at Taylor with fury etched into his features, and those long-hidden horrors I felt resurface. "You love her. Does she know how dangerous that is for her? Is she your family, pet? Does she know what happened to your last one?"

Closing my eyes, I swallow my pride as the past rears up to haunt me, the one I've never told anyone. "Please." The words are like glass. I told myself I would never beg this man for anything again, but when it comes to them, I'll do it. I'd rather be made a liar than lose them.

"Fine, fine, I won't harm her. Does she know?" he repeats gleefully, and when I don't answer, he laughs. He swings around to the Sai brothers, and I can't meet anyone's eyes, knowing he's going to do it just to hurt me. I tried to kill this when I killed him, but I guess there is no escaping blood. "Do you know who you kept under your roof? Shall I tell them, pet? Shall I tell them I wasn't the first person to break you? Shall I tell them how I saved you?"

He looks at Taylor. "You're scared of me, but you should be scared of her. Tell them, pet. Tell them who you really are and what you did."

I stay silent, horror clawing at me as the room spins, the past I buried deep ripping through me.

He laughs as he steps toward me, focused on my reaction. "Did she tell you that she killed her parents? I bet she didn't. Poor little thing never could accept she was to blame. I didn't kill them. She did. I found her later. She was so beautiful, covered in blood and tears, so little, breakable, and moldable. My little killer."

"Stop," I croak. I'm frozen to the spot like not moving might make the words go away.

"Isn't that what you used to beg your dear old daddy to do? Or your mom, who was too busy getting high to care what he did to you? How about when she handed you over to my men in payment for drugs? You still loved them, though, because little kids always love their parents. What set you off that night? I've always wondered. What made you finally snap?" I feel a tear leak from my eye, and he grins at my pain. "But she did snap," he yells, turning to look at the others. I don't look away from him. I can't. I can't meet their eyes as he spills my bitter truth for everyone to know. "Her daddy was a bigwig, even knew dear old Sai, but he liked to hurt his little girl, didn't he, Rebecca North?" I swallow at my real name, and I hear someone whisper. "That's right, the missing daughter of the great, mighty Norths. She changed her name to Bexley while she was in my care. I guess she wanted to forget. How is that working for you?" When I don't give him what he wants, he pulls his gun out and points it at Zayn. "Tell them what you did or he's dead."

Blinking quickly, I look at Zayn, who shakes his head slowly. He realizes what this will cost me, and he's telling me not to, but I can't let him die, so I tear open my soul. "I killed them," I whisper.

"Louder," Butcher yells happily.

"I killed them!" I shout, my fists clenched.

"How did you do it, pet?" he taunts.

"I took the gun from my father's holster when he was busy getting his pants off, and I shot him point blank. He looked surprised," I admit. It's an expression I've seen in my memory for years. He never thought I'd do anything to stop him. Like Butcher, he thought he had broken me.

"And your mother?" he asks, his eyes narrowed on me.

"She was waking up from her high when I came for her in the living room. She got my name out before I shot her."

"She did, and then her good old uncle swept in and saved her from me and them and raised her, framing me for their murders. I, of course, had to get revenge. All this bloodshed for one little girl who killed her mommy and daddy."

I say nothing as my world comes crumbling down around me. I feel like I did back then—terrified and broken. I'd been with my uncle for a little while. It was where I met Taylor for the first time and hoped I could have a normal life. Taylor asked what happened when I disappeared for years and came back, but I never told her the whole truth. I couldn't bear to see her lose the innocence in her eyes.

"Good," Kane spits and grins at me.

"I hope she made it hurt," Taylor adds, and my shoulders relax slightly.

They don't think I'm a monster. They still want me.

It's obviously not the reaction Butcher wants.

"And who am I, pet?" he demands. "You know, don't you? I thought you figured it out. Is that why you tried to kill me?"

"No, I—" He smacks me, and I tumble to the floor. I feel Lauren's hand slip into mine, and I look at her for a moment before raising my eyes to his.

"Say it! Say who I really am!" he roars.

"My half-brother." The words make me sick. I didn't know for a very long time.

"That's right." He crouches before me, tipping my chin up. "My dear little sister . . . Did you know that's why I came that night? I was going to kill them myself for what they did to me, sending me away, hiding me in the dark, only giving me some small piece of the drug business to run to keep me happy. I wanted more, and then I saw you . . . but then our uncle took you away. You! No one ever protected me like that. I was nothing to them, a mistake our father made. When I saw you and you didn't even know me, something in me snapped." He strokes my face. "My perfect little sister was pampered and given a better life, one I could never have." He squeezes my throat before relaxing. "But now it will be okay. We will reclaim what our family lost. You have already started on those streets of yours, and we will run it together." He kisses me softly, and I fight my gag.

No, no, no.

"But you can only have one family," he says to me as he looks at Taylor and Lauren. "There isn't room for anyone else. They are collateral, a weakness—" Standing, he pulls me with him. "Kill them both and hang them outside for everyone to see."

"No!" I yank myself from his arms, grab his gun, and aim at him, panic gripping my chest. "They are not collateral damage in your war, nor my weakness!" I scream as I step forward. For a moment, I'm back to being a kid on that quiet night, my hand shaking under the weight of my father's gun as I looked at him and said no more, but then I hear Taylor, Lauren, Kane, Neo, and Zayn all struggling to get to me, and I know I'm not alone. I'm not her anymore. I'm not Rebecca or even pet . . . . I'm Karma. "She is not collateral damage. She is my sister. She is my best friend. She is not a footnote in your rise to the top. She's the best part of my story, and you tried to take her from me."

"I am your family!" he roars.

"No, you're my nightmare, and do you know what they say about nightmares?" I ask slowly. "You have to slay them." I pull the trigger, but the gun clicks, and terror grips me.

Chuckling, he grabs it and tosses it away. "I knew you'd do that." Stepping around me, he pulls out a blade. I hear the Sais struggling now, but they are fighting a losing war.

Besides, this is my battle, not theirs.

Butcher knows he isn't making it out of here alive, but he's determined to take me and those I love with him. I can't let that happen. This is all my fault. If I killed him back then, no one would be hurt. It's my job to keep them safe and fix my mistakes.

He's my family, my responsibility.

I step into his way as he swings the knife toward Taylor, who is bent over, protecting Lauren. The blade finds its home in my side, and his eyes widen for a moment. His shock gives me the time I need to yank the blade free and slam it into his chest. "You're right." I feel blood pouring down my stomach. "We are tied together. I might die tonight, Butcher, but so will you, and the last thing you will see is me, knowing you lost."

I hear gunshots and Kane's, Neo's, and Zayn's voices, but I don't look away from Butcher.

"I killed our father. It makes sense that I kill his evil spawn as well," I sneer as I press the knife deeper before he rips away, my blood loss allowing him to stumble back. He presses his hand over the gaping wound. For a moment, fear fills his eyes and he glances around. I follow his gaze to Kane, Neo, and Zayn, who lead the charge with Dodge to kill the mercs. He's losing, and he knows it.

He looks back to me, then I see the second he makes his decision. He's going to run and hide and lick his wounds.

Fool me once, shame on you. Fool me twice, shame on me . . . but fool me three times? Well, it isn't going to happen. I'm going to eradicate our bloodline tonight.

He stumbles toward the door. Someone wraps something around my waist, and I hear frantic voices, but I'm watching Butcher hurry out of the open front door to a car haphazardly parked outside. He throws one of his own from the vehicle and stumbles inside.

Not again.

He's not getting away again.

"Keep them safe!" I yell, trusting the Sai brothers as I dive outside after him. My bike is to the right, where I was doing donuts this morning on the grass. I sprint toward it and climb on, quickly firing it up, shoving my helmet down, and shooting out onto the street.

I hear my name screamed, but I don't look back.

This ends tonight.

44

BEXLEY

He's trying to outrun me, but I'm faster, and he doesn't even realize that I'm chasing him where I want to—far from my family and into my streets. He's right, this is my town, but he was wrong about one thing.

I'm not alone with him, and there can only be one of us. We rush across junctions that are mostly empty this late, running red lights. I don't know where he thinks he's driving to, but he's like a cockroach, so if he leaves, he'll be back. I can't let that happen.

Swerving through the line of cars at the next road, I pull up at his side but have to fall in behind him when an oncoming truck honks. He manages to slip ahead, and I snarl, ignoring the warmth in my clothes from my blood as weakness starts to spread through my body. It's a deep wound, which means I don't have much time.

As if reading my thoughts, the light turns red ahead. He either doesn't care or doesn't notice and speeds through the four-way intersection.

I watch his car jerk and spin, the crunch loud as an SUV plows into its side. The light was green on its end. Driving around the crash, I look into the driver's seat as Butcher climbs out, clutching his chest as he stumbles away. I leave my bike and take off after him. He's fast despite his wound, but I catch up with him around the corner and tackle him. His elbow catches my injury, and I grunt in agony, but I'm used to pain. I grab the gun he was reaching for and stand, swaying as I taste my blood in my mouth.

"On your knees," I order.

He slowly kneels, his hands at his side as he eyes me. The world is dark around us, but I recognize the familiar small park where I brought Lauren. It's deserted now, which is good.

He looks up at me, bleeding and pathetic. "Pet—" I cock the revolver, and he gulps. "Sister, we're family."

"We aren't family. We are enemies, and my enemies do not live." I shoot. I don't need his pleas. I don't need anything but his death.

I watch a hole appear in his head. He sways on his knees for a moment before falling back. The gun drops from my hand, and I step forward, my legs buckling. Looking down, I see blood soaking through my shirt and all the way down my jeans.

That isn't good. He must have done more damage with his elbow. Crawling closer to Butcher, I check his pulse, needing to be sure this time, but there's nothing, and the right side of his face is a bloody, mutilated mess.

He's dead.

He's really dead this time.

Crumbling over his body, I look up at the night sky as everything becomes floaty. My body is cold, and I feel weaker than I ever have. Not even the satisfaction of victory is enough to stop me from falling to my back. I can't feel my arms and legs anymore now that adrenaline is leaving me. I know that's not a good sign, since that's what kept me going, but it pumped more blood from my wound.

I'm dying, but my family is safe and Butcher is gone. It's almost a relief.

All these years of fighting just to survive are over, and at least the people I love have a chance. I'm finally free of the nightmares that have scarred me since I was a girl.

I must miss some time because when I blink, I hear sirens in the distance and the roar of engines. When I blink again, Kane's worried face is above me.

"I've got you, hellion," he says softly, sliding his hands under me and lifting. A scream of agony tears from me, and his eyes tighten. "I know, baby. I know. I'm sorry." He's running. When I blink again, I'm upside down, or maybe that's Neo's face. Rolling my eyes down, I find Zayn at my feet, and Kane is kneeling next to me, his hands holding something against my stomach.

Shouldn't that hurt?

"You're okay," I croak.

"We're fine," Neo promises, "and you will be as well."

"Step on it," Zayn yells. "She's losing too much blood."

"Taylor . . . Lauren?" I ask, my voice weak even to me.

"Fine, Dodge has them. They are safe," Kane assures me as he lifts his bloody hand, takes mine, and kisses it. "Just hold on, hellion. We are getting you help."

"You're going to be fine, Bex," Neo says, leaning down to kiss me. I try to turn away, not wanting to get my dirt on him since Butcher kissed me, but he turns my head back and kisses me forcefully.

"Don't you dare give up," Zayn snaps. "You hear me, Bexley? You're too fucking strong to die, so don't you dare. Taylor needs you. Lauren needs you . . . . I need you."

"Knew you liked me . . . ," I try to tease, but it comes out as a whine of pain.

"Nah, I just like annoying you," he responds, but when I meet his eyes, they are glassy with tears. "I need you, *cariño*."

"We all need you," Neo murmurs, stroking my face, "so don't you dare leave us yet. Your contract isn't finished."

"I think . . . I think I might not be able to complete this one."

"Like hell you won't," Kane snarls, angrier than I've ever heard him. "You're going to be fine."

"It's okay," I murmur, shutting my eyes. My eyelids are just too heavy to keep open. Nothing hurts anymore, which is nice. "He's dead. Everyone is safe. It's okay if I go now."

"No, it isn't." The pressure on my stomach registers, and I

whimper as pain splinters through the numbness and keeps me tied to this body. "This world needs you, Karma, so fight."

"I'm tired," I admit.

"Just fight one more time," Neo pleas, "and then we will fight for you for the rest of your life. One more fight, Bex. What do you say?"

"Hellion, don't be so fucking weak. Are you really going to let us win?" My eyes narrow in annoyance as I fight not to fall asleep, and Kane smirks. "That's my girl, not long now."

I must miss time again because when I come to, I'm being carried by Neo, with Kane and Zayn in front of me, and I realize why. There's a crowd, a mob, with masks on. They have guns, bats, and every weapon you can imagine. It's a familiar area, but I can't figure out why, and then a whisper goes up.

"It's Karma!"

The crowd suddenly parts, creating a passage that we take hesitantly. I see familiar faces as hands reach for me, pushing us forward, and then I see Reacher.

"My girl," he murmurs. "Go. We've got this. His men won't get to you."

His men? I can't think. It's too hard. When I come to again, I'm staring at a bright light, and then Willow's face is above me, streaked with blood. "There she is. Bexley, I had to manually start your heart. Stay with us, okay? I need to stop the blood and give you a transfusion."

"Willow?" I try to move, but hands are on me. I turn my head to find Kane, Neo, and Zayn at my side.

"She was the closest person. She's going to save you," Kane promises.

"Say with us, baby," Neo begs, and I try to nod, but everything goes black as their frantic voices fill the air.

"Her heart is failing again. She's lost too much blood. Get in here!" Willow shouts, but it's the brothers' voices that chase me into oblivion.

Three familiar, loving voices all call out to me, but even they aren't enough to save me this time.

45

KANE

S he looks so little on the metal table. Bexley has such a big personality that sometimes I forget how small she really is, but right now, she looks tiny. Willow and her assistant cut her clothes away, so now she's in a gown under a blanket. Machines beep at her side.

We could take her to a hospital, but no one would take better care of her. Besides, we have a situation outside, so it's best not to move her. Willow said she's lucky to be alive. She nicked her liver, but Willow managed to patch her back up. Her heart stopped a few times, but the doctor got it restarted, and Bexley is looking a little better with blood and whatever else Willow is giving her. She's still unconscious, but I watch the rhythm of her heart on the monitor without blinking.

"There was fluid in her lungs. I had to drain it," Willow explains softly. "She's a strong motherfucker. Anyone else would have died, but not our Bexley," she mutters as she checks the monitors and then the IVs. "She'll be out for a while, which is probably good. She needs to rest. It's all up to her now."

Nodding, I keep hold of her hand and brush some hair from her face. "Hear that, hellion? It is up to you. I know you can do it. Come back to us. We are all here, waiting."

"Brother," Neo murmurs, but I ignore him. I even ignore my ringing phone. I know by now the police will be there. With that much destruction and that many bodies, not even Dodge could hide it before they arrived, but nothing matters right now other than Bexley.

"Kane," Zayn murmurs.

"No," I snap, not looking at them. "Not right now. I'm not Kane or Sai or the leader. I'm just a man who's in love with this woman and is terrified of losing her, okay?" I look at my brothers, drowning in grief and panic, and they crowd around me.

"Lean on us," Neo says.

"We've got this," Zayn assures me as we look at her.

"She'll wake up, won't she?" I ask out loud.

"Bexley? Of course. She wouldn't let us win like that. Our girl is petty." I smile, knowing Zayn is right.

There's a bang outside, and we all jump, pulling our guns out, but when it comes again, I realize there's someone at the door.

"I got this. You stay with her," Zayn orders. Usually, that would ruffle my feathers, but right now, I'm lost. I can't be who they need me to be, so I let him take over and sit with Neo in front of our girl.

Nobody will hurt her again. We'll make sure of it.

Zayn

Stepping outside, I raise my eyebrows at the crowd gathered there. A plump, older, oil-stained man barges through with Reacher at his side. "How is our girl?"

"She's resting. Willow thinks she will be okay, but she needs as much sleep as she can get," I admit, the words pulled from a place deep inside me. The fear I felt the moment I saw that blade go in . . . it didn't compare to the terror I experienced when I saw her collapse and knew I would be too slow to catch her.

That's the issue with loving a woman like Bexley. She's so strong and determined that we can't stand in her way, but watching her suffer while protecting everyone else is worse than her hatred would be if I had.

"Don't worry, we'll make sure no one disturbs you," Reacher says. I don't know if I believe him, because rows of police cars line the streets. The officers hesitate beyond the mob, even if they know they need to talk to us. I have no idea how they found us, but it doesn't matter. They aren't taking any of us from her or her from us.

Pulling my phone out, I shoot off some texts and nod at Reacher and the other man. "You'll have backup who will talk to the police. I've also called in some favors. Their forces will be split with some fires, hostage situations, and robberies spreading across the city to distract them."

"Smart." The other man nods. "But get back in there with her and keep her safe. We'll protect her from here." He hesitates, looking at me. "Did she do it? Did she finally get her closure?"

"She killed him." I have no idea who this man is, but I can see the love he has for her in his eyes, and that's enough for me. All these people are here for her because of who she is to them. We control people with money and fear, but she controls them with love without even realizing it. Every single person here is ready to use themselves as a human shield to protect her from the law.

She was right. These are her streets. She bled to protect them, and now they will do the same.

I want to help, but I'm antsy about being away from her for so long. I need to see her, touch her, and know she's okay. She looked so small and broken in the back of the car, and even now, my hands are speckled with her blood. I know I will never forget the way her heart stopped, because mine stopped with it.

What started as a game and then a contract between us is so much more. Bexley stole my heart, just like she stole my brothers', whether she wants it or not, and now I don't want to live without her.

I can't.

"Good, that's my girl." He nods at Reacher. "Let's give them the time they need."

I slip back inside and head toward Bexley like a magnet. My hand seeks hers, gripping her callused palm, and I kiss it softly. Kane holds her other hand, while Neo paces by her head. He's tense and furious, but I see his fear and how he softens every time he looks at her. Kane tugs her blankets up, fussing over her comfort.

"Police are here. No idea how they found us—"

"There are videos online," Neo snaps. "I'm getting them taken down as we speak. They are at the house too. Dodge is dealing with it. I called in our other lawyers. Hope that's okay."

I shrug. "She's all that matters," I say as I kiss her hand again. "The mob is creating a blockade. They'll have to fight their way through if they want to get to us. Right now, that need doesn't outweigh the risk. They'll need backup, and they won't have any. Their numbers will be spread thin when my contacts are through with the city. The police can't get through to get to us," I tell my brothers. "Every single person in the area is flooding the street in front of the house. The authorities will need to remove them all to take us from her."

I press her hand against my face and close my eyes, absorbing her warmth. "You hear that, baby? Everyone is here to protect you, so you don't have to worry. You just have to rest. Let us be strong for you for once."

She doesn't answer, of course, and I reach up and brush some of her hair aside, hating that she doesn't open her eyes and glare at me. I would do anything to fight her right now, anything for her sass and spitting words.

Bexley is larger than life, has been since we first met her, but even queens fall, and these kings will make sure she finds her way back home.

"At least she's finally free," Neo says. "Maybe now she can move on and be happy."

The thought makes my heart clench. She's spent her life running from her nightmares and fighting to free herself of their grip. Will she let herself be happy now? Will she settle down as much as a person like her can, and if she does, will it be with us?

I don't know, but I do know she'll fight us tooth and nail along the way, and I can't wait. She's worth it. If she would give us a chance, my brothers and I would spend the rest of our lives sheltering her and making her as happy as possible. We don't want to clip her wings. We just want to be along for the ride.

"She's not going to make it easy when she wakes up," I admit out loud. "She's going to fight to get away from us. You saw her in that house and how his words broke her apart. She's going to run from us. She thinks she's better alone, thinks she doesn't deserve love."

"She won't make it easy," Neo agrees. "But then again, we've never done anything the easy way. We'll just show her that we aren't going anywhere."

I look at Kane, but it's like he doesn't hear us. Kane Sai has no weakness, or he didn't until her. I'm not even sure if she is a weakness, more like a strength, but for him? He would destroy everything he carefully built just for her to look at him again.

He was joking when he brought her home, or so we all thought, but he wasn't. It was a plot to tie her to us and keep her. He knew if we all loved her that we would do anything to make her stay. That manipulative bastard made sure we had time to crave and love her like he does so he doesn't have to let her go.

It should make me mad, but if anything, it just makes me smile. My brother always does what is best for the family, and he was right. She is what is best for us. She is the only person who could ever make us whole and love us.

No, she won't make it easy, but if she thinks she could ever escape us, then she's a bigger fool than we are. We control this city, and there isn't a place she could hide from us.

Kane says nothing, which surprises me. He's usually so in control. By now, he'd be barking orders and controlling the situation, but he doesn't seem to care. Instead, he rests his head on her chest and closes his eyes as he listens to her heart, his fingers seeming to tap the beat on his thigh, a habit from his piano days. I know he's haunted by the fact that it stopped before.

I've never seen Kane like this. Even at the worst times, he's calm, but right now, he's anything but. He looks . . . human. My infallible brother is scared, which is something I've never seen, and when I share a look with Neo, I know he sees it too, so we step up and take over. Kane has spent his entire life protecting us, and now it's our turn.

Pulling my phone, I start through the texts there. The first one isn't a surprise. Oliver and his sister are gone, it turns out the woman Butcher brought along was the one Oliver was searching for and in the madness after the fight they have disappeared. I hesitate, should I ask them to search for them? However, when I glance back at Bexley, I decide to let them go to live their lives, just like we are hoping to do.

Neo

"Where's my sister?" comes a yell, and then the door bursts open. Taylor pushes me out of the way, ordering, "Move, asshole." When she reaches Bexley's side, a choked sob leaves her throat. "Bex," she whispers, "what did they do to you?"

I have no idea how she got through the mob, but judging by the furious look in her frantic eyes, they probably simply got out of her way. Like Bexley, Taylor can be terrifying when she wants to be, and there's nothing scarier than a woman when it comes to her family.

"She's going to be okay," I say as softly as I can. I check my texts to find that Dodge sent some guards with her, and Lauren is with him at the house. I breathe out a sigh of relief. They are Bexley's family, and right now, we have to protect them, even if she turns those furious eyes to us.

"This is all your fault!" Taylor shouts, and we let her. Poking my chest, she backs me toward the wall. I look down at the pint-sized woman and raise a brow. "She never should have gotten involved with you. She was fine, and now look at her!" Some of her bravado fails when she glances back at Bexley, but she shakes it off and turns her angry gaze back to me. I let her because I see her fear and grief, and she's taking it out on anyone she can.

"Yeah, back away, pretty boy. I'll fucking end you."

"Your sister is scarier," I respond truthfully.

Her scream of anger is impressive, and her fist swings up. She has control and power, but she lacks speed.

Catching her hand before she touches my face and hurts herself, I gently squeeze it before I let it go. "Bex will have my head if you hurt yourself trying to hit me."

"She taught me how to fight," Taylor hisses.

"No doubt," I reply. "But if you have a single scratch on you, she will cut me to pieces, so please, let's not go there. If you still want to scream at me, maybe we can go outside so we don't disturb her rest."

"Don't you try to control me, you oversized, walking, talking penis!" she yells, throwing her hands up as she sweeps her gaze across the room to encompass us all. "You're supposed to be so scary and powerful, but look at her! You didn't protect her!" Her chest heaves, and none of us deny her accusations. She's right. We failed her. It won't happen again. Tears bloom in her eyes. "She sent me away to protect me, and she could have died." Taylor wraps her arms around herself for a moment, and I look at Zayn for help. The only crazy woman I know how to deal with is Bexley. I don't think what I do to her to calm her down would help Taylor. She wouldn't enjoy fighting me or sparring it out.

"Taylor," Zayn begins, holding up his hands like he's talking to a wild animal, "she is going to be okay. Be mad at us, that's fine—"

"Don't you tell me what I can and can't do. All men like you are good for is what's between your legs."

"Your sister agrees, though she quite likes my mouth too," I add, and her glare turns to me as I grin.

"Not helping." Zayn sighs, being surprisingly serious while I'm being more like him. "Taylor." Her attention refocuses on him. "Would you like me to hit my brother for you? He's right. If you do it and Bexley finds out you hurt yourself on his stupid face, she'll kill us.

While we enjoy the special brand of torture our baby gives us, she's in no shape for it at the moment."

"Our baby?" Her eyes narrow. "Our baby? Did you touch my sister?"

"Many times," he answers truthfully. "We love her."

Taylor freezes, her eyes blowing wide.

"It's true," I admit. "We're in love with her. Look at him." I jerk my head at Kane, and she follows my gaze. "You've undoubtedly seen him before on the news. Look at how broken he is. We know we failed Bexley, but we won't ever again. We love her for who she is and everything that means. We couldn't stand in the way of her choices, nor would we ever do that, but we should have protected her back better, and we will from now on. You can hate us, but please don't try to push us away from her. You won't like what happens if you try to take the woman we love from us."

Her eyes narrow at the very clear threat in my voice. "Bexley doesn't do love," she snaps. "She does sex. That's it."

"Maybe, but it doesn't stop us from loving her." I need to change my approach. It's obvious Taylor's opinion will be important. If we can win her over, then Bexley won't stand a chance, so I try to force a smile, but it must come across as terrifying because she steps back before turning away.

"Of course she'd get three mad dogs to follow her home," she mutters, then she seems to remember her anger and collects herself. "You're missing the point. This is your fault," she hisses, turning her finger toward us as she seems to amp herself back up. "She was safe, she was okay, but then you got her involved in all of this—"

They say sisters are alike. I know Taylor and Bexley aren't biologically related, but her rant would suggest otherwise.

Oh yes, Taylor is certainly someone we need to win over.

46

BEXLEY

I don't know what death is supposed to be like, but I recall nothing until my eyes open again. What woke me up?

Then I hear a familiar voice.

"I'll fucking kill you all for what you put her through! She was safe all these years, and then you got involved—"

Turning my head, I watch Taylor scream at three pale-faced Sai brothers who make no move to stop the tiny five-foot woman pacing before them. "She's all I have, and look where she is because of you!"

"You're always so loud," I mutter, and she spins, her jaw dropping when she sees me. All her anger dissipates, and she rushes to my side. Tears slide down her face and she sniffles, snot dripping from her nose. "I was so scared. Don't you dare do that to me again." She smacks my arm. "You just fucking let him stab you! Then you left!" I let her rant, knowing she needs to get it out. She's fine, and I breathe a sigh of relief then look at the brothers. They are frozen with their eyes on me, and their bodies are tense, as if they are ready to pounce on me at any moment, but from the haunted looks in their eyes, I know they feel the same as Taylor.

Wincing, I look down to see I am covered in heaps of blankets and in Willow's operating room. "Huh, so I didn't die," I scoff, and Taylor smacks me.

"You weren't even listening to me!" she shouts hysterically.

"Babe, you were talking in a pitch only dogs could hear," I tease, and her eyes narrow. "I'm hurt, be nice."

"Whose fault is that for getting stabbed?" She shakes her head, dropping into a chair next to me. "Is it over?"

"It's over," I promise as I take her hand. "Lauren?"

"She's fine. A hottie with a serious mean face offered to show her their toy room, and she went with him, the traitor." I look at the brothers, and Kane nods.

"Dodge?" I guess, and she nods.

"Who names their kid Dodge? What is he, a movement or a car?" she mutters before shaking it off. "We are all fine."

"How did he get you?" I ask, needing to know. I can't bring myself to say his name, and I lower my eyes, not wanting to look into hers or theirs.

"Some men found us. Shelly said the guy who betrayed you from down the road was a client of hers a long time ago and knew about the house. She fought, but they overpowered her. She was fine when we left, just out cold. I'm sorry. I tried to fight and keep Lauren safe—"

"Shh, you did well. You stayed alive, and that's all that matters. Sometimes it's better not to fight," I tell her, and her eyes soften, having seen too much. Glancing down, I try to pull my hand away, feeling filthy now that they all know. The room shrinks as panic grips me. They know. They all know, and now I'll be soiled to them.

"You heard him." It slips out, and the room falls silent. "I didn't tell you. I couldn't bear to. I couldn't even think about it. My own brother. He was my brother, and he—" Shaking my head, I close my eyes and look away, feeling disgusted with myself.

He planned to make me rule at his side, to break me and keep me with him. All this time, it was my fault.

Her tightening hand makes my eyes snap to her. "You listen to me, Bexley, you stupid bitch. You are my sister, not his. I don't give a shit about what he said or did. You are Bexley, our Bexley." She hiccups.

"It doesn't matter, do you hear me? We are your family, but if you try to die on us again, I swear to fucking God, I will find some voodoo priestess to bring you back, and then I'll kill you myself."

"Then you'd have to clean up the mess instead of me," I tease, and she smacks me, tears sliding down her cheeks, but she smiles.

"I'd bribe Lauren." She holds my hand tighter. "I don't want you to ever look like that again, okay? Nothing else matters. We're family."

"But what he did—" I whisper.

"Doesn't matter," Kane interrupts, and I stare at Taylor, unable to look at him even though I felt him round the bed. Reaching down softly, he tilts my chin up until I meet his eyes. "You survived so much, hellion. Do you know how proud of you I am? I can't take it away, but I will never let anyone hurt you again. None of us will. Your sister is right. Nothing else matters. You are our Bexley. It's that simple."

"Besides," Zayn adds, but his eyes are sad and relieved, "you're too stubborn to let him win, and if you keep thinking like that, then he will."

"Stop the fucking pity party." Neo's harsh words snap my attention to him. "You're alive, we're alive, and that is all that matters. Who are you to sit there, moping and feeling sorry for yourself?"

"I will kill you," Taylor growls, but I cocoon myself with his words and the harsh truth.

"Fuck him," he continues. "You're alive, and he isn't. That's all that matters. Are you really going to lie here, feeling sorry for yourself, and let him win? If you do, you're not the person we thought you were."

"That's it—" I keep Taylor seated as I smile at him.

"You're right," I admit as I take a deep breath and let the panic pass. They aren't treating me differently, they are still here, and they are right. If I let these feelings take root once more, then Butcher wins. I'm too petty to let that happen. "I don't suppose you have any good drugs, though, because my body hurts like a son of a bitch."

"No more drugs," Willow interrupts, and I look at her as she sweeps into the room. "Sorry, but I don't want to keep you dosed up forever. I needed to know you were okay. I gave you some ketamine."

"Ah, the floaty drugs. That shit was good," I joke, and she grins as she checks my vitals. "So, am I going to die, doc?"

"Nah, seems you're too stubborn for that." She pats my hand. "You should know they didn't leave your side. Hell, I even saw them crying. Some tough bastards they are."

"Crying, really?" I grin as her eyes sparkle. "That I can use."

"Thought you could." She looks around then back to me. "I don't want you moving yet. Rest."

"The bodies—" I start, looking at Kane.

"Shh, we will deal with everything. You heard the doctor. You need to rest, nothing more. Besides, hellion, who do you think you're talking to? You don't think we can cover up a little mass murder? Please."

As he speaks, I see some life return to his eyes, and it makes me relax. They really were worried. I panic for a moment at what that means, but he's right. I'm tired, and before I know it, sleep claims me, taking me away from any concerns of bodies and men who may or may not love me.

A horrifying thought, even more so than the dead.

Two days later, I am still bed bound by Taylor and the Sai brothers. They fuss over me and argue with me when I start to get annoyed.

I'm over it.

"I got stabbed, not torn apart by dogs. People get stabbed all the time."

"I don't care," Zayn snaps, crossing his arms. He's playing the bad guy this time since I argued with Kane and Neo all morning. I managed a pretty good shot with a bedpan they tried to make me use, and his cheek is red. "You're staying here."

"I'm going home," I snarl. "Move or I'll stab you too."

"Go for it." He shrugs. "We have a doctor here."

"Sai," I snap.

"Bexley," he teases.

"Enough, children," Willow says. "One more day and you can go home on bed rest. I mean it—bed rest. I'll check on you every day."

"She'll be with us. I can send the address," Kane begins.

"Like fuck I will be," I scoff, trying to sit up. Neo and Kane pin me down. Taylor is watching, chewing on a sandwich. She seems to find this way too amusing. Traitor. I don't know when they started wearing her down, but she's almost . . . civil toward them. Maybe it's the fact that they bought Lauren so many toys, we'll need a new house, or the bodyguard or the new car and protection on our house. It seems the Sais aren't above bribery. I have no idea why they are trying so hard to win her over, but I don't like it.

"You will, so we can keep an eye on you," Kane demands before sighing. "Please, hellion."

"No," I growl, eyes narrowed. "I'm going home. I need my own bed and house. Besides, our contract is complete. It's done."

"We aren't done," he warns. "You're running away from us."

"I'm not running anywhere," I taunt. "Besides, I only run from zombies. I'm just going home. We had a contract, and it's finished. We have no reason to be near each other."

"No reason?" Neo mutters, but I sense his hurt. I try not to let it get to me. It's for the best. "Seriously?"

"None," I add, the word feeling like a lie.

"Bexley, we lo—" I throw the cup near my head, hitting Neo in the face and bruising his nose before he can say the words. They've been hovering around since I woke up. If they say the L-word, then every-thing will change, and I can't deal with that.

We were just having fun. That's all.

"This is better than TV," Taylor remarks, and I glare at her. "Alright, boys, it's clear Bexley is coming home with me." She holds up her hand. "How about we compromise? You help us get her home, and I'll update you on how she is whenever you want to know, and you can visit."

"Like hell they will!" The idea of the three Sai brothers in my tiny bedroom is enough to break me out in hives. There would be no escape, which is exactly what they want. I started this with them because I wanted them, but it's obvious they have no intention of letting me go.

They were serious when they said I was theirs.

I don't run, but a bitch can walk away fast when faced with these three idiots.

"No, she will come with us—" And so the arguments begin. It goes on like this for hours. The police were finally allowed through, and they took our statements. I played dumb, using my wound to say I didn't remember anything, and since the bodies mysteriously disappeared from the morgue, they have no case, so they left. I have no idea what they did with the mercs and Butcher, and honestly, I don't fucking care.

It's over, and I'm going home.

Everything will go back to the way it was . . . but the thought almost makes me sad.

47

BEXLEY

It's been two weeks since I came home. I rested for another week before I started to go crazy from Taylor and Lauren's fussing. I love them, but if they tried to sponge bathe me one more time, I was going to stab myself just to get away from them. I just want everything to go back to normal.

The police left us alone, and the streets are like nothing happened. I'm free to be who I was before, yet as I climb onto my bike, I hesitate. Was my life always this . . . lonely?

I miss them. I miss attacking them and winding them up. I miss their arms and laughter. I shouldn't, it was just sex, but this stupid thing in my chest won't listen to me.

I might have to carve out the traitorous organ.

I know they have been talking to Taylor every day, and she almost seems to like them now. I have no idea how they managed that, but I don't ask, and I don't answer when they text or call. If I do, I will be dragged back to all that. No, it's better this way. They have too many enemies, and I have too many issues.

I don't belong in their world, no matter what we want.

Shoving my helmet on, I turn the engine over and pull onto the road, speeding up to outrun my wicked thoughts. I need a good fight, which always cheers me up, but everyone is being so careful with me. I finally got Reacher to tell me that the Sai brothers put out word that if they saw me sparring or fighting, they would come after whoever it was. The pricks. They are taking all my fun away. What am I supposed to do without murder and mayhem?

My stomach aches as I turn the corner, careful of my stitches. I'm still healing, and if I don't want any complications, then I need to be careful. Willow comes to see me every day, and I don't want her to get angry with me, so I slow the bike. I'm still over the speed limit, but at least I'm not pulling my side anymore.

When I pull up at Reacher's, I glance back just in time for a black SUV to pull into the lot and park. My eyes narrow as Dodge gets out and opens the back door. Kane slips out and leans against the passenger side. His phone is in his hand, but his eyes are only for me.

What the fuck is he doing here?

I expect him to say something or come after me, but he just watches, even when I go inside and talk with Reacher. When I come out, he's still there, and when I climb onto my bike to head home, the SUV follows me the entire way.

It's like I'm being hunted.

Over the next few days, I see them everywhere I go. They either don't care that I can see them or they just gave up being discreet.

The Sai brothers are stalking me. Usually, I enjoy a bit of light stalking, but it's starting to piss me off—mainly because they look so good while they do it.

I glare from under my sunglasses as Neo waves, leaning against a familiar black Mercedes parked across the road from the shop I was in, grabbing food for our girls' night tonight. This morning, I saw Zayn in the gym I warmed up in, and he winked. Last night, I looked out of my window and saw Kane sitting outside my house. He pointed back to bed and blew me a kiss.

They are insane.

I try my best to ignore them as I climb back on my bike, hoping they will get bored and leave me alone. By the time I'm home and the movie is on, I can't stop thinking about them.

"They are crazy," I grumble, and Taylor looks at me in question. "Those Sai assholes are stalking me."

"Of course they are." She shrugs. "Have been since you got back. You just didn't see them."

"Idiots. What do they think will happen? They need to take a hint and go back to their lives."

She sighs, focusing on the movie.

"What's that noise for?" I ask.

"I love you, Bexley," she says as she mutes the TV, "but you weren't having any fun until you met them. I saw the way you were with them. You enjoyed fighting with them, enjoyed their company. You looked happy. You have protected Lauren and me for years, and you've earned enough so we can have the life we want. You've fought so hard to be someone people can depend on, but you were never happy. I'm not saying you didn't have days where you were, but under it all, you weren't. You were sad and lonely and scared. When I saw you with them, you weren't. Did you even notice that you still look around, and when you see them, you relax? Stop being an idiot and accept it."

"You hate them," I mutter, ignoring her other comments.

"They are . . . okay. If anyone was going to put up with your crazy ass, it would have to be someone as batshit as you. They are, and they are obviously serious."

"They bribed you." I narrow my eyes, feeling both pride and annoyance.

"Maybe. The gifts were nice, but honestly, all the money in the world wouldn't matter if you didn't love them, but you do. You can fight it all you want, but I know you, Bex, better than anyone, and you miss them. Stop being so stubborn. The world won't fall apart if you allow yourself to love them." She pats my hand. "We're not kids anymore. You don't have to take on the world for us. It's time to move on and make a new life. I want you to be loved. I want you to be with someone who can stand at your side."

"I have you," I grumble.

"You do, but it's not the same. I can't walk by your side, Bexley.

I'm not the same as you, but they are. They know all of you, and yet they are still here. That means something. Trust me, no one else would put up with your reckless ass. Besides, they are rich, and there are three of them. When they annoy you, you can simply kill one and still have the rest."

I smile then admit, "I'm scared. I don't know how to . . . love or let someone love me. My parents didn't, Butcher . . . I'm broken, Tay. That part of me is broken. It scares me how deeply they want me."

"Because you're worried they'll leave one day and you'll be alone all over again," she surmises, and I turn my head to her. "You aren't so mysterious and hard to read. No one can predict the future, Bexley, so stop hesitating because of what-ifs. Besides, you'll never be alone. You'll always have us."

"They love the fantasy of me, not me."

"No? Because they are still here after everything. They love you. Give them a chance. They might surprise you. It's time to stop being so scared, Bex. It's time to be as brave with love as you are with every other part of your life. Being alone is fine if that's what you want, and you did before them, which is why I never pushed it, but you don't want to be now. I see you searching for them every day. You might not be ready to admit it, but you love them. Stop living for everyone else. Live for yourself now. Be happy. That's all we want."

"They are overgrown brats, rich, and stuck-up. They are insane and think they are the best—"

"Sounds like someone I know," she interrupts.

"They are killers, mafia leaders—"

"Then be theirs," she teases. "Keep them in line. Stop finding excuses. You don't need to find reasons why you want them around. You don't have to justify how you feel, Bexley, not even to me."

"Taylor is right," Lauren says, looking at me seriously. "I like them. They are good for you. Now either kill them so they stop scaring my friends when they come over or get it on with them. Either way, decide, and let's finish this movie before I have to finish my homework."

"Kids," Taylor grumbles.

"She never changes," I mutter, but I hit play, and she settles in. Taylor's hand covers mine, and I look at her, seeing her smile softly.

"We want you to be happy. Figure out if they make you feel that way. Figure out if they are worth the risk. Give yourself a chance." She focuses on the movie, and I glance out of the front window to see all three of them watching us. It's eleven at night and freezing, yet they stand there like they would wait forever.

Would they?

Are they serious about me?

And is Taylor right? Do I care for them? Even the thought sends a shudder of dread down my spine, but I have to admit I miss them.

Someone fucking kill me now, I think I might have fallen for the brothers.

The horror.

48

NEO

The front door opens, and I sit up, my heart racing when I get my first look at my girl today. She looks good enough to fucking eat, but I check her for any signs of pain. She still isn't okay after her wound. She walks fine, and she isn't pale, so I relax and check her out before my eyebrows rise. She wears a gray skirt that reaches mid-thigh, with two buckles across the right hip. Her usual black boots fit her legs perfectly, and her top is an oversized sweater. Bexley's hair is loose, and her makeup is more dramatic than normal. She looks like she's going all out.

Something is different today. Usually, she's trying to outrun us and looks annoyed, but today, she appears happy. There is a mischievous glint in her eyes when she glances at my car as she heads to her bike.

She has been ignoring the new one we bought her a week ago. Hers is scratched up from her chase with Butcher, but she doesn't care. Now, though, she hesitates before she walks to the new one and climbs on, making me sit up as she starts it, letting it purr to life.

My chest clenches. Does this mean something? I think it does.

Lifting my phone, I hit dial. "Get here now." I hang up and leave them to figure out where I'm going. I start the engine in my new lime-green Porsche that matches her new bike and pull out after her. She doesn't speed too much, apparently going slow for me to keep up. She's usually trying to outrun us.

Is she luring us into a trap to kill us? Maybe, but I still go willingly.

It's the most attention she's paid us in two weeks, and I'll take it. My patience has been wearing thin. I miss her too much to keep this up forever, even if we have a plan.

By the time we pull into the aquarium, the others are with me. Kane parks his car to my left, and Zayn pulls into a spot to my right. We get out as she looks back at us before heading to the ticket kiosk.

"What's going on?" Kane asks.

"Not a clue."

"It's a trap. She's probably going to feed us to sharks," Zayn supplies. "Let's go." He hurries toward the kiosk, so we follow.

"Three adults," I say, craning my neck to look around and see her inside, even as I speak.

"Here." The bored kid slides three tickets over then stamps our hands as we reach for them. "Head inside. Have a nice day exploring our oceans," he recites boredly.

"We didn't pay." I frown, pulling out my wallet.

"The hottie before you did. She said, and I quote, "There are three mean-looking assholes coming after me. Don't worry, I'll keep them in line. Give them their tickets."" He shouts, "Next," and we have no choice but to move on. We share a worried look and walk inside.

She bought us tickets. It's definitely a trap.

I've never been so excited. My steps speed up as we head past the photographers. "Do you want a picture with a seal?" they call after us, but we ignore them as we step through the automatic doors, the air conditioner hitting us. There are kids screaming and running around, with frazzled parents chasing them, but we are on the lookout for a familiar black head of hair.

"Split up and text when you find her," Kane orders, going left to the Arctic exhibit. I go right to the tropics, and Zayn heads outside. I've never been before, but Tommy always asks to go. It's busy as hell, but once I'm inside the winding exhibit, the brightly colored fish and jellies make me stop for a moment before I remember why I'm here.

I find her in the next section. She's in front of a giant tank, staring at some iridescent jellyfish. There's no one around her as she stands with her hand on the tank, her neck craned back. She looks so beautiful that my feet carry me to her before I remember and swerve to a fish tank instead.

Neo: Found her.

I shoot off the text and location, and then I watch her. My brothers join me not long after. She doesn't seem to be in a rush as she wanders through, reading the information and looking at the fish and animals.

We stay one tank away at all times, standing before it like we are looking, but in fact we are watching her, no matter how amazing the animals are.

She takes her time at each exhibit. "Where is the trap?" Zayn whispers. "It has to be around here somewhere."

A kid bumps into us, and Kane tries to sidestep him, but the little brat narrows his eyes and kicks Kane in the knee. "Move, old man."

"Old man? You little brat. Where are your parents? I'm going to teach them manners." I watch my brother argue with the child, who sticks his tongue out before running away. Hiding my smile, I look up and realize she's gone.

Fuck.

I race forward and finally find her outside, looking at otters and seals. Breathing a sigh of relief, I walk around with my brothers so I can stare at her across the way. She has to know we are here, but she studiously ignores us like we aren't. That or she's biding her time. Who knows with her, but Zayn is right. I'm excited.

When she's finished wandering around an hour later, she heads to the gift shop, picking things up and putting them back down. I glance back and find Kane and Zayn have a basket overflowing with items. "She obviously liked them, so we are buying them for her."

"Bribery won't work on her. She's too smart for it," I remind them. "Though, she might be impressed that you are trying."

Kane simply shrugs, and when we get to the cashier, we have eight overflowing baskets. I end up paying because they are right. It can't hurt. When we get outside, she's sitting astride her bike on her phone, so we dash to our cars and follow as she puts on her helmet and pulls out into the busy, midday traffic. She typically weaves through traffic and speeds to avoid us, but she's currently driving leisurely. The slow pace only amps up my anticipation that she's up to something. Maybe I should be scared, but if anything, I'm eager.

Even if it's a trap to kill us, I'd thrive under her attention.

The next place she stops is even more surprising than the first—a multistory cinema. By the time we get inside, thanks to Kane parking his car way at the back, she's holding a tub of popcorn, heading past the barriers to the screens. Hopping over the ropes, we skip the line. Kane goes to the servers while I yank out my wallet and throw some bills at the people grumbling unhappily at us for cutting.

When I join Kane, he hands me a ticket. "Three tickets waiting again like last time."

"Definitely a trap," I mutter, especially when I see the film title and realize it's the new zombie horror movie. She'll probably wait until we are focused on the movie before she slits our throats.

How romantic.

"Here." Kane hands over a stack of bills. "Rent out the entire theater. I don't want anyone in there but us."

He's obviously thinking the same thing I am and reducing the risk . . . or he doesn't want anyone to see him get scared since he hates horror movies. Holding my ticket, I turn back as Zayn whines, "I want popcorn."

"Fine." Smashing down more bills, Kane grumbles. "Give him the largest bucket you have, and a drink too or he'll whine more."

Goods in hand, we find the screen and head down the dark ramp. The advertisements are already starting, and she's sitting a few rows back from the front. Her boots are kicked up on the seat in front of her as she munches on her popcorn. We take three seats directly behind her a few rows back.

Despite the film playing, I watch her the entire time, noticing her small pout about halfway through when she finishes her popcorn. I'm on my feet before I know it, ignoring my brothers as I return to the concession stand and get what I need.

I sneak back in and wait. A few moments later, the now five-hundred-dollars-richer server brings her more popcorn, a drink, chocolate, and a hotdog. She doesn't seem confused, but she does eat it.

Zayn chuckles. "Really?"

"Bribery." I shrug. "Like you said, it's worth a shot, and the only way to that woman's heart is family, money, or food."

"Don't forget weapons," Kane adds, covering his eyes with his fingers. "Why couldn't she pick something else to watch?"

"Maybe she likes seeing you squirm," I tease as I shove a fistful of popcorn in my mouth. I wait for her to make her move the entire movie, but she doesn't do anything, and when it's over, she collects her trash and leaves, getting back on her bike.

What is happening?

I can tell my brothers are equally as confused, but once again, we follow her. This time, she parks outside of an Italian restaurant downtown. It's within an old steamworks building and covers three floors. It's a trendy new place in an up-and-coming area—I know because I've been trying to convince my brothers to come here for weeks. Their burgers look incredible.

She heads inside like she doesn't have a care in the world, so we park our cars and follow.

"I think we should talk to her," I suggest as I step into the dimly lit interior. The mix of brickwork, modern, and old works for the place. It's filled with tables on different levels and down wooden stairs, and it has a homey vibe.

"She might still be mad," Zayn cautions.

"I think we should anyway."

"Let's see what she does first," Zayn suggests.

"No, he's right. She's leading us around for something. Come on."

A bright, bubbly male server pops up in front of us. "Sai brothers?"

"Um, yes?" I reply.

"This way to your table." Blinking at his back, we have no choice but to follow. We wind through the partially filled restaurant then up a wide staircase to a smaller dining area where booths line the walls, looking out at the bay. What surprises me most, however, is that he leads us directly to a booth where Bexley sits. She wears a smirk on her lips as we hesitate at the end. When the server leaves, I finally slide in. My exit is blocked, which is why Kane hesitated, but honestly, I don't care. I'm across from her, and it's the closest we've been in weeks. Zayn slides in next with Kane taking the end.

"I heard you mention this place once." She nods at me. "Figured you might like it."

"Are you going to poison us?" Zayn asks, but he doesn't seem upset by the idea.

"Not today. Besides, if I was going to kill you, I would make it more spectacular than that." She shrugs.

"Okay." Splaying my hands on the table, I lean forward, and she looks at me, capturing me and not letting go. "What's going on?"

"What do you mean?" she asks too innocently, and that's when I notice her eyelashes. They are tinged pink toward the outside, like her hair. The effect leaves me speechless, and she arches a brow. "Problem?" she purrs.

"You're too beautiful," I whisper.

"Yes, I know, now back to your question," she taunts.

"What's going on? You knew we were following you at the aquarium, the movie, and now here."

"I wanted to watch the movie," Zayn says, and she grins like he said the right thing. "Wait, I think I told you about it coming out and how I wanted to go with you."

Her grin widens.

"I mentioned I used to go to the aquarium all the time with my mother," Kane says slowly. "All these places . . . are for us?"

"Like a last meal before you kill us?" I grin, unable to help it.

"More like a date," she replies just as the server arrives. We stare in shocked silence as she orders, and we scramble to do the same. When he leaves again, I lean forward.

"A . . . date. Today was a date with all three of us?"

"Yup." She leans forward and sucks on the straw in her drink. For a moment, I get caught up looking at her lips, and she grins.

"Hellion, most people ask someone on a date," Kane says.

"I'm not most people," she responds.

"So that means you're not ignoring us and pushing us away. You took us on a date," Zayn concludes, sounding happy.

"I might go back to ignoring you. I haven't decided yet, but I might be considering giving you a chance, hence the date."

"A date," Kane repeats, shaking his head. "Only you would date us like this."

Sighing, she pulls her phone out and turns it to us.

"See? I even took pictures like it's a real date." She turns her phone around, scrolling through the photos. She's posing at the front, grinning, and we are in the background. There's one of Kane arguing with the child at the aquarium, us pretending to look at the fish, one of us standing opposite her across the seal exhibit, and another with us behind her at the movie.

"I didn't even see you take these," I admit.

"I'm sneaky." She shrugs.

"Hellion," Kane states seriously, "don't do this if you don't mean it. You know how we feel about you. We've made it very clear. All three of us are in love with you and want to be with you. You can't play with us when it suits you then drop us."

"We'd let you," I admit, and Zayn nods.

"But it would hurt," Kane finishes. "So what is this?"

"Maybe I've decided to give you a chance," she repeats. "I'm not saying it will last forever or will even work out, but maybe you're right. Maybe I don't want to go back to being nothing. Maybe I like spending time with you and playing with you. I won't say . . . that L-word you seem to throw at me a lot, but I like all of you. It just took me some time to realize it. I hate myself for it, but there you go, so I'm here. Isn't that enough? Or is it too late?"

"We'd wait a lifetime for you," I reply seriously. She is the only one for us.

"We were waiting for you to come back through that door yourself. I would have let you go if that's what you wanted. We never wanted to take your choices away from you. We wanted you to choose us, choose this. We can be patient, but now that you have walked back through this door, we aren't letting you go again," Kane warns her.

She swallows hard, looking between us before shaking off the serious thought, her lips tilting in a cunning smile. "What if I'm only with you for your money?"

"I don't care as long as you're with me," Kane responds, and my brother stares dreamily at her, so happy he's almost bursting with joy.

"You hate gold diggers," she retorts, looking between us. I simply grin, letting Kane handle this, so does Zayn.

"I could never hate you. Here." He hands over a stack of cards. "The pin is your birthday. Buy anything you want, it's yours."

"What if I want an island?" she jokes, no doubt testing him, or maybe she really wants an island. It's hard to tell with Bexley.

"Then buy it." He shrugs. "I have enough money to take care of you for a million lifetimes, and even if you somehow manage to spend it all, I can always earn more."

"And if that isn't enough . . ." I hand over my wallet, and Zayn does the same. "Take our money. We don't give a shit, baby. All we care about is that you stay with us. No contracts, no games, just us."

"You know, you're all a lot cheesier than I expected," she says, looking at the wallets, which she pockets. "I expected the big scary Sai brothers to fuck me and then drop me as fast as you could, yet here you are, chasing after me. Your father was right. You're romantics."

"You've been speaking to our father?" Zayn asks curiously.

"Hedging my bets. I want a sugar daddy," she teases. "He kept telling me how you were all moping and how I should come back and kick or fuck your asses because if he had to deal with one more sad-eyed 'I miss her at breakfast,' he was going to murder someone."

"We did miss you," I tell her as the food arrives. I won't be ashamed of moping around. The house was empty without her. Zayn's always enjoyed life, but even he seemed tired without her, and Kane? He's always so serious, yet she brought him laughter. She's good for us, but it's more than that. She fits with us, and I'll do whatever it takes to tie her to us for life. While Kane and Zayn were bribing her sister, I was being smarter.

Grabbing my phone, I turn it around and show her the document. "This was my backup plan in case you took too long to come back to us." She scans it, her eyebrow rising.

"Is this a lawsuit against me?" she asks dangerously.

"For services rendered." I smirk.

"You claim I blackmailed you, harassed you, and injured you? This is ridiculous," she scoffs. "You know I would never pay damages for that."

"Exactly. Read the settlement."

She does, and her eyes light up. "If the defendant is unable to pay back the Sai family, she can work off her debt by living with them."

I expect anger, but she bursts into laughter, pride in her eyes. "I'm impressed," she admits. "Smart boys get rewards. I like it when you play dirty."

"That would never stick in court." Zayn chuckles.

"I didn't need it to, just kick up enough fuss to get her attention." I wink as I take my phone back. "Can you send me the pictures from today? I want to change my lockscreen."

Grabbing my phone, she turns it, takes a picture, and hands it back. I can't look away. She is so fucking cute. Her fingers are pressed to her cheek in a peace sign as she blows a kiss. Hunching around the phone, I grin down at it as I set it as my lock and phone screen, then I go one further and log into my work socials and upload it there. I don't have a personal one. Zayn does, but Kane and I felt like it was asking for trouble, but I still want the whole world to know I'm hers.

"What about mine?" Zayn grouses, handing her his phone.

She rolls her eyes once more. "You know, you're making my eyes roll a lot on this date, and not in the way you should be, like into the back of my head."

I choke on my drink as she continues eating innocently.

"This is quite tame for you. I expected gladiators or death," Kane remarks as I continue to choke and splutter. Zayn hits me on the back a couple of times.

"That comes later." She shrugs. "Besides, I wanted to show you I care." She shudders in horror. "And if you ever repeat this, I'll cut out your tongues and stuff them into a dildo."

"I'd gladly welcome it," I rasp, taking a drink to soothe my sore throat.

The rest of our meal is uneventful and so fucking amazing, I don't want it to end. She talks with us just like before, making Kane light up with laughter. Zayn and Bexley lean together mischievously, and when she grins at me, including me, it's like my world is whole again.

The burger is really good. She demolishes hers and then finishes mine as well, and when it comes to the bill, Kane puts his card down.

"I'm not against you using your own money, but not when you're with us," he says as the server goes to run it.

"You're so sweet. That's why I like you, and because you're filthy rich."

"Mainly the sweet thing though, right?" I ask with a grin.

"Sure, let's go with that," she says, patting my cheek condescendingly as she gets up. We hurry after her, Kane grabbing his card, and once we're outside, he heads to her bike.

Do I ask when our next date is? Do I follow her home? I have no idea, other than I don't want to watch her walk away from me again

"Now for the final part." She grins at us, oblivious to our worries. "If you catch me, you can have me. I'm a lady like that." She's straddling her bike, and the engine roars to life.

"I think our girl forgets who we are," I say.

Zayn chuckles as he twirls his keys.

"I agree. Let's remind her, shall we?" Kane suggests as he heads to his car.

49

BEXLEY

The bastards are not playing fair. I can't help but laugh as I come to another road closure. It's clear they've been calling in favors across the city. So far, I've run into three police blockades, four private ones, and two closures. They are trying to corral me. I can't see them behind me or even hear their cars, but I know it's what they are doing.

Three against one. The only problem is, they don't seem to notice it's exactly what I want. I have to make them work for it, but I want them as badly as they want me. I want them to catch me, but it doesn't mean I'll make it easy.

Spinning my bike in a cloud of smoke, I shoot down an alley meant for pedestrians and cross the next street. Cars honk as I intersect their paths and drive into the next alley, which stretches horizontally from my original street that would take me to the highway.

Once I'm five blocks over, the road is open, and I speed toward the highway, but when I get to the on-ramp, I see it's completely blocked and closed.

Lifting my visor, I laugh at the LED sign with four men in high visibility vests blocking the road.

TRY AGAIN, HELLION.

Pulling my visor down, I turn once more and head the opposite way toward home, but the streets are once more closed.

The rich pricks have shut down the entire city just to get me. Fuck, I love rich men who know what they want. My pussy clenches at the foreplay, knowing I have no chance of getting away. I'm going to do the opposite and secretly give them what they want.

Speeding up, I drive straight to their house, avoiding any major roads where they'll be watching. I have no doubt they are tracking my bike, so once I'm two blocks over, I hide it in someone's driveway, cut through back gardens, and slip into theirs. Taking a running jump, I scale the wall and roll onto the balcony. I startle a guard there and grin, lifting my finger to my lips.

He smiles and nods. Most of them now answer to me, thanks to Kane's orders. Strolling into their house like I own it, I open the door to the dining room, pour myself a drink, plant my ass on the dining table, and wait.

It doesn't take long. I hear them storm into the house. They know I'm in the area, but they have no idea where. They are good, but I'm better.

I can hear their frantic voices as they make calls, searching for me. Chuckling, I lean back on the dining table—the very same one I once perched on after our first meeting. So much has changed since then, it's insane. I'm shivering with anticipation, just like then, but unlike before, I want their attention, not their lives.

The door finally opens, and they freeze. Déjà vu hits me for a moment as I lift my glass and cross my legs. It's clear I surprised them.

"Technically, I caught you," I brag as I raise the glass and take a sip. I expect arguments or teasing, but my eyes widen in surprise when Kane prowls toward me. I could get away, but I don't want to, and when he knocks the glass out of my hand and yanks me to him, I groan.

Our lips crash together as we sprawl down on the table.

Hands grab my wrists, and I'm pulled up and away. My eyes open, and I look from side to side to see Neo and Zayn as they slide me to the head of the table. Kane is already seated there. They pin my hands to the wooden surface as Kane slides a knife down the front of my clothing. It's so sharp, it doesn't even catch the fabric, and the pieces fall away, leaving me naked and shivering under their greedy, watchful gazes.

Neo and Zayn hand my wrists over to Kane as the table rocks. I look between the two brothers as they climb onto the table on either side of me. Neo takes my mouth, kissing me hard and fast, while Zayn starts at my feet. He kisses and licks my foot and then up my legs, skipping my pussy before kissing my chest, then my mouth. Neo moves away and down, and he takes his place, kissing me hard. The change makes my head spin, but this time, Neo stops at my breasts, sucking until I cry into Zayn's mouth. Neo continues down, licking my stomach then lapping at my cunt as I arch up. Zayn's mouth breaks away, and he moves down, playing with my breasts while Neo's mouth expertly tastes me.

My head falls back, and I roll my eyes up to see Kane holding my wrists above my head. I'm sprawled across their dining table like a feast, with Neo between my legs, doing just that.

He keeps my eyes prisoner as his brother's tongue circles my clit at a maddening pace that he knows will get me off. I toss my legs over his shoulders without looking away as Zayn tortures my breasts. Both of them drive me toward my release, all that anticipation only helping them along until I cry out, coming all over Neo's mouth. He doesn't linger, sliding up my body. Zayn moves closer, licking my cunt as Neo kisses me, letting me taste myself on him.

They don't give me time to think, just keep me needy and high until my hips are lifted and Zayn pushes into me. I scream into Neo's mouth as I grip Kane's hands, holding on as Zayn fucks me, the table rocking from the force.

Neo pulls away as I bite his lip, and then his cock brushes against my mouth. His hand grips my chin as he glares at me. "No teeth, baby," he warns. "You wanted this."

Too fucking right, I did. I open my mouth, and he smirks, slipping past my lips. Within seconds, he matches his brother's pace until he fucks my mouth in the same rhythm.

My wrists are freed, but Neo keeps me pinned, my face pressed to the wood as he drives into my mouth. Zayn's piercing hits a spot that has me whimpering, and then something hot and hard touches my hand.

Kane wraps my hand around his length and jerks himself with it. All of them touch and caress me, using me for their pleasure.

"Share, brother," Kane orders, and Neo pops free of my mouth and turns me to Kane, who surges in. My cheeks hurt from the force as he fucks my throat hard and fast before I'm turned again. I'm dizzy from being passed between them, and when Zayn pinches my clit, I scream as I come.

Luckily, whoever is in my mouth pulls out so I don't bite them, and once I relax, they carry on. Their grunts are loud, and the table rocks. Someone groans, and I feel their release shoot down my throat. It's only then I notice my eyes are closed. I peel them open to see Neo fall away before Kane jerks my head around, forcing himself into Neo's place. The brutal pace makes my neck and face hurt, but in the best way, and the magic Zayn is working between my thighs makes this pleasurable rather than painful.

When I feel him swell between my lips, I open my mouth, and when he comes, it overflows onto my chest as he strokes my throat, making me swallow the rest, and then he takes my hand again. Neo grabs my other hand as my head bangs back onto the table so I can see Zayn. He smirks like he's been waiting for it then surges into me so deep, I realize he was holding back.

He fucks me ruthlessly until I'm coming off the table, screaming his name with a hoarse throat as he drives me into another orgasm. I claw at their hands as they restrain me. When he roars his own release and I come again, I slump.

Every inch of me aches in the best way as I pant. Zayn covers me with his body as his brothers hold my hands, and I stare at the ceiling when a thought crosses my mind.

"We need to clean this before your dad eats here."

They laugh, and my lips quirk as I settle into their hands and touch. As long as they don't stop, I don't care.

59

ZAYN

When my eyes open, I roll over and sigh as I burrow into warmth before freezing when I feel all the hard muscle. Sitting up, I glare down at Neo, who is snoring, his arm thrown over his face. Kane is behind me, facing the windows. The space between us where Bexley was is empty, and I panic. Falling from the bed, I ignore their groans. She clearly wore them out.

I stride naked down the corridor, shouting her name. Our guards simply chuckle. I hear a few yelps as maids turn away, but they point farther down, so I continue.

I end up in the kitchen, sliding on the tiles and grabbing the door-frame to stop my fall when I find her. She's making a mug of something. When she turns, surprise fills her eyes as she takes in my naked body and heaving chest.

"Zayn?"

"I thought you left," I exclaim as I stare at her.

"No, I was hungry," she replies.

I thought she ran again.

Covering the distance in four steps, I scoop her up and put her on the counter as I press my forehead to hers. "Don't do that again. I woke up and you were gone."

"Zayn," she whispers, sliding her hands down my bare back to give me comfort. "I'm not going anywhere. Once I make up my mind, I never change it. You know that. I'm all in this now, until you annoy me, and then I'll simply kill you."

"Of course." I sigh, pressing my head to her shoulder and letting my heart calm down. She lets me take a moment before smacking my ass.

"Okay, enough cuddling. Feed me," she orders.

"Not yet," I murmur as I kiss her. Her eyes stay on mine, wide before narrowing as she bites my lip. I hiss as I pull away.

"I'm hungry," she mutters.

"So am I." I slide my hands up her thighs, and she shivers under my touch. I love her reaction to me, and she knows it, her smile turning cocky as she leans back so my hands slide higher.

"Well, we can't have that, can we?" she teases, playing with the edges of one of our stolen shirts and raising it until she shows me there's nothing underneath.

I tighten my hold on her thighs. "You walked around like this? What if someone saw?"

"I don't care—"

"I do," I snap, interrupting her, and her eyes widen as I open the shirt, her nipples tightening in the air as I press my nails into her bare thighs. "If you let anyone else see you like this, I will kill each and every one of them. Do you understand me, *cariño*?"

"Possessive much?" She laughs, trying to redirect our conversation, but I narrow my eyes and pull her forward so she tumbles into my chest.

"I mean it." My voice is cold, and I expect her to be scared, but I should have known better. She simply smiles and leans into me, sliding her hand down my body so she can cup my hard dick.

"I can see that," she murmurs. "You're hot when you're angry. I should piss you off more often."

"Try it," I growl, fighting not to thrust into her fingers, but then she releases me and lies back across the counter, parting her legs and showing me heaven.

"Weren't you hungry?" She cups her pussy with her hand and strokes herself, moaning loudly for my benefit.

My muscles shake with the need to knock her hands away and take over, but I'm not letting her off that easily. Her lips purse in a pout. Never one to lose, she reaches up and strokes her glistening fingers across my lips. My tongue darts out, tasting her, and all my fury morphs into desire until I fall upon her like a starving man, making her laugh in victory. I no longer care because I get what I want. I bury my tongue in her tight cunt, and her laughter changes to cries of pleasure as I thrust it in and out until she comes all over my face, then I drag her down and thrust into her. She's still tight, even after her orgasm, and she cries out as she arches up for more. Bending down, I lap one of her rosy nipples into my mouth, suckling until she bucks below me, taking me deeper. Her sharp claws drag down my back before she bites my shoulder, leaving marks I'll proudly wear. Still, I don't relent, fucking her hard and fast. I slap one palm to the counter, the other on her hip to lift her into a better angle.

Her pussy drips down my length as I twist my hips and slide my hand between us, slapping her clit. She cries out, but I don't yield. Bexley comes again, but I don't stop. I push her higher, knowing she can take more.

Her chest is red and her eyes are wild as she meets my thrusts, begging for more. Her moans are loud and unchecked, and I know everyone will hear what we are doing.

Good. Let them know who she belongs to, so the next time she walks around like this, they won't look.

"Zayn!" she screams, gripping her perfect breasts. The sight causes my balls to draw up. I fight off my pleasure, but it drips down my spine, demanding to be felt, and when she cries out again, I'm lost. I yell my release, dragging her with me until she's coming again, even as I pump my cum deep inside her pretty cunt. I want it to drip from her while we eat breakfast.

Slumping into her, I kiss her heaving chest as I recover. When my legs feel stable enough to hold me up, I straighten and carefully button her shirt as she watches me with amusement. Her soft expression is my undoing, and all my jealousy dissipates.

"Now feed me," she demands breathlessly.

"Gladly." I steal a quick kiss and step away.

That's how my brothers find me ten minutes later, in nothing but a frilly apron as I cook breakfast for our girl. They say nothing, but their amusement is evident. Kane kisses her before he sits at the table, while Neo simply lifts her, sets her on his lap, and goes back to sleep, his head buried in her shoulder.

"We have some meetings today, hellion. Will you be here when we are done?" Kane asks casually, but I can tell he's anything but. This is new territory for us, and we are trying our best not to give her orders or control her, but we all want her here at all times, just like before.

"I have to work today," she says, "but if I finish at a normal time, I'll come after."

"You should just move in," I interject. "Our house is big enough. Bring Taylor and Lauren, then we don't have to spend time apart."

"I like my house," she scoffs, "and my streets."

"Then we'll move in with you," I reply as I plate breakfast and sit opposite her.

"Like fuck you will. I agreed to date you, not marry you."

"Same thing," I reason as I prop my head on my hand. "You'll figure it out eventually."

"Crazy, all of you," she grumbles, but she starts to eat. "Look, I plan to have my own life. We'll find a middle ground, but don't push it too much."

"Not yet," Kane agrees, "but one day, you'll wear our family ring, so you might as well accept it."

"I will still stab you," she warns, pointing a fork at us.

"Wouldn't be the first time." Kane winks, covering the knife with his hand. "And we both know I enjoyed it. Go ahead, hellion."

"And everyone says I'm crazy." She drops her knife and fork. "I'm off to work."

"Enjoy hunting," I call with a wave.

She flips me off but kisses my cheek. "Enjoy being warlords," she responds before she walks out of the door.

I watch her go until Neo, who woke when Bexley got up, glares at me. "Did you not cook us breakfast?"

"Make your own," I scoff, stealing some scraps from my girl's plate. "She is the only one I'll cook for."

"Favoritism," he grumbles. "Fine, I have court anyway. See you later."

Kane watches him go and then glances at the mess on the counters then me. "Clean up your mess. Don't let the cook see her ass print on his counter."

Laughing, I slap his shoulder as I get up. "You're just jealous, old man."

"Damn right I am. I want her for breakfast too. You're right. We need her to move in."

"Baby steps," I caution as I grab the cleaning spray. "She'll move in eventually. We just have to make her think it's her idea. Don't worry, brother. I have a plan."

"That's what worries me."

51

BEXLEY

I need a hunt to distract me from them. They are overwhelming me, and if I'm not careful, they will smash through all my walls and take over my life. I don't plan to let that happen. I'm still Karma. I still have a job and responsibilities. I won't be their trophy, and they accept that, which I'm glad for.

A man came to me last week, said he was out of options and heard from a friend that when everyone else failed, I would be there. The whispers on the streets told him that. When you're out of options and desperate, come to me. All it took was one look at his dead eyes to know he needed me, and when he told me why, I immediately got to work.

Research was key for this one, as was planning. This isn't just a rival gang member or a theft, this is so much more, and I want to give this man the justice he deserves. Leaning into my bike, I glance down at the picture on my phone then back at the man. It's definitely him. I followed him a few times last week to get his schedule down. The idiot sticks to it like it's written in stone—gym, breakfast, then home and work.

Starting my bike, I squeeze into traffic a few cars down from his imported British car and follow him home. When he pulls into the fancy gated driveway of his big house, I park down the street and wait to give him enough time to get inside.

I could take him away and do it elsewhere, but I want them to find him here. I want them to see what happens when the law fails.

Five minutes later, I stroll down the driveway to his front door and ring the bell. Not a minute later, he answers, still sweating from his workout. He's in his late forties with graying hair. I would have considered him attractive if I didn't know what he was. He's in a suit in all the photos of him online, which as a CEO of a major pharmaceutical company makes sense. They've had him at home recently since the case was leaked online to contain the bad press, but he smiles when he sees me like he doesn't have a care in the world, and that annoys me more.

"Delivery?" he asks in confusion, looking me up and down.

"Of a sort." I grin before I slam my fist into his face. He stumbles back with a shout, his nose broken. I step over his body and kick the door shut as I grab the neck of his shirt and drag him down the hallway to his sitting room.

His wife isn't here right now. She's on a spiritual retreat in Cabo—more like to get away from it all. There's no way that woman didn't know what she married, yet she stayed, protecting a monster like him. She'll get her own justice, I made sure of that, but he's my victim today, not her or the others who failed everyone.

His shock finally gives way when I throw him into an armchair. Pulling my bag around, I grab ropes as he recovers and goes to tackle me. We hit the floor, and I roll us then press my knee to his neck. Within seconds, he's out cold. He isn't used to fighting with adults.

I take my time to find a good chair. It's a metal one from the kitchen, not wooden. I've had someone escape from them before, but not this time. I haul his heavy ass up and bind him. "All that time spent at the gym for muscles, and you still got taken down by little old me, idiot," I mutter before strolling into his kitchen, filling a glass with ice water, then heading back and throwing it into his face.

He wakes with a sputter and yelp, tugging at his bindings as he screams at me. I let him get it all out. They have to conclude they are captive on their own, and breaking their hope is the best part. I let him rant and rave.

Anger.

Placing my bag down on the sofa, I open it, letting him watch as I lay out my tools on the perfectly organized cushions. That's when his anger starts to give way to fear. "Please, please, what do you want? Money? I have lots."

Bargaining.

"So do I." Lifting a knife, I let it catch the light for him to see. Mental torture is sometimes more successful than physical. "However, you couldn't pay me enough to stop this." I cover the short distance between us and stand close enough to smell his sweat, tapping his cheek with the sharp edge of my blade. "I'm here on behalf of every single child whose innocence you stole. That's what you did, didn't you? You hurt them. You're a pedophile, and you thought you'd get away with it."

His eyes widen as I press the knife to his throat. "I know everything, and there's no one to save you this time. No money. No connections. No one is coming for you. It's just you and me and my bag of toys. I'm betting you have one of those. It will be a little like that. Did you tell them it wouldn't hurt much? I bet you did. You probably even told them they might like it. Don't worry, you won't like this at all, but I will."

Tears roll down his face as he shakes and fights his bindings, terror removing rational thought when faced with his own mortality. This is my favorite part—the moment the mask is stripped away, revealing the animal underneath.

"Did you touch them with these hands?" I ask as I hold the knife up.

"Please, it was wrong. I can make this right. I'll turn myself in," he argues.

"Not what I asked." I grab his chin, force his mouth open, and shove the wide edge of the knife in until he's choking on it. When he's about to pass out from panic, I pull it out. He coughs and gags as I step back. "Answer the question. It will make this easier for you."

"Yes, yes," he sobs. "I touched them. I'm sorry. I couldn't stop myself. They were just so pretty, so perfect and small—" I smash the knife into his face before he can carry on. I don't want to hear it. Flipping the knife, I stab it into each hand as he screams and writhes. As I pull it out, I make sure to twist the blade so his fingers will no longer work, and then I get to work with bolt cutters. I take every single finger off until his hand is just a stump. He passes out a few times, but I always bring him back—Willow made me a perfect concoction of drugs that will keep him alive and feeling all the pain, which I injected the second time he passed out.

While he's still crying, I get creative. I cut off his clothes so he's naked. It's a mental warfare trick, leaving him vulnerable and off-balance. He cries like a child. "Look at you, pathetic. Did you take pictures of your victims?"

When he doesn't answer, I slice off a nipple, and he howls. "Videos, digital."

"Of course," I snarl as I grab the camera and take one. I make sure to use my voice modulator just in case as I move it close to his red, snotty face. "Cry for me like your victims did." He sobs harder as I run the camera down his body. "Beg like they did."

"Please, please, I'm sorry. Please don't hurt me," he whines. He broke quicker than I thought he would, but most predators do. They are used to being the strongest, most dangerous person in the room, and their victims are young and helpless. When they are faced with someone who can look after themselves, they don't know what to do.

They prey on the helpless.

I keep recording. "Tell me what you did to them."

"I hurt them. I'm so sorry—" Fisting his hair, I lift his head and shove the camera in his face.

"No, tell me what you did." He doesn't get to escape this time.

"I raped them. All of them. I couldn't help myself."

"Where?" I demand.

"Here, upstairs, a secret room," he admits, looking at me through the camera. "Please, call the police. I'll go to jail. I'll admit it all."

346

"No, jail is too good for you." Putting the camera down, I move back. "You like both boys and girls, correct?"

His eyes close as his head falls. "Yes," he whispers.

"Do you know some of them will never recover from what you did? Not just mentally, but physically? Their bodies will never be the same from what you forced them to endure, and now neither will yours." Heading to my bag, I pick up a long poker as fury unlike anything I've felt before guides me. The slats on the metal chair give me a good angle as I step in front of him, kicking him until he's face down on the carpet. He struggles, begging and crying, but I tune it out as I shove it into his ass. He screams and bleeds, but I don't care. I keep it buried in him as I lift his chair again until he's sitting on it and facing the camera.

He's passed out. Grabbing Willow's next concoction of drugs, I inject it straight above his heart like she told me to. When I described what I needed, she didn't even question it. He'll stay alive and conscious.

He jerks awake with a gasp then screams. "Shut up," I bark, and he falls silent. "Tell me about the room."

"Hallway between my bedroom and office. The panel is hidden there." I kick the chair slightly, and it must move the poker because he starts screaming again. I video it once more before getting annoyed. He's giving me a headache.

Grabbing a huge knife, I show it to him before I get to work carving off his manhood. I wear gloves, not wanting to touch him, and when I'm done, he's losing too much blood. I blowtorch the edge of the blade and cauterize the wound. It won't hold forever, but just for what I need. I shove his bloody member in his mouth for him to gag on. It silences his screams, and I point in his face.

"Don't die yet," I admonish as I grab the camera and stalk up his staircase to the second floor to find this room.

He abducted his victims. He even knew some of the parents. He tied and blind-folded them and brought them here. He raped them, sometimes for days, and then let them go—at least at first, but he killed the last few. He was getting careless and worried the police were closing in on him.

I find the edge of the panel. If he hadn't told me, I wouldn't have noticed, but it swings outward. The room is exactly where he said it was. Either when they searched his house, they didn't look hard enough, or they didn't care. From the research I did, I'm betting it was the second. He's in good standing in the community with ties to a lot of important people. When he was arrested, they even apologized to him. The case was not investigated properly at all. They failed those children and their families, but I won't.

There's a lip that I step over, and then I recoil. I want to throw up, but I don't.

There's a bed to the left with ankle and wrist bindings tied to the metal headboard, and toys are spread across the mattress. I notice a bucket in the corner, offering no privacy. There's also a camera on a tripod at the bottom of the bed, and in the back corner is a computer. It's obviously been shoved in here hurriedly, so I head its way. There's only one thing he would hide.

I left his penis in his mouth to shut him up since the sound of his voice makes me want to carve him to pieces, and it seems to be working, since I still can't hear him.

I kill and hurt people, but him?

He's evil, pure and simple. He took the most innocent people in the world and hurt them for his own pleasure, and then he got away with it while his victims and their families never will. They will live with it for life.

The computer isn't even password protected. There's an open web browser, showing a site on a dark web, with photos and videos of children so disturbing, I minimize it. There are so many around the world, I would never be able to stop all of them. The desktop folders are neatly labeled with names, and I don't want to look, but I have to be sure, so I pick the one I know.

The man who came to me had a daughter named Sarah. They caught a clip of her getting into his car. They knew it was him, but they never looked until her body turned up, abused and naked in the local river three weeks later, and he still got away with it. Apparently, all DNA evidence was washed away or unusable. The police said they couldn't prove it. I don't think they wanted to. I think they were paid not to. I'm not foolish enough to believe the police can't be bought, considering the Sai brothers do it all the time.

I'm nearly sick when I turn on the first clip. She's wearing the same pink frilly dress she was last seen in. Her little matching socks are missing, and for some reason, that infuriates me. Before she starts to scream, I can't take it anymore. Shutting it off, I leave a note stuck to the computer instead.

ALL THE EVIDENCE YOU NEEDED, YOU FUCKWITS. DETECTIVES OLIVERA AND WRIGHT LET THIS MAN GET AWAY TO OFFEND AGAIN. HOLD THEM RESPONSIBLE OR I WILL COME FOR THEM AS WELL.

KARMA

Heading downstairs, I take my fury out on him. When I'm done, he's nothing but an unrecognizable, bloody mess. That evil room is leaking into me. I need to get out of here. I can't be here any longer. Besides, he can't take any more. It's done.

Once I'm packed, I walk into his hallway, pick up his landline phone, and dial.

"911, what's your emergency?"

"He'll be dead in under two minutes. Save him if you can." I hang up, knowing they'll trace the call. It isn't enough time for them to save him, but it will get their attention, and before morning, it will be on the news. I already put in a tip, called an old friend at the gazette, and sent him some pictures. He'll have all the graphic, gory pictures of this man up on his blog before then.

He'll live on infamously online just like his victims did.

I leave the same way I came in, through the front door, and head to my bike. I ride the high of my successful hunt, even as my stomach clenches in sickness at what I saw. When I open my phone and the app I need, it shows me their locations. They don't know I did it.

Zayn is at their company, as is Kane, but Neo is close by at the courthouse, so I drive there.

I feel dirty and sick, and I need them. I need them to wash me clean of that filth and evil.

By the time I get to my destination, I'm feeling a little better, but not much. I know this world is filled with people like that, but it never gets easier. Pulling into the lot, I spot one of Neo's cars a few rows down. It's a fancy new black Mercedes, nothing showy but enough to let them know who he is. I'm just getting off my bike when I hear his familiar laugh. Spinning around, I spy him on the steps near the parking lot. He looks really fucking good in his suit. He holds a brief-case in one hand as he smiles at someone, but a car is blocking my view. It's a good smile, friendly and nothing more, but I don't like the little giggle that responds. Climbing silently from my bike, I round the car and stop.

There's a woman next to him in a tight black skirt and white blouse. She reaches out and lays her hand on his arm, saying something, but he steps back, that smile still in place. She doesn't take the hint, however, and moves closer. His smile tightens, but he doesn't do anything else.

He's a dead man.

Does he think because we are just dating that he can let anyone flirt with him? She eventually leaves, and I'm prepared. I still have some of Willow's drugs, and when he bends over his trunk to put his bag inside, I inject him in the neck. He spins, his eyes widening before he collapses.

"Shit, remind me to thank Willow. This is good," I mutter as I grab his legs and start to lift him. I have to roll, and it takes a lot of maneuvering before I get him into the trunk, completely passed out.

I may have overreacted since I'm already in a mood from the day I've had, but I stand by my actions as I shut the trunk with him inside.

I leave my bike there for now and drive to my house.

Neo and I need to talk.

52

NEO

My head aches like a son of a bitch, and my eyes are heavy. What happened? I rack my brain. The last thing I remember was winning the hearing then heading out with my client. She kept trying to pressure me into a thank you drink . . .

Bexley.

I remember seeing her before everything went dark.

I force my eyes open and frown when my body doesn't respond. Looking down, I realize I'm chained to a bed. It isn't one I recognize, but when I look up, Bex is there with her arms crossed, leaning against a door.

"Hey, baby," I croak, coughing to clear my voice. "Where are we?"

"My house, where no one will disturb us," she snaps, her tone freezing cold.

"So this is your bed?" I grin, still a little groggy.

It's now obvious what happened. She kidnapped me. I relax and smile at her. "You didn't need to drug me. You could have just asked. I would have gone with you anywhere."

"You needed a reminder of who I am and what I am capable of," she warns, her voice deadly. I realize she's furious. I search my memory, trying to figure out why.

"Baby," I cajole, "what's wrong?"

"You smiled at her," she hisses.

I roll my lips inward to stop myself from telling her how fucking cute she is when she's jealous. "I won't let it happen again," I state sincerely. "Now, can we get rid of the chains? I want to touch you."

"No." She's unmoving, and I know I'll have to try harder.

"Okay then," I flirt. "How about coming here, baby, so I can touch you and show you how you're the only one for me?" My voice is low and soft, the one I know she likes. It's a low blow, but I'll use whatever I can to get her near me.

"You aren't touching me for a very long time," she threatens, even as she steps closer. Fuck, she's magnificent when she's angry. My cock hardens as I jerk my legs up.

I pout. "I thought you were flirting with me."

"I kidnapped you," she responds.

"Exactly." I grin as I lean back. "Isn't this foreplay? Or do you want me to bleed and scream first?"

"I came to you because I wanted . . . wanted something after what I did this morning." She stabs a knife into the pillow beside my head. I don't even flinch, just raise an eyebrow. "Yet there you were, flirting with someone else."

She came to me for comfort? I feel like I could take on the world.

"Not flirting. Not ever," I say slowly, wanting her to really listen. "She's an important client, so I couldn't get angry, but I rejected her multiple times. Why would I ever want anyone else? Your many personalities are enough to keep me busy."

Her nostrils flare in fury as she straddles my body, her heat and weight making me lift my hips to get her to slide down to where I want her. "You're being very arrogant for a man who is drugged and chained."

"And in your bed." I lick my lips. "You're jealous, and I love it, but it's not necessary. You are the only thing I see."

Snapping my hands up, I show her the bindings I broke out of. Her eyes widen, but then I'm on her, rolling her to her back and pinning her so she can't escape. I slam her hands above her head as she snarls like a wild animal, bucking and fighting. "Listen to me, baby—there's no one but you. I will ensure no one ever touches me again, not even in passing. Now let me make it up to you."

She frees her hand and slaps me, my head jerking from the blow. I lick my split lip as she glares at me, so I grab the bindings and tie them around her wrists. "If you can't be good, then I'll tie you up until you listen."

She tugs on them, her eyes flashing in anger as she kicks at me. "Let me go, now."

"Not a chance." I smirk as I strip her clothes off despite her twisting and bucking body, but when I come down on her, she manages to get one hand free, and there's a knife in her hold. I block it, feeling it slice into my forearm. It wasn't a killing blow, which tells me she isn't really that mad, just warning me.

Retying her, I pull her thighs up and press her knees to her chest, keeping her like that as I free myself and drag my length across her folds. Despite her anger, she tilts her hips to give me better access. Smirking, I wind her up until she's glowering, and when her sassy mouth opens to tell me off, I slam into her. The bed frame shakes, and her eyes roll back. Pulling free of her tight, wet cunt, I thrust forward, setting a hard pace that has her gripping the bindings above her rather than fighting them.

She cries out so sweetly, relaxing into her pleasure.

"Good girl. If you kill me, you won't get to fuck me again."

"Fine," she says, lifting her hips, "but next time, you're dead."

"Thank you, my magnanimous baby," I praise as I lift her hips higher. She comes for me, and even then, I don't hold back. She whimpers, and her pretty cunt flutters around me as I drive into her, forcing her to take it. I want her to know this body, this man, is hers. I never want her to question it, and I'll make sure she doesn't. Bending over her, I force her legs higher until she moans loudly.

"This is yours," I snarl, fighting my release. I want to feel her come again. I want to stain her bed with it so when she runs away from us, it's all she'll think of. "No one else's. I'll remind you as often as you need."

Her eyes open, but she nods, and when I slam into her again, that previous annoyance is completely forgotten. Her hips lift as much as possible to take me deeper, and our lips meet in a feral kiss. No more words are needed as both of us fight to get as close as possible.

Biting her lip until I taste blood, I press my arm there so our blood mixes, the sight making me swell inside her, her red lips parted in a pant.

"Neo," she whispers, and I know she's close. I dive into her until she screams, clawing at her bindings, and then I pull free, and with a roar of my own, I pump my release across her body, covering her with my cum.

She's riding her high too much to care, and I slump down at her side, spent. Reaching up, I undo her bindings, and she curls up at my side, making my lips twitch. She's always like this, so strong, bold, and crazy, but when she's sated and happy, she's like a spicy little kitten who wants cuddles.

I stroke her back as she moves closer, and my heart eventually slows as I look around her room before a question comes to mind.

"What happened to my suit jacket?" I ask casually after seeing everything else.

"She touched it, so I burned it," she answers.

Laughing at how adorable she is, I kiss her cheek and tug her closer, never wanting to let her go. "I love you, my crazy girl."

53

KANE

Three weeks later . . .

I've been working nonstop for weeks. We ran into some issues in one of our parent companies, with someone embezzling and selling company secrets. It's the most boring part of my job, but it means I've hardly spent any time with Bexley or my family. I haven't even seen my dad and Tommy despite them being back from their vacation, so when I get home, tired and ready to head to my office to continue working, I'm expecting chaos, but the house is empty.

"Where is everyone?" I ask as I put my shoes away, and the guard closest to me hands over my phone. Frowning, I scroll through the messages and images I've missed during my meetings as I wander to my office.

Sai Family Group Chat

Bexley was added to it the day after our date. She usually just sends GIFs or argues with Tommy, but it's nice seeing her in there.

Bexley: I was bored, so I kidnapped your father, brother, and guards. We are at Terrace Park.

The amusement park with roller coasters? My eyebrows rise, and then I open some of the pictures and burst into laughter.

It's one of those ride images. Bexley is in the center with her hands in the air, and next to her is my dad, who is screaming. My little brother is on her other side, laughing, and every other seat around the three of them is filled with our guards, all trying to stay stern-faced and failing.

Scrolling through the images, I find more of photo booths and rides. They are in teacups, boats, and even in the gift shop, dressing up. The last one is of them in matching hats and shirts, even my guards.

Chuckling, I quickly dial Dodge. He picks up a minute later. "Sir," he says, and I hear screams behind him.

"What are you doing?"

"I am currently on a winning boat," he mutters. "Your future wife is insane." His voice is soft, though. They all have a soft spot for her.

"Are my dad and Tommy okay?" I ask.

"They are loving it," he admits as gently as he can. "I'll make sure they are okay, sir, so you can work."

I look at my office and consider it before I change my mind. "I'll be there in twenty minutes. Don't tell them." I hang up and call my brothers and head to them.

Life is too short to work to death while my girl and family are having fun. Instead, I join them with my brothers.

They all had an amazing day and went to bed exhausted. I even had to carry Bexley to bed. I leave her in my room between my brothers and head back to my office to finish the work I missed this afternoon. I don't regret it. Watching them laugh and enjoy their day was worth it. I haven't seen Tommy or my father light up like that in such a long time. Life is about sacrifice. I'll work this hard if it means my family can spend every day like that, not worrying about anything but enjoying life.

Sitting heavily in my chair, I get to work, and hours later, a noise has my head jerking up. Bexley is at the door, wearing my shirt and nothing else. "I woke up and you were gone." Leaning back in my chair, I open my arms, and she walks my way. Sighing, I embrace her and bury my face in her shoulder, reclaiming my strength when all I want to do is sleep with her.

"Sorry, I have so much work to do," I murmur. "Go back to bed. I'll be up as soon as I can."

"Is it because you skipped out to play with us today?" she asks, pulling away and stroking my cheeks. I love her when she's soft and sleepy. I love fighting with her, but I love it when she takes care of me as well, especially since we are the only people who see this side of her.

I'm learning my little hellion wants to be spoiled and treated like a princess, but she has the mouth of a sailor and the reactions of an assassin. It's just another reason I love her.

"Don't worry about it, hellion, I can handle it. Go get some sleep." I kiss her, but she grabs my cheek and deepens it. "Hellion," I whisper when I pull away. Hunger steals the rest of my words, but I swallow it back. This isn't just about sex with us, and I never want her to think that.

"I'm awake," she murmurs as she licks my lips, making my self-control fritz. "And you need a break. You need to let go for a moment." She bites my lip, and I let out a grunt as my cock hardens. "Let me help." Her breathy plea has me rising with her in my arms, despite all my good intentions, and I walk around my desk, but I don't make it far because she sucks and licks my neck, and I can't take it anymore. Dropping her on her feet, I spin her and press her against my office door.

She presses her perfect ass back, taunting me, and the smirk she throws over my shoulder tells me she knows exactly what she is doing. Smacking her ass, I watch her eyes flare in hunger, so I do it again, watching it jiggle. I do it again and again, harder each time, until her creamy ass is red from my touch and she's pressed to the wall, moaning softly.

"Kane," she murmurs. "Fuck, that feels good. Do it harder."

I never have to be told twice. I stop holding back and give her the full force of my hand. The resounding smack is so loud, I wonder if I went too far, but the breathy moan she lets out tells me otherwise, so I do it again, kicking her legs open so when I smack her, I catch her pussy. She pushes back, dripping for me, and I can't do it anymore.

"Hold onto this," I snarl, lifting her hand until she grips the ridge in the door. I lift one of her legs and press her knee to the door, then I bury myself inside her in one swift thrust.

She cries out, trying to pull away, but I pin her and slowly pull out before I thrust back in. Each time, my hips hit her perfect ass and my marks, the pain mixing with her pleasure as I speed up.

She wanted to be fucked, and that's exactly what she'll get, but I should have known my girl gives as good as she gets. She kicks back, and I stumble, grabbing a table and knocking it over as I go. There is a crash, but then she's on me, sinking down my length again. I roll us and thrust deeper until she cries out, but we roll again, this time hitting the bookcase. I hear it wobble, and then books start to fall. Lifting my arm, I block any from hitting her, ignoring the sharp pain as I roll us back the other way, pin her, and fuck her hard and fast as she laughs below me.

Her arms drape around my neck as she grins at me, and before I can react, she flips me over her head. I hit the floor hard, shaking off the confusion, and then my face is pressed to the wood as she slides her hand down my back, across my ass, and then to my wet cock. "I like you like this," she admits, biting my ear. "All that perfect civilization is stripped away for me, and nothing but the beast is left. I'm not afraid of you though. It gets me hot. Stop holding back."

I knock her back, and when she tries to crawl away, I drag her to me with one hand and impale her on my length. She claws at the floor as I kneel behind her on all fours and take her harder than I ever have.

She's just as wild as I am, meeting me thrust for thrust. The room is wrecked around us, but neither of us care. We only worry about getting our pleasure from one another, and when it becomes too much, she shatters with a scream. Her perfect cunt clenches around me, milking my cock until I let go with a yell.

My back bows, and I pin us to the floor, my dick buried deep as she pants and whines. I kiss her face and neck until I can move, then I pull free and kneel, watching my cum drip from her pretty pussy. The sight is so fucking sexy, I reach for my phone and snap a picture, then I send it to my brothers before gathering her in my arms. She sighs happily, curling up as I wrap a blanket around her before sitting in my chair. Her head notches on my chest, her smile small but happy. "Sleep now, hellion."

Kissing her softly, I swallow her hum of agreement and stroke her back as she closes her eyes and gets comfy. Not ten minutes later, she's asleep, and I move my mouse until my computer comes back to life.

I work around her, happy to have her here with me, even if she's asleep. It's nice not to be alone, for someone to see me and how hard I'm trying to understand.

Everything I do is for this family, but her?

She's all mine.

"Where are we?" I grumble for the tenth time. My girl knows I have control issues, but she doesn't care as she grips my hand and leads me blindfolded down what feels like stairs. The floor is squishy, so carpet maybe? I didn't have much choice other than to follow. She kidnapped me from my office, tied me up, and blindfolded me—not that I care. I'd happily let her kidnap me any day. I'm just hoping it ends with her with the blindfold on.

"Stop moaning," she says as the floor changes to what feels like hardwood, and then she helps me up some stairs before letting go.

"Hellion?" I call when I no longer feel her touch. My voice seems to echo, and that makes me frown, my hands itching to reach for a weapon.

"Okay, you can look." Her voice is soft and faraway.

Reaching up, I yank down the blindfold and frown. I'm standing on a wooden stage, and she's sitting in the front row of what looks to be a theater. As I take in the gilded molding and upper boxes, I realize it's the Palace Theater, which is usually filled with performances every night of the week. Not tonight. It's empty, and there is a spotlight shining to my left. When I turn, I find a Steinway there.

"Bexley?" I ask, even as my fingers twitch, aching to caress the keys. It's been too long since I played. Between the kidnapping and then her coming into my life, I haven't had a chance to indulge in my guilty pleasure, not to mention the occasional ringing I still have in my ear from Butcher's knife, which makes me think I wouldn't be able to play as well.

"I wondered why your fingers were always tapping until Neo told me. You dreamed of playing professionally, but you might never get to do that since you're so dedicated to your family. I figured I could give you one night, one performance, with me as your audience. Play for me, Kane, and live your dream."

I look from her to the piano and back again. Neo told her? For a moment, I'm back to being thirteen years old and told by my teacher that I'm a prodigy. My father was so happy but also scared to dash that dream away. It was only two years later when I realized that would never happen. My family needed me. I had a duty I was born in to. I didn't have the luxury of chasing that dream, but as I stare into my girl's hopeful gaze, I know she's trying to give that back to me.

I wander over to the piano and sit, unbuttoning my jacket as I do so. My fingers reach out to caress the keys. "I haven't played in a long time. It might not even sound the same with my ear—"

"Stop making excuses. I can tell you love it. You might never get to perform around the world, but I want you to perform for me for the rest of our lives, starting tonight. Come on, baby, show me what you've got."

Unable to deny her or the need to play, I sit taller as I press the first key, and it comes back. Before I know it, music fills the empty theater. It's a piece I practiced many times with my teacher. I have to adjust with my ringing ear, but before long, my eyes are closing, and I pour myself into the song. When it's over, the last note dying, clapping makes my eyes open, and I turn to find Bexley on her feet, cheering loudly. She grabs a huge bouquet of flowers from the seat next to her, hops onto the stage, strides over to me, and lays it on top of the piano.

"I don't know much about piano music, but even I know that was incredible."

I wrap my arm around her waist and tug her between my legs on the bench, leaning my chin against her shoulder. "Thank you."

"Always," she murmurs, pressing into me. "Play me another piece?"

My smile is genuine as I reach for her hands and press them to the keys. "Let's play it together."

In the empty theater I once dreamed of performing in, I play my final song with the woman I love. The younger me achieves his dream, if only for a night, and it's all thanks to her.

54

BEXLEY

Two months later . . .

"I took a bullet for you," I grumble in annoyance as the doctor cleans the wound. It was a through and through, and it didn't cause much damage since it hit my arm, but Kane is glaring at me. Zayn is at my side, holding my other hand, while Neo strokes my hair. I don't bother telling them I've been patched up many times before because they don't care. Even the slight hint of my pain puts them in a tizzy. I once stubbed my toe and they called the fucking doctor. They are insane.

"Baby, you are the reason we were being shot at," Zayn teases, but it's soft.

"So? I still took a bullet," I snarl. He was aiming at Kane.

"You're right, baby. You're so right." He nods as we all look at Kane.

"You're grounded," he growls. I know it's all out of concern for me, but I narrow my eyes to match his glare. "I mean it, hellion. You started a fight with a group of assassins. What were you thinking?"

"I was bored, and I wanted to see who would win," I mutter, but then I point at him with my good hand. "And you don't get to ground me. Try it and I'll destroy the house so there's nothing to ground me to."

"Bexley," he warns.

"Kane," I snap.

"Alright, alright, what's done is done," their father says as he wags his finger at me. "No more playing tag with assassins." He grins at Taylor. "Come on, dear, let's finish our game of chess. I'm sure with Bexley's teaching, you will win against me one day."

Taylor nods, glaring at me. "Grounded," she mouths, but she follows him out. Lauren and Tommy are playing in the garden with Dodge, and I watch through the window as Taylor waves at him, stopping to chat. He grins, something he's started to do more, and always at her. I suspect they are fucking, but every time I bring it up, she hits me. I'll find out one day. I put cameras in his room, so we'll see.

I don't know how it happened, the sneaky bastards, but I'm living with them. I blame Taylor and Lauren. The brothers must have gotten to them, and before I knew it, I had my own room, which they spend more time in than their own. Taylor and Lauren have their own wing and are loving life. They are spoiled rotten, the traitors. I still have my house, and I stay there when they annoy me, but it's become normal to come here before I even realize it. After all, my family is here.

"All done. You'll be fine in a few days," the doc declares, and the brothers remain silent until he's gone, then Kane sighs, pinching his nose.

"You'll be the death of me, hellion," he grumbles.

Popping to my feet, I kiss his cheek as I walk by to watch Taylor lose. "But it's so much fun." I leave them to it, escaping before they can remember they are mad at me for getting hurt.

As I head outside to find my sister, I look back to see Kane smiling, even as he's shaking his head, and I grin. I fought tooth and nail when they dragged me here to live with them, but I'll admit it's fun. I even told them I loved them last night. It was during sex, so at least there's that, but they won't let me live it down. If they carry on, I'll have to kill one of them to make a point, or maybe I'll let them get away with it. I have a reputation to uphold, after all, but they might be the exception to my rules.

Not that I'll let them know that.

The door bursts open, and I meet Kane's worried gaze as he raises an eyebrow in question.

"Settle our argument. Your brother thinks that Godzilla with no arms or legs would win against King Kong with no eyes or ears."

He strokes his jaw as he thinks, and I tread closer. "King Kong," he states.

"Thank you!" I yell before there's a cough. Craning my neck, I peek at his screen to see rows of people reflected back. "Oops, were you in a meeting? Hi, business people."

Chuckling, he drags me onto his lap. "Stay while I finish."

Huffing, I settle in, but I zone out until I can't take it anymore. "This is boring," I mutter, expecting him to ignore me, but he leans around me, his voice sharp.

"Meeting over. We'll conclude next week."

"But, sir, we just started," someone begins before he ends the call and turns me.

"You're bored? Want to go kill people with me instead?"

"No, I like this outfit. I don't want to get blood on it." I sigh as Neo and Zayn follow me into the office and sit down, an idea coming to mind. "There are other ways to fill boredom though."

"I thought you liked your outfit," Kane scoffs, but he's already reaching for me as I dance out of his reach.

"Well, duh, I'll take it off." I stare at them, my brow furrowed. "I think I'm in love with you—not because of orgasms or in the moment confessions, but I love you," I admit before I slam my mouth shut, my eyes wide as I look between them, horrified at what slipped out.

"We know, baby," Zayn says softly. "We don't need to hear it to know you love us, though it is nice."

Neo quickly stands and blocks the door, understanding I was about to run. "Uh-uh, no running just because you realized what we all know."

I turn, ready to throw myself out of the window, but Kane is there, grinning. "You know we love you too, more than life, now let's show you before you decide to bolt."

The suckers think they have me cornered. I spin, drive my foot into Zayn's cock, and leap over him as I hightail it out of the door, knowing they will chase me.

I love them, but I won't make it easy.

EPILOGUE

BEXLEY

FOUR MONTHS LATER . . .

I am so fucking late. If I thought Lauren was bad at scolding me for tardiness, I was wrong. Those three assholes will have my head and then kiss it better. I didn't mean to be late. I just got distracted at Reacher's, kicking the new guy's ass. By the time I realized what time it was, it was an hour later than I was supposed to leave. I shoved on my dress and heels and jumped into the Lamborghini I stole from the garage this morning. They say I have access to everything. Hell, they keep filling the garage with new toys for me to play with, but I think they know I like to steal them more, so they started hiding them. This is Neo's brand-new car, but when I looked at the key, I saw it was pink with hearts saying, "Bite me," so I know he got it for me.

The cute idiot.

Speeding up, I run a red light. It's our anniversary. I'm not big on that stuff, but apparently they are and I have no choice. They wouldn't tell me what we are doing, wanting to surprise me, but I know it's important to them, and I don't want to upset them, so I drive as fast as I can. Taylor and Lauren worked so hard to pick my outfit, so I know they would be angry too. They have backup now when they are mad at me, and having the entire family glaring at me in disapproval is not the way I want to spend my night.

I'll just have to fuck their brains out until they forget they are mad.

Swerving through traffic, I wave at the police car. They know better than to stop me or the Sai brothers. I'm forced to slam on the brakes, however, when a dark Mercedes slides into my lane at the last second. Something familiar about it bothers me until I remember . . .

"You've got to be kidding me." I slam on the horn, but he ignores me, and when the light turns green, he doesn't move. He waits for it to turn yellow then shoots off.

The idiot picked the wrong bitch. I speed after him and easily catch him. This time, I block him and leave the car running as I get out. I stride toward him in my knee-length black dress. The split allows me to move fast, and the lace edge slides across my skin like a snake. I know I look good, and I'm betting I won't even make it through appetizers before they have their mouths on me.

The man in the Mercedes sees me coming, his eyes widening, and I chuckle.

It's the same idiot from all those months ago when I was on my way to pick Lauren up from Tommy's birthday party. Talk about serendipity.

I raise my hand to knock on his window, and the light catches on the rock on my finger. The diamond ring they bought me is beautiful, but I hardly ever wear it. It's not practical, but I can't take this one off. It's dainty and gold, with the letter S entwined with a K for Sai and Karma. It's ornate, like their family crest, and inlaid with small diamonds that make it sparkle.

Glaring down at the ring, I barely feel the small spikes that dig into my skin, meaning I'm unable to remove it since they knew I would try to. I blame them. I was distracted by dick when they put it on. We aren't married per se, but to them, we are. It means the world is even more afraid of me than before. They all know I hold the leashes of the three Sai brothers.

When the man continues to ignore me, I roll my eyes. "I don't have time for this."

I smash my fist into his window. It shatters as he screams, taking cover as I reach in.

"The police won't save you this time." I grin at him. "You're just lucky I'm late and in a good mood since it's my anniversary. Next time, I'll kill you." I steal his key and jump back in my car and rush off, leaving him stranded.

I make it to the address ten minutes later. Frowning, I climb from the car and walk across the gravel toward the red carpet leading to a yacht, which has the name "Karma" proudly painted on the side. "Hello?" I step through the sliding door, confused. It's empty and dark.

Candles explode to life, and I turn in shock as all three familiar men appear from the shadows. Neo is carrying the biggest bouquet of flowers I have ever seen, and he struggles to carry it. Kane has a glass in his hand, which he offers to me, and Zayn has a bag. He places it on the table, which is sprinkled with rose petals. Soft music fills the air.

"Well?" Neo asks nervously. "Happy anniversary."

"Do you like it?" Zayn asks excitedly.

"My feet hurt," I admit, which makes them laugh, but I yelp when Kane lifts me effortlessly. Neo and Zayn lower to their knees, and within seconds, they pull off my heels. Their hands stroke my legs and feet before Kane kicks off his shoes, and they help me into them. They are too big but so much comfier.

"Better?" he asks.

"Better," I whisper, and he grins, kissing me.

"Open your presents, hellion." I move away from them and open the black bag, and my eyes widen as it rolls out like a mat. There are blades, guns, and everything a girl could need for a hunt, all in black and pink, with elaborate silver Ks engraved on them.

They bought me weapons.

That's so hot.

"I love them," I whisper as I stroke the handle of a wicked knife. "I only got you me as your present."

"Better than any gift you could give us," Zayn whispers into my ear as I shiver.

"So we're dining on a yacht?" I ask curiously, changing the subject before I tackle them.

"Your yacht, with all your favorite foods, and then after, the crew will lock themselves in the bridge, and we are going to hunt you through the boat," Neo teases with a grin.

My eyes light up, and they chuckle. "Exactly." Zayn grins. "You better hide well."

"Hide? I don't hide, but I'll make you regret hunting me," I retort.

"Never," Neo murmurs as he kisses my hand. "Now do your worst, Karma."

Stepping back, I grin, sliding my hand down my chest. All three watch the movement, their eyes filled with liquid fire and hunger. The same desire pools within me, not for food, but for them. "Why wait?"

I can't help but laugh as they lunge toward me.

We don't bother waiting for food, none of us having the patience. Kane sends up a message, and I grab one of the new guns on the table and take off, leaving Kane's shoes behind as I race through the boat. I break out to the top deck, and just as I do, fireworks explode on shore in our colors. I know it's for me. Excitement fills me as I hear them coming for me.

The chase is beginning, but they should have known better. Clutching the gun, I turn and slip into the boat to hunt them.

I'm their karma, after all.

ABOUT K.A. KNIGHT

K.A Knight is a New York Times Best Selling Author trying to get all of the stories and characters out of her head, writing the monsters that you love to hate. She loves reading and devours every book she can get her hands on, and she also has a worrying caffeine addiction.

She leads her double life in a sleepy English town, where she spends her days writing like a crazy person.

Read more at K.A Knight's website or join her Facebook Reader Group.
Sign up for exclusive content and my newsletter here
http://eepurl.com/drLLoj

OTHER BOOKS BY K.A. KNIGHT

CONTEMPORARY

LEGENDS AND LOVE *CONTEMPORARY*

Revolt *RH*

Rebel *RH*

Riot *MF*

Resist *MM*

PRETTY LIARS *CONTEMPORARY RH*

Unstoppable

Unbreakable

PINE VALLEY COLLEGE *CONTEMPORARY*

Racing Hearts *MM*

Crashing Hearts *MM*

Bleeding Hearts *FF*

DEN OF VIPERS UNIVERSE STANDALONES

Scarlett Limerence *CONTEMPORARY*

Nadia's Salvation *CONTEMPORARY*

Alena's Revenge *CONTEMPORARY*

Den of Vipers *CONTEMPORARY RH*

Gangsters and Guns (Co-Write with Loxley Savage) *CONTEMPORARY RH*

FORBIDDEN READS *(STANDALONES)*

Daddy's Angel *CONTEMPORARY*

Stepbrothers' Darling *CONTEMPORARY RH*

Book 3 - *coming soon..*

HER MONSTERS SERIES *PNR RH*

Rage

Hate

Book 3 - *coming soon..*

COURTS AND KINGS *PNR*

Court of Nightmares *RH*

Court of Death *MF*

Court of Beasts *RH*

Court of Heathens *RH*

Court of Evil *RH*

THE FALLEN GODS SERIES *PNR*

Pretty Painful

Pretty Bloody

Pretty Stormy

Pretty Wild

Pretty Hot

Pretty Faces

Pretty Spelled

Fallen Gods - the omnibus 1

Fallen Gods - the omnibus 2

FORGOTTEN CITY *PNR*

Monstrous Lies

Monstrous Truths

Monstrous Ends

SCIENCE FICTION

DAWNBREAKER SERIES *SCI FI RH*

Voyage to Ayama

Dreaming of Ayama

STANDALONES

Crown of Stars *SCI FI RH*

SHARED WORLD PROJECTS

Blade of Iris - Mafia Wars *CONTEMPORARY RH*

CO-WRITES

CO-AUTHOR PROJECTS - *Erin O'Kane*

HER FREAKS SERIES *PNR Dystopian RH*

Circus Save Me

Taming The Ringmaster

Walking the Tightrope

Her Freaks Series - the omnibus

THE WILD BOYS SERIES *CONTEMPORARY RH*

The Wild Interview

The Wild Tour

The Wild Finale

The Wild Boys - the omnibus

STANDALONES

Kingdom of Crowns and Daggers *Dark Fantasy RH*

The Hero Complex *PNR RH*

Dark Temptations *Collection of Short Stories, ft. One Night Only & Circus Saves Christmas*

CO-AUTHOR PROJECTS - *Ivy Fox*

Deadly Love Series *CONTEMPORARY*

Deadly Affair

Deadly Match

Deadly Encounter

CO-AUTHOR PROJECTS - *Kendra Moreno*

STANDALONES

Stolen Trophy *CONTEMPORARY RH*

Fractured Shadows *PNR RH*

Shadowed Heart

Burn Me *PNR*

Cirque Obscurum *PNR RH*

CO-AUTHOR PROJECTS - *Loxley Savage*

THE FORSAKEN SERIES *SCI FI RH*

Capturing Carmen

Stealing Shiloh

Harboring Harlow

STANDALONES

Gangsters and Guns *CONTEMPORARY*, IN DEN OF VIPERS' UNIVERSE

OTHER CO-WRITES

Shipwreck Souls *(with Kendra Moreno & Poppy Woods)*

The Horror Emporium *(with Kendra Moreno & Poppy Woods)*

AUDIOBOOKS

The Wasteland

The Summit

The Cities

The Nations

Rage

Hate

Den of Vipers *(From Podium Audio)*

Gangsters and Guns *(From Podium Audio)*

Daddy's Angel *(From Podium Audio)*

Stepbrothers' Darling *(From Podium Audio)*

Blade of Iris *(From Podium Audio)*

Deadly Affair *(From Podium Audio)*

Deadly Match *(From Podium Audio)*

Deadly Encounter *(From Podium Audio)*

Stolen Trophy *(From Podium Audio)*

Crown of Stars *(From Podium Audio)*

Monstrous Lies *(From Podium Audio)*

Monstrous Truth *(From Podium Audio)*

Monstrous Ends *(From Podium Audio)*

Court of Nightmares *(From Podium Audio)*

Court of Death *(From Podium Audio)*

Court of Beasts *(From Podium Audio)*

Court of Evil *(From Podium Audio)*

Unstoppable *(From Podium Audio)*

Unbreakable *(From Podium Audio)*

Fractured Shadows *(From Podium Audio)*

Shadowed Heart *(From Podium Audio)*

Revolt *(From Podium Audio)*

Rebel *(From Podium Audio)*

Riot *(From Podium Audio)* Coming soon…

Cirque Obscurum *(From Podium Audio)* Coming soon…

Kingdom of Crowns and Daggers *(From Podium Audio)*

Diver's Heart *(From Podium Audio)*

Racing Hearts *(From Podium Audio)*

Crashing Hearts (From Podium Audio)

FIND AN ERROR?

Please email this information to thenuttyformatter1@gmail.com:

- *the author name*
- *title of the book*
- *screenshot of the error*
- *suggested correction*

Printed in Dunstable, United Kingdom